MORTAL:
Surviving the
Zombie Apocalypse

SHAWN CHESSER

CONTENTS

ACKNOWLEDGMENTS

For Mo, Raven, and Caden, you three mean the world to me ... love you. And thanks, Maureen Chesser, for all of the support you've given me through this incredible journey called life. Love you. I owe everything to my parents for bringing me up the right way. Mom, thanks for reading ... although it is not your genre. Dad, aka Mountain Man Dan, thanks for your ear and influence. Cliff Kane, RIP. Daymon, thanks for introducing me to Grand Targhee *and* Jackson Hole! Thanks to all of the men and women in the military, past and present, especially those of you in harm's way. Thanks to all LE and first responders for your service. To the people in the U.K. who have been in touch, thanks for reading! Lieutenant Colonel Michael Offe, thanks for your service as well as your friendship. Larry Eckels, thank you for helping me with some of the military technical stuff in Mortal. For answering my questions concerning the Hercules: John O'Brien, Norman Meredith, James Wallace Holdstein, Robert Kagel, Dennis Lyons, Michael Offe, Larry Eckels. Any missing facts or errors are solely my fault. Beta readers, you rock, and you know who you are. Thanks George Romero for introducing me to zombies. Steve H., thanks for listening. All of my friends and fellows at S@N and Monday Old St. David's, thanks as well. Lastly, thanks to Bill W. and Dr. Bob ... you helped make this possible. I am going to sign up for another 24.

Cover by Jason Swarr of Straight 8 Photography. Thank you sir!

Special thanks to Craig DiLouie, John O'Brien, and Mark Tufo for continuing to provide me with invaluable advice when I come a' knocking. David P. Forsyth, thanks for including me in the Permuted Press published anthology, Outbreak: Visions of the Apocalypse. Being published and all of the proceeds going to charity = WIN+WIN. Also thanks for inviting me to ApocaCon2 in Long Beach. Had a blast and met some other cool folks ... Craig DiLouie, Saul Tanpepper, Peter Clines, A. American, Julie Randolph, and Christopher J Fennell, to name a few.

Once again, extra special thanks to Monique Happy for her work editing "Mortal". Mo, as always, you came through like a champ! Working with you has been a seamless experience and nothing but a pleasure.

If I have accidentally left anyone out ... I am truly sorry.

***

Edited by Monique Happy Editorial Services
www.moniquehappy.com

Chapter 1
Outbreak - Day 16
Draper, South Dakota

Jasper heard the screams well before he committed the left turn onto Cemetery Road, and as the springs supporting the overburdened truck squeaked and crushed stone popped and crunched beneath its balding tires, the shrill animal-like warble rose above it all. Suddenly the volunteer undertaker longed for the old yellow earmuffs he usually kept in the truck's bed and without fail donned when weed whacking the church grounds at Father O'Reilly's behest.

But sadly, the hearing protection and the rest of his lawn equipment had been supplanted by the Omega-ravaged bodies of the Vasquez family—all six of them—mom, dad and their four girls, aged three to ten.

He braked fifty yards short of the wrought iron fence surrounding the cemetery, pressed the tiny binoculars to his face, and focused on the smoking wreckage.

From his vantage point, which was nearly straight on, he spied the massive crater where the black helicopter had impacted the ground at the far north end of the cemetery. The dark brown chasm it had plowed as it bled airspeed ran through a hundred yards worth of dirt and grave markers, and also a good number of his neighbors' corpses, before finally coming to rest with its angular nose partially buried under the tilled topsoil.

He removed the field glasses momentarily, squinted against the sun's harsh rays, and ran his forearm across his brow to wipe away the beaded sweat. "Hell is getting hotter," he said softly to himself. After performing a thorough visual check of his surroundings and seeing none of the walking corpses nearby, he replaced the binoculars and stole a longer peek at the wreck.

The hubcap-shaped rotor disc atop the listing aircraft was in one piece; however, it appeared that the initial contact with the ground had reduced the whirring blades to nothing but stubs sprouting streamers of some kind of high-tech wispy fiber. The violence of the crash had rent a gaping hole in the craft's upturned right-hand side and had compromised the cockpit glass, leaving the screaming pilot pinned in his seat and fully exposed to the flesh-eaters.

He slammed the transmission into park, set the brake, and killed the engine. Deciding against the shotgun, he fished the graphite-black .22 semi-auto pistol from the glove box, and retrieved his machete from the passenger side footwell.

After taking a little more time to scan all four points of the compass, he slid from behind the wheel, eased the door closed, and made off in a crouch toward the cemetery's easternmost edge.

The guttural pleas for help continued in earnest while he covered the thirty yards between his truck and the graveyard at as close to a sprint as his forty-five-year-old legs would propel him. Once he reached the far fence line, winded and gasping for breath, he took a knee behind a large headstone denoting the final resting place of one *August Piontek 1884-1941*.

Sweat dripping from his brow, he brought the binoculars to bear on the crash site, and from the new and improved viewing angle saw that both pilots were still strapped into their seats. The one suspended a dozen feet off the ground appeared to be dead, head and arms hanging limply. The one making the racket was at ground level, bucking and thrashing against his flight harness.

Jasper turned the focus ring and held his arms steady, trying to discern how badly the man was injured. He saw the man's mouth contorting under the smoked visor—a ghastly visual finally mated with the nerve-jangling peals filling the air. Then he panned the

2

binoculars down to where the helicopter's fuselage merged with the ground. Suddenly his blood ran cold when he realized that a lone ghoul had beaten him to the crashed aircraft. The shirtless creature worked its feet furiously, digging into the browned grass, succeeding ever so slowly in squeezing its upper body through a jagged fissure in the cockpit glass.

Through the Plexiglas, Jasper could clearly see the screamer's gloved hand performing a rapid sort of pageant wave as the pallid creature shook its head and rent a mouthful of fabric and glistening meat from the man's forearm. Averting his eyes from the horrific sight, Jasper moved his pistol over his chest, a makeshift sign of the cross.

After speaking with his God, he chambered a round, *snicked* the safety off and tapped the courage necessary to put the wailing pilot out of his misery.

Breathing through his mouth in order to keep a rising tide of bile at bay, he rose, skirted the weathered stone marker, and tiptoed through the morass of Omega-infected bodies he'd been dumping there since the plague began ravaging his corner of the world. And though the doomed pilot wouldn't be the first human he'd been forced to put down before reanimation, he was certain nothing about this one was going to be easy—especially if the dying man made eye contact. For it was that *knowing* twinkle, the spark only present in the eyes of the living, that made the final act of compassion so difficult for him to fulfill.

God give me the strength, he thought as the keening continued unabated. Head ducked, he flitted between headstones and approached the ghoul from behind and to the right. He paused for a tick, long enough to bring the binoculars to bear, and counted the trudging corpses he'd passed on Cemetery Road a couple of minutes ago. *Twenty-two*. A far cry more than the small manageable groups of twos and threes usually attracted to the graveyard by the noisy carrion-feeding birds. And though the throng was still a good distance away, the danger their large numbers presented meant he had to get a move on. *Should have known the crash would draw a crowd*, he told himself as he fought off an overwhelming urge to bolt for his pick-up and head for home.

3

But his upbringing wouldn't allow it. *Country folk always help their fellows*, had been his father's mantra.

Put the dying one out of his misery first, a little voice in his head urged.

The simple act would take but a second and leave him with a clear conscience when answering to St. Peter at the Pearly Gates—if he didn't first succumb to the ever-present apocalypse-induced urge to eat his shotgun—an act that would surely resign him to eternal hellfire. *Damned if he did, and damned if he didn't*, he mused. But first he'd have to deal with the zombie.

Shifting his gaze back to the helicopter, he saw his hopes of an easy out dashed when the other pilot, who he'd thought was dead, brought his gloved hands up and began batting away the tangle of wires hanging in front of his face. Then, obviously fighting both gravity and the weight of his bulky flight helmet, the pilot lifted his head to horizontal and held it there for a tick before once again going limp in his harness.

"Your mercy mission just got more complicated," Jasper said to himself, as he silently picked his way through jagged wreckage resembling pieces of honeycomb ripped from a scorched beehive. His approach undetected, he stood over the lower half of the prostrate creature's squirming body, feet a shoulder width apart, and thrust his pistol through a crack in the cockpit glass. Heart racing crazily, he took a deep breath and aimed for the rear of the abomination's skull—just above the base of the neck where the pencil eraser-sized .22 caliber bullet had the best chance of penetration. And as he said a silent prayer and drew back the final half-pound of trigger pull two things happened simultaneously. First, the pilot went deathly quiet, all of the fight leaving his body. Then, from somewhere deep inside the helicopter, someone bellowed, "*Hold your fire!*"

Complying with the barked order, Jasper eased off the trigger, and put his pistol in a back pocket.

Then the disembodied male voice calmly added, "There is a fuel leak. You smelling it?"

Jasper clamped his mouth shut and breathed in through his nose. Sure enough, barely perceptible, under the oppressive carrion pong, was a hint of kerosene. "Yeah. But just barely," he replied.

"Your gunfire would have ignited the vapors, killing us all."

Stunned into silence by the revelation of just how close he'd come to finally making St. Peter's acquaintance, Jasper shifted his weary gaze to the lurching troop, still half a football field away, and vectoring unwaveringly towards the wreckage.

With a calm air of authority, the male voice asked, "What's your name?"

Dividing his attention between keeping a tab on the deadly creature near his feet and probing the chopper's gloomy interior for the source of the voice, he answered, "Jasper ... Jasper Hasp."

"OK, Jasper Hasp," said the voice. "Do you have a knife?"

"A machete," answered Jasper.

"Then *kill* the thing," the male voice stated calmly.

Chapter 2

Jasper hinged at the waist, looked under the pilot's visor. He noticed the man's eyeballs darting around behind closed ashen lids. "Sorry friend," he said softly. "You're going to turn and there's nothing anyone can do for you now." Then the big-boned undertaker regarded the zombie. He shuddered at the sight as the thing continued burrowing—pulling its emaciated body forward—inch by inch past the broken glass and twisted metal of the shattered cockpit. Finally he bent down and wrapped his calloused hands around the zombie's cold, clammy ankles. He hauled back and straightened his legs, and tugged the soulless monster through the jagged glass, inflicting deep half-moon shaped lacerations along both sides of its ribcage. Then, after dragging the writhing abomination clear of the pooled fuel, he crushed his knee against its knobby spine, took a handful of matted hair, and behind a short economical swing, buried the machete inches deep into its exposed temple. "It's done," he said as gray matter and brackish blood bubbled around the blade.

"Good job," called the person from inside the helicopter. "What kind of shape are the pilots in?"

"The one who *was* screaming nearly lost his arm to one of those *things*," Jasper said. He crouched down and peered through the glass and the space between the two pilots and finally caught sight of a man-shaped silhouette deep in the bowels of the aircraft. "I'm sorry ... it'll only be a matter of time before he turns."

Save for the moaning and hisses of the nearby dead, there was a short silence. Jasper felt very alone. He wanted the stranger to

6

keep talking. To tell him what to do. He stood up and looked the length of the wreckage, walked a half dozen feet to his right, and regarded the underbelly of the aircraft. Weeds and grass hung in clumps where they had been worked into panels split presumably upon impact. That Jasper could see no markings on the craft's fuselage, and the fact the man inside of it was wearing some sort of camouflage uniform that he didn't recognize, left a whole lot up to his imagination—most of which made him wish he'd followed his gut instinct and hadn't gotten involved. Ignoring the flight impulse, he took a sidelong glance towards the advancing flesh-eaters and said, "What are *you* going to do about the infected pilot?"

"Unless you've been under a rock the past three weeks," the shadowy form said, "you know what must be done. But first things first. My foot is trapped, so I'm going to need your help in here. Then I'll see to Durant's condition and do what's necessary."

"He could turn any second," said Jasper excitedly. "His fingers are beginning to twitch."

Hearing this, Ari's head again levered sideways and his entire body went rigid. He mumbled something indecipherable and shot his gloved hands to the safety harness suspending him at a precarious angle mere feet from harm's way. "*Durant's hurt ...*" he called out frantically, eyes fixed on his good friend to his left. "I need to help him. I think he's bleeding out ..."

"Ari, *stand down*," the shadowy form bellowed. "Durant is *gone*. He's infected, and if you unbuckle yourself now you will be too."

"Do something then," Ari said sharply.

"He's beyond our help," answered the voice from within the helicopter.

Nodding in agreement, Jasper flashed the inconsolable pilot an empathetic look, and once again performed the sign of the cross.

Apparently resigned to the fact that he wasn't going anywhere anytime soon, Ari composed himself and reached down near his feet, manipulating something there. He hinged back up, swiveled his head left and yelled back into the cabin, "I took care of our leaking fuel problem."

Not gonna help us much now, Jasper thought to himself, looking at an ever-widening moat of fuel and other viscous fluids forming around the aircraft. He backed up a step and shifted his gaze to the right, spotting the body of a man lying several yards away. The prostrate form was wedged up against the iron fence surrounding the cemetery, but didn't look to be in an advanced state of decay like the infected citizens of Draper that Jasper had been depositing here for days. This one looked newly dead and was wearing some kind of tan fatigues that rendered him nearly invisible amongst the sun-scorched grass. And if it hadn't have been for the wide-open staring eyes, which were now merely black dots sunken into a slack ashen face, he would have missed seeing it entirely.

Projecting his voice into the fuselage through cupped hands, Jasper called out, "We've got more pressing problems out here."

"What kind of problems?" the man asked from deep within the wreck.

"Your friend Ari here says he stopped the leak, but I'm afraid there's still a fairly deep pool of gas that's formed up around the helicopter." He went silent for a second, took a deep breath. Then, wishing he'd lugged the shotgun along, added, "Also ... there are more than twenty of those dead things heading our way, and no doubt more following behind them. I reckon that's way more than I can handle by myself ... with only my pistol and a machete."

"How far away are the Zs?" croaked Ari, trying to crane his head around.

"Quarter mile ... give or take. I figure we've got two ... three minutes tops to get you two out of there and get around to my truck. But there's also something else you need to know."

There was a short silence, after which the voice inside the fuselage said, "Spit it out."

"There's a dead man out here ... and he's wearing the same camouflage get up as you. Anybody missing from inside there?"

There was another short silence.

Finally the man inside the helicopter replied, "My name is Cade. And I need you to forget about everything out there for *now*. I have plenty of problems of my own and I need your help inside here. Right now I've got a man trying to bleed out on me and three more who are either unconscious or dead ... hard to tell 'cause they're wearing body armor and helmets."

After casting one last furtive glance at the approaching pack of dead, Jasper walked his gaze over the jagged metal edges still dripping with the zombie's blood. Then, noting wisps of acrid smoke wafting from the rear half of the wreckage, he said, "How do you expect me to get inside there?"

"*Improvise*," Cade said sharply.

Chapter 3

Utilizing the titanium frame like the rungs of a ladder, Jasper scaled the listing helicopter. When he reached the top—which was really the helicopter's right side—he saw a gaping hole where some kind of a sliding door had once been. He ducked under a drooping slab of rotor blade, lay flat on his stomach on the warm black fuselage, and stared down into the crumpled crew compartment. Instantly he was hit full in the face with the reek of fear-laced sweat and the metallic tang of spilt blood.

Arms blood-slickened and fighting a losing battle to hold Ronnie Gaines' guts in, Cade looked up at the man whom so far he'd only seen reflected in miniature scale on Ari's smoked visor. "Jasper, I need you to jump on in here and start seeing to them," he said, gesturing with a nod of his helmet towards the limp forms strapped in across the way. "Check for a pulse, and if you don't find one right away, move on to the next person."

Jump? Yeah right, thought Jasper. *I'm forty-five going on sixty.* Gingerly he scrabbled over the edge, placed his feet on the frame of the shattered flat-panel display mounted to the fore bulkhead, and then reached for the neck of the closest of the three still strapped-in bodies. The second his fingers grazed the man's carotid, a gloved hand shot upward and grabbed his wrist in a vice-like grip. Then the soldier—who was clad head-to-toe in black body armor and matching helmet—opened his eyes and whispered two words: "What happened?"

Good question, thought Jasper as he pulled free from the man's clutch, and with a flick of the eyes deferred the question to the man calling himself Cade.

"I'm certain I heard Durant say *"Bird strike"* and the cockpit went black just before the helo went lawn dart on us," replied Cade. "None of that matters now. How are *you* doing, Cross?"

"I don't think anything's broken," the man responded. "Probably gonna have some serious whiplash. Maybe gonna need a massage when we get back to Schriever."

With a dog-like tilt to his head, Jasper followed the conversation.

"We've got to make it out of here alive first," intoned Cade. He ripped another trauma bandage from its packaging, tossed the blood-soaked one aside, and pressed the fresh item into Gaines's abdomen, eliciting a groan from the ashen general. "Cross, my hands are full here ... you're going to have to triage Lopez and Hicks."

"Copy that," answered Cross as he gripped the airframe above his head and released the harness that had most likely saved his life. Holding all of his weight with his upper body, he ducked his head around a dangling wiring harness and lowered himself down, careful not to step on Cade or the general. Carefully, he placed the sole of one boot on the hand grip of the port side mini-gun, and then toed the other securely into some nylon webbing hanging off the aft bulkhead. Then he wrestled his gloves off, reached up and grabbed Sergeant Hicks' wrist. He worked his fingers under the glove and detected a very strong pulse there. He let go of Hicks' arm, and then, like some kind of aerial contortionist, or an astronaut in space, performed a slow motion pirouette. Now in a position where he could reach Lopez, he grabbed a handful of webbing to steady himself, lifted the operator's limp arm and wormed two fingers under his glove and blindly felt his wrist in search of a radial pulse. *Nothing.* The operator's skin was cool and slick to the touch.

With a sick feeling washing over him, Cross released the dead man's arm and let gravity take it. As he watched it fall away, a flash of purple showed between the man's camouflage sleeve and his tan tactical glove. Then a conversation he'd had with Lopez prior to boarding the Ghost Hawk at Schriever came rushing back. He remembered the stocky operator saying that since the CDC mission during which Desantos ordered him to carry the decaying Alpha specimen up thirteen flights of stairs, he *always* wore at least two pair of surgical latex gloves underneath his tactical gloves. *Protects against the demonio blood*, Lopez said as he snapped them on. So Cross reached over and checked the man's carotid and felt a strong pulse there. "These two are alive," he said, looking about the cabin, "but where the hell is Tice ... anyone see the Spook?"

"Could be the body I saw out there—near the fence," Jasper said to Cross. "I'm certain that he's dead. He was pale as a ghost and his eyes were stuck wide open."

"*Dead? Are* you certain?" asked Cross incredulously while holding the compress to the general's abdomen with one hand.

"Positive," the undertaker replied from his perch atop the wreck. "He's all contorted and hasn't moved a muscle since I first saw him."

"What happened?" asked Lopez groggily.

"Multiple bird strikes," answered Cross.

Hicks was stirring now. He shook his head side to side and instinctively ran his hands over his extremities, checking his bones and joints for fractures.

Hicks looked over at Cade. "How long have I been out?" he asked.

"Just a few minutes, I think," replied Cade.

"Did Ari and Durant make it?" Hicks pressed.

"Durant bought it," answered Cade. "Ari's lapsing in and out of consciousness."

"Fire?"

"Not yet," said Cade. "Ari took measures."

Hicks inched up his visor. "Radios?"

"I'm sure the shipboard comms are down," Cade said. "I already tried the general's sat-phone ... it won't power on. And mine's in my ruck ... if we can locate it in all this mess."

Trying to take this all in, Hicks closed his eyes for a beat. When he reopened them he popped his harness, bent down and shimmied past the debris and into the cockpit.

Cade called out, reminding the crew chief to steer clear of Durant. Then he checked Gaines's pulse again. It was very weak and fading. Gently he eased up on the compress. He dug around in the medical bag and brought out a syringe filled with morphine, and set it aside. "I need another bandage," he grunted as he reapplied pressure to the grievous wound.

A few seconds after Hicks disappeared into the cockpit he slithered back out, clutching Ari's emergency radio. He powered it on and started sending a silent distress signal which would be picked up by either an overhead satellite, nearby aircraft—or hopefully a combination of both. Then he tried to hail Jedi One-Two on the emergency dust-off band. *Nothing.* "Looks like there'll be no dust-off bird for the general," he said, slumping against the bulkhead.

"No dust-off," Lopez added morosely.

Cross ripped open another clean compress and pressed it next to the one Cade was holding. "I've been thinking," he said. "If I know President Clay like I think I do ... we're secondary. She'll push for the scientists' safe return before diverting any assets to look for us."

"As will Nash and Shrill. They have to. The anti-serum is more important than any one man. That means we're on our own for now, boys," Cade replied. Then he went on and filled the operators in on all that they had missed while unconscious.

"Mierda," said Lopez. "Tice is dead?"

Cade looked down and bobbed his head. He unsheathed his Gerber and, with short precise strokes, sliced through the first half dozen laces on his left boot which was still inextricably wedged under the general's extremely mangled seat frame. He gazed up at Jasper, who, from where he sat, had a clean view into the cockpit and the cabin. "How's Durant now?" he asked through clenched teeth as he twisted and pulled on his leg until finally it corkscrewed free.

Jasper disappeared for a second and then returned and said, "He's *in-between.*"

"Do you mean he's dead but hasn't reanimated yet?"

"That's my opinion," answered Jasper.

Adjusting his grip on the blood-soaked plug of gauze, Cross said, "Gaines is slipping away now too."

"Shit ... shit, shit," chanted Ari from the right seat. "If Durant turns I *need* to be the one who puts him down. I *promised* him as much."

"Ari, pull it together," barked Cade. "Save the worrying for later. That is an *order*."

Ari muttered, "All my fault ... it was all my fault. Durant and now the general." He uttered a flurry of expletives, unplugged his flight helmet, and fast-balled it through the cockpit glass. It bounced a few times and then, without warning, the sky went dark. All eyes looked skyward as the beating of feathered wings announced the return of the raptors responsible for downing the Ghost Hawk. After squawking ardent displeasure at having their mealtime disrupted, some of the birds lit on the downed chopper while the majority sank their talons into the town folks from Draper and resumed picking away at their festering corpses.

"Didn't take them long," said Lopez. "Pinche mirlos."

Returning his attention to Gaines, Cade checked his friend's neck for a pulse. *Nothing.* Then he grasped the general's forearm, ruffled up his ACU sleeve, and searched his broad wrist for a radial pulse. *Still nothing.* He looked around the cabin, met everyone's gaze for a tick, and then said quietly, "Gaines is gone."

Cross removed his hands from the wound below the general's body armor and immediately a loop of pinkish intestine wormed out, followed by a torrent of crimson blood which only lasted until the dead man's blood pressure fully ebbed—a couple of seconds at most.

Wasting no time, Cade unlaced Gaines's left boot which had to be two or maybe even three sizes too big for him. He worked it off and slid his foot inside, where he could feel his size-nine swimming inside. He cinched the desert-tan boot tightly, looped the laces around twice above his swollen ankle, and then tucked the extra deep down inside. He wiggled his toes and realized that he would— literally and figuratively—never fill the general's boots. *Good to go.*

Jasper banged his palm on the fuselage, getting everyone's attention. "The dead are here," he said in a funereal voice. "And we're nearly surrounded."

Looking up at the undertaker, Cade said, "I need you inside here and *everyone* needs to remain quiet and out of sight."

Feeling a bit like a Jack in the Box, Jasper lowered himself back into the crowded crew compartment where, standing upright looked to be a difficult endeavor under normal circumstances, let alone with the floor nearly vertical, while rubbing elbows with four fully outfitted soldiers.

Cade adjusted the tiny voice-activated throat mike, powered it on, and said "Mike check."

"Good copy," replied Cross.

The other two men made eye contact, nodded silent affirmatives of their own.

After tightening his MOLLE gear, Cade cycled a round into the M4. He felt blindly for the reassuring outline of his Gerber combat dagger, then patted the holstered Glock 17 riding low on his left thigh—both automatic rituals he'd performed a million times before going *down range*. He looked at the men who were leaning and sitting on any flat surface available. Lopez, who was now fully conscious, was wedged tight into a nook worn smooth from seeing its fair share of combat boots.

Brandishing the compact MP7, Agent Cross stood next to Hicks, both of their helmets close to brushing the starboard mini-gun. The President's man appeared confident, albeit a little jittery—no doubt itching to get out into the open and *get some*. Hicks was his usual stoic self—red-rimmed eyes staring out from under the flight helmet's retracted visor.

Cade set his gaze on Ronnie's body. Inexplicably, the general's eyes were now open, and his skin had gone ashen—a dingy gray pallor—like a chalkboard in need of a thorough cleaning. His face was waxen and had started to slacken, the flagging skin forming jowls beside his dangling chin straps. Cade looked away and muttered a few choice expletives under his breath. *This unfortunate event is going to do a number on Ari*, he thought to himself. First a murder of birds had ruined their day, and now he could hear the Zs' raspy hissing rising above the steady thrum of beating wings cutting the air. A couple of beats later, he opened his eyes as the hungry throng began raking their nails along the craft's outer skin, sending spine-tingling scratching noises echoing through the cabin.

Chapter 4
Schriever AFB
Colorado Springs, Colorado

All conversation in the mess hall ceased as a group of *outsiders*, undoubtedly just released from quarantine, filed in ahead of their handlers—a pair of stern-faced soldiers who had been given the unenviable task of chaperoning the haggard civilians about the base. They passed out aluminum trays to the men and women who were standing in a ragged line, fidgeting and casting furtive glances about the dining area. Bathed in the blue-tinged light thrown from humming overhead tubes, the avocado-green institutional-style chairs and faux wood grain on the table tops lent the Schriever mess hall all of the charm of an inner-city hospital cafeteria.

With the late night chow line attack fresh on her mind, Sasha cast a worried look at the forming queue and sank into the molded plastic seat. She tore her gaze away momentarily and hissed under her breath at Wilson, who was busily shoveling gravy-soaked bread into his maw. She repeated his name three times, and when he finally acknowledged her she added a rapidly recurring nod that looked more like some kind of spasmodic episode than a gesture imploring her brother to take in the unsettling sight.

Pretending for a moment that he hadn't seen her unwitting Arnold Horshack impersonation, he finished chewing the mouthful of food and then nonchalantly looked over his shoulder at the newcomers. "So what Sash," he replied, shooting her a quizzical look. "Not long ago that was us."

"You think they're *infected?*" she whispered without taking her wide-eyed gaze from them.

"Every single one of them are. I'm *sure* of it," said Taryn, causing Sasha to visibly shudder. The tanned and toned brunette had been standing and watching the procession from a blind spot directly behind the redheaded siblings. She winked across the table at Raven while avoiding eye contact with Brook, who didn't seem to be onboard with the juvenile behavior. Then she leaned in between Sasha and Wilson, her long black hair brushing across both of their backs and added, "I'm sorry Sasha. I was just pulling your chain since your brother here won't reciprocate. What's that phrase that I'm searching for?"

"I'm sure it will come to you," said Sasha, straightening up in her seat.

"What goes around comes around," Taryn said, adding a wan smile.

"So there's *no* chance of one of them turning?" asked Sasha, ignoring the earlier comment and casting a skeptical look over her shoulder.

"*None,*" answered Taryn. "If those people received half of the *welcome aboard* treatment I did, there's a good chance they might be *brainwashed* ... but surely they are not *infected.*" She skirted the table and placed her tray next to Raven's, and as a smitten Wilson stared across the table at her, trapped her hair at the nape of her neck with both hands and deftly secured it into a snakelike ponytail with half a dozen black hair ties.

"What *exactly* do you mean by brainwashed?" Wilson asked, as feelings of insecurity and inadequacy bubbled to the surface. *Maybe she had been brainwashed*, his magical magnifying mind needled as the molehill grew exponentially into a monument to worry and despair.

Meeting Wilson's gaze, Taryn reached across the table and took his hand in hers. Instantly his face flushed hot, the visible cues to her effect on him concealed beneath his already sunburned dermis. Then his heart started hammering, wanting to leap from his chest. He was certain she could hear its telltale thumping in the nearly empty mess hall. "I'm OK," she said with a quick smile. "And I think it's so sweet that you're concerned about me."

"What did they do to welcome you aboard?" asked Raven, shattering the Harlequin moment.

Conscious of the fact that Brook was staring in her direction, Taryn released Wilson's hand, sat back and crafted her answer carefully. "A thorough strip search followed by a thousand and one questions," she said slowly. "And then they asked me a hundred more questions about someone I didn't know. At first I thought they were believing the stories in the tabloids and were searching for the *real* Elvis." She winked at Wilson, throwing more fuel on the twenty-year-old's smoldering desire. "I almost told them he was cashiering at the K-Mart in Denver but thought better of it—because my captors had guns."

Taking this literally, Raven said, "Twelve hours straight of nothing but listening to someone like my dad talking about *old* music. No thanks." Then she realized which *Elvis* her new friend was referring to, went silent, and returned her attention to the *food* on the plate in front of her.

The flock of newcomers, trays filled with something brown concocted with unknown ingredients into something barely edible, filtered past and commandeered a number of tables nearby.

Brook regarded the people with a look filled more with pity than fear. Still, she nudged her tray toward the center of the table and retrieved the battle-scarred M4 carbine from the shiny linoleum floor.

Earlier in the day she and Raven had passed by another contingent of refugees from Pueblo. The group, numbering somewhere north of twenty, had been standing in the beating sun near the parade grounds, their thousand-yard stares fixed on the red-faced airman who was busily pointing to the areas where they were welcome while issuing stern warnings and singling out the places that were *verboten*—completely off limits to civilians.

To Brook, the whole affair smacked more of a prison induction than the assimilation of American citizens—survivors of what might be mankind's extinction level event—onto an air base just outside the new capitol of the United States of America. *Thanks Elvis*, she'd thought at the time. Just like Bin Laden had been to America before the raid in Pakistan—Elvis was to Schriever now. He was the *new* boogeyman. Gone, but not really *gone*. Kids whispered his

18

name without a clue as to who the man was, what he looked like, or who his namesake had been. The perception of safety afforded by the high fences and armed men and women of Schriever had been shattered by the attacks that had taken place on the base during the past week, and short of the public execution of the man who some people feared still lurked in the shadows, this palpable sense of vulnerability would continue to be the *new normal*.

Hopefully, she thought, Robert Christian's execution—supposedly set to take place the next morning—would satisfy the need for revenge openly called for by the handful of outbreak survivors. *Surely*, Brook thought. *Absent the real perpetrator of the attack—cutting off the head of the snake would be better than nothing.*

Beginning the day before, scores of injured and badly-burned civilian refugees had begun arriving from the south, fleeing the dead by car, bus, and pretty much anything with wheels ahead of raging fires that she had overheard one shell-shocked man describe as *a great conflagration*.

Most of the survivors, because of infection, injury, or a combination of both, were still in quarantine and might never make it out alive. Explaining to Raven why and where all of them came from had been a little difficult. On the one hand she hadn't wanted to sugarcoat their new reality with half-truths or generalities. But if the twelve-year-old was going to be a hardy survivor going forward, downplaying even the smallest detail would only prove to leave her at a disadvantage—especially if she faced something similar in the future. So Brook used their flight from Fort Bragg as an example; however, she did downplay the numbers significantly since she had been told the ferocity of the undead attacks on the living during their diaspora from Pueblo would alarm even the most seasoned combat veteran. Just last night at dinner she'd overheard an older officer likening the scene on Interstate 25 to the aptly-named Highway of Death between Kuwait and Basra on which thousands of Saddam Hussein's Republican Guard had been savaged by the full might of the United States Air Force, Marine, and Naval airpower.

Apparently several thousand survivors had been holed up and hunkered down, scattered throughout Pueblo, probably cut off from the outside world and hoping to wait Omega out, Brook explained.

Until finally the raging fires and advancing dead had literally eaten their way north, consuming buildings and flesh alike. The ones arriving now, she warned Raven, were the first of many. What she didn't say was that she had overheard the same officer mention that tens of thousands of walking dead were shambling north towards Colorado Springs in hot pursuit of the survivors. Raven would find out the hard-to-swallow facts soon enough. Hell, thought Brook. Mother and daughter might just find themselves standing shoulder-to-shoulder picking off the dead from within the same guard tower— a family affair indeed. She shuddered at the thought.

"Finish up, Raven," Brook said, chair legs screeching as she rose and policed up her trash. "You *kids* still want to learn to shoot?" she asked, her gaze lingering mostly on Wilson.

Raven was up first, obviously eager to resume her *studies*. "Can we bring Max?" she asked excitedly, referring to the stray Australian Shepherd she had adopted the day before.

"Wouldn't have it any other way," replied Brook. "He can't stay in the barracks all day." Besides, she thought to herself. If Cade was going to allow the dog to come along with them to Eden, then it would be nice to know how the stray reacted to prolonged gunfire.

"Yippee," cried Raven. "Can I ride my bike?"

"Yes you may."

On the way out the door Sasha sidled next to Raven and whispered in her ear. "Can I get a turn on your bike?"

Grinning ear to ear, Raven answered, "You can go first. On one condition."

"What is it?" Sasha replied, trapping a strand of red curls behind her ear.

"You have to agree to let my mom show you how to shoot my rifle. It's little ..."

Rolling her eyes, Sasha said, "I'm not *afraid*. It's just we're not really a gun family."

"You'll have to learn to be comfortable around them if you and Wilson want to go to Eden with us."

Listening in, Brook slowed her pace and corrected her daughter. "Sasha, as far as I'm concerned, you and Wilson and Taryn are welcome regardless. I think what Raven is trying to convey is that

Cade would probably be more comfortable with the idea of you coming along if at least one of you knew a little about firearms. At least the safety part."

Throwing her hat in the ring, Taryn blurted, "Count me in." Then as the group exited the mess and stood outside awash in sunlight, the dominos began to fall.

"Me too," added Wilson, even though the awful memory of the shotgun-blasted arm gripping his red locks instantly sprang to mind.

"If they all go first ... I'll give it a shot," Sasha added quietly, pun not intended.

"We're off then," Raven said, tapping her newfound friend on the elbow. "You can ride my bike for as long as you want."

Chapter 5
Draper, South Dakota

"*Now* we *are* surrounded," whispered Jasper. "You sure I can't pop a few of them from up top? It's only a little .22."

"*Positive*," said Ari. "JP-8 is *very* flammable. We'll go up like a Viking funeral pyre if you do."

"Surrounded by *demonios?*" Lopez rasped. He cracked his neck and then rubbed his neck and shoulders. His back throbbed where the vertebra had been compacted during the jarring impact and subsequent rapid deceleration. Like he'd just awoken from a nightmare, he surveyed the damaged cabin with a worried look on his face. He shook his head, trying to clear the cobwebs from what he guessed was a minor concussion, and asked Cross in a near whisper, "Where did we go down?"

"Somewhere in the middle of *nowhere* South Dakota," answered Cross as he unbuckled the stocky operator and helped him down to the floor.

Lopez unclipped his M4, set it aside, and covered his face with gloved hands. "Tice, Durant, and Gaines ... all dead," he said quietly. "Where'd that guy say Tice's body ended up?"

"Outside somewhere," Cross replied. "Somehow he got thrown out when we went down."

After scrutinizing the seat where Tice had been sitting, Lopez pointed to the harness and said, "Looks normal to me. Nothing torn... clasps look OK."

"Freak accident... just like the bird strike," replied Cross shaking his head. "Murphy's got our number today—"

"We ... are ... *hosed*," Ari called back matter-of-factly. "There are at least a dozen Zs up here ... and Durant's just turned."

"Can any of them reach you?" Cade asked.

"Negative ... I'm about a foot above their reach," replied Ari. "But Goddamn they stink."

Welcome to our world, thought Cade as he swiped his fingers down Gaines' face, closing his staring eyes forever.

Hoping to hear a different opinion than the one already voiced by Cade and Cross, Hicks said to Ari, "How long before Ripley misses us and turns her Osprey around?"

Ari shouted back, "She has a big jump on us. So I don't expect her to give us a second thought before she gets the scientists back to Schriever ..."

Hicks removed his helmet, hung it by its strap on the mini-gun grip. "Fuck," he spat, obviously disgusted by the predicament they were in.

"Shouldn't a crash beacon have been activated or something?" inquired Cross.

"Should have," Ari called back. "But did it? That's the million dollar question. I have no way of telling because my electrical is dead. We can only *hope* that *if* a signal went out, there was a satellite up there to bounce it back to Schriever." But after witnessing the Chinese satellite destroy the ISS at the pre-mission briefing, and then subsequently learning that Major Nash's fleet of spy satellites had suffered losses due to similar attacks—Ari was very reluctant to pin his hopes on a hope filled assumption.

As if he knew what was going through Ari's mind, Cade piped up, "Me and Cross are of the same mind back here. Ripley can't come back until she's over the wire and wheels down and her customers have been delivered safely."

"I concur," said Cross. "Not to cast blame on Ari or Durant or the general for allowing it, but the fact that we deviated from the flight path on that low level shakeout means we cannot wait in place ..."

"He's right," said Cade, locking eyes with Lopez, who was the
last living member of Desantos' original Delta Unit. "More Zs *will*
show up if we loiter here. And when enough of them gather they'll
start to climb over each other. *Eventually* the tenacious bastards *will*
get in here. And when they do, I intend on being someplace else."

Cross shifted his gaze upward, looking beyond Jasper who
was still prostrate near the tear in the starboard fuselage. He regarded
the birds swirling like a black tornado overhead and then leaned back
against one of the helicopter's internal support members and met the
Delta operator's gaze. "So, Captain Grayson—tell me—what's your
plan?"

Cade waited a beat before answering, and when he finally did,
he had to raise his voice to compete with the unsettling sound of
bone and nail grating on the metal behind his head. He went over his
plan in detail and then asked the survivors to take inventory of their
ammo. All combined, for the M4 carbines they had just shy of three
hundred rounds of 5.56 hardball loaded into ten magazines. Each
man also had his own personal sidearm with at least two full
magazines for each. Lastly, the *lone wolf* of the team, Secret Service
Special Agent Adam Cross, had two extended thirty-round magazines
fully loaded with 4.6x30mm cartridges that were unique to his
suppressed HK MP7 auto pistol.

"I'm going to need your weapon, Agent Cross," Cade said
quietly. He knew the stubby carbine like the back of his hand, and
had used one like it on hostage rescue missions when CQC—close
quarters combat—was imminent, and necessitated a quick takedown
of multiple targets in confined spaces. He figured its compact size
would be perfect for the looming task, allowing him to move freely
between the headstones. It made no difference that there were only
two magazines left for the weapon. Because if the sixty rounds they
held wasn't sufficient to get him to the truck in one piece, then he
had no business calling himself a member of Delta.

Without a word, Cross shrugged off the MP7 and handed it
over, dangling it by its single-point sling. He removed the spare mag
from his now empty MOLLE gear and passed it over as well.

"One more thing," said Cade, looking up through the starboard doorway at the rectangle of blue South Dakota sky. "I'll need a leg up."

Quick to comply, Lopez laced his fingers like a stirrup and braced his shoulder against the seat, ready to accept Cade's full body weight.

But before Cade stepped up, he called forward to Ari, "You better play possum until I get back or this thing might backfire on all of us."

Hearing every word Cade had said, Ari made no reply. He'd been thinking ahead, and already his eyes were shut and his breathing slowed—all in an attempt to fool his undead co-pilot into thinking he was already dead.

Chapter 6

The dead were congregated mostly near the helo's nose when Cade emerged from the gash in the fuselage where the impact with hard Dakota soil had sheared off the sliding door and a portion of surrounding airframe along with it. He looked closely at the brown sod and scraps of decayed flesh clinging to the jagged edges near where Hicks had been sitting, marveling at the fact the crew chief was still among the living, while Gaines, who had been on the port side opposite the damage, was the one who was dead. He also found it strange how the man on the proverbial white horse had chosen to take Tice's life while sparing the two operators who had been strapped in on either side of him. Even after having served in multiple combat zones and surviving many firefights in which others around him had not, it still never ceased to amaze the Delta operator how unpredictable the hand of fate could be when it came to dealing out the death card.

With the black composite skin radiating warmth through his gloved hands, Cade crawled aft along the fuselage. Pausing next to the angular engine nacelle, he came up on one knee and swept his gaze in a wide arc until he picked out Tice's still form lying exactly where Jasper had said it would be. Twisted up next to the fence a number of yards off of the ship's nose, arms and legs jutting at unnatural angles, the camouflage-clad body looked more like a kid's discarded G.I. Joe doll than the affable warrior who, for the better part of a week, had been a recipient of the Delta team's hazing.

Cade said a prayer for Tice and tore his eyes from the surreal sight—from the shell of the man he'd just been talking and joking with minutes ago. He regarded the ancient cemetery, most of which remained pristine save for the dark furrow the helicopter had made when it went down. Fifty yards beyond the initial point of impact, which had to be a football field's length from where the helo came to rest, was a sizeable white church that he guessed had been standing sentinel over the deceased of its congregation for the last hundred years.

He turned and gazed past the clutch of dead gathered around the nose of the helicopter, judging the distance to Jasper's truck to be about seventy-five yards, most of which was hardscrabble earth patrolled by shambling Zs drawn in as a result of the crash. Then he looked at the grass between where he stood and Tice's body, judging it to be no less than twenty feet. He shifted his gaze to the fence line off of his right shoulder and placed his money on seventy yards—just a few shy of the truck. Lastly, he ticked off the twenty-two rows of graves stretching away from the crash south to north and then added up the columns running west to east. Making a quick calculation, he realized that interred within the four sagging runs of fence were at least two hundred and twenty of Draper's past residents, each of who had been memorialized by small squares of marble, pointed monoliths, and dozens of chest-high slabs of natural stone hewn into all manner of shapes: crosses, round tops, pillars, cherubs, and the occasional Star of David. Scattered randomly among the carved tributes to lives past were dozens upon dozens of dead bodies, the majority of which had already turned and thankfully now bore gunshot wounds from having already been put down.

After taking into account the number of flesh-eaters between him and the truck, and the fact that the helicopter sat on fuel-soaked ground, he came to the conclusion that there was no easy answer. And as he knelt atop the aircraft calculating his odds of survival if he made a dash for the truck, the solution came to him. As usual, the answer wasn't exactly what he wanted it to be. He knew in order to make a clean break while luring as many of the dead away from the wreck as possible, he would have to take the long route north towards the church, and then double back outside the fence to the waiting set of wheels—all the while with *only* a couple or three dozen hungry Zs giving chase.

One step at a time, Grayson, he reminded himself. Then one of Mike's favorite phrases—of which there were many—popped into his head. *The first step is always the hardest*, the hard-charging Delta commander usually said prior to going down-range. And in the teams, that *first step* was making certain all of the available info was known up front and then running the mission over and over until each team member could execute his job flawlessly—but also could step in and execute any one of his teammates' jobs if the need arose.

But unfortunately for Cade, he didn't have the luxury of physically running this thing through even once—let alone multiple times until it was rote. So he did the second best thing: he visualized the route he'd take. He ran it a dozen times in his head before he was confident and ready to take the plunge—literally. Then he reran it a dozen more times—after all—the first step in this instance would be for him to get off the helo and on the ground in one piece and without further injury. Then *all* he needed to do was convince the dead into following him away from the wreck all without getting surrounded and eaten alive.

Piece of cake.

Chapter 7

Still reeling from the loss of Maddox, and lamenting the fact that they had been forced to leave his corpse on the tarmac at Grand Junction, the Delta team, to a man, had decided days earlier that they would leave no man behind—and though he had already turned—that pact also included Durant.

While Cade had been plotting his egress, inside the cabin Cross unbuckled Gaines and replaced his entrails, wrapping everything up with some kind of first-aid tape taken from the med kit. Then, with a little help from Lopez, they manhandled the general's body into a sitting position.

Meanwhile Hicks busied himself preparing a makeshift sling out of high tensile nylon rope, the idea being that when Cade returned with the truck they would combine their muscle and use it to haul the general's two-hundred-plus pounds of dead weight out of the helicopter.

"Any way I can help?" whispered Jasper who had wedged his considerable frame against the cockpit bulkhead, and up until then seemed content just listening and watching.

After stripping the backpack and MOLLE gear from the general's body, Lopez liberated the seven full magazines and handed them across the cabin to Jasper. "Put these up top ... quietly," he said. "And we'll need his weapon." He went through the motions of clearing the chamber and set the general's SCAR carbine back on safe before passing it over to Jasper.

"So you are serious about taking the bodies with you?" asked the undertaker.

"We *do not* leave our fallen behind," Lopez said sharply.

"And the infected one?" asked Jasper, furrowing his brow.

"We are going to move Heaven and Earth to bring Gaines and Tice home. And Durant goes too, *if* we can get him untangled," replied Hicks, adding a no-nonsense look that ended Jasper's line of questioning.

"Captain Grayson will be back in a few minutes and that's when you come into play," Cross said, tapping Jasper's well-developed bicep.

Chapter 8

Crouched atop the helo, Cade counted seventeen Zs moaning and jostling for space, pressed two deep against the cockpit glass. Watching them, he could almost feel their hunger as they reached excitedly into the helo, bony fingers kneading the air, straining to grab ahold of Ari, who Cade guessed had to be shitting in his flight suit right about now.

"Fresh meat," Cade bellowed as he rose. Then, to *really* get their attention, he waved his arms wildly and half walked, half limped towards the tail assembly, hollering at the top of his lungs. "Ding, ding, ding. Dinner time. Come and get it!" He continued hollering and carrying on loudly while inwardly hoping he wasn't laying it on *too* thick. The last thing he wanted was for them to get overly excited and infuse some kind of extra pep into their normally slow step.

He went silent, stood hands on hips, and observed the Zs freeze in place. Then, predictably, their heads panned in unison and their rheumy eyes fixed on him. *Good*, he thought to himself, noticing that they had, at least for the moment, forgotten about Ari.

Next, in order to get them moving in his direction, he belted out a few choice expletives unbecoming of an officer. *Mission accomplished*, he thought as he watched the entire lot of them file around the Ghost Hawk's undercarriage, dead eyes locked solely on him.

He paused and steadied himself with one hand on the upthrust rear canard, which, stabbing skyward, looked quite a bit like an Orca's black dorsal fin. After stealing a final glance over his left shoulder, and seeing that the Zs had covered half the distance to his position, he shifted his gaze and studied the ground for a flat landing spot free of crash debris. *Now or never*, he told himself as he dipped his hips, stepped forward, and committed to the twelve-foot drop.

With the Zs crowding his peripheral vision on the left and the ground rushing at him from below, he concentrated hard on coming down on the ball of his right foot with his body canted at an easy angle. In theory, if performed correctly, he could then fold over and roll out without further injuring his left foot—or anything else for that matter. The technique, known as a *paratrooper's landing fall*—or PLF—was taught to every airborne soldier before ever setting foot in an airplane.

The descent was rapid leaving him little time to shift on axis, let alone focus on his desired landing spot. But as luck would have it, Mister Murphy was occupied elsewhere. *Three good men dead*, Cade thought darkly. Apparently the damage here had already exceeded Murphy's expectations, because, bum ankle and all, his landing was perfect. He barrel-rolled fluidly to the right, slowed himself midway with both palms flat to the earth, and sprang upright, slightly gimpy. Shifting his weight to his right leg, he adjusted the MP7 on its sling so that it dangled out of the way behind his back, and drew the Gerber combat dagger.

But before he could check his surroundings—let alone take that first step towards the church—Mister Murphy changed his mind. The carrion birds went deathly quiet as if they had been watching with bated breath, excited at the prospect of sharing in the fresh kill. A millisecond after he sprang up and the birds went mute, a subtle intermittent rasp of fabric chafing against fabric and the soft firework crackle of brittle grass underfoot reached his ears. He whipped around and found himself face-to-face with one of the monsters. At first he supposed it had unwittingly chased his silhouette as he walked the length of the tail boom. Then a shiver traced his spine when he realized it was likely that he was witnessing a bit of cunning at play; the fact that it had stalked him without making a sound was the biggest tell of all.

For a tick the monster stood stock still, shark-like eyes staring, seemingly sizing him up with a sort of quiet determination

Cade had yet to see one of them exhibit. A good thing, because in its condition, the sight of the thing alone froze Cade for the duration.

Most of the Z's skin had sloughed off, leaving tufts of hair and glistening muscle clinging to its bare skull. All of the soft fleshy bits were gone: ears, nose, cheeks, and lips, the loss of the latter leaving it with a devilish toothy grin.

After the split second staring contest, the decaying abomination raised its arms and attacked.

Ducking, Cade avoided the cold embrace, and countered with backhanded roundhouse that left the black dagger buried half a foot into the thing's brain. He stepped aside, allowing the achingly-thin zombie to slide free from the steel, and watched it crumple to the ground, a tangle of bony arms and legs like something out of a wartime newsreel.

Out of the frying pan and into the fire, Cade thought as a claw-like hand, bony nubs trailing ribbons of flesh and sinew, flashed by an inch from his face. Instincts kicking in, he backpedaled and moved to his left under the tail boom while two hundred and fifty pounds of moaning flesh-eater plodded toward him.

Cade regarded its blood-spattered tee shirt swaying with each uneasy step and recited the words stitched across the chest, "World's Greatest Grandpa." Instantly he thought of Brook's mother and father and the grisly details surrounding their final day on Earth.

"Sorry, sir," Cade said in a low voice. Feeling a twinge of empathy usually reserved for the living, and with all one hundred and eighty pounds behind the thrust, he rocketed off his right foot, the Gerber accelerating towards Grandpa's left eye socket. The point on the finely honed blade sliced through the fat layer surrounding the clouded eye, and glanced off the rigid orbital bone before finally penetrating the creature's low functioning brain. He followed through with a sharp elbow strike to the right side of its mottled gray face, freeing the dagger and redirecting Grandpa's forward motion left and away. As the plastic cap on Cade's tactical elbow pad resonated from the delivered blow, his torso rotated on the follow through, saddling his left foot with the combined body weight of both he and his assailant.

Swallowing hard, he fought off the unexpected flood of nausea as the three bones making up his ankle balked at the maneuver. An explosion of white hot pain came next. Coursing up his left leg, the intense stimuli transited his sciatica and rippled like a fast-moving tsunami through his spine to a spot just behind his right eye, where he was certain a nasty little imp was fileting his optic nerve with a rusty razor blade. Normally 20/20, his vision suffered at the periphery, and as he fought the urge to pass out the world went soft around the edges; he could just barely make out the next echelon of creatures closing in doggedly, unstoppable and insatiable wraiths fading along with his eyesight.

Chapter 9
Schriever AFB

Annie leapt to her feet, nearly breaking her neck trying to acquire the source of the shrill screams carrying across the quarter-mile oval track.

Reacting instantly and instinctively, Brook snatched up her carbine and in one fluid motion jumped cat-like from the bleacher seat to the sun-baked ground. She took a few steps forward and then visibly relaxed upon realizing the spine-tingling sounds, which of late had mostly been associated with death and doom, were merely the by-product of a healthy game of tag. For Annie's benefit she shouldered the M4 and scanned the foreground through the rifle's optics.

"The twins are just playing tag. Everything's OK," she said. A few seconds slipped by and the screams turned into peals of laughter. Keeping her cheek to the stock and her eye close to the 3x magnifier, Brook swept the rifle from left to right along the fence line where she could see the monsters clutching the fence and Max jumping and snarling protecting his new *sheep* the only way he knew how.

"What do you see?" asked Annie, strain evident in her voice.

"The girls are playing. The Zs are still right where they're supposed to be—on the other side of the fence. And it looks like Max thinks he's the only thing standing between the girls and the Zs."

Releasing the breath she'd been holding, Annie followed the action as her twins ducked and dodged through the lengthening grass, trying their best to elude their new friend Sasha, who was reaching and swiping and corralling nothing but air. *Two against one*, she thought. Good odds, but not great, considering her eight-year-old girls were still truly eight and hadn't yet been forced to run for their lives. In fact, just after Mike's passing, she'd made a solemn vow to herself to shield Sierra and Serena from the horrors of this new world for as long as humanly possible, even going so far as resisting the constant invites to *"Learn the ins and outs of shooting,"* as Brook had taken to calling her daily target practice on the living dead that lurked just outside the wire. Paper targets were one thing, Annie had decided after declining Brook's first overture. But shooting something that used to be a human just wasn't in her. And she sure as hell wasn't going to force it upon her kids in order to condition them to the real world outside-the-wire.

Until she was certain there was no danger, Annie kept one eye glued on her kids in the foreground and the other on the gathered undead clutching the fence a dozen yards beyond. Finally, forcing a tight smile, she sat back down and shifted her gaze to Brook. Searching for something meaningful to say, she locked eyes with her friend, but came up empty. Then, like a crashing wave, the realization that she and Brook had spoken on but a handful of occasions since Mike's passing hit her. And those conversations—centering mainly around the how's and why's of surviving the apocalypse, of which they each held widely differing opinions—were far from their *normal* shoot-the-shit types of chats about their men and kids. Something had changed between them. The feeling that she and Brook were growing apart had started as a barely perceptible twinge deep in the pit of her stomach the day she'd put her husband into the ground, and had been ever-present, growing like a widening chasm splitting the common ground between them ever since. It was nothing calculated on Brook's part, of that Annie was certain. She supposed Brook's metamorphosis was a by-product of some kind of innate defense mechanism triggered by Mike's untimely death. Truth be told, both of them always thought it was going to happen to someone else's husband, that the hand of fate would never touch their lives. But now that it had, and in such an intimate way, Annie was afraid their relationship would never be the same—if it survived at all.

Ignoring the uneasy silence that hung thick between her and Annie like some kind of invisible force field, Brook propped her rifle against the bleachers and watched with a widening smile as Raven whizzed by, one hand on the bars, four fingers thrust into the air indicating what lap she'd just completed. "*Go girl,*" Brook called out as her daughter rounded the far corner, pigtails flapping and the shimmering heat waves lending the impression that she was gliding over hot coals. Sure enough, the day had shaped up just like the last three or four, another scorcher to add to the record books. Why she had agreed to let Raven take her new metal steed for a spin under these conditions, during the hottest part of the day, escaped her. In hindsight, however, a little toughening up and acclimatizing the girl to the heat before their upcoming cross-country trip to Utah would do more good than harm. For there would be no 7-Elevens or Dairy Queens providing a plethora of cold drinks along the way. And rest areas with complimentary Styrofoam cups of piping-hot coffee provided by some fraternal order named after an eagle or an elk were a thing of the past. *No,* Brook thought. *There'll be nothing but unforgiving territory and God only knows how many Zs between us and sanctuary once we're outside the wire.*

"Come in for a pit stop, sweetie. You need to stay hydrated," called Brook. Then she looked to the far end of the bleachers where Wilson and Taryn were crushed together presumably sharing thoughts and dreams about their new future. The blissful sight suddenly made Brook pine for her man's return. She reached into her cargo pocket and rooted around until she felt the sharp edge of the death letter. She wanted nothing more than to rip the thing into a million pieces. Or burn it and pretend it had never existed. But superseding and dwarfing both of those kneejerk reactions to something that symbolized a possible outcome to the mission that she never wanted to face—yet was a risk that she knew came with the territory—was her desire to have the family back together for good.

As if she had been reading Brook's thoughts, Annie asked, "When is Cade supposed to return?"

"Depends upon who you ask. Nash and the President led me to believe it would be a quick in and out. Half a day tops—"

"Are they ever?"

"No, and I'm *fucking* sick of it," Brook spat. She collected her carbine and Raven's rifle and jumped to the ground, her boots creating a puff of dust.

There was silence for a moment. Both women knew innately that they were going in two different directions, so neither made an attempt at small talk. They stood close but not too close and watched the twins playing for two or three long minutes.

"Let's go, girls," Annie hollered as she held the swaddled Mike Junior close and began walking away from the parade grounds and towards her quarters.

"Raven and Sasha," Brook bellowed. "Time to shoot."

"OK, Mom. Just a second," Raven called out as she tackled one more lap.

"Now!" Brook added, raising her voice substantially. Then, without another glance in Annie's direction, she strode toward the lovebirds, tapped Wilson on the shoulder and with an arch to her brow and a silent nod of her head, requested the pair to follow.

Chapter 10
Schriever AFB

The cheer that resonated inside the 50th Space Operations TOC—Tactical Operations Center—when Marine Aviator Major Loretta Ripley announced that her Osprey, call sign Jedi One-Two, was *wheels up* with the scientists safely aboard shook every flat panel monitor in the room on its stand.

Then, a handful of minutes later, when word came down that Jedi One-One—with General Gaines and all of the Delta customers safely aboard—was also *wheels up*, an equally rousing round of applause circled the TOC and the previous feeling of accomplishment and joy Nash had felt was trumped tenfold. And as the sound rippled into silence, Major Freda Nash smiled; she couldn't remember ever having been this elated over one event in twenty years of running satellite overwatch over *her* Special Operations boys.

But seeing as how the possible fate of mankind hinged on rescuing and returning with enough brainpower to decipher the data contained on one tiny thumb drive, Nash expected nothing less than ecstatic jubilation from her young Air Force staff.

She, on the other hand, was reserving the right to celebrate at a later date. For the jury was still out whether the three scientists from the National Microbiology Laboratory—Canada's answer to the Centers for Disease Control in Atlanta—would be able to reverse engineer Sylvester Fuentes's Omega antiserum. The possibility, she would tell anyone foolish enough to ask, was a longshot at best.

However, the fist pump President Valerie Clay delivered upon hearing the good news was going to go down in the history books—hopefully on the first page of a chapter telling how Omega was finally defeated and how the country had rid itself of the walking dead.

But that chapter in history had yet to be written. The helicopter carrying the Delta Force shooters was overdue to check in and couldn't be hailed. The mood inside the computer-filled room had instantly crashed, going from a palpable air of hope and exuberance to an atmosphere akin to that of a wake—the only thing missing: the casket and the funeral dirge.

Nash massaged her temples, then impatience got the better of her. "Has Jedi One-One checked in yet?" she asked for the second time in the last five minutes.

"No, Ma'am," said a baby-faced communications sergeant sitting off to the major's right.

"Keep trying," barked Nash. "But do not lose contact with Major Ripley's bird."

"Yes Ma'am."

Fearing the worst, Nash kept her game face on. Keeping up the appearance on the outside was easy. Stilling the Mothra-sized butterflies in her gut was not. She placed her elbows on the podium and formed a steeple with her fingers. Staring out over her hard-working staff, she ran the many different scenarios through her head. After two or three minutes of this she'd boiled them down to three, and not one of them pointed to any kind of a good ending.

***

West of the Rockies

Bishop tossed the empty can aside and opened another, poured the entire five gallons from the plastic container into the generator's oversized tank.

Second chore of the day done—cutting a half a cord of firewood being the first—he walked around to the rear of the chalet-style house and sat down on his favorite chaise. With a world-class view spread out before him, he retrieved the sat-phone from the low cedar table, thumbed it on and checked the display. *Three missed calls.*

Two were from Elvis. Recent. Annoying. The other was left two hours prior by Carson, his second-in-command. He scrolled down, ignoring the two messages from Elvis, and selected the one from Carson. But instead of listening to it he hit send, calling him back.

Three rings later the connection was made and always businesslike his number two simply said, "Carson."

"Bishop here," he said, sparing the formalities for face-to-face communications. "What kind of progress are you making?"

"We loitered in Boise overnight."

Slightly taken aback, Bishop said, "In the city?"

"No," replied Carson. "It burned pretty hard. We're at the Air National Guard base—"

Bishop interrupted. "What's the undead situation ... have you come across any of those large hordes?" he asked, running a shaky hand through his dark hair.

"Boise is thick with them ... the fencing here is keeping them out, for now. Figure when we bug out, so will they."

Carson paused for a tick, trying to decide how to word the rest of his answer.

"And?" said Bishop, sensing Carson had more to add.

"We overflew a very large horde near the Tri-Cities in Washington. Nowhere safe to put down there."

There was another long silence and Bishop changed the subject. "Did you find any aircraft where you're at?"

"A couple of A-10 Thunderbolts in the middle of repairs. The few helos the Guard left behind are a total loss—"

Bishop rose from the chaise and paced the lawn. "Fuel?"

"All of the underground storage tanks were spared from the fires."

"Personnel?"

"Aside from a few deadheads, the place was deserted when we landed."

"And today?" asked Bishop.

"Today we'll recon Salt Lake and then we'll square the box and head north to Ogden."

"How much more time do you need?"

"A day or two. Then you'll know exactly what we're up against. Both the living and the dead."

"Carry on," Bishop said. He stabbed a key ending the call, pocketed the phone, and walked down to the lake's edge where he could see going up on the other side the first of many crosses he was having erected.

The tithing had stopped coming in, yet he and his men continued to keep the place free from the roaming dead. He feared that if the locals continued to be ungrateful for all that he'd done for them in such a short span, then an example would have to be made of someone.

Chapter 11
Draper, South Dakota

As the pain doubled down, harsh waves of nausea returned in direct proportion. Fighting the urge to puke, Cade bent over, bracing his palms on his knees, and took a number of rapid breaths, expelling each one more forcefully than the last until the pain ebbed and the blue tracers affecting his vision began to fade.

He rose, shook his head vigorously, and with the monsters nearly on top of him informed the men in the helo, in rather optimistic fashion, that he was *on the move.*

More as an afterthought, the word *maybe*, usually forbidden from the Delta warrior's lexicon, stayed trapped in his head as he took the first tentative step. And as the seven crucial bones and the spiderweb of tendons and ligaments supporting them compressed under his full weight, the resulting pain was sharp and unyielding. Sweat beaded on his forehead, yet he willed himself to put one foot in front of the other. With more than a dozen Zs on his heels, he continued trudging forward; there was no need for him to check his six—it would only slow him down, he reasoned. Besides, in dribs and drabs, during brief lulls in the cacophony made by the feeding birds, he could hear his pursuers' low-timbered moans interspersed with the sound their footfalls produced trampling the brittle grass. In a last-ditch effort to slow their pursuit, he zigzagged between a pair of waist-high tombstones, using them like static blockers in a high stakes game of graveyard football.

At the midway point between the helicopter and the fence separating the church from the cemetery, Cade took a knee and leveled the MP7 at the ghouls. A thought suddenly occurred to him, and he tried to recall the exact wording on the warning stickers plastered all over the gas pumps back home. He knew that any kind of open flame was forbidden in their immediate vicinity. And if he remembered correctly, the warning stickers stated a safe distance, a radius measured in feet, inside of which an errant spark was likely to set off any lingering gas vapors and possibly produce a gigantic fireball.

But his memory failed him. He had no idea how fast or how far from the source flammable fumes wafted, nor if there was some kind of half-life he should consider. He supposed every accelerant had its own properties, but the one he was dealing with was JP-8—a kerosene-based aviation fuel—highly flammable with its own unique properties that set it apart from the stuff that used to flow from gas pumps at stations on every other street corner in the United States before Omega culled the people and stilled their petrol-thirsty cars and SUVs.

With that in mind, he said a silent prayer, snugged the carbine in, and tensed his finger against the trigger. The red holographic pip hovered on the kid's face. Sunlight glinted from some kind of steel caps concealing an upper and lower picket of presumably rotted baby teeth—assaulted in life from too many sweets or merely bad genetics—whichever the culprit was, Cade had no idea. However, he was certain that he still hated nothing more than the idea of going to the dentist. And aside from the long dead politicians of the old world, the *trying-to-converse-with-you-with-their-hands-in-your-mouth* head drillers hovered somewhere around second or third on his list of people he would *not* miss.

In the half of a heartbeat Cade used to steady his breathing and take up some trigger pull, he regarded the metalwork someone had performed on the kid in life. During the second half of the same heartbeat he decided the shiny beacons were a perfect target to aim for.

The two rounds he squeezed off entered the creature's parted mouth, and after contacting enamel and metal, the bullets tumbled upward and, with an audible pop that could be heard even over the avian din, created a horrific exit wound. The upper two-thirds of the undead kid's skull spun through the air, an uneven wobbly arc of bone and fluttering hair followed by something resembling moldy cottage cheese—*large curd.*

Save for the pint sized Z's dome, there was no secondary explosion. Thankfully his prayer had been answered—he had in fact been a safe distance outside of the mysterious danger zone, and his teammates had *not* been instantly incinerated inside the earthbound helo.

As the headshot body spun, its lifeless arms flailing like a rag doll, Cade snapped the barrel to the right by a degree and dinged the next two walkers with precise head shots.

A double tap. Two soft chugs from the suppressed sub gun. Eye and forehead on the first Z. An implosion and a black dimple, separated by only a millisecond—the former started its head spinning; the latter, centered equidistant between brow and hairline, lifted the geriatric off of the ground. The two nearly simultaneous impacts were followed at once by an aerated cloud of gray matter that drifted to the ground with a wet patter.

Another perfect double tap. Temple and ear on the second creature as it cornered a large, cross-shaped tombstone. The damage escaped Cade's notice because the creature had dropped quicker than his eye could track. Faster than gravity by itself could tug on a falling human body. Terminal velocity aided by two sizzling chunks of 4.6mm lead penetrators.

But the aftermath was evident. Gelatinous chunks of brain painted the cross. *Nothing survivable*, Cade told himself as he left the rest of the shamblers to figure out how to move around the newly-fallen obstacles blocking their path.

Without a backward glance, he navigated the last two rows of graves, finally emerging from between a pair of very large monuments to a couple of long dead people.

The pink marble head stone on his left came up to just below his sternum. It was the perfect height to lean on, allowing him to take the weight from his bad ankle for a few precious seconds. He steadied his weapon, drew a bead on a female first turn, and double tapped her in the forehead. As the body collapsed, he unleashed a dozen rounds downrange, pausing slightly between every other pull of the trigger to acquire a new target. He fired until the bolt locked, and then with a fluidity gained from years of putting practice to work dumped the mag and inserted a fresh one containing the final thirty rounds for the MP7. By feel he charged the weapon, and then padded across the open ground. He entered the shadow cast by the towering church, crabbed sideways through the gate, and scooted under the ornate wrought iron archway.

The patina of dirt and moss accumulated over decades of changing seasons had left the cemetery's name—*Saint something or other,* which was spelled out in an arc of flowing script atop the gate— mostly unreadable to his military-trained eye. He had always been partial to the simple blocky font *The Big Green Machine*—the United States Army to the layperson—labeled everything with, and though he couldn't tell whom the graveyard's anonymous saintly namesake had been, he was one hundred and ten percent certain the man would be spinning over in his grave if he knew the undead were treading on this sacred ground.

Dispelling the thoughts of who's or what's pertaining to the church's history he turned left, hobbled a number of yards in shadow, made another left, and then shot a glance over his shoulder at the trailing creatures. The carrion bottleneck that formed as they tried forcing their way through the gate in unison would have been a funny sight if this were some stupid Super Bowl commercial or one of those horror comedies that popped up every so often at the local Cineplex, back when zombies were but figments of someone's vivid imagination and made real by a few talented makeup artists. But this was no film shoot. There was no crew. No director. No sandwich wagon waiting to feed the extras. This was life and death, not only for him but also for the men in the Ghost Hawk, and he derived no pleasure from watching the clumsy creatures—wanting nothing more than to strip the flesh from his bones—struggling with the simplest of obstacles. In fact, he was grateful for the diversion that had allowed him to gain a few more precious feet of separation.

Chapter 12

Cade reached the southwest corner of the cemetery with the dead close behind and made a tactical decision. Before covering the open ground to Jasper's dusty truck, once again he took a knee and emptied half of the little MP7's final extended magazine into the staggering clutch. Putrid bodies thudded to the dirt as the initial fifteen rounds, rocketing at 2,400 feet per second, found undead flesh, bone, and brain. The next flurry of controlled head shots added more dead Zs to the trail of twisted corpses outside of the fence line. *Three left*, he thought to himself as he unclipped the smoking weapon and dropped it near his feet.

Now free of the added weight of the MP7 he was able to move a little faster. Shielding his eyes from the sun, he cast a quick glance toward the helicopter. The simple fact that the perimeter around the downed craft was clear of walking dead told him his ruse had worked. He flicked his eyes back to the still-shambling cadavers and tore the Glock from his shoulder holster. Deciding he'd only use the unsuppressed pistol as a last resort, he held his fire and commenced a slow speed dash for the safety of the truck.

After gingerly traversing the minefield strewn with sun ripened-bodies and bits and pieces of rotor blade and fuselage, he reached the pickup. Dizzy and winded and sweating profusely—but relieved his grueling ordeal was about to pay off—he grasped the handle, wrenched the door open, and flung his body headlong onto the sagging, burgundy vinyl bench seat. Without a backward glance he hinged up and slammed the thin-skinned door home, an action accomplished mere seconds before the ghouls made its acquaintance.

Sharp reports of ashen palms slapping the window were followed instantly by a trio of sneering faces. Teeth clicking against glass, the insatiable Zs got an eyeful of the meat inside and instantly began to head-butt the driver's side window. Cade couldn't believe what he was seeing as the trio stepped back and flung themselves against the vehicle. Hollow thuds resounded as each new impact caused thick black fluid to flow from their pulped noses. Inexplicably they seemed to be cooperating, coordinating and delivering each blow simultaneously with a vigor that sent a chill up his spine. He thought back to the multitude of times he'd encountered the walking dead since Z Day and couldn't remember having ever seen them exhibit such determined, purpose-driven behavior. Sure he'd seen them *accidentally*, through sheer numbers, blast through a plate glass window. He'd been in an old farmhouse when a large group of dead knocked a four-inch-thick oak door and its casing and door jamb asunder as if it were constructed of Styrofoam. From inside the Ghost Hawk in a steady hundred foot hover he'd witnessed a sight he'd never forget, as the Denver horde—which had been traveling down the freeway packed tightly several hundred thousand strong—tossed SUVs, passenger cars, and multi-ton fire trucks around like plastic toys. It had struck him at the time because of the way they moved, like army ants on a mission. *And if they* are *becoming aware*, he thought grimly, *even one iota, and then start hunting in the kind of numbers that were present on I-25 that day—then the remaining pockets of humanity worldwide are fucked.* As the dead banged against the window again and again, he asked himself a single question he hoped would never come true: *Were they learning?* As if his thoughts had been tapped, one of the ghouls stopped assaulting the glass and turned its milky eyes and undivided attention from him to something on the outside of the door. Blood turning to ice, Cade cast his gaze left and down and noted a subtle movement to the interior door handle. Just a halfhearted jiggle, but enough to nearly stop his heart. Then he heard a clicking noise identical to the sound the latch had made seconds ago when the door slammed shut behind him.

He lashed out with his left elbow, popped the rounded locking knob down, and groped the steering column searching for the keys. *Way to go Jasper*, he thought, a thin smile curling his lip.

Dangling from the ignition was a purple rabbit's foot attached by a beaded chain to a small complement of silver keys—the most important of which was still in the ignition right where the man said it would be.

"Let's see if any of you have learned the fine art of the duck," he said, turning the engine over. The engine roared to life and instantly the male first turn that had been worrying the door handle reacted by flinging its arms over the top of the cab. *Perfect*, thought Cade as he powered the window down a few fingers width and stuck the compact Glock's business-end into the opening. "Who's hungry?" he asked, chiding the flailing creature in a sing-song voice. It took a handful of seconds, but the time spent waiting and inhaling the eye-watering stench up close and personal paid off as the *quick learner* moved its open maw near the flat black muzzle.

Cade did two things at once: he plunged the pistol into the ghoul's throat and then twisted his wrist clockwise in order to angle the barrel up so the discharged round had no chance of reaching the helicopter. He caressed the trigger twice and winced as the Z's eyes momentarily bulged from their sockets, then retracted and followed the rest of the cranial contents out the gaping exit wound in the rear of its skull. Contained within the cab, the back-to-back reports were deafening. One of the spent shells struck the metal edge of the visor then ricocheted back across Cade's face, grazing his nose before disappearing behind the bench seat. The other followed the curve of the windshield and disappeared down the window defroster. Ears ringing, he pulsed the window all the way down and with the Glock in a two-fisted grip moved the weapon's muzzle to the left, firing several more shots into the remaining pair of creatures. Watching them fall, he powered the window shut, slammed the transmission into drive, and hauled the wheel hard to the right. Bouncing over arms and legs and small pieces of debris from the wreck, he worked at loading some G-forces to the tail end of the truck. Slowly but surely the stiffened bodies Jasper had been hauling made the inevitable slide from the truck's bed onto terra firma. He flicked his gaze to the rearview and watched as the bodies of two full-sized adults and what had to be nearly half a dozen children-sized cadavers tumbled out and bounced and skidded, kicking up puffs of ochre dust in the process. Straightening the wheel, he said a prayer for the family and aimed the pickup for the opening in the nearby fence. Barely wide enough for one vehicle, the gravel access road splitting the graveyard in two stretched north nearly all the way to the church's steps. If Cade had to venture a guess, the road had been used primarily to bring in occupied caskets and the digging equipment necessary to inter them.

As he nosed the Chevy through the gap in the fence, the mirror on the passenger side folded back with a screech and a bang. Ignoring the noise and the temporary loss of a good portion of his situational awareness, Cade craned his neck, glanced over and spotted Cross and Jasper atop the black chopper. Each man had a hold of one of Gaines' gloved hands and together they were slowly lowering the fallen operator's body into the outstretched arms of Hicks and Lopez.

As the truck swayed left and right on tired springs, Cade slalomed around the pallid corpses lining both sides of the road. Once parallel to the chopper, he spun the wheel right and bumped over the firm ground between two rows of headstones. There was a bang and the right front fender groaned when he failed to split the goalposts and a centuries-old cement marker disintegrated in a spray of pebbles and sand. Cade winced at the transgression but stayed the course.

"I'm retrieving Tice's body," Lopez said over the comms.

"Be careful, Lowrider," Cade said sharply. "One of the Zs almost got me. Seemed like the bastard planned to ambush me. Oh, and while you're back there keep an eye out for my backpack."

"Copy that," replied Lopez as he looped around the chopper's nose.

"Someone give me a situation report," Cade called out to anyone who was listening.

"I didn't see your ruck ... but you were correct, Captain," replied Lopez. "I just dropped a lurker behind the helo. Collecting the Spook's body now. Back at the chopper in one mike."

"Copy that. Pulling up now," Cade called back as he ground the getaway vehicle to a stop a good distance from the wreckage, where a stray spark or its hot catalytic converter had no chance of touching off the fuel. Head on a swivel, he slammed the shifter into park and set the brake.

Suddenly Cross's voice overrode everything. His words were clipped and to the point like he was reporting a threat to the President's life—big important life-changing words delivered in a controlled, easy-to-comprehend diction. "Hurry up, gentlemen. I'm looking at a herd of Zs coming our way."

"Looked like only thirty or forty to me," replied Lopez between labored breaths.

"I know crowds," said Cross, who was still standing atop Jedi One-One. "And what I see is not thirty or forty ... there are at least two hundred on the move."

"Two hundred Zs," Cade said incredulously. "From which direction?"

"They're vectoring in from the interstate," answered Cross. "Jasper says they've been moving between Sioux Falls and Rapid City. Says they pace the road and normally don't venture into Draper unless there's a reason. And the helo going down was plenty of *reason*. I estimate we have five mikes, *tops*, until the lead element is upon us."

That gives us three if we're going to transit the gravel road ahead of them, Cade thought to himself. He cast the miserable thought aside and shouldered open the slime-covered door. He tried swinging his feet over the raised channel and nearly passed out as a lightning bolt of pain flared in the ankle, that now, even in the general's size twelve boot, felt like a bowling ball stuffed into a marble bag. "I'm no help," he gasped, beads of sweat cascading from his brow. "Ankle's shot. You'll have to bring the bodies to the truck by yourselves. I only have a few dozen rounds left so *double time* it."

"Copy that, Captain," said Lopez as he tapped his inner strength and hauled Tice's dead weight around the helo's shattered nose while consciously diverting his eyes from the snarling Z that was once Durant. He paused for a tick to steady the load and caught in his side vision the still-suspended Ari giving him a look that seemingly said: *Get me the fuck out of here.*

Back at the truck Cade cast his gaze to the rearview, noted a growing cloud of gray-brown dust. Then he scanned every degree around him for threats, paying close attention to the helo and the church in the distance. "Clear to the north, west, and east," he said to the men whose grim task of putting down Durant, extricating Ari, and moving the bodies to the truck had just begun.

Finally, resigned to the fact that he was merely an observer—and hopefully a successful getaway driver—he looked to the mirror, locked his eyes on the expanding haze to his six, and waited for the cards to fall where they may.

Chapter 13
Schriever AFB

The air temperature inside the TOC had risen steadily all morning. Now, with the hottest part of the day upon them, and two dozen human bodies and twice that many electrical devices all spewing hot air into the room, the atmosphere inside mirrored that of a pressure cooker— super-heated and volatile.

"Will someone *please* get me an idea of when Jedi One-Two will be wheels down," Nash called out as she paced a hole in the burgundy carpet directly in front of the lectern.

"On it," one of the junior members of her staff called out.

"Let's get this right, folks," she said. "The President wants to personally greet our guests from the NML when the bird puts down." She looked around the room, searching for Airman Davis, and issued another order to the group of Air Force personnel who had been parked in front of their computers and communications gear for the better part of ten hours. "I want answers. Someone *please* tell me why Jedi One-One missed checking in."

"I just tried to hail One-One to set up the final refueling rendezvous with Oil Can Five-Five," stated a tired-looking airman, his once-pressed uniform looking the worse for wear and an out-of-place five o'clock shadow beginning to show on his face. "But there was still no reply, Ma'am."

"Good job," she said, knowing full well everybody in the hot TOC was doing their best and those two simple, morale-boosting words would be noticed by the other hardworking men and women. "Just keep trying," she added.

"Give it some time, Major," said Colonel Cornelius Shrill as he strode into the room. "These men and women are doing their best."

No shit, Shrill, she thought as she hovered over a young captain who for the moment was in charge of the 50th Space Wing satellite operations. "Jensen, how long until you can bring a KH-12"—a highly advanced U.S. satellite that carried an array of powerful sensors and optics onboard—"into a stationary orbit over Jedi One-One's last known position?"

Brunette hair snaking from under a navy ball cap, the captain consulted the two, twenty-four-inch screens arranged on the desktop before her. "Thirteen minutes, twenty-two seconds, Major Nash," she stated confidently.

"Not good enough. I have a feeling we've been paid a visit by Mister Murphy. Everyone listen up," Nash said, adding a fair amount of bass to her voice. She was in her element and it showed as she began formulating a response to these new developments. "Until we hear from the flight crew, we are going on the assumption that One-One suffered a catastrophic problem ... meaning, ladies and gentlemen, that we have a Black Hawk down situation outside of the wire. Captain Jensen, I want you to have Oil Can Five-Five link back up with the KC-135,"—a larger, jet-powered version of the prop-driven Hercules—"then, once Five-Five is topped off, have Dover reverse on Jedi One-One's last known heading and begin a track-crawl search pattern along that route. I want the KC-135 orbiting on station until further notice or until they are on fumes and need to RTB—return to base—to refuel themselves."

"Copy that," said the captain as she began updating all parties involved of the rapidly-changing mission profile.

After taking in the entire exchange, and admiring Nash for her rapid fire decision-making, Colonel Shrill made an executive decision and quickly dispatched another airman to fetch him a fully-charged satellite phone from the equipment room. Then he ambled forward; as he stepped up onto the small briefing platform, his lanky frame blocked out the lights overhead and cast a shadow on the diminutive major.

"I think you are jumping the gun, Nash," he said. "I wouldn't worry too much about Ari. He probably started telling dirty jokes and the general ordered him radio silent because of the mixed company here."

"Doubtful," said Nash immediately. "He's brash and cocky and Night Stalker through and through. But he's no dummy. Orders or not, he wouldn't willfully go black."

Shifting from one foot to the other and totally unwilling to acknowledge what his gut was telling him, Shrill looked away from Nash's piercing gaze and removed his cover. He didn't want to pull rank and override her in front of her staff, so he rubbed his bald head and pinched the bridge of his nose in order to buy some time to think before trying to sell Nash his glass-half-full scenario.

"Better to be safe than sorry," Nash pressed.

"A precedent has already been set," Shrill said. "Ari and Durant only checked in with the TOC a handful of times during the Jackson Hole mission. And correct me if I'm wrong, but that mission had *zero* satellite overwatch because we were involved in a protracted engagement with the Chinese."

Nash was about to lobby Shrill to take a more proactive approach toward finding the Ghost Hawk, but was preempted when the airman returned with a thin satellite phone in hand.

Shrill took the phone, handed it over to Nash, and went on talking. "Major, you and I both know how finicky those Gen 3 rides can be. That's all I hear Whipper talking about. *I have to fix this ... Ari broke that ...*" he said, bringing his normally baritone voice up several octaves in order to accurately mimic the owlish first sergeant's voice.

Suppressing a chuckle, Nash cut him off. "To refresh your short memory, *Sir*. The Robert Christian snatch-and-grab was conducted under strictly NOE—nap of the earth—flight rules while maintaining *strict* radio silence."

Shrill made a face that mirrored his resignation. He knew the facts and he also knew that Nash was right in acknowledging and preparing for every worst case scenario.

Nash covered the hot microphone with one hand and said, "I hate to correct you, Colonel, but what I think you meant to say is, 'all that Whipper *complains* about,' right?" She thumbed on the phone and waited until it produced a tone indicating it had made a connection. She consulted her clipboard, keyed in an eleven-digit number, and pressed the sleek black handset to her ear. After thirty seconds, she said, "*Nothing*. Gaines isn't answering." She made a face and killed the call. Grabbing another set of numbers from the sheet, she keyed them in. She hit send, then, an antithesis to the frenzied motion of people working all around her, she stood stock still, listening for one full minute. She grimaced, removed the handset from her ear, and powered it down. She shook her head and said, "*Nothing*. Captain Grayson isn't picking up either."

"Listen Freda," Shrill said quietly, trying to remain positive, "I know how protective you are of your boys, and I know how much is riding on the success of this mission, but I'd be willing to bet they've got their sat-phones tucked away, snug as a bug in a rug, inside their packs by now. Besides, even if the general had one of those things sitting on his lap, he's not going to be able to hear it ringing or feel it vibrate inside of the moving helo."

"I don't like it," intoned Nash. "Compared to a UH-60"—the basic Black Hawk platform—"the Ghosts are super quiet inside. *One* of them would have heard the phone or at least felt the vibration."

"Helos are nothing but one big controlled vibration. If I know Ari as well as I think I do, then it's safe to say he's just hot dogging like I told you a minute ago," Shrill said, doubling down on his first argument. "Him and Durant are brushing up with some low level stick time just in case the Chinese or Russians try to take advantage of the Omega situation."

"Still doesn't feel right," Nash countered, shaking her head vehemently.

"It's a new *toy* to Ari," Shrill said, remembering the one and only time he'd had the pleasure of riding in the troop compartment of a Black Hawk with the cocky SOAR—Special Operations Aviation Regiment—aviator at the stick. In fact, whenever he recounted the story of his introduction to the bouncing and jarring that was the reality of low level NOE flying, he always conveniently left out the fact that *he* had earned one of the not-so-coveted puker patches the Night Stalker pilots enjoyed doling out.

"Still, I've got a bad feeling about this. A gut feeling that I need to listen to," the usually unflappable major persisted, her voice cracking a bit. Abruptly she turned and locked eyes with Airman Davis who had just rolled in from outside. "Davis ..."

"Yes, Ma'am?"

"Go find Brooklyn Grayson and bring her here. Alone. Unarmed. I want her here *five* minutes ago."

"Yes, Ma'am," he said, and turned on his heel and sprinted for the Cushman he'd left parked outside.

Shrill dabbed at his forehead with a yellowed handkerchief and then cleared his throat. "I know I'm just a bystander when it comes to this delicate orchestra of man and machine you are conducting here, but I do have one final question I need answered, Major."

"Yes, what is it?" Nash said, turning back to face him.

"I asked Captain Jensen if there had been an emergency distress call and she indicated there was none, and conversely I haven't heard you or anyone else mention anything about a distress signal. Shouldn't we have had some kind of indication if something had gone wrong?" Shrill asked, hitching an eyebrow.

Except for the hum of computers and the low murmur of people talking quietly, the proverbial calm before the storm had fallen over the TOC. But that was all about to change as Shrill and Nash commenced in a battle of wills. *Two men enter; one man leaves*, a voice sounding eerily like Tina Turner echoed in Nash's head. Thoroughly committed to fighting for the Delta Unit she squared herself away, brushing some lint from her blue uniform. Hoping she was going to be that victorious *man,* she tucked a strand of graying hair under her ball cap and walked headlong into a spat with a *full bird* colonel. "Colonel Shrill," she said. "With all due respect, Jedi One-One is missing and presumed to have gone down. Unfortunately the usual suspects ... any locals in the vicinity that would hear and see an aircraft go down and render aid, are all dead and gone. Furthermore, the FAA and local municipalities, police, or fire ... first responders who would normally receive and respond to any kind of distress signal—are also nonexistent. There are no manned control towers or even so much as a little Podunk one-person radio center servicing a dusty airstrip between here and the Canadian border. Colonel, the country has gone dark. And adding to that, as you already know, we're a little hamstrung in the satellite department. So until the Hercules and or the KC-135 closes the distance to Pierre, which was where we last had radio contact with the aircrew, *we* are also in the dark."

Realizing he was in the petite major's domain, and though he was her superior in rank and tenure, Shrill merely winked at his old friend and colleague. *Lady's got it all figured out*, he thought to himself. Then, maintaining his silence, he about-faced and stalked the room in search of a chair in which he intended to get comfortable, sit quietly, and watch the drama unfold.

Chapter 14
Draper, South Dakota
Six minutes prior to Cade returning with
Jasper's truck.

After overhearing the men in the cabin say that Cade was on the ground and on the move toward Jasper's truck, Ari opened his eyes and watched with glee as the Zs lost all interest in him and ambled lockstep away from the helicopter and out of sight.

But he wasn't saved yet. A handful of feet away, Durant had just turned, and was reaching and swiping at him.

In order to keep his numb left arm from dangling near the Zs snapping teeth, Ari tucked his hand under his safety harness, and with only one hand to work with cinched it down as tight as he could.

Hurry the eff up, Delta, he thought as he fought tooth-and-nail to remain still and play the role of a dead man.

***

Several long minutes battling gravity and trying to tune out the snarling one-armed mess strapped into the copilot's chair was beginning to take a toll on Ari's sanity. To pass the time until the Delta captain returned with the vehicle, he did his best to remember what Durant had been like in life. He'd known the man since they'd attended flight school together at Fort Rucker. Nestled among rolling and wooded hills in Southeast Alabama, the sprawling base had been almost too small to contain the two. They were placed in the same training squadron and their careers followed similar paths, but for reasons unknown, Ari had always been given command of whatever ship they'd both been assigned to. And that was how it had been since Omega dealt the nation a death blow—him on the stick and Durant his copilot. But there had been no animosity on Durant's part, and this trait was what Ari had most appreciated about the man. He was humble until the very end, and now that trait was causing Ari a great deal of pain. For it was his fault Durant was dead, and it was on him to make it right. To end his friend's suffering.

Ari shot a sidelong glance at the pale cadaver that used to be a living, breathing man. He reminisced over the countless hours he'd passed shooting the breeze with Durant in the cockpit. A tear formed as he thought about all of the scrapes they'd gotten into and out of all over the world. Then, grasping the buckles holding him in place, he uttered a short prayer. He figured when he released himself and succumbed to the pull of gravity, one of two things would happen. Either he'd fall into the undead creature and get bit and join him for a time in whatever purgatory the undead endured. Or he'd fall, and somehow succeed in avoiding the creature's snapping maw. Then he figured he'd flip up the smoked visor and plunge the locked blade of his Leatherman multi-tool into the Z's eye socket.

Seconds away from punching free of the four-point harness and letting fate run its course, he saw Lopez sprint in front of the helicopter. Moving from right to left in a low crouch, holding a black tanto-style blade in his right fist, the stocky operator was focused laser-like on something near the fence line.

What the hell, thought Ari as he watched Lopez weave and bob through the gravestones and bodies until he was out of sight. Then, after a few seconds or minutes had ticked by (Ari's perception of time having been skewed since the crash, so he wasn't certain), he picked up a flash of movement from the left.

But unfortunately the Z that used to be Durant had also noticed the flash that was Lopez and instantly began to buck and flail against the restraints. The hissing and moaning and clacking of teeth coming from below rose to a crescendo as Lopez—weighted down by a camouflage-clad body held firmly over his shoulders in a fireman's carry—trudged slowly by.

"Shut the fuck up," Ari bellowed as the sound of an approaching vehicle helped drown him out. "You guys gonna get me out of here?" he hollered to no one in particular. He craned his stiff neck all around, searching for a friendly face, listening hard for a reply.

"Hang tight," Hicks called back from his blind side.

Instantly a wave of relief hit Ari as he began to tick off in his mind the names of the passengers and crew that he knew had survived: His flight engineer Hicks, Captain Grayson, Sergeant Lopez, and Secret Service agent Cross. However, the feeling of dread returned when he realized that he hadn't heard the general's voice since Cade left to get the truck. So using the logic of deduction, he came to the conclusion that the body Lopez recovered had to be the spook named Tice. *Goddamnit.* Three dead because of him. The urge to martyr himself alongside Durant returned—only this time, the desire was a hundred times stronger than before. "I'm tired of hanging tight," he called back to no one in particular. He was about to punch out of the harness holding him when the sound of brakes squealing met his ears. A tick later a pair of black boots entered his side vision. They were quickly joined by two pairs of tan combat boots. He looked up, as difficult and painful a task as it was, and spied Cross, Hicks, and Lopez form up in front of him and begin conversing in hushed tones. The look on their faces told him they were forming a plan to extricate him and somehow find a way to honor his earlier request. They were standing side by side, tallest to shortest. Cross, Hicks, and Lopez—left to right, looking like something out of an old AT&T commercial. Absurdly, the tagline *got bars* popped into Ari's head. He embraced it, welcoming anything and everything that would take his mind from the burden he was going to carry with him for the rest of his days.

They stood there for a few seconds and then abruptly separated, each trotting off and following a different point of the compass. When they returned, each man was carrying something different. Cross had someone's bloody uniform blouse which he placed over Durant's head and upper body. Before the newly turned Z could brush it aside, Lopez and Hicks each placed a fairly large piece of carbon fiber rotor blade atop the camouflaged ACU top.

Lastly, Hicks reached his gloved hand through the metal framework that once held cockpit glass and gave Ari his Cold Steel blade. "However you want to do it ... it's on you, Warrant Officer Silver," he said, turning his back and looking away.

***

Three minutes later

Looking at the bodies on the back of the truck was surreal to say the least. Cade consulted his Suunto. Thirty minutes ago, give or take, Tice had been bantering with Lopez and he, Captain Cade Grayson, had delivered his first and last fist bump with a sitting general.

Tice's slack face showed no signs of the terror he must have endured the last few seconds he was alive. His helmet had been ripped from his head and his neck was broken, the latter a certainty judging by the fact that the man was lying chest down on the truck's bed and his wide open, glazed-over eyes were peering skyward.

The general on the other hand, Cade noted, had passed from this life with a pain-filled grimace frozen on his face. His brow was furrowed, his lips were pulled back over clenched teeth, and minus his body armor and blouse top the cause of death was wholly evident. Between where his body armor had stopped and his belt line there was a jagged, foot-long gash from which a fair amount of his internal organs were protruding. Flies buzzed and settled. Took a meal and flitted off.

Shifting his gaze from his deceased brothers-in-arms, he did a quick scan of his surroundings. *Clear*, he thought to himself and was about to verbalize the same to the others when something on the south horizon caught his attention. Soft and hazy. Not quite roiling, but still clearly visible, a gauzy curtain of fine, airborne dust was rising from the ground.

"We've got company," Cade barked. "The Zs are on the gravel feeder road now."

"Copy that," said Lopez. "We're extricating Durant's body now. Wait one."

"That's about all you've got. Pulling around front," Cade said over the comms. He turned the ignition over, then let the idling

62

engine pull the truck forward. Keeping the same safe distance from the pooled aviation gas, he cut a half-circle around the wreck and pulled abreast of the remainder of his team. He caught Lopez's eye and mouthed the words: *Burn it.*

In no time, with Jasper lending a hand, Hicks and Lopez had placed Durant's lifeless body in the back alongside the bodies of Tice and Gaines.

Having a hell of a time moving around thanks to the continuing numbness in his extremities, not to mention the pounding his body took in the tumble from the seat in the Ghost Hawk, Ari slid his frame gently into the truck's cab. *Riding bitch*, he thought, fondly remembering the ribbing Tice had taken so gracefully. Interrupting the moment, Jasper wedged in tight next to him and slammed the door with a resonant bang. The truck jounced, a kind of diagonal shimmy on its suspension, and then the horizon through the windshield dipped slightly as Lopez, Cross, and Hicks, loaded down with their guns and gear, piled in back and settled in amongst the fallen.

Cade heard a loud clang followed by a couple of hand slaps on the sheet metal. He glanced at the mangled and canted side mirror and registered a thumbs up from Lopez, who was sitting on the wheel well and brandishing his M4. "Better hold on," Cade shouted. "Ride's going to get bumpy." He wheeled to the right, zippered the truck between a couple of headstones, and then to complete the haphazard loop through the cemetery, hung a left on the access road. The moment the bucking Chevy passed through the iron gate Cade hit the brakes—a move that caught everyone but Lopez by surprise. Without stating his intentions the stocky operator rose, engaged the 3x magnifier in front of the Eotech 553 holographic sight on his rifle's monolithic upper rail, spread his feet incrementally, and then snugged the weapon to his shoulder. "Going hot," Lopez called out to no one in particular.

Literally, Cade mused, a millisecond before the sergeant opened fire. He watched Lopez methodically walk a half dozen rounds from right to left down the length of the matte black fuselage. *Nothing.* Then Lopez paused for a tick, , leaned in against the recoil, and as rapidly emptied the mag at the point where the chopper met the glimmering fuel.. Sparks flashed as the two dozen 5.56 rounds penetrated the chopper's skin, leaving a snaking line of dark holes just above the fractured hatch where the port wheel was stowed away when retracted.

The explosion, though intended, was instantaneous and violent. Two things happened simultaneously: Lopez yelled, "Go, go, go," and was slapped down from the superheated shockwave. Subsequently, heeding the words piped into his ear bud, Cade pinned the accelerator to the floorboard. Meeting Ari's gaze, the Delta captain offered up a sheepish grin and shrugged a shoulder. "If it gets us rescued, it was worth the risk."

"Not if a cooked-off stray round finds your head or this piece of crap's gas tank," stated Ari. "Where'd you get this *thing*?"

Reflecting in the rear view, seventy yards away, the fireball had mushroomed, dwarfing the mature trees east of the wreck.

"She's mine," Jasper said in response to Ari's query.

"And who's this?" Ari said to Cade.

"Jasper," he said. "While you were unconscious, he nearly incinerated us."

"How?"

"He was about to shoot Durant to put him out of his misery..."

"How did you see me from where you were?" asked Jasper, craning his head in order to look Cade in the eye.

"Saw you reflected in Ari's visor. You're a big guy ...pretty hard to miss. Thanks for the help. By the way, the guy riding *bitch* is Ari Silver."

"Pleasure ... I think," added Jasper.

Noticing the gold wedding band on the man's ring finger, Cade asked, "Where's your family?"

"Buried them last week."

"I'm sorry to hear that," said Cade. "Who were the folks in the back of your truck?"

"Neighbors of mine ... they held out the longest."

Cade took his eyes from the road. Asked, "You put them down?"

Jasper nodded subtly then looked out his window.

"Do you intend on going back ... to your home?" asked Ari.

Jasper's hand clenched around the butt of his pistol. Knuckles going white he said, "I was thinking hard about joining them."

"I've had similar thoughts since the crash," Ari conceded.

With these two new revelations out in the open, Cade's gaze ran the bases, going from the road to the pistol in Jasper's lap up to Ari's face and then back to the road. The round trip took three seconds at most but left him only half of a heartbeat to mash the brakes and slew the truck sideways, an unexpected but lifesaving maneuver that nearly pitched the rest of the team onto the road.

"Oh my God," stammered Jasper. "I've never seen so many of them in one place."

Save for the moaning wall of dead in front of them and the low rumble from the roiling fire behind them, inside the cab it was deathly silent.

Looking past Ari at the local, Cade blurted, "Which way?"

After a second Jasper said over the rattle clatter of the Detroit V8, "Draper is to the right if you can get us to the road."

Cade made a face. Flicked his gaze over his shoulder and registered a snapshot in time. Sitting, back against the wheel well, legs across Durant and his rifle propped between them, Hicks was looking neither at the conflagration that used to be their ride, nor the monsters spread out across the road and sallow fields to the left and right of it. Instead, he had a thousand-yard stare fixed on the dead he was sharing space with. Cross, however, stared back at Cade stoically, a calm look parked on his broad features. And Lopez was looking at the rearview mirror and spinning his finger in a lazy circle pointing towards the heavens—his way of saying: *Captain, we need to be Oscar Mike—on the move—now.*

***

Twelve miles away, north by east, Lieutenant Ben Dover nudged the lumbering Hercules into a gradual left hand turn. With the first leg of the search pattern completed, the new heading would have them skirt south along the same route but five miles to the west so the crew in back could effectively scan the new ground below for any sign of Jedi One-One or her crew.

In his headset, Dover overheard the radio chatter as Captain Jensen back at the TOC instructed Major Ripley in One-Two to swing wide to the southwest side of the base and land her Osprey on the far western edge of the tarmac when she arrived. Presumably, the unorthodox landing pattern was to keep the passengers from seeing the layout of the base and he guessed the final landing spot had been chosen to keep her *cargo* away from prying eyes—civilian and base personnel alike. Then, he figured, some kind of vehicle would be waiting to immediately whisk them away on the final leg of their journey, their ultimate destination no doubt more Gitmo than Club Med. And taking the earlier terrorist attack on the base into consideration, Dover agreed wholeheartedly with whoever made those decisions. However, in the hours since he'd attended the pre-mission briefing, he'd been wondering how the Canadian citizens aboard the Osprey were going to handle being shanghaied by their big brothers to the south. And if he were in their shoes, he'd want to be given a goddamn good reason why he shouldn't be demanding and then receiving an immediate return to Winnipeg. *Real flower leis would be a good start*, he thought to himself. *Maybe some cold Molsons and a smoking fifty-five gallon drum full of BBQ beef brisket.* Anything but being greeted by grim-faced soldiers on a hot tarmac and then the mandatory fourteen-hour stay in solitary confinement that was sure to follow. *No way to endear yourselves to the folks who might have the skills to replicate the antiserum*, he thought. *No way indeed.*

As soon as Dover brought the Hercules out of the turn and back to level flight, he spied a wispy finger of black snaking up from a copse of trees far off in the distance. "I have a visual on the ground. Smoke plume at one o'clock, approximately ten to twelve miles," he said, informing his co-pilot Second Lieutenant Norman Meredith as well as the folks monitoring the search and rescue operation from the TOC back at Schriever. "Taking us closer to investigate," Dover stated. Next, he rattled off his new heading, current altitude and airspeed for whoever was keeping tabs on him in the TOC, then, tempering any kind of expectation, gently nudged the stick forward, keeping his eyes on the drifting gray smudge on the horizon. And given the fact that on every mission of the dozens he'd flown out of Schriever, every single one—without fail—included the sighting of at least one out-of-control structure fire—sometimes dozens—he doubted the smoke on the horizon had anything to do with the missing helicopter.

***

A handful of minutes passed and nothing he saw was working to change his mind. Probably a gas stove left on had finally touched off. Or a faulty water heater. Or maybe someone was burning their dead; all plausible explanations.

He leveled Oil Can Five-Five out at one thousand feet, keeping the rising column of black smoke slightly off the plane's nose on the starboard side, throttled the engines back somewhat, and then began a final gradual descent to five hundred feet.

Chapter 15

Two minutes later Lieutenant Dover contacted Schriever. "Preparing for our first pass. Maintaining five hundred feet AGL," he stated, holding the bird on a straight heading that would take them within an eighth of a mile of the target. Close enough to get a good idea of the source yet still a big enough buffer in order to avoid the swelling cloud. To his right Meredith trained a pair of binoculars on the ground and after a couple of seconds described the white church in detail. He panned the binoculars left and mentioned the cemetery littered with dozens of presumably Omega-infected bodies.

"Do you have eyes on any kind of wreckage?" asked captain Jensen who had been maintaining constant contact with Oil Can from the TOC back at Schriever.

"Negative," replied the co-pilot.

Someone's burning bodies, thought Dover.

"Wait one," Meredith said excitedly as the plane's right wing dipped a few degrees to starboard. "Affirmative," he said. "I can see an impact zone and an extended debris field. The tail boom has separated and is partially intact. I see the tail rotor disc and the forward swept horizontal canards. I can say with high confidence that what I'm seeing *was* Jedi One-One—"

Captain Jensen cut in. "Are there survivors?" she asked.

Dover banked the Hercules sharply and began a tight orbit of the crash site.

Startled by the loud engine noise, the flock of birds still feeding on the corpses took flight and the sky over the graveyard went dark but soon cleared as the raptors dissipated and then lit on the fallow fields bordering a nearby road.

"Negative," replied Meredith as soon as the sky had cleared. "The helo is fully engulfed and I am seeing secondary explosions on the ground. How copy?"

"Solid copy, Oil Can," Jensen intoned. "Zero survivors and ongoing secondary explosions," she repeated, presumably for the benefit of Nash and whoever else was following the ongoing rescue efforts back at the TOC.

"Captain Jensen, we've got a full tank," Dover said. "I want to stay on station for a little while longer just in case."

"Wait one," replied Jensen.

In his mind's eye, Dover imagined the paper-pilots and desk jet-jockeys who made most of the decisions back at Schriever consulting their actuarial tables and weighing the expenditure of JP-8 over the value of human life. Always the pessimist when it came to higher ups making the right decision, he held his breath and waited for a response.

***

Schriever TOC

Glued to the largest monitor in the building, Nash bellowed, "Where's my sat feed?"

"In 5 ... 4 ... 3 ... 2 ... feed coming online."

"Thank you, Captain Jensen," replied Nash, who appeared to be calming down a bit.

Jensen said, "Zooming in," and the specialist next to her hit the appropriate key strokes and made it happen.

There was no steady pan or video game-like drama or silly clicking sounds as an image grew larger in steps before finally filling up the screen. This was instantaneous. A snap of color and the screen was dominated by flames and the wreckage of what no one in the TOC doubted was the Ghost Hawk—or rather what remained of it. Nothing but a melted lump of exotic black fiber and pooling molten alloy.

The TOC went deathly quiet.

"Pan out," said Nash. "I've seen enough." The screen quickly snapped out so far the downed chopper was lost in the ground clutter.

Nash looked over at Shrill who remained seated. He mouthed, "I'm sorry," and buried his face in his hands.

"Major Nash," said the TOC controller Captain Jensen. "What are your orders for Oil Can Five-Five?"

Nash said nothing. With a look of utter dejection on her face she simply shook her head side-to-side.

***

Oil Can Five-Five

After a long, uneasy minute of silence the radio crackled back to life. "Negative," Captain Jensen replied with a flat affect. "You are to RTB at once."

"Copy that," said Dover. "Returning to base." He looked over at Meredith and mouthed, "Bullshit." Then muted his microphone and said aloud, "We owe it to them to go around one more time. Someone might have been thrown clear or maybe survived the impact and crawled away."

Taking his time while Dover flew the Hercules in an ever tightening circle, Meredith trained his binoculars on the wreckage. Flames, orange and red, leapt high, licking at the nearby trees. Thick oily smoke tendrils coiled hundreds of feet heavenward. He panned the entire crash site, paying close attention to the surrounding fencing and the two groves of trees on either side. After a couple of minutes and three futile laps without seeing anything moving on the church grounds except for a couple of walking dead and a large flock of birds, he dropped the field glasses into his lap, looked over at Dover and shook his head.

In response, Dover said, "Nothing?"

"Someone has been depositing their dead down there, but I didn't see anything to make me believe anyone walked away from that crash. No clothing. No discarded weapons."

"Gotta give them the benefit of the doubt," said Dover. "I know Ari would us if the tables were turned."

"There were no survivors, Ben."

Dover said, "Second Lieutenant, we're staying on station for five more minutes."

There was another long uneasy silence and then Meredith nodded his head in agreement.

Dover brought his mike back on line and said, "Copy that. Oil Can Five-Five returning to base." And then contradicting his last transmission, continued scribing a wide circle in the sky while keeping the white church with the rising steeple the center of attention.

Chapter 16
Draper, South Dakota

"Take a right on 16 ... that's the intersection dead ahead!" Jasper bellowed over the roar of the overworked engine and the constant din of flesh slapping the vehicle's sides. "Then a few hundred feet and you'll need to take the next left. County Road 13 shoots to the south under the Interstate."

Great number for an escape route, thought Cade. *Lucky number thirteen.*

"There's an exchange on the left goes up to the 90 that will take you east to Sioux Falls. You probably don't want to go that way."

"From the exchange on 90, what major city lies to the west?" Cade asked as he jerked the wheel hard left in order to miss a lumbering three-hundred-pounds of undead American.

To keep from banging into Ari, Jasper held the grab bar near his head in a white-knuckled death grip. "Rapid City," he replied, looking past Ari to meet Cade's eyes. "It's about a hundred and fifty miles. But I heard it's crawling with those things too."

Having only been through there as a kid while on a family driving trip to see Mount Rushmore and the Black Hills, the pertinent details such as the city's population and whatever intersecting thoroughfares that might run through the area was unknown to Cade. "How many people lived in Rapid City before the outbreaks, and which interstates connect with the 90?" he asked.

Like a carnie guessing someone's weight or a contestant on the Price is Right trying to decide how much a Caribbean cruise aboard the Pacific Princess might set him back, Jasper looked up and away, obviously concentrating very hard. "Give or take ... about seventy thousand souls," he said. "I'm a country boy so we didn't get down that way very often, so I can't speak to which Interstates run south out of the city."

"And to the east?"

"Sioux Falls," replied Jasper. "But there are dozens of cities just like Draper between here and there. And the Missouri is that way. And a neighbor said the National Guard dropped the bridges to try and contain the outbreak. That's why I said it'd be best you avoid that route."

"Ellsworth Air Force Base is just this side of Rapid City," added Ari. "We might find another helicopter or a fixed wing there. There's probably plenty of fuel as well. I think it's worth a shot."

Tightening his hold on the grab bar as Cade swerved the truck around a couple of putrefied first turns, Jasper shook his head and said, "It's twenty miles this side of Rapid City."

"Perfect."

"You don't understand, Ari," said Jasper. "That still leaves a hundred and thirty miles of I-90 for you to travel ... and the closer you get to the big city, the more of these things will be on the road. And all of the stalled cars too."

Not good, Cade thought as he fought with the truck's mushy suspension to keep the rig on the road. Simultaneously he jinked left and right, dodging walking corpses, and tried to orient himself by picturing a virtual map of the United States in his mind. He put an imaginary pin in Pierre—the under-siege capitol they had overflown a couple of hours ago—the same city that had just received an airdrop of much needed supplies thanks to the highly motivated First Sergeant Whipper.

Clipping the man on the chin, Cade thought to himself, *was the best thing I've done in ages.* It had felt good and just at the time, but thinking back on it, he supposed he'd been a bit out of line. Still, he wouldn't take it back for anything. He could only hope the violently-delivered message would continue to pay off in the form of a multiple aircraft search party. Or at the very least, a tanker would be recalled to top off Jedi One-Two so Major Ripley could return and conduct a thorough search. Furthermore, he found comfort in knowing, with or without Whipper's help, that the second Nash realized how much time had elapsed since Ari's last radio communication, a search of some kind would be mounted—if one hadn't been already.

But for now, survival was a second-to-second, one move at a time affair. Continuing to map their current location in his head, he visualized the flight path that was supposed to have taken them south by west from Pierre directly over Draper and onward, overflying the bottom quarter of South Dakota and a good chunk of flat, treeless, Nebraska prairie before finally arriving at Colorado Springs which lay roughly four hundred miles southwest as the crow flies.

Jasper's confirmation that Sioux Falls was to the left and Rapid City was off to the right meant that there would be large numbers of dead trudging the 90 between the cities. Tens of thousands of them would be stretched out over a hundred miles in small groups and bigger herds, Cade guessed, but thankfully nothing comparable to the Denver mega-horde.

What to do? he thought. Following the straight gray ribbon of highway for any duration would be risky, while sheltering in place awaiting rescue in the vicinity of the burning wreckage would be tantamount to him signing all of their death warrants.

Then an alternative came to him. They would have to get from Draper, South Dakota to Colorado Springs the same way he got from Camp Williams to Hanna, Utah a few days after the outbreak— by following back roads, avoiding the dead at all costs, and relying on a whole lot of luck. Sure it would be risky—almost stupid, he supposed. To deviate from the area rescue craft would most likely overfly went against every shred of training he'd absorbed.

"We're going south. Cross country. Take back roads and resupply along the way."

"With all due respect, Captain," Ari said. "We have got to stay near the crash site."

"We'll be surrounded in minutes," said Cade. "Hell, we're damn near surrounded now."

Ari said, "You *really* think we can survive a five-hundred-mile hump through Indian country?" He removed his sidearm from the horizontal holster affixed to the front of his vest, ripped back the Velcro flap and removed the survival radio that Cross had returned to him before boarding the truck. He verified it was still on, and double checked to make sure it was tuned to the proper *dust-off* frequency. "This is Jedi One-One requesting dust-off at Draper, South Dakota. How copy?" He released the call button and waited. *Nothing.* He tried again and still received only static. "This thing is damaged. Probably made in China."

"South it is. Which way, Jasper?"

"I still think Ellsworth is the answer," pressed Ari.

Shaking his head, Cade replied, "Too many dead between here and there." Suddenly he eased off of the pedal. "Hang on," he blurted a second before the rig passed over the raised railroad tracks that just happened to run parallel to the interstate. Hitting the crossing at the speed they were traveling launched the truck, putting a few inches of daylight between its tires and the ground. Then, upon landing, the three men in the cab bounced into each other like ball bearings in a kinetic sculpture. The men in back, however—dead and alive alike—fared much worse, going weightless momentarily before coming back down with a series of hollow clunks followed by the discordant clatter of gunmetal and the shrill squeaking of springs that had lost their temper long ago. "Sorry," Cade called out. "Saw it at the last moment. Couldn't be helped."

Rubber squealed as he hauled the Chevy into a hard right turn, taking them onto a two-lane splitting the tracks and the 90. Gazing past Ari, Cade hitched a brow and looked a question at Jasper that said: *Tell me where to turn next.*

"Next left is State Route 13 South," Jasper announced. Then, as if he had mulled through their options utilizing the same thought process as the Delta operator, he told Cade in no uncertain terms to stay away from the 90 and continue driving straight.

Hearing this, Ari shook his head but said nothing.

With the low sun glancing off the dirty windshield making it difficult to see the road ahead, let alone the sign indicating where he needed to turn, Cade decided to roll down his window and stick his head into the slipstream.

"Turn here," hollered Jasper.

The balding tires chirped trying to maintain their tenuous purchase as Cade pulled his head inside and guided the truck into a hard left at the intersection. He stole a look over his shoulder at the black smoke roiling from the burning wreckage and couldn't help noticing the telltale flashes of rounds cooking off. From experience, he knew that lead cutting the air unexpectedly and indiscriminately was nearly always a losing proposition. *No kind of place for anyone to be near*, he thought.

"We're so fucked," Ari bellowed. "If you *do not* turn onto the 90 here we are as good as dead." And since he didn't have a throat mike, and there was a great deal of competing ambient noise as well as a quarter-inch of rear window glass between the cab and the bed, his words, and the worry inflected in them, were lost on everyone save Jasper to his right and Cade to his left.

Caught in a moment of indecision, Cade stood on the brakes and brought the truck to a jarring halt. Listening to the grating tick of a bad lifter, Cade cupped his chin with a gloved hand and tapped the fingers of his other hand on the steering wheel. He stroked his goatee and watched the dead amble around the arcing stretch of oil-stained blacktop leading up to the eastbound freeway. "You have fifteen seconds, Night Stalker. Sell the interstate option to me," he said sharply.

In the back, unaware why the truck had stopped so abruptly, Agent Cross got his feet underneath him and popped up to scan their surroundings. He placed the SCAR rifle he'd taken off of Gaines over the truck's roof, flicked its selector to fire, and about shit himself when he saw the predicament they were in. *Make up your mind, Delta*, he thought to himself. To the left and right of the freeway underpass, dozens of walking dead were making their way from the elevated roadway via their respective off-ramps. Eastbound. Westbound. Do Not Enter. None of the signs meant a thing to the hungry Zs. They were fixated on two things: the sight and sound of the Ghost Hawk and its remaining ammunition firing off in the distance. And the new attraction —the decrepit, idling truck which was full of meat, obviously closer, and quickly becoming a much stronger draw. Then, without warning, rotten creatures began raining down around them from the overpass overhead.

With his hands kneading the wheel at the proper ten-and-two, Cade closed his eyes and let his chin hit his chest. He remained that way for a handful of seconds, during which Ari and Jasper watched his head rock side-to-side. It didn't take a rocket scientist to know that he was mentally working on some kind of equation in which life and death were more than just random variables. He was making some kind of decision, that much was clear.

Too many deaths on my watch, Cade thought. Too many walking dead on the freeway to make it the logical escape route, and judging from the unmistakable sound of meat slamming to the roadway in front, the monsters must be hurling themselves off of the I-90. In his mind's eye he relived the wave of Zs pouring from the shattered skywalk at the NML in Canada and the cacophony from hell that it had produced. He snapped his eyes open and was not surprised to see what his other senses had already confirmed. In addition to the falling forms and the broken shapes crawling and scrabbling and painting the gray road with crimson blood and who knows what else, there was a sizable contingent of Zs about to block their path ahead. Like a single cell organism, the river of flesh and bone marched the gently curving arc that would put them on a collision course with the idling truck.

Agent Cross tapped the sheet metal over Cade's head. "Better do something," he said into the comms. "We've got Zs raining from above." Then, trying hard to ignore the heavy thuds and rifle-shot-like cracks from flesh and bone impacting concrete, he looked beyond the heavy shadow cast by the overhead stretch of I-90 and spied two very large knots of walking dead filing off the other pair of freeway ramps. "I now have eyes on sixty-plus Zulus inbound from the south at twelve o'clock."

"Roger that," Cade said back.

"Permission to fire?" Lopez called out, as he had already followed Cross's lead and had his M4 lined up, bracketing the northbound dead in his crosshairs.

Cade's terse reply, "Wait one," sounded immediately in his ear bud. Nonplussed, Lopez hinged over and shot an impatient look through the truck's rear window at the inside of the crowded cab where an animated discussion was currently underway. Then he shifted his gaze to Cross, who remained stoic and solely focused on the building mass of moaning walkers threatening to surround them. Disregarding the reek of death thick on the air and an overwhelming impulse to empty his carbine into the dead, Lopez performed the sign of the cross over his body armor and prayed for his acting commander to come to some kind of decision. He peered through his weapon's optics and targeted a tottering female first turn, centering the floating red pip between its staring eyes. *Better do something quick, Wyatt*, he thought, taking up a few pounds of trigger pull.

Suddenly the distinctive rapid clatter of a weapon's bolt opening and closing, coupled with the telltale whispers of subsonic lead leaving a suppressor, drew their attention to the rear where Hicks was engaging a cluster of Zs that were *danger close*. The brassy tinkle of spent shells added to the lethal soundtrack as he steadily swept the beefy-looking barrel in a flat left to right arc. "Couldn't wait, Captain," Hicks stated over the comms as the constant accurate fire from the business end of his M4 created a slow motion aerial display of bone and brain. Simultaneously, smoke drifting from the carbine's hot barrel, he slapped a new mag in the well, chambered a round, and called out, "I've got our six cleared ... for now."

In utter disbelief that they were sitting in an idling vehicle in the middle of the road with dead raining down a few yards in front and behind them, Ari finished explaining to Cade why they *must* back up and risk the westbound freeway and the large numbers of dead they were likely to encounter there.

Cade nodded and yanked down on the shifter. "Hold on," he ordered as the transmission caught and the truck lurched sharply in reverse, bouncing up and over half a dozen rotted bodies and grinding them into the street. He worked the gas, brake, and transmission in a finely-choreographed sequence to put the rig into a not-so-graceful low speed bootlegger's reverse; when the truck finished the J turn and came to a complete stop, they found themselves facing the Z-choked westbound onramp.

With a firm set to his jaw, Cade levered the transmission out of reverse and into drive. He looked his friend in the eye, paused a beat, and said, "Are you sure of this, Ari?"

"Positive. Just get us past the Zs on the ramp and the rest will be manageable," Ari said, displaying an air of confidence unbefitting a man who had just crashed a multi-million dollar top-secret helicopter, killing three in the process.

"Roger that," Cade said, while in his ear Lopez's voice was urging him to drive.

But before he could comply, a house-sized shadow flitted by, causing a good number of the monsters to look skyward, lose their already compromised balance, and fall to the roadway like dominos. A half second later the blue sky was blocked by a swiftly moving mass producing a deafening noise that was instantly recognizable to everyone but Jasper.

Chapter 17
Schriever AFB
Grayson Billet

Having just stepped out of the shower, dripping wet and naked, Brook heard the screech of rubber on asphalt and a tick later the telling cough and sputter of a Cushman's engine dying to silence. She snatched a towel off the hook near her head, wrapped it around herself, and padded towards the window to see who had come calling. But before she could make two wet footprints across the floor, someone was banging loudly on the front door.

"Give me a second," she hollered.

After returning recently from giving Wilson, Sasha, and Taryn a primer on firearm safety followed by a hands on, live fire introduction to her M4 and Raven's Ruger 10-22, she had wanted nothing more than to lay on her cool bunk in the dark and await Cade's return. Now, more than a little irritated, she donned a black tee shirt, stepped into a pair of Cade's shorts that fell well below her knees, and wrapped the damp towel turban-like around her head. Tucking the loose end in, she crept to the door, peeled the heavy curtain aside, and peeked out. *Airman Davis,* she thought to herself. *What the hell does he want?* A millisecond after the question popped into her mind, an icy fist gut-punched her as she remembered Cade's death letter. *No, no, no,* she chanted in her head. Suddenly she felt like she was on the summit of Mount Hood at 11,237 feet, in thin air, with someone sitting on her chest. Trying to head off the rising anxiety attack she bent at the waist and sought to relax her diaphragm. *No help.* "Raven," she rasped. There was no answer. The girl had ridden her bike hard for the better part of an hour, making seventeen laps around the jogging track, which when added up amounted to four and one quarter miles. Raven was sound asleep and snoring atop the four bunk beds she called *Raven Island*.

After a long sixty seconds, finally composed and breathing somewhat normally, Brook unlocked the door and stepped into the afternoon sunlight. She looked at Airman Davis, who was one of the few people on the base whom she'd gotten to know fairly well during the past week, yet without the comforting heft of the M4 clutched in her newly-calloused hands, she still felt somewhat naked and vulnerable. *Stay frosty*, she heard Cade whisper in her head as she waited for Davis to deliver the bad news.

But he said nothing. Instead, he broke eye contact, tilted his head and smiled.

Brook followed his gaze and spotted Raven, face pressed to the glass, mugging at the airman. "Spit it out, Davis," she said sharply. "What happened to my husband?"

"I'm sorry, Ma'am," he said, wearing a sincere Sergeant Schulz look on his face. "I don't know anything."

Brook didn't believe him, but did notice that he held her gaze. In her experience, most liars usually looked away. But he didn't shift or shuffle or fidget and, most importantly, maintained direct eye-to-eye contact. By all outward appearances he was telling the truth—but Brook's gut still led her to believe the opposite.

Again she looked over her shoulder and saw that Raven was no longer peering through the window. Fearing the inquisitive twelve-year-old was preparing to join the party, Brook reached behind her, grasped the door handle firmly, and leaned forward with all her weight so it wouldn't budge even if she tried. "I don't believe you," she whispered. "Not for a second."

Davis sighed, looked at the ground, and shook his head. "I've been ordered to say nothing."

"That I believe," she admitted. "Then who do I thank for the pleasure of your company?"

"Major Nash. She ordered me to come and get you."

"Are we going to her office?"

"No. She's at the TOC ... I mean the command center," Davis said. He removed his cover and wiped his brow. "It's hot, Ma'am. Can we go now?" He replaced his hat and squared it away and then shot her a look that said: *I won't be leaving without you.*

Taking just enough time to convey the message that she was the one in charge, Brook uncoiled the towel from her head, tousled her damp hair, and said, "I'll need five minutes. You'll have to wait out here."

After consulting his watch, Davis nodded and mouthed, "Five minutes." And as he watched Brook go back inside and close the door, he wondered to himself how she was going to take the bad news. Would she calmly accept the facts and melt down later in private? Or would she instantly attack the major, the President, or both for goading her husband into accepting the ill-fated mission?

Loathing the fact that he knew what he knew but couldn't share, he returned to his vehicle and slumped in his seat, wiped the sweat from his brow, and then waited patiently on the newly-widowed woman.

***

In three minutes, not five, Brook was standing in the doorway, hair pulled tight into a high ponytail. She had on the same black short-sleeved tee shirt with newly-formed puddles of sweat under her arms and a damp strip down the middle of her back. The shirt was tucked into the waistband of a pair of women's slate-blue and gray digital tiger-striped Air Force issue camouflage pants, the cuffs of which were stuffed neatly inside her fully broken in desert tan combat boots. In her right hand, she clutched the short barrel M4 carbine, its muzzle trained near her feet. Crushed in her left hand was a stark white envelope crisscrossed with a roadmap's worth of creases.

Leaving the square patch of shade provided by the Cushman's small roof, Davis dismounted and approached Brook. Noticing that Raven was within earshot he leaned in and said, "There's something else I need to tell you and I don't think you're going to like it." Detecting a degree of worry settle on the petite woman's features, and reading the look of dread in her eyes, Davis stated Nash's two conditions as delicately as possible. "Two things.

One, you're going to have to find someone to watch your daughter ..."

"And?" Brook asked hitching a brow.

Davis said, "Since the President will be in attendance, you won't be allowed to bring any weapons into the command center."

Brook made a face. "You mean the TOC," she said, correcting him. "As far as weapons go ... you're looking at it. And I feel damn naked without it—" Then, turning and addressing Raven who had been hovering in the doorway, she asked, "You want to hang out with Sasha, Taryn, and Wilson until your dad comes back? It might be late when he does, so it could *end up being a sleepover.*" Even though Brook thought Raven would jump at the chance of hanging out with the cool crowd, still, she stretched out the latter half of her offer, making a once-ordinary occurrence seem like some kind of forbidden fruit.

Instantly the first traces of worry dissolved from Raven's face and, as any pre-teen would, she immediately began planning her night of freedom without a second thought as to why it was being offered in the first place. "Affirmative," she said with a wry smile.

In the brief seconds between question and answer, inexplicably Brook's mind flashed back to the last sleepover Raven had attended, or hosted for that matter, and sadly the details eluded her.

The events of the past two weeks had also blurred together into one long stream of consciousness consisting of combat-induced spikes of adrenaline sandwiched between way too many emotional valleys for her to count, and if she could print out a graph detailing them it would undoubtedly resemble a cardiac patient's EKG strip with a little red arrow stating *you are here* at the very lowest axis on the readout. That's how far down the scale the airman showing up at her doorstep had just taken her. And if she were to sink any lower emotionally she feared that the reptilian part of her brain—the lump of gray matter also known as the *basal ganglia* that drives innate survival-related instincts such as aggression, dominance, and territoriality, which had not only been switched on, but ratcheted up a few hundred notches—might never return to its normal state.

Lately she'd started noticing dangerous situations a few steps before they devolved into deadly ones. Reacting to those threats had become an almost instantaneous muscle-memory-type of response—a far cry, she admitted, from her pre-Omega protocol of observe, analyze, overanalyze and then *maybe* act. She mused sadly that the things that *used* to come naturally, like remembering the names of two dozen of Raven's friends and classmates from school, or who had been slated to be her daughter's fifth grade teacher, were all lost to her. Brook had known sooner or later she'd start forgetting the minutiae from her old life, but the fact that it was happening just two weeks out left her worried whom she would be once she finally reached Eden. The last thing she wanted to be was a cold, emotionless lump of flesh able to protect Raven but nothing more. That led to the question she'd been meaning to ask Cade; yet, despite his open door, ask anything policy, she'd never worked up the courage to do so. Had he been taught some kind of technique that allowed him to switch off his combat instincts each time he walked back into their home after a mission, or was it something that came naturally?

Suddenly Brook was yanked off the couch, figuratively speaking, and snapped out of her Sigmund Freud moment when Raven slammed the door and bounded down the steps with all of her worldly belongings stuffed into one oversized canvas leave bag.

"Grab a change of clothes just in case?" Brook said with a chuckle.

"This is stuff I need for the sleepover, Mom."

"See if Davis can help you with that. And don't forget to tip the man."

Raven made a face and handed the bag to the airman, then hopped aboard the golf cart. "I don't have any money, Mom. Besides ... where would he spend it?"

From the mouths of babes, thought Brook. She took a seat next to Raven, placed her rifle between her knees, and exchanged a look with the driver that begged him not to say anything to further complicate matters.

"I'm the same as your dad. I work for the government, therefore I can't accept tips. It's the thought that counts though.

Thanks all the same," he said with a little wink meant for Brook. He returned his gaze forward, set the engine sputtering, and after a lurch they were barreling across the base towards a cluster of squat gray buildings bristling with antenna and a number of VW-sized satellite dishes.

Chapter 18
Ovid, Colorado

Two fucking days, Elvis thought. That's how long he had been
trapped inside the two-story house outside of Ovid, Colorado. With
no one else to talk to and nothing to keep him occupied, he was just
about at the end of his rope.

Two and a half days thinking through his options in this
house seemed like a year. To pass the time and remain somewhat
sane he'd taken to reading Harlequin romance novels he'd found—
hidden like some kind of contraband—in a brown grocery bag in a
corner upstairs, behind an old fashioned push-pedal sewing machine.
They had already been thoroughly thumbed through, spines cracked,
pages dog-eared. Obviously the interactions on those pages had kept
someone else company for quite some time.

He looked out the kitchen window at the bobbing heads.
Watched the zombies pressing against the waist-high chain-link. Over
time they had thoroughly trampled the shrubs and flowers the owner
of the house had planted there, leaving only churned-up earth in their
stead.

He looked down at the kitchen table. In front of him were
three items.

The black .45 he'd taken from Private Farnsworth and
subsequently killed him with was there. With only eight bullets
remaining in the single stack magazine, it was all but useless against
the numbers he faced. At this rate, he figured, one would suffice.

He'd stick the pistol in his mouth. Do it right the first time so there would be no chance of him coming back as one of them.

Then there was the Iridium satellite phone, now all but useless, its display a blank gray crystal, its keys darkened. He'd made his final call to Bishop less than an hour ago. And for the tenth time today the call had gone unanswered. And then the phone had died. And the charger was in the truck, in the glove box. Worthless. As was the truck now, seeing as how there were thirty of the things between it and the fence blocking the path leading to the back door.

Lastly, there was the scrap of paper with a set of GPS numbers scrawled in silver pen in his hand. Also worthless.

And then there was the road where even more flesh-eaters were shuffling by in what Elvis preferred to call *packs,* which he thought a better term than *herds* as the soldiers at Schriever preferred to call them. Hell, he thought, herd just sounded too bovine in nature—docile—almost as if you could stand back and let them pass and you'd be totally ignored. *Bullshit. What did the stupid soldiers know anyway.* Though the creatures around the perimeter and trudging the road did move slow, in a herd-like follow-the-leader manner when there was no prey around, Elvis knew nothing could be further from the truth once they got sight of meat.

And that's what had happened two days ago. Thirty seconds out back taking a piss was all it had taken for him to get noticed. At first the group of offending creatures had been inconsequential. But by morning he was General Custer and the Sioux were all but knocking down the fence. And to make matters worse, he had company in the cellar. Every so often he'd tread on the floor wrong, producing a squeak not too uncommon in a house a century or so old, and each transgression elicited a whole new round of banging against the cellar door.

Casting furtive looks at the dead walking the road, he wolfed down the last of some kind of meat-filled raviolis straight from the can. Finished, he tossed the spoon in the can and the whole lot in the sink which was piled to overflowing with dishes, dirty and rancid.

He rose from the table and pocketed his belongings, putting the .45 in the small of his back, then moved through the kitchen to the living room, its airspace cut up by bars of afternoon sun. To the left was the front door, a substantial piece of oak inset with three thin works of stained glass which he had already deemed sufficient protection against one or two monsters but no better than rice paper against many more. Next to the door, facing east by south, was a plate window bordered by heavy drapes in burgundy with a paisley print. To his right was a hall that he'd already explored. It led to a small powder room, and, of no use to anyone over four feet, a tiny bedroom painted pink that housed a princess-themed toddler bed, atop its taut bedspread a pair of frilly pink pillows adorned with Snow White and Cinderella, respectively.

Drawing his attention to the fore was a brick fireplace he'd not yet given much scrutiny. It was mantled with a two-foot by six-foot golden slab of old growth that had been polished to a high luster. Arranged on its top with surgical precision were a dozen pictures, some of an elderly gray haired lady—probably a widow, he guessed. Or the world's oldest carpet muncher. He chuckled and looked over the rest of the framed pictures, most of which chronicled nearly every watershed event during the first few years of some little girl's life. One was of the girl as an infant in the arms of a pretty hot-looking nurse, swaddled in a pink blanket, readied for the first handoff. *Come to mommy,* mused Elvis, eyeing the nurse while ignoring the baby. His gaze fell on another photo of the same baby reclining in a plastic tray of some sort in a kitchen sink, wearing a perplexed look that clearly said "What the hell is going on?" *First bath.* He replaced the frame and regarded the next—the obligatory picture of the infant spitting up baby food. Cute and disgusting all at once. Lastly, he eyed the inevitable photo of the anonymous tot's first wavering steps, her little hand fully enveloped by a wrinkly, liver-spotted, hand. *Grandma, is that you downstairs?* thought Elvis. *Are you alone?* he wondered. He hoped so. Just the thought of the toddler in the photos banging around, all rotten and slimy in the root-cellar, brought on an involuntary shudder.

Eyes tearing, Elvis remembered how on every birthday and holiday nearly identical photos starring him and his sister would materialize out of Mom's secret stuff-from-the -past vault. And how she would reminisce for hours over a bourbon hot toddy about the good old days and openly wonder where they'd all gone. Sadly, Elvis knew the answer to that question, and it had been eating him alive since that final phone call—the mother of all dropped calls—when his family had been sent via demolition charges set off by the California National Guard to their watery graves, along with most of the San Francisco-Oakland Bay Bridge.

He removed the *first-steps* photo and tossed the frame to the floor, eliciting a fresh barrage of flesh impacting the cellar door beyond the kitchen. Though the pig-tailed girl in the photo wasn't really his younger sister, she would have to suffice. He folded the photo in two and put it in his pocket, where it would remain until the smoldering ember of hatred within his heart grew dim. Then, with his resolve beginning to waver, he'd unfold it and stoke that ember with the memories of days gone by.

He plopped down on the overstuffed earth-tone *daveno. An absurd old folks' name for a sofa if he ever heard one.* He put his boots on the veneer-topped coffee table, scattering ornamental figurines and spilling a bowl full of age-hardened ribbon candies in the process. Once settled in, he pressed the field glasses to his eyes and adjusted the focus ring. Immediately the virtual river of walking dead filled his field of vision, lurching and bouncing along the shimmering blacktop. Men, women, and kids were all represented in the mix. Not a horde but deadly just the same.

He panned up and left and acquired US-138, which snaked in front of Ovid feeding Sedgwick to the west and Julesburg to the east, and was but one small piece of the asphalt marvel of engineering the hundreds of dead had taken to following.

Bracing his elbows on his chest helped stop the minute shaking that was keeping him from seeing the whole picture. And once he focused on the scene it was evident he was looking at a true horde in all sense of the word. Hundreds of monsters all headed in the same direction with no discernable destination. He keyed in on a telling piece of information. A good number of camouflage-clad zombies were scattered amongst the civilian shamblers. He made a cursory tally of bodies from the shoulder across to the passing lane. Eight was what he came up with. Then he swept the binoculars to the left, ticking off a quick head count along what he guessed to be about a quarter-mile of westbound 138. Eight multiplied by forty.

"Let's call it two fifty," he said softly. Two days ago the sheriff and her merry men of Julesburg had turned him away. But that had been a good thing in hindsight. There was no doubt the city had been overrun. Fine tuning the focus, he walked the binoculars from right to left, noticing that the majority of the walkers appeared to have turned recently. Their skin wasn't flagging off in places like the weeks' old first turns.

He heard it before seeing it. And so did the dead. Ashen faces turned cheek in unison, looking east towards the sound.

Elvis trained the binoculars on a spot where 138 made a bend and adjusted the focus ring. A tick later a flatbed truck with three people crammed into the cab came around the corner, geared low, slowly zippering through the dead, swerving from shoulder-to-shoulder, seeking the path of least resistance. He could see fear and stress and all manner of emotion set on the trio's faces as the dead tried to close ranks on the rig.

"Thank you," blurted Elvis. He rose from the *daveno* and went back into the kitchen and peered out the window; he noticed that the dead out back had forgotten about him and the house and trampling the shrubs. Now all he could see was the back of their heads as they negotiated the drive towards the road beyond.

Hustling back into the living room, he caught the tail end of the truck, brake lights flaring, as it bulled through the front end of the herd, then the reassuring droning of the motor as it disappeared from sight. *Now or never*, went through his mind as he stowed the binoculars. Leaving the case behind, he shouldered the pack and pushed through the kitchen, heading for the back door and the woodland camouflaged GMC he had parked in the detached two-car garage.

But on the way past the cellar the thing bashed against the door. Then the glass knob jiggled ever so slightly. Finally, curiosity got the best of him. Leaving now would be akin to leaving a Husker's football game at halftime. The need to know what had been periodically bumping the door and taking up space in his head over the last sixty-some-odd-hours was gnawing at him.

He stood there gripping the door handle for a few minutes with the rational side of his brain urging him to walk out the back door—to sprint to the pick-up he'd liberated from the Fonz and make his way through the dead and go to wherever the silver GPS numbers would deliver him.

But the irrational side of his brain spoke to him—a sick mantra, the words, *do it, do it, do it* resounding in his head. Manifest Destiny be damned. Getting ahead of the *herd* or *horde* would have to wait. And locating a GPS unit in order to play Bishop's silly game would also go on the back burner.

Do it.

And he did. Like a lion tamer, he held the kitchen chair horizontally in front of him, left arm threaded through the back slats, four sturdy legs ready to counter the creature's inevitable first lunge. He leaned forward and *snicked* the lock with his right.

Bang.

Do it.

That the door would open towards him was a given. Whoever designed the first cellar stairway long ago had come to the conclusion that opening a door into a darkened hole where the footing was uncertain and lighting a luxury was likely a losing proposition. So Elvis pulled the door towards him, releasing a sickly sweet stench of carrion and damp soil and old rotted timbers. Then from the darkness, hunched over and gray, the toddler's granny fell up the top two stairs, landing face first on the kitchen floor, the impact sending its dentures skittering across the floor and loosing a torrent of squirming maggots from its toothless maw. Sidestepping the glistening white larva, Elvis trapped the writhing creature to the floor. Picturing a soccer ball at his feet, he torqued his hips and drew his right leg back to half-mast. "Sorry, Ma'am," he said as he dipped his right shoulder, starting a chain reaction as the energy coursed through his back muscles, unloaded his cocked hips and focused every ounce of inertia down his leg, culminating in the introduction of shoe leather to bone.

Following through with a final twist of the hips, Elvis drove the reinforced steel-toe of his boot through the monster's septum and into its brain. A sickening crunch reverberated through the galley kitchen and Elvis hopped in a circle around the chair, struggling to dislodge his boot from the stilled creature's caved-in face.

He finally resorted to stepping on Grandma's stick-thin neck, grinding the vertebra there to a pulp while working his right foot free.

Fighting the urge to puke, he stepped over the body and stared down into the void. Listened hard. *Nothing.*

He pulled a mini-Maglite from a cargo pocket and twisted the bezel until he had a nice wide cone of light to work with. Leading with the pistol clutched in his right fist, flashlight held in the left, he took the stairs two at a time. He stopped four strides later. Eight stairs down—mid-flight. Starting at his four o'clock he swept the white light over the packed dirt walls right to left. Freezing the beam at roughly ten o'clock, he gasped as what he was looking at was rejected momentarily by the rational side of his brain.

The little girl whose short life was on display in pictures on the mantle upstairs was dead. She'd been killed and partially eaten by Grandma. Her thick blond hair had stuck fast to the floor in the blood that had pooled and dried where she had been ravaged and then finally reanimated.

What a pitiful sight it was, watching it struggle and twitch, its tiny teeth clacking together.

Unable to check the rising surge Elvis hinged at the waist and vomited on the stairs below him.

Chapter 19
Schriever AFB

"Boardwalk with one house ... that will be two hundred big ones," crowed Sasha, palm out. "Rents due, big bro. Pay up."

"Dice are broken," Wilson mumbled, ripping the paper band holding the two-inch-thick stack of twenties he'd surreptitiously pocketed after the imploding windshield encounter with the undead Wells Fargo driver days ago. Why the stone-faced soldier had given the bricks of cash back after quarantine was the sixty-four-thousand-dollar question. Maybe the Army's *don't ask, don't tell* policy could be applied in more than one way, he'd thought at the time. Especially after a society-crushing viral outbreak. No matter, he gave Sasha a well-earned dose of stink eye, licked his thumb, and then flicked away ten of the crisp, aromatic Andrew Jacksons.

"You're just unlucky, Wilson. Don't pout, give it here," she said gleefully, waggling her fingers in the universal gesture that meant *fork it over.* As he handed her the worthless bank notes, his gaze shifted to Taryn and he reflected on how lucky he'd been to have crossed paths with her. How an unfathomable, yet serendipitous chain of events—like some kind of fated butterfly effect—had thrown them together. How in an you-cannot-make-this-shit-up kind of story she had been trapped in an airport full of the dead, only to be rescued by a stealth helicopter full of Special Forces led by the husband of someone he had recently met. Like he was living out a plot device in a James Cameron movie, he fantasized that he'd somehow been chosen to survive the initial outbreaks and then meet

93

Taryn and conceive and raise a child with her. *Their* child would then grow into a man and eventually save the world. With a dreamy smile on his face, he was rudely yanked from his flowery fantasy by Sasha's whiny voice. "Snap out of it, Wilson," she said, mouth hovering a hand's width from his ear.

"What were you thinking about, Red?" Taryn said softly into the other ear from an equal distance.

"Zoning out I guess," he said, bending the truth enormously. "I guess I got way too much sun the last couple of days. Probably overdosing on vitamin D or whatever it is in sunshine." In truth, he surmised, the vivid daydream had nothing to do with how many times he'd watched the Terminator movies. He was no Kyle Reese and Taryn was not his Sarah. Fact of the matter was, he was still grappling with the romantic repercussions of the previous night. A night of bliss he'd never forget and hoped to replicate before leaving for Utah. *Hell*, he thought, *if Captain America aka Captain Grayson wanted to go on a few more missions, he was OK with that.* The window of opportunity was as wide as it would ever be, and he harbored a considerable amount of fear it was about to start the downward slide. Hell, as far as he knew the ink on the inevitable Dear John letter was probably still wet and the piece of rotten news was tucked away in the top drawer of the desk sitting against the wall under the warbling air-conditioning unit. *On the bright side*, he thought to himself—as Taryn's iPhone which was sitting atop said desk caught his eye— there was no way he'd be experiencing another one of those dreaded *I'm dumping you* text messages which had been all the rage before the world went to shit. And the thing that had really pissed him off about the ones he'd received was that there had been no way for him—the dumpee—to cajole, plead, or argue his case with the thousands of cold and indifferent pixels on the tiny screen telling him in more ways than one: *You are not worthy.*

So he had told a little white lie. Big deal. He couldn't have just blurted out—*I was fantasizing about you and me living together forever, Taryn.* Followed up by putting his irrational thoughts into words—*And please don't dump me, Taryn. You're all I have to live for.*

Melodramatic?

Yes.

But with the loss of his mom, and the swift and sudden disappearance of the human race to the unforgiving Omega virus, the fear that he would never find someone as beautiful and sweet-smelling as Taryn again was visceral—and of late—all-consuming.

So he closed his eyes, hoping to live in his fantasy world for as long as possible.

"You're doing it again, Wilson," Taryn said, delivering a peck on his sunburned cheek.

And never the one to let her brother enjoy himself, Sasha said, "Your roll, Miss Tattoo."

Shooting Sasha a look that said, *Don't push it,* Taryn threw the dice. "Lucky seven," she said as she did a little dance in her seat and moved the pewter gray roadster the appropriate number of spaces. "I passed Go ... and that means I collect two hundred dollars. Pay me, banker man." She flashed a quick smile at Wilson, who was peeling off twenties and glaring at Sasha, and concluded that there would be no better time than the present to address the thousand-pound gorilla in the room. Scrunching her brow, she took a deep breath and asked, "What did you two think about taking target practice on the zombies?"

Without missing a beat Sasha piped up. "That creeped me out big time. Especially how comfortable Raven was with the whole thing ... popping them in the head like that with *her own gun* ... almost seemed like she was enjoying it or something."

"Apple doesn't fall very far from the tree," said Taryn. "Because it was crystal clear to me that Brook *was* enjoying every second of it." She shuddered visibly, went quiet for a good long beat, and then went on. "Something about the way she calmly put down one after another of those things didn't seem normal. I had to stop counting after about ten."

"She offed twenty-six of them," Sasha said proudly. "I was counting. And she didn't even blink when she was shooting at the little ones."

Taryn nodded but said nothing.

"A bite from a kid Z will kill you just as good as any," Wilson proffered. Then he threw the dice, strictly because they were there in front of him. He watched the bones bounce around and finally come to rest showing double sixes. Box cars. Good a sign as any.

Disregarding their ongoing game, he let his gaze fall on Taryn and decided to dig a little and see if an earlier observation he had made was correct. "Looked like *you* had no problem shooting the handful of deadheads that you did," he said. "*Granted* ... Miss Grayson seemed to think we all needed our *firearms* and *double hit* merit badges."

"Double tap," Sasha said, correcting Wilson. "*Two shots to the head. The double tap ensures that they go down and stay down,* were her exact words."

"She doesn't scare me a bit," said Taryn, inclining her head a degree to punctuate the statement.

"At all?"

"Not one iota, Sasha. So she's comfortable with her role. Momma lion protecting her cub. I get it. But she's still human like you and me. She puts her pants on one leg at a time."

Breaking out in a big grin, Sasha said, "Which side you think she lets it hang?"

"Grow up, Sasha," said Wilson. He screeched his chair back and looked Taryn square in the face. "I have to know something."

"Go ahead. Shoot," said Taryn.

Wincing at her choice of words, Wilson removed his hat. He listened to the A/C rumble for a tick as his inner voice waged a losing battle with itself, one second screaming, *Ask the question,* and the next begging him to tell her to forget about it because he'd lost his train of thought. After a few seconds the mental volley became too much and he popped the question he assumed he already knew the answer to. "Did *you* enjoy it?"

"*Me?*" Taryn said incredulously. To Wilson her response sounded rehearsed. Almost theatrical.

"Yeah, you," he said back. "Did you get any *satisfaction* from ridding the earth of a few more of those infected things?" And to drive home the seriousness of his question, he donned his hat and smashed it down to its customary position, put his elbows on the table, cupped his chin, and stared at her awaiting a reply.

"Not so much," she answered softly. "I killed Dickless 'cause he had it coming. He was a pervert when he was my boss and he wouldn't quit staring at me after he got bit and turned into one of those things."

"They all do that after they turn."

"I know, Sasha. But you weren't there to see him leering. *Your* skin wasn't crawling twenty-four-seven just knowing he was out there dry humping the door trying to get in." Suddenly, as if she'd run out of gas or blown a fuse, she went silent, lowered her eyes and bowed her head.

"Must have been awful," Sasha replied sincerely.

There was a long moment of silence.

Lamenting the fact that Taryn was revisiting her darkest moment because of him, Wilson fidgeted in his seat, praying for Sasha to rest her case and conclude her line of questioning.

"It was," Taryn said, lifting her head enough to shoot a sidelong look at Sasha. "When I shot him in the face I was happier than I'd been in days. Happier than when I found those two granola bars behind a porno mag in his lower desk drawer. Shooting those burnt creatures by the fence today was *not* the same ... I got *zero* satisfaction from that. Just makes me have to think about how they died the first time around. Who they were. Who they left behind. Made me think about my mother. My father, and my brother. Reminds me of the hot rod we were gonna restore together ... as a *family*. Just makes me think, and right now the last thing I need to do ... is fuckin think."

Wilson peeked from under his boonie hat. "Speaking from experience, shooting them is a lot easier than killing them with a bat," he intoned, remembering how he'd been forced to brain his undead next door neighbors at the Viscount Arms in Denver. "And now that I've got a feel for that M4 of hers, there is *no* way on earth I'm ever going to use that Louisville Slugger again. That thing is retired ... unless I have to use it as a last resort."

"So a convert, huh?" Sasha said. "Mom always was against *guns*."

"Says my *sister* who won't brandish *anything* except for her knockoff Fendi and Louis Vuitton handbags," countered Wilson.

"You didn't even shoot Raven's rifle ... did you?" he added accusingly. "No reason to fear it. Thing's about one notch above a BB gun."

More than a little embarrassed to debate her fear of firearms let alone her total inability to touch one, Sasha wisely made no reply.

Sensing the chink in her armor, Wilson turned the tables and pushed *her* buttons for once. "I suggest you put a couple of non-quarried rocks in those pleather bags of yours and swing away. Then you could say you're a certified, green, organic, natural-born, free-range zombie killer," he quipped.

"Better than being a *gun nut*," was the best Sasha could come up with.

"One day this *gun nut* might save your bacon with a ... oh my gosh ... a *gun*." *Touché* thought Wilson. Living away from home for a decent stretch before the outbreak had softened his delivery somewhat. But the longer he found himself cooped up with his little sister, the sharper his witty verbal comebacks had become.

Chapter 20

There was a knock at the door. Staccato, machine-gun-like pops of knuckle on wood containing a certain sense of urgency.

Everyone stopped talking at once, but it was Taryn who rose and took a few tentative steps toward the door.

After a few beats it came again. Only louder, like someone who was being shadowed down the street by a stranger and had just so happened to have randomly chosen Taryn's billet for refuge and wanted in ... *now.*

"Who is it?" Taryn called out, even as she peeled the blackout curtain from the narrow window beside the door. The air conditioner rattled on and a voice, barely audible above it, called back, "It's Brook and Raven's with me. Can we come in?"

Taryn let go of the curtain and looked over her shoulder at Wilson and Sasha and whispered, "It's them. And there is a guy sitting in a golf cart. He's wearing some kind of uniform." She took care to smooth the curtain into place, making sure no outside light shone in, then hinged up and worked the lock.

Brook and Raven stepped inside with a few bars of sunlight and the faint smell of death close on their heels.

"Game's over," Wilson said to Sasha. The wheeled office chair he had been sitting on emitted a pneumatic hiss when he rose. He stacked the three unwrapped packets of twenty dollar bills totaling six thousand in all, rustled up the loose bills and was about to stuff the whole lot into one of his cargo pockets when he caught himself. *Old habits die hard*, he thought with a smile upon recognizing the absurdity of giving a shit about leaving the cash lying around. He tossed the worthless money on the table, watching it fan out and then slide onto the floor.

"What did you go and do Wilson ... rob a bank or something?" Brook said as Taryn shut the door and snapped the deadbolt into place behind her.

Ignoring the quip, Wilson regarded her with a serious look and said, "I thought you'd be down at the flight line by now welcoming your husband back."

Making no reply, Brook fixed her gaze on him, hitched a brow, and tilted her head towards Raven, conveying the universal message that what needed to be said wasn't appropriate to voice out loud with young ears around.

Seeing the looks exchanged between Brook and Wilson, and correctly guessing their meaning, Taryn grabbed Raven's duffel bag and guided her to where they'd be out of earshot from the others and vice-versa. "I've got just the thing for you," Taryn said to Raven. As she led them around the makeshift gaming table, they passed by the trio of desks pushed tight against the right side wall. She snatched up her fully charged iPhone and the white tangle of wires that passed for earphones. Then she directed Raven to one of the furthermost bunks, sat down and patted the mattress next to her. "I've got *everything* Lady Gaga ever recorded on this thing," she added, hefting the smartphone in her hand like it was the last one on earth. "Want to give it a listen?"

"Heck yeah," blurted Raven, eagerly accepting the device that was nearly identical to the one she had hoped to receive for her twelfth birthday but had not. Like an old pro, she plugged the buds into her ears and began thumbing her way through the digitally-rendered album covers.

After Raven and Taryn had moved out of sight, Brook commandeered the chair that Wilson had relinquished. She made herself comfortable, looked up at him, and said slowly and succinctly, "I need you and Taryn to watch Raven for me. It might even end up turning into an all-nighter."

TMI—too much information— thought Wilson as he struggled to believe that Brook would even consider leaving her daughter alone for a few minutes, let alone overnight, considering the dead gathered outside of the wire and the other dangers—real or imagined—still lurking inside the base. Giving her the benefit of the doubt, he took a deep breath, hid his fomenting disgust, and instead began to calculate the odds of him surviving a night of Monopoly against three members of the opposite sex.

But in the time it took him to exhale the breath, he read the worry on her face and realized that she merely wanted to protect Raven from seeing or hearing something she wasn't prepared to deal with, not unload her in order to have a night alone with *Captain America*. "What's going on?" he asked, concern showing in his voice.

She made no reply.

Then he noticed something about her body language that set an alarm off in his head. It seemed like she was carrying an invisible baby grand piano on her back. Her shoulders sagged and the way she was sinking in the office chair was totally unlike her. He'd seen her in action, and in his book the lady was no slouch—literally and figuratively. Thinking the worst, he finally asked, "Is Cade OK?"

Brook hitched her brow and tilted her head towards Sasha in the same manner that she had with Raven a moment ago.

Wilson said, "Sasha ... can you give me and Brook a second alone?" And though it was worded as a question with an option, it had been delivered more like a parental order, leaving no room for discussion.

"Do I have to?" she asked. Then, after shifting her gaze from Wilson to Brook and receiving only a cold stare from the visitor, she pushed her chair from the table and stormed away in a huff, mumbling something about her and Wilson being equals now that their mom wasn't here and how she better not be asked to babysit someone else's kid.

Brook watched Sasha leave and then said, "The only thing I can tell you is that Cade went out on a mission and hasn't returned yet."

"I gathered as much since we didn't leave for Utah today." He paused, waiting for an answer. When none came, he asked, "So why do you need us to watch Raven?"

One hand knuckling out a slow cadence on the tabletop and the other clutching Cade's death letter in her pocket, Brook replied, "They sent a man to get me. He said I was needed in the communications room ... wouldn't elaborate."

"Who is *they?*"

"Major Nash. She's the lady we gave the thumb drive to."

Not good, thought Wilson. The fact that Cade had so abruptly changed his plans meant that the mission had something to do with the information contained on the thumb drive. That Brook couldn't divulge what kind of mission and was now being summoned in for a face-to-face with the crotchety major told him more than he needed or wanted to know. So he said nothing. Just looked at her face, hoping she'd crack a smile and say everything was going to be alright, and that they were still leaving the dismal base in the morning. But she didn't, and judging by her deepening worry lines, he surmised she'd already arrived at the same conclusion he had. He said, "We'll entertain her then. And try our best to keep her occupied and her mind off the fact that you're both gone."

"She's gotten used to her dad being gone. But once the allure of the iPhone wears off and it sinks in that she's *really* alone, she'll probably get fidgety. If I don't return she might not fall asleep right away. She'll talk your ears off instead of closing her eyes if you let her. But she's a resilient kid ... she'll be OK."

No shit, thought Wilson. Resilient doesn't even begin to cover it. Hardened. Calloused maybe. He could probably go on and list a half-dozen other adjectives usually associated with steely-eyed-shooters in the old Westerns—because when it came to blasting the dead, the stoic four-footer made him look like a pussy and Sasha seem like an emotional infant. "Take as long as you need," he said. "And I hope Nash has nothing but good news for you." *You dumbass, Wilson*, he thought to himself, knowing full well from what he'd seen in the movies and on television that nothing good was ever attributed to a somber-looking man in uniform coming to an Army wife's door. "What I meant ..."

"Save it," said Brook. "You'll only succeed in digging the hole deeper. If I don't come back tonight, there are some MREs and a change of clothes in her bag."

"MREs? We'll take Raven to the mess hall in an hour or so."

"I don't want her going outside. Period."

"I'll bring something back then."

Fixing her gaze on Wilson, Brook said, "After I leave I don't want you to open the door for anything or anyone. I don't care if it's Shrill, Nash, or President Clay herself." There was a moment of silence. "The door remains locked. Is that clear?"

Staring into the woman's determined eyes reminded him of the time not long ago when he had found himself peering into the gaping muzzle of an automatic rifle in the hot confines of a U-Haul's cab. This time the stare was just as icy, but thankfully the M4 didn't factor into the equation. "She'll be in good hands," Wilson said. "I promise."

"Mom!" yelled Raven as she fumbled to remove the ear buds that were still pumping some kind of bass heavy track which Brook could hear from roughly thirty feet away. "Can I hang out with Taryn and Sasha for a while?"

"It's OK with us," said Taryn. "Right Sasha?"

"Should be fun," countered Sasha meekly.

"Sounds like a plan. Sweetie," Brook called back. "Come give Mom a hug and a kiss before she leaves." She turned her head and palmed a couple of tears away, and then received her not-so-little-girl with open arms. Embracing Raven tightly, Brook rested her chin on the top of her head and slowly drew her girl's silky pigtails through her fingers. "We need to get this hair trimmed," she said absentmindedly as tears welled up fat in the corners of her eyes. She stood up and turned away before the wet trails on her tanned cheekbones gave her away.

From his seat at the game table, Wilson got misty-eyed watching the two share words which were drowned out by the conditioned air buffeting his back. And speaking from experience, having grown up without a father, he'd be lying if he said he wasn't more than a little worried for the both of them. In fact things would probably never be the same once they were reunited. Because his gut was telling him that the news Brook was about to hear was going to affect Raven—resilience not withstanding—much harder than anyone could imagine.

SHAWN CHESSER

Chapter 21
Draper, South Dakota
SR 13-I 90 Juncture

"What the heck was that?" said Jasper.

Eyes tracking the glorious sight across the sky, and hearing Lopez in his ear bud thanking God for their apparent about-face in fortune, Cade answered, "That, my friend, is our ride home."

Craning his neck in order to follow the source of the shadow that had just moments ago blotted out the sun, Jasper asked another question that Cade was already contemplating. "Where is a plane that *big* going to land around here?"

"You would be surprised," came Ari's unsolicited reply as the airplane's retreating engine noise was supplanted by the snarls and hisses of the dead and an out-of-place whine coming from poorly-meshing synchros in the transmission just inches below his ass.

Saying nothing, Cade pinned the accelerator to the floor and put the two wheels on Jasper's side parallel to the rumble strips on the right shoulder. There was no guardrail on the onramp, only a gently sloping once-manicured expanse of long-dormant grass running the entire length of the incline that fed into the two westbound lanes. In his side vision he saw the parchment-colored swath of grass and the ragtag groups of dead flash by. He flicked his gaze to the airplane, which had climbed to a point where it was seemingly suspended, like one of the many plastic scale models that had once been thumbtacked to the ceiling of his childhood room back in Portland. Only this was no model, and the props were spinning, clawing the air, trailing zephyrs of pewter gray exhaust, a testament to how hard the four engines were working. Then it nosed up as the pilot made a subtle course correction to the south, further showing off the top of its fuselage, a gray blue 'T' silhouetted against the sun.

For a split second Cade worried that the dust- and grime-coated Chevy had gotten lost in the ground clutter, and perhaps they hadn't been spotted. He thought he might have screwed the pooch. Loitering in the lip of shadow thrown by the overpass had been foolish and, however improbable the case may be, might have occurred at the exact moment that the minuscule patch of ground had received its split second's worth of scrutiny from the search and rescue plane. However, that notion quickly passed, giving way to a more plausible explanation—perhaps the pilot, co-pilot, and the other half of the four-man crew had been fixated on the burning helo northeast of them and the KC-130 that was supposed to be their salvation was now returning to Schriever.

Pushing all of those negative thoughts from his mind, Cade kept his attention locked on the gray ribbon of oil-stained cement four or five car lengths ahead and plotted a course that would deliver them onto the 90 without getting their ride high-centered on a mound of squirming corpses. And while his concentration was focused on steering clear of the groping claw-like hands of the dead, Mister Murphy was working the bellows, heating and folding the metal, fashioning a very big monkey wrench to throw into the Delta operator's plans. "Shoot me a path through these things," he bellowed, even as the report of silenced machine guns and the tinkling of brass skittering across the roadway reached his ears.

One hand working the wheel, he punched the window down and went for the Glock suspended under his arm. The polymer pistol slipped from the holster fast and easy, and once comfortably in his left hand, he stuck the muzzle past the side mirror, drew a bead, and tracked a pair of recently turned Zs—one male and one female. Barking twice, the semi-auto pistol delivered a lethal one-two punch, cratering the male's face. As the creature pirouetted into the truck's path, Cade shifted aim by a degree and eased back on the accelerator. The Glock bucked twice more, sending a lead double-tap careening towards the female Z's face. Snapping the pallid Z's head back like a Mike Tyson uppercut, the first round struck the strip of skin just below its upturned nose and spread a rose-tinted haze containing splintered teeth and pulped flesh into the air. A fraction of a second later the rotten corpse's clouded eyes disappeared, punched through the back of its head as the second 9 mm Parabellum entered on an upward trajectory directly between them. At last, the combined kinetic energy from both slugs threw the lifeless corpse into a backward half gainer. In all, less than two seconds had elapsed, and as dumb luck would have it, both Zs smacked the concrete less than a yard apart, succumbed to the combined effects of gravity and the engineered cant of the onramp, and rolled into the path of the Chevy's left front wheel. Pulling his arm back into the truck, Cade set the smoking Glock on his lap and grimaced as a pair of muffled pops reverberated through the floor pan as both of the Zs' skulls lost the battle with the steel-belted radials.

Close to retching, Jasper motored his window down and brought his pistol to bear on the pale creatures scrabbling through the expanse of knee length grass to his right.

"Make 'em count," Ari called out, trying to cover his ears. But thanks to the ongoing numbness because of the cinched-down harness, lifting his arms up even an inch was a monumental task. So, myth or not, in an effort to protect his hearing against the dueling reports to his left and right, more necessary at this point than combating the stench of death enveloping them all, he opened his mouth to equalize the pressure in his ears. *Bullshit*, he thought, as a stabbing pain settled behind his eyes and a shrill buzz akin to overhead high voltage wires on steroids blared inside of his skull. Whoever had fed him that line of crap—probably some artillery officer bragging over beers—deserved to be punched in the mouth. So he sat there, hands in his lap, and split his attention between watching the big undertaker to his right deal out second death and keeping a watchful eye out for additional rescue aircraft he hoped had been dispatched. And as he hoped and prayed for Jedi One-Two to materialize on the horizon, he tried hard to remember how much landing strip a fuel-laden Hercules needed to land. He knew from running joint operations with the Air Force Army and Marines that the durable aircraft could land most anywhere, on roads, unimproved grass, or dirt airstrips. He also knew its four engines were designed with counter-rotating props which provided a considerable amount of reverse thrust. Enough to begin slowing it down immediately after its wheels hit the ground.

"You think she's going to be able to land on the interstate?" Cade asked, casting a quick glance at Ari.

"If we clear a spot for them," answered Ari, thinking to himself how eerie it was to have Cade reading his mind at nearly every turn. "Road's pretty choked," he added. "It's gonna take some work."

"Can you drive?"

"I couldn't scratch my balls even if I wanted to," said Ari, both arms still numbed out of commission from hanging inside the helo like a meat piñata for the dead.

"We better get to it then," said Cade, downshifting in order to power through a phalanx of ambling Zs. "Whatever you do, Jasper. Make sure when you pop them they fall *away* from the truck's path." Then, practicing what he preached, Cade retrieved the Glock from the seat. Swerving right, he squeezed off half a dozen rounds, dropping four of the dead that were doing their best to get in front of the truck. Finally seeing a sliver of daylight, he nosed the truck through and flicked his gaze south of west, where far off in the distance he recognized the unmistakable form of the Hercules crossing the sun on a wide banking turn.

"They're coming back," said Cade into the comms.

***

Onboard the Hercules, Dover thumbed through his mission briefing paperwork and found the communications page that listed all of the call signs and the frequencies the different packages were broadcasting on. He located the frequency the Delta team had used to communicate with the Jedi flight and amongst themselves while they were on the ground at the NML. "Meredith, take this." He handed the clipboard to his co-pilot. "Since you're not getting a copy on the dust-off frequency, why don't you try and hail them on their RF comms."

***

Cade had one eye on the approaching plane and was sighting down the Glock with the other, when a voice with a slight southern drawl utilizing a calm, business-like syntax said in his earpiece, "Oil Can Five-Five here. Anvil Actual, is that you in the civilian vehicle at my eleven o'clock ... how copy?"

Containing his enthusiasm, Cade answered back, "Anvil Actual ... I have a solid copy. And it's very nice to hear your voice."

"Well it just so happens to be your lucky day, Anvil," replied the pilot. "Because you, my friend who has already been written off as dead by the brass, are the very lucky recipient of one off the record and highly insubordinate final pass."

"Roger that, Oil Can. We'll be sure to keep this off the record. And rest assured if I have to go outside the wire for it—you'll be getting more than the case of beer Ari already promised you—" Cade ceased talking mid-thought and jerked the wheel hard left to avoid a pair of Zs making one of their patented slow speed lunges into the path of the creeping pick-up.

"That was close," said Jasper, flinching away from the window. Then he asked Ari with a quizzical look on his face, "Who is he talking to?"

"His imaginary friend ... talks to him *all* of the time," answered Ari in his best deadpan. "He hears voices as well. And sees dead people." Ari wanted to make the universal finger-circling-the-ear gesture implying Cade was cuckoo, but didn't want to bring on another wave of nausea by trying to move his arms. So he said, "Jasper ... I'm fucking with you."

To which Jasper said nothing. Instead the undertaker powered his window up and stared straight through the windshield.

Searching for a suitable stretch of road or tract of land for the plane to land, Cade looked over his shoulder at I-90 stretching off to the east. *No good.* It was choked with walking corpses and vehicles. Too many to navigate in this ride. And switching vehicles wasn't an option. He glanced in the rearview at Cross, who was kneeling on one knee, swaying to and fro like he was in a tiny skiff fighting rough seas. The Secret Service man had one hand wedged under the lip on the passenger side of the bed and the SCAR carbine gripped tightly in the other, pulling it taught against its sling in order to steady the front heavy weapon. Hicks was switching magazines while Lopez was opposite Cross—a near mirror image—his suppressed M4 held steady, squeezing off snap shots at the creatures within reaching distance.

With the merge to the 90 at the top of the ramp getting closer one hard-fought uphill yard at a time, Cade pushed off against the sagging springs and craned to see what lay ahead before committing fully.

"This is Oil Can Five-five," said Dover in Cade's ear bud. "We didn't pick up a distress signal on the *dust-off* frequency. Is your transponder activated?"

"It wasn't at first ... but that's a long story," Cade said back. "It is activated now."

After fiddling with the radio's switches for a second, Ari said, "It's powered on and looks to be transmitting normally." Then, after inspecting the stocky antenna and noticing a fair amount of abnormal play at its base, he finally conceded that it had probably been broken either in the crash or when he had unclasped his harness and hinged forward into the choppers mangled HUD—heads up display.

"No matter," Dover said back. "Let's put our heads together and think of a way to get you all aboard."

Already several steps ahead in his mind, Cade nosed the pickup onto the 90 and felt his heart skip a beat when the entire picture unfolded. As far as he could see, cars, trucks, and SUVs were spread out at intervals resembling some kind of a static Indy 500 staggered start. Dotting the lanes every hundred yards or so were vehicles piled high with worldly belongings, some of them occupied with moving, festering corpses.

After travelling a dozen yards moving at a school-zone clip, Cade had an idea. He pulled in tight next to a white panel van that had taken quite a beating. The rear bumper was hanging precariously, and the three corners he could see were battered and rounded off, presumably from striking metal and meat alike during a mad dash from Sioux Falls. Crimson hand prints marked every square inch of the Euro-styled van, and as he stopped alongside, the distinct smell of sun-baked carrion wafted from the passenger window. Cade looked left at the swollen inanimate corpse. Feasting on a gray hunk of rotting tongue, flies darted in and out of its drooping mouth. *What's your story,* he thought, as the sweet treat hinged forward and bumped against the inner door, sending a buzzing black and green cloud into the air.

Ignoring the nearby creature and its vain attempts to get a hand on him, Cade said, "Cross, get up on the van and tell me what you see."

Instantly the gunfire from the bed diminished and the truck lurched upward on its springs, relieved of a portion of its burdensome load as Cross launched his two hundred and fifty pound frame at the panel truck, made a handhold out of the sleek black rail atop it, and easily scrabbled aboard.

A few seconds elapsed before Cross said, "Wait one. Adjusting optics."

Then there was another long moment during which no words were exchanged and everyone seemed to be holding their breath. The only sounds, dry hisses of the dead and a rhythmic coughing coming from the truck's bed as Hicks and Lopez pumped 5.56 rounds from their M4 carbines into the dead.

Finally Cross relayed in detail what he was seeing.

To Cade, none of it sounded good.

Chapter 22
Schriever AFB

Catching Airman Davis unaware, Brook hopped from the Cushman before it had come to a complete stop. Without a backwards glance, and fully expecting an admonishment from the uptight driver, she set her jaw and squared her shoulders to lend the impression that she knew exactly where she was going as she strode towards the rear entrance to the wide, low-slung building.

Built of cinder and glass and finished in a dull battleship gray, the fifties-era structure housed all of the different elements comprising the 50th Space Wing, including the bustling TOC which was her ultimate destination.

Having already been warned that President Valerie Clay would be in attendance, as would her protection detail, Brook left her M4 behind a withered bush and shouldered her way through the door without regard to who or what stood in her way.

The door swung shut behind her, closing with a soft squelch. She paused for a moment to get her bearings, listening hard for any sounds she imagined might be associated with a command center: barked orders, the bustle of bodies in close proximity to one another, perhaps fingers tapping out commands on computer keyboards. *Nothing.* The only noise evident as she stood stock-still was the muted hiss of overhead fluorescents and the nearly subliminal whoosh of conditioned air transiting conduits hidden behind the ceiling's drop down tiles. And overriding the building's mechanical noises was the steady cadence of her beating heart. She let her gaze follow the hall off to the left and then she took in the nearly identical view to the right. The floors were covered with a battleship-gray, institutional-type low wear carpeting— easy on the feet but not on the eyes—and breaking up the linear flow of the wood paneled walls, photos of men and women looking important in blue uniforms were affixed at regular intervals. She ignored their squared-away plastic smiles as she filed past, instead focusing all of her attention on finding signage that would point her to the *top secret* satellite command center.

After a winding and fruitless search of the left half of the building, and finding absolutely nothing, she went back the way she had come. The entry door passed by on her right, and she padded down the narrow corridor experiencing a niggling sense of déjà vu. Minus the low-hanging pipes and wires snaking overhead, this part of the building reminded her of the interior of a submarine she'd once toured. Wondering why she hadn't come across any Air Force personnel or a submariner or two, she walked a straight line past a handful of closed doors and came to another 'T' where another decision loomed. *Left or right?* she asked herself.

To the left was more of the same: dark wood, gray flooring, and harsh lighting. To the right, past a stainless wall-mounted drinking fountain, the hallway doubled in width and continued on for another twenty or thirty feet before ending at a sturdy-looking door of brushed metal with no visible handle or hinges. Affixed to the door at eye level was a sign that said *Authorized Personnel Only,* and coming from the other side were subdued voices engaged in serious-sounding conversation. *Gotta be here*, Brook thought as she ignored the sign and leaned against it, leading with her shoulder. *Locked.*

She stood there for a moment wondering what could be so important for Nash to summon her to the back door of the TOC a number of hours prior to Cade's supposed return. Maybe the Delta team was coming back empty handed. Perhaps Nash wanted to put her off balance in order to try and convince her to allow Cade to go on another mission. She would be in a foreign environment—not necessarily hostile—but still staffed by Nash's people which would surely lend the major the upper hand in any kind of negotiations. *Stick to your guns*, she told herself. Then she came up with a couple of mental bullet points to use if she was in fact ambushed: *You can't be swayed this time because your debt to Nash and Shrill has already been paid in full—twice. President Clay is a person, nothing less, nothing more.* With the fear of finding out Cade's fate pulling her from the door like some kind of invisible tractor beam, and her newfound *'moxie,'* something her mother had called *the rare commodity a female needed to survive in a man's world* urging her to confront that fear, she deliberated for a second outside the door.

And as she worked the pro and con columns in her head, she remembered her mom speaking highly of the women pilots who flew the newly-built fighters from the assembly lines near Boeing Field in Washington State to their respective jumping-off airbases during World War 2. According to Mom, those women had *'moxie.'* Mom had always used *her* mother as an example of a courageous woman blessed with the very same trait. Gloria had been one of the famous women known collectively as *Rosie the Riveter*. They were the women who dropped everything: kids, husbands, a teacher's job in Grandma's case, in order to assist the war efforts by helping to build the Liberty Ships in the Van Port shipyards.

Brook smiled at the good memories she had of her mom, the woman who had been her best friend in life. Then, dredging up enough courage to confront Nash and possibly the President in front of a room filled with Air Force personnel and Secret Service agents, she closed her fist and pounded resolutely against the door.

A second later it was opened by an unsmiling man whose eyes were hidden behind wraparound glasses with lenses that appeared honed from obsidian and reflected a half-dozen moving images from the flat panel screens scattered about the room. At six-and-a-half feet tall and easily north of two seventy-five—except for catching a casual glance at one of the *athletes* in a WWF match on television—this wall of flesh was undeniably the biggest man Brook had ever seen. And as a nurse who'd had to transfer many a patient bigger than her from one bed to another, she possessed an uncanny knack for guessing, rather accurately, these kinds of attributes. There was no doubt in her mind that if this were a hospital setting and he one of those patients, two or three burly orderlies wouldn't be able to budge him.

For a few long seconds he didn't move or react to her presence in any way. He just filled the doorway like some kind of bouncer at a Manhattan nightclub. Resisting the urge to knee the Golem in the nuts and scream *I'm on the VIP list*, Brook instead, in as nice and cordial of a tone as she could muster considering the circumstances, demanded to speak to Major Freda Nash.

With no visible display of emotion, the stony-faced mountain bent his elbow and said a few hushed words into a microphone secreted somewhere in his sleeve. He went silent for a tick and then nodded, listening to a string of orders coming through his earpiece, Brook supposed. She craned her head to see around the barrel-chested specimen and noticed a somber-looking affair. Heads were bowed. A few people were fixed intently on something taking place on the monitors on the room's far wall. Most everyone had lines of worry etched on their stark features. With goose bumps forming on her arms, and half expecting a funeral hymn to emanate from the speakers inset in the drop down ceiling, she turned back to face the agent.

"Identification," the Golem finally said in a voice with a deeper register than Colonel Shrill and James Earl Jones combined.

Brook made no reply. Clearly agitated, she shook her head in an exaggerated manner.

"Name?"

"Brooklyn Grayson," she said, peering defiantly into the eyes she couldn't see but knew were there, somewhere, sizing her up from behind the dark lenses.

Upon hearing her name, the man's head tilted down a degree, and he looked at her through the paper-thin sliver between the top rim of his shades and the chiseled ridge of his Cro-Magnon-like brow.

Noticing some kind of recognition and perhaps a split second of deliberation betrayed by a subtle squinting of his eyes, Brook held his gaze and the thin thread of hope that she wouldn't have to go the knee-to-the-groin route to get past him.

After what seemed like half a lifetime, the Secret Service agent seemed to have made his decision, and shifting his weight nearly imperceptibly from one foot to the other, he pivoted with an ease that belied his size and waved her on by.

He recognized my name, Brook noted as she side-stepped into the dimly lit space. *Or most likely the latter half I took from Cade thirteen years ago*, she conceded, as a cold chill of anticipation traced her spine.

Chapter 23

Nash watched Brook as she entered the room. As the woman stood near the outermost ring of desks, seemingly on the edge of commitment, Nash tried to read the petite woman's body language.

But there were no dead giveaways. No tells as to the woman's demeanor. She appeared calm and relaxed. Nash expected nothing less. So she stepped from behind the lectern where she had been watching the action on the trio of screens. Moving with no sense of urgency, the equally petite major navigated the pair of stairs, sidestepped a tangle of wires, and moved slowly in Brook's direction.

After taking a few tentative steps into the busy TOC, Brook stopped and made a calculated decision to go nowhere near the President and force the major to come to her. *Keep her on the defensive,* she thought.

Finally, after a couple of minutes, Nash had wound her way between the desks and was standing a foot away, hand extended, expecting a reciprocal handshake.

Fighting an almost irresistible urge to plant an elbow on the woman's chin, Brook ignored the overture and said icily, "Why am I here?"

A noticeable shudder rocked Nash. She let her arm fall to her side and said quietly, "Because I didn't want you to hear secondhand through the base grapevine what I'm about to tell you. That's why I had Davis bring you here." Visibly shaken, Nash steadied herself on the chair back in front of her, swallowed hard, and went on. "The helicopter that General Gaines, your husband, and six other men were aboard has gone missing."

Brook's face blanched. She shook her head side-to-side. "What do you mean, *missing*. As in misplaced ... or did it *crash*?"

Save the steady percussion of fingers working keyboards and the soft chirp from the hard drives inside the multitude of computers, the room was suddenly a vacuum of sound.

Time seemed to stand still for Brook. Her attention was drawn to one screen in particular. A grainy, moving image featuring a rising column of thick black smoke was bracketed in the center, and whatever was filming it seemed to be creeping closer ever so slowly.

"There has been no distress signal as of yet, and up until a couple of minutes ago we have had no visual confirmation of wreckage on the ground."

"What the hell is that," blurted Brook, pointing a finger at the large center screen.

"The pilot on station thinks it's a burning house. Says he's seen more than he can count. I've got hope," Nash lied. "If anyone can bring the team home in one piece once they're wheels up, it's Ari Silver."

"What if they crashed?" blurted Brook.

"I'm not going to go there," said Nash as the lies piled up.

"So if that's not a crash site. And those aren't rotor blades, and that black 'T' there isn't the tail section, then *that* ..." she pointed to the huge flat panel on the right near where the President stood rooted, staring intently, following the action. "Then *that* isn't another mega horde approaching from somewhere that looks eerily similar to the desert and clogged freeway system south of Springs." Putting one hand on her hip, she turned and stared daggers at the major.

Nash remained silent.

"Looks like Clay gives more of a shit about whatever she's watching than the burning house that you've apparently already ruled out as my husband and his team's final resting place."

Still, Nash didn't reply. She looked away and seemed to be trying to get the attention of a woman airman sitting behind a trio of smaller computer screens.

"No answer? Cat got your tongue?"

Clearing her throat, Nash turned back towards Brook, inclined her head and removed her cover, placing it atop a desk cluttered by laminated topographical maps and grease pencils every color of the rainbow.

Sensing the scrutiny leveled at her, Brook moved her gaze from the President and the pressing situation on the monitor and locked eyes with Nash. It was instantly apparent to her that the major was thinking of a way to deliver a pertinent piece of information diplomatically so as to avoid releasing the tension bubbling just below the surface that Brook had so far successfully held in check. In fact, the major seemed to be concentrating so hard on conjuring up the right combination of words that Brook could almost hear the sound of eggshells being crushed underfoot.

"OK," Nash said. "That *is* the wreckage of the stealth helicopter that carried Gaines and Cade and the rest of the team. This is satellite footage from a couple of minutes ago. There was a refueling tanker in the area with eyes on. After a couple of passes with no sign of life on the ground, I recalled them."

"You *what*," spat Brook, veins bulging in her neck.

"Listen ... I made a call."

"A call? You *need* to send that plane back. Send another helicopter. Do something—"

"I need to focus on recovering Jedi One-Two and the scientists aboard," Nash said coolly.

Steadying herself on the desk to her right, Brook seemed to shrink. Her shoulders hunched and she let out a low moan. Her worst fear had apparently became real. Now she and Annie had *everything* in common. Both widows. Both solo moms in a terrifying new world. Nash's words yanked her from the *what ifs* swirling through her mind and back to the room and the present.

"There was not a distress call when it went down, and we've received no communication from the ground."

On the monitor, there were licks of fire and the cherry-red skeleton of the helicopter glowed hot.

"How can you be certain they're all dead? That Cade is dead?" Brook said, her voice rising and cracking as she averted her eyes from the apparent funeral pyre.

The President turned at the sound of Brook's outburst, while at the same time, rising from his seat, Shrill grabbed his cover and took a step in Nash's direction. But she waved him off with a casual flick of the wrist that was lost on everyone save Brook and the colonel.

Clenching her fists tightly, creating red half-moons on her palms where her trimmed nails met flesh, Brook said under her breath, "You're going to need Shrill to save your ass if you don't tell me the truth. And I want to know *everything*. We should probably sit down, don't you think?"

Nash made no reply.

Just then a female captain sitting nearby whipped around, hand cupping her boom mike, and said excitedly, "Oil Can stayed on station—"

"What?" replied Nash.

"Oil Can has a visual on a vehicle moving on the ground. They have made contact over air-to-ground radio frequency."

"Is it the general and his team?"

"Roger that, Major."

A ripple of excitement jumped from person to person making the rounds of the room.

Nash removed her cover. Plopped it on the desk before her. "Bring the satellite feed up on three. Cycle it back five minutes if you will."

"Roger that," replied the captain.

"I'm sorry Brook," said Nash. "We've all been under so much pressure the last twenty-four ..."

Making no reply, Brook stalked closer to the wall of monitors.

"Wait one ... The feed is compiling and coming up on three," said the captain, tapping out the correct combination of keystrokes to make it happen. She rose and delivered the headset to Nash.

Then, several separate yet wholly connected events happened simultaneously. Monitor three to the right of President Clay flicked to life and displayed in full color HD a moving vehicle that, from the satellite's orbit, looked like a toy Hot Wheel creeping along a strip of highway amid a converging crowd of zombies. Closer still, cutting the

120

airspace over the recorded scene, and appearing twenty times larger than the pick-up, was some kind of slow-moving airplane. Gray and wide-bodied, with a bulbous nose and a tail Shamu would be proud of. Brook knew instantly that it was most likely the same plane she had witnessed take off from Schriever's westernmost airstrip prior to Cade's departure earlier in the morning.

Monitor two on the wall in the center position suddenly came alive with movement as the camera broadcasting the scene in black and white panned and zoomed in. Now the marching Zs were more defined. That they were washed by sunlight from the right, which cast long shadows away, led Brook to believe that the lens was pointed south, thus confirming her hunch that the horde was marching lockstep from Pueblo. To Brook it was obvious the footage was being shot from something hovering at a distance. A helicopter was her best guess. Why the event was being monitored didn't fully dawn on her until the pair of rockets lanced from the aircraft, their white contrails and shimmering heat signature momentarily obscuring the camera as they streaked towards the creatures on the ground.

"We're trying to slow them until our ground units are fully prepared to take them on."

Thinking about Raven now, Brook said slowly, "When will the horde arrive here?"

Nash said nothing as more rockets left the pods of whatever was beaming back the unsteady silent images.

Brook cleared her throat.

"Sometime in the next couple of days. Good news is they aren't irradiated. Bad news is there are twenty or thirty thousand of them following the survivors out of the burning city."

"And the Delta team?" asked Brook. Locking her gaze on monitor three, she watched the old footage as the tiny, rust-colored pick-up reversed from the shadows of an overpass and conducted an abrupt J turn. Then the vehicle paused as creatures plummeted from the overpass in front and behind it. Brook ignored the one-sided aerial assault playing out on the center monitor and stared and prayed and then prayed some more that Cade was in the truck, which stayed stopped for a long minute and then inexplicably motored up a freeway ramp already choked with walking dead.

"Who is the pilot talking with on the ground?" asked Nash.

"Anvil Actual," replied the captain. "He says there are three casualties."

"Fast forward the sat feed to real time," Nash said sharply. "And Captain, bring me a headset."

At first the call sign Anvil didn't ring a bell. But Brook was certain she had heard the strange combination of code words before. Sometime in the not-so-distant past. Maybe Cade had uttered them during one of his frequent nightmares. Perhaps she'd heard someone use the call sign when she was on one of her *'official'* yet *'unofficial'* forays off the base. Then her hopes buoyed when she recalled Cade mentioning he'd been assigned the very same call sign on the recent snatch and grab mission to Jackson Hole. During an intimate moment he'd even elicited her help in trying to determine why Nash would want to refer to him as Anvil.

Instantly she cast aside all previous worries and watched the footage cue to real time. Nash was pacing back and forth in front of the three displays, gesticulating with her hands, mouth going a mile a minute. Standing beside Colonel Shrill, President Clay suddenly seemed to be fully invested in the rescue.

On monitor three the image zoomed in and showed the pick-up stopped next to a much larger white van. And standing atop that van was a person clad in all black, who appeared to be sighting down the barrel of some sort of rifle. Looking closer, Brook noticed a trio of prostrate bodies in the truck's bed. And nearly lost in the van's shadow were two more figures clothed in lighter-colored fatigues. Judging from the glittering projectiles raining to the blacktop, the two Delta soldiers were pouring a good volume of rifle fire into the wall of walking corpses to their six.

Looking directly at Brook, Nash said matter-of-factly, "Cade is driving the truck."

After hearing, processing, and embracing the five spoken words, everything else Nash said was garbled as the part of Brook's brain associated with feelings of joy flooded her entire body with endorphins. As if suffering a bad case of vertigo her head began to spin and her legs turned into a couple of overly-boiled noodles. Ignoring everything and everyone in the room, she succumbed to emotion and went to her knees, watching the fate of her family unfold on a nameless road somewhere between the Colorado border and Winnipeg. Suddenly she felt so close yet so far away. Like a ghost, ethereal and powerless. Watching from the sidelines, unable to say or do anything to affect the outcome of the drama playing out in front of her eyes.

So she pulled a chair near, levered herself into the seat, and watched, helpless and detached, trying to maintain a modicum of hope that Cade was coming home to her and Raven.

Chapter 24
Colorado Springs, Colorado

Sergeant First Class Larry Eckels cracked his door a few inches and took in a deep lungful of air heavy with the odor of carrion, freshly churned earth, and diesel exhaust. The resulting sensory bombardment instantly took him back to the 'Stan, providing him a subliminal combat tingle though he was presently in little danger. *Strange how the human brain is wired*, he mused. Even more baffling to the veteran of multiple tours of duty in the Middle East was how what remained of that same mass of once-living gray matter could possess the Zs with such an intense drive and insatiable hunger for human flesh.

He pressed the Steiners to his face, fine-tuned the wheel on the field glasses, and studied the foothills several miles off his right shoulder. Shaped by an ancient glacier grinding into them behind a billion pounds of brute force, the fingers of red earth snaked up hundreds of feet on both sides, forming a canyon split by a twisting steeply graded highway leading to the turn-of-the-century mining town called Manitou Springs.

While Eckels had been watching the heavy earthmoving machinery tear up the quarter-mile stretch of I-25 in front of him, he'd heard on the tactical channel that a squad of 4th Infantry Division soldiers who had been conducting a door-to-door search and rescue operation west of Springs had apparently disturbed a nest of Zs and had been cut off from their MRAPs (Mine Resistant Ambush Protected vehicles) with the drivers still inside them. And as the squad leader had sheepishly admitted over the net, in front of God and everyone, his vehicles had been unable to intervene, thus forcing him to lead his dismounted squad into the basement garage of an adjacent building in order to seek refuge from the undead mob. On the bright side, he had added, his men had suffered no casualties. *Yet*, Eckels had thought as he listened to the exchange.

Then, a few short minutes after the call had gone out requesting air support and an immediate extraction for the MRAP drivers and the embattled squad, Eckels spied a pair of Black Hawks cutting the air east to west, wicked-looking guns protruding ominously from their open doors, a sense of urgency evident in their haste. The Black Hawks were shadowed closely by two smaller AH-6 Little Birds, black and nimble and carrying a quartet of Hellfire missiles on one stubby wing and a tubular pod containing seven Hydra rockets on the other.

Knowing second death was about to visit the Zs, Eckels smiled as he brought the Steiners to bear. Wavering perceptibly in the optics, rising and falling with his breathing, the distant cluster of unimpressive apartment buildings didn't seem worthy candidates for a survivor to hole up in or likely objectives for any type of clearing operation. But orders were meant to be followed, and judging by the actions of his superiors these days, he surmised they were mostly deskbound paper-pushing weenies blindly out of touch with the hardcore realities outside the wire. *If only I was in charge*, thought Eckels, *I'd be conducting razing operations instead. Give me a couple of HMEEs—High Mobility Engineer Excavators—and a handful of D-9 dozers, and this combat engineer will have the outskirts of Springs knocked down and Z free in no time.*

But seeing as how he was still a few pay grades below the President, who seemed to be calling all of the shots from the hip these days, he kept his eyes glued to the ongoing rescue op and waited expectantly for the first telltale signs of delivered ordnance. *Softening up the target.* The thought brought a broad smile to his face. Then, as if on cue, red smoke marking the location of the encircled squad wafted up and the smaller helos broke orbit, taking on a more aggressive, nose-down attitude.

And as the Little Birds rolled in, the fact that he was commanding a large meaningful ground operation of his own hit him full force. He watched the first volley of Hydra rockets lance groundward, their motors burning yellow, and imagined the distinctive whooshing sound he'd heard up close a handful of times. Like breaking waves, the white smoke from the rockets curled through the second helo's rotor wash as it moved in and hovered a short distance from where the crimson signal smoke was spreading. A tick later a Hellfire missile dropped from the hovering Little Bird and blurred towards the ground, jinking and course-correcting minutely as the operator in the helo guided it on to the target.

A few seconds passed before the multiple reports traveled the distance and reached his ears. The Hydra rockets, which undoubtedly carried flechette warheads that peppered the enemy with hundreds of small, razor-sharp projectiles, exploded with a rippled series of soft pops, sounding like a kid working a sheet of bubble wrap. The Hellfire's eighteen-pound warhead, however, produced a wasp-like cloud of shrapnel and a bass heavy note, subtle and distant, like rolling thunder following a storm. Finally, Eckels observed the two slower-moving Black Hawks descend and troll back and forth for a couple of minutes, presumably engaging the Zs on the ground with their side-mounted mini-guns. *Prepping the landing zone at six thousand rounds a minute*, he thought as he witnessed plumes of ochre dust rise and mingle with the diminishing contrails from the rocket motors and the red smoke still rising skyward from somewhere between the squat buildings. While he sat there in the safety of his M-ATV with his explosive-sniffing German Shepherd Hudson by his side and a half-dozen soldiers from the 4th ID securing the perimeter nearby, Eckels suddenly felt sorry for the squad leader who had, for whatever reason—maybe fatigue caused by mission creep or perhaps a bit of bad intel—miscalculated the situation, and was now calling in *danger close* fire on top of himself.

It is what it is, thought Eckels. His fate had been signed, sealed, and delivered by one hell of a similar poor decision made by a captain named Phelps. Why the captain insisted on riding around in a soft top Humvee instead of an armored M-ATV, a Stryker, or a Bradley Fighting Vehicle beat the hell out of him. Choosing a vehicle damn near one step up from a convertible over anything up-armored and high-clearance when travelling outside the wire was a JFK faux pas if he'd ever heard of one. Eckels shook his head in disgust. *Just one bite is all it takes*, he thought darkly. And that's exactly what got Captain Phelps killed; an unfortunate event that led to Combat Engineer Sergeant First Class Larry Eckels being given the unenviable task of stopping the Pueblo horde in its tracks.

Hell, bring it on, he'd thought at the time. He'd been making it up on the fly since Z-Day plus one anyway, so the instant battlefield promotion—minus the actual bump in rank and the ceremony and fist-pumping that came along with it—really meant little in the big scheme of things. Something he'd overheard a much younger and inexperienced sergeant say a day earlier, *Here one day and gone the next*, popped into his head. He didn't subscribe to this kind of fatalistic thinking—never had. Nor was he prone to offering unsolicited advice. But at the time he'd gone ahead and broken his own rules, ripping the young sergeant—who coincidentally happened to be Captain Phelps' driver—a gaping new asshole, punctuating the dressing down by telling the soldier that if he didn't *adapt* to the new realities and *improvise* accordingly, he *would* be '*gone the next.*' And he was. Apparently the captain's soft top Hummer had been swarmed, and before help could arrive the Zs had wormed into the vehicle and ripped into the sergeant's guts. Captain Phelps, as the evidence later suggested, had valiantly fought off the Zs with his sidearm until he was grievously wounded and down to his last two rounds, one of which he used to put down the sergeant who was close to reanimating—the other he pumped into his own brain to avoid the same fate.

Here one day, eating a bullet the next. Hell of a way to go, thought Eckels, giving Hudson a thorough scratching behind the ears. "Chaos theory rules in the land of Mister Murphy, Huddie," said Eckels. "And don't you forget it." The admonition was received with a tilt of the Shepherd's head, and answered with a yelp which Eckels took to mean, in Huddie speak, '*Understood.*'

It truly was a brave new world with a different set of rules, and that's why he had been thrust into this position. Utilizing the best man for the job had suddenly become the gold standard. And in just a few short days that best man—Sergeant First Class Larry Eckels—had found that being on this side of the action was more to his liking. Sure, tooling around Indian country finding and disabling IEDs—Improvised Explosive Devices—responsible for killing and maiming so many of his brothers had been rewarding, and had helped save more than enough lives over there to justify the risk he'd shouldered upon re-upping. But during those two tours, he'd grown to abhor the cowardice shown by the enemy, a ragtag group of religious fanatics who favored roadside bombs and hit-and-run guerilla tactics to a fair fight. Thus, the prospect of toe-to-toe engagement with the enemy was exhilarating to say the least—for the Zs not only stood their ground—they shambled directly into the fray in pucker-inducing numbers.

Taking on this horde, tens of thousands strong by most estimates, needed to be approached differently than the Denver mega-horde which was thought to have numbered somewhere north of half a million. Eckels concluded the only way to engage this horde would be surgically, like excising a malignant tumor, only on a much larger scale. But he didn't have the *luxury* of using a couple of nukes—nor were there enough Zs to justify such an action. That the fallout from the Castle Rock event had dispersed to the north and east and had been beaten down by a lengthy rainstorm was attributed by most to just plain dumb luck. But Eckels liked to think it had been divine intervention, of which he could use a little right about now. So he decided to go another route and employ a tactic that had been used effectively elsewhere in the early days of the outbreak. But the first order of the day was to make sure the horde stayed together. A small handful of Zs—squirters as they were not so affectionately called—breaking away from the main body would trigger larger clusters into doing the same, setting off a chain reaction that would flood downtown Springs and eventually see Schriever to the east having to deal with numbers of the dead that hadn't been seen since the first days of the outbreak. Therefore, in order to keep the aforementioned Pied Piper scenario from occurring, Eckels had deployed, for the lack of a better name, '*squirter teams*' on either side of the freeway. For half of the day and the better part of twenty miles, the eight CROW-equipped M-ATVs shadowed the Zs like sheepdogs, keeping out of sight and only dismounting and engaging the stragglers with silenced weapons as a last resort.

***

Eckels brought the field glasses up, snugged them in tight, and focused on a point far off in the distance where northbound 25 dipped underneath a westbound arterial leading into downtown Springs. Phase two of his plan would commence at this junction, and to ensure that the Zs played into his hand when they finally came into sight, he pre-positioned three teams operating M-ATVs equipped with remotely operated CROW systems—top-mounted belt-fed M240 light machine guns capable of delivering 7.62 mm lead at a rate of 950 rounds per minute. He gazed at the team deployed closest to his position. Settled and alert, their boxy M-ATV was backed up against the white cinderblock wall of a Krispy Kreme Doughnuts whose darkened neon *Now Serving* sign would never flare red again. *Good to go.*

Then he panned right and scrutinized the second team; their M-ATV was parked, quiet and inert, a hundred yards to the west in the shadows of a dormant fast food joint whose yellow and red sign still proudly crowed the billions served by Ronald McDonald.

Finally, he shifted his gaze up and locked onto a pair of silhouettes: a sniper and his spotter fresh from the 'Stan. His *eyes and ears,* nestled amongst the ventilation equipment atop the McDonalds. And even as highly trained and disciplined as the combat-hardened shooters were, every once in a while Eckels would see one of the forms shift a little and a head would bob up and furtively scan the ground surrounding the building—a definite no-no in a hostile environment where the bad guys employed counter snipers who shot back. But that wasn't the case here; Eckels had just witnessed firsthand the disconcerting affect the Zs had on even the coolest of individuals, who at this point in the operation, with their manned getaway vehicle a mere five foot vertical drop away, had a better chance of getting heatstroke than being eaten by a Z.

Dropping the Steiners to the seat, he consulted the Blue Force Tracker display—a GPS-derived digital map of the area, showing all friendly forces in blue and all known enemy concentrations in red. He zoomed out in order to see all of his teams, which were represented by a blue icon labeled with their unique call sign. He gazed at the spiderweb of streets, focusing on the yellow pixelated stretch of I-25 splitting the screen vertically. He adjusted the crosshairs over a position to the south, toggled the *zoom out* key a couple of times, and as the screen fully refreshed what he saw there warranted an immediate double take. Represented by brilliant red pixels overlaying a large segment of I-25, the computer-generated zombie horde crept continually north towards his position, a seemingly unstoppable juggernaut he was about to meet head on.

He noted the locations of his men and war-gamed the scenario in his mind one more time. When the dead reached his forward deployed M-ATVs, the crew would engage them with the turret-mounted 240s. Next, the drivers would bump their lightly-armored vehicles down the nearby embankments and onto the freeway, two at a time, and begin a series of low speed hit and run maneuvers designed to entice the dead and lead them north on the 25 to the prepared stretch of highway that—if all went as planned—would become their final resting place.

Should have named this thing Operation Cattle Drive, he mused as he turned up the volume and listened to the ongoing rescue operation to the south and west of him. The pilots, who were alternating between calling out targets on the ground for the door gunners and offering up reassuring words to the men on the ground, sounded calm, cool, and collected. Every once in a while the squad leader on the ground would ask, in a clipped, almost frantic voice, for a situation report, which the Black Hawk pilots promptly delivered while painting a much rosier picture than the men on the ground most likely faced.

Lamenting the fact that there was nothing he could do for the surrounded squad but pray, he turned the volume down and rested his helmet against the seatback, a move that earned him a wet sloppy Huddie kiss.

"Thanks buddy. I needed that." After giving the German Shepherd a much deserved scratch between the ears, he snatched his last can of Amp from the console, finished the tepid energy drink in one gulp, and chucked the empty on the floorboards. "Gotta stay frosty, boy."

In full agreement, Huddie added a clipped guttural growl of his own.

"Let's see where the enemy is." He glanced at the BFT, noting the ever-present red inchworm of death had moved considerably northward. Then, with the reassuring knowledge that the horde was several miles away and the first contact of Operation Toll Booth likely an hour in the future, he closed his eyes and recited a prayer he'd memorized for just such an occasion.

Chapter 25
I-90 West of Draper

Sitting behind the wheel, left ankle throbbing madly, Cade listened intently to the conversation between Cross and the flight engineer in the Hercules circling overhead. And in just a couple of minutes he overheard Dover relay to Cross all kinds of information pertinent to the hastily cobbled together rescue plan. Finally Dover wished Cross and the Delta team good luck, and signed off.

Craning his head, Cade witnessed the Hercules perform an exaggerated wing waggle and break orbit. He twisted around in his seat and watched the Hercules fly off on a southbound heading.

Seriously doubting the agent atop the van could hear him over the tinny screech of dead hands raking against the rusty hood and fenders, Cade asked, "Cross, did you by chance get *all* of that?"

"Roger that. Did you forget I head up the President's detail or something?"

"What's that got to do with it?" Cade shot back.

"To do my job, you have to have a near photographic memory and possess a very high IQ," Cross stated, sounding neither cocky nor full of himself. "I had to remember a lot of faces and a ton of operational details. Can't be consulting notes with the big boss's life on the line."

"Yeah ... stay frosty," said Cade half-heartedly. "So what are you seeing now?"

"Looks better from up here than it does from the back of the truck," answered Cross over the comms.

"No shit," Lopez replied as he shot a pair of Zs in the head at point blank range. The haze of pink mist blossomed and drifted sideways before fading to nothing. "Madre," cried the deeply religious operator. "They just keep coming."

"We're almost home free," answered Cade reassuringly. "Keep shooting them."

"I'm down to one mag and my sidearm."

"What about Tice's ammo?"

"Burned through his last two mags while you were arguing with Ari," said Lopez.

"I was lobbying," Ari said sharply, shooting a glare through the back window. He swiveled his head forward, made eye contact with Jasper, and asked the question he supposed everyone aboard was dying to know. "How in God's name did all of these cars end up stuck on the interstate here in Draper?"

"Human nature I suppose," said Jasper. "Before all of this we used to have the busiest Dairy Queen east of Rapid City and west of Sioux Falls. Hell, our two little gas stations did a brisk business too. People are creatures of habit, and with our little town sitting nearly halfway between two of the biggest cities in South Dakota, I gather it was just a natural place to stop and stretch, gas up, and get some fries and an ice cream cone to keep the kids happy."

Ari kept his gaze fixed on Jasper for a beat. "Doesn't answer my question," he finally said.

"Right after the outbreak, just about the time the people on the East and West Coasts were looting and acting crazy, the bad elements in Rapid City and Sioux Falls jumped on the bandwagon." He went silent for a beat. Made a face and swallowed hard. "And as if the zombie outbreaks broadcast on the news weren't bad enough, the cities started burning. They were showing massive fires on the TV."

Ari noted the faraway look on the undertaker's ruddy face, as if he were attempting to recall something pertinent to the conversation. "So these folks ended up in a place they knew," he added, helping to fill in the blanks. "But Draper didn't know them. Especially didn't want them bringing their infected loved ones around."

"You hit the nail on the head, Ari. In a matter of hours both stations' tanks were bone dry. Texaco first and then the Astro station. My good friend Bernie died defending his pumps ... bunch of animals. They looted the Thriftway after that." Jasper pinched the bridge of his nose. Took a deep breath. "Sheriff got the guy who killed Bernie. Apprehended a few of the looters and then ran out of room in the jail. Then he set up a roadblock and started turning folks away. Some left their cars but most drove as far as the fumes in their tanks would take them ..."

"Which wasn't very far from the looks of things," Ari said.

Jasper nodded. "And then they walked," he added quietly. "And they kept walking even after they got bit."

"The remnants of that same human nature I'd guess," Ari stated.

Jasper made no reply. Just stared straight ahead, ignoring the sneering ashen faces of the walking corpses.

Suddenly the gunfire ceased, leaving only Jasper's labored breathing to compete with the ticking engine and the fingernails of the dead scrabbling against the skin of the truck.

With his back pressed firmly against the white van and the M4 pointing at his two o'clock, Hicks reached out with his left hand and rapped his knuckles on the back window. Once he had Cade's attention, he spun his finger and raised his M4, a wisp of smoke curling from its muzzle. "I'm nearly *winchester*," he bellowed. "We gotta *go*."

Just then a loud clang shivered the truck and the shocks compressed as Cross landed in the bed after having jumped down off the panel van. Simultaneously, Cade heard the man holler, "Go, go, go," in his ear bud. He slipped the transmission into a gear meant for towing, probably last used well before the rattletrap had a quarter-million miles on the odometer. A time when the big V8 engine could still transfer all that horsepower in the form of torque down to the asphalt. Now, judging from the sounds coming from under the hood, he doubted the rig could drive its way out of a wet paper bag, let alone through a handful of determined Zs.

But he gave it the old college try, and when the Chevy failed to deliver any kind of forward progress, slammed the rig into reverse and accelerated backward with as much speed as he could coax. Hands groped and metal screeched, and paint was traded as the two vehicles parted ways.

"Go around the Zs and continue until you pass the next three vehicles," said Cross. "Then you'll see a silver compact, and just past it there's a school bus and a red SUV with a bunch of crap piled on top ... the only clear passage is between the two. After splitting the bus and SUV, you have to move to the left and pass a yellow VW Bug ... but keep to its driver side. Then once you clear the VeeDub you move left to the breakdown lane and you'll have a clear path for ... let's call it a couple of hundred yards."

"Since I don't possess a photographic memory like yours ... *who* is going to help me remember all of that?" asked Cade.

"I've got your back," answered Cross.

"So ... what exactly happens after we pass the VW?" Lopez asked out of the blue, a touch of sarcasm to his voice.

"We've got our work cut out for us," answered Cross, who went on to explain in detail what the air crew in the Hercules was planning and what role each one of them had to play so everyone could get home to Schriever with a steady core temperature as close to ninety-eight-point-six as possible.

Chapter 26
Schriever AFB TOC

Propelled on rubbery legs, Brook made her way to a chair and kept her eyes glued to monitor number three. Judging from the graininess of the image, she guessed the camera recording it was perched on a satellite in a very high standoff orbit. The footage also lacked a sense of depth, which made it difficult to see details like dimension, angles, and direction. However, the unmoving bodies and black splotches of spilt blood painting the roadway were unmistakable. *Cade and the boys have been busy*, she thought, narrowing her eyes in order to read the scrolling and constantly changing series of monochrome letters and numbers at the bottom of the screen. But they told her nothing. In fact, they only added to the confusion of the constantly moving, vertigo-inducing, real-time feed.

Then, catching her attention, the image on the vivid display abruptly refreshed. Everything was still in color but the distance from lens to ground seemed to have been cut in half. Consequently the truck now looked more like a Tonka than a Hot Wheel in size. And instead of jersey barriers she could see some kind of cable separating the two directions of travel on the four-lane highway. Then the new and improved resolution revealed a defined shadow falling behind the stationary pick-up. And though she was no detective, its mere presence told her the truck was heading west—towards the lowering sun. Suddenly a cold chill traced her spine as she realized there was much more movement on the roadway than she had previously noticed. Given away by defined shadows all their own, the slow-moving figures homed in on the truck from every point on the compass. Whether they'd been drawn in by the engine noise of the truck, the gunfire, or the airplane that had already buzzed the pick-up twice, she hadn't a clue.

Oblivious to the others in the room, she walked a few steps closer to the screen and tracked a path with her eyes from the pick-up down the onramp, where crushed bodies and severed limbs and glints of brass offered proof of the fight her husband and whoever was with him had already put up. She made a cursory inspection of the freeway and the road feeding it. *More bodies.* Then her eyes moved on to the crash site which was a smoldering dark spot in the lower left-hand corner of the screen. And though it was removed from the camera's primary area of focus and grainier than the rest, she could still see dozens more corpses scattered near what had to be a graveyard fronting some type of church. She flicked her eyes back to the seemingly immobilized vehicle. Saw the bodies in greater detail. Stretched out, limbs askew, and still unmoving in the truck's bed. Cade had to be hurting after a crash like that. She longed to comfort him. *What are you doing, Cade? Where are you going?* Suddenly she wished she were on the ground with him more than anything on earth. Fighting alongside him. She wanted to hear his voice again. Hear him say something. Offer up a clue as to what he was planning. She also wanted some insight into how the major planned to redeem herself and rescue the team before they were overrun. She shifted her gaze to Nash and Shrill, who had both donned headphones sprouting boom mikes with little black sponges positioned inches from their lips. And to add insult to injury, after being summoned to the TOC out of the blue, and having been lied to, she was now being ignored entirely.

She cast scrutiny on the first monitor where the other rescue mission was playing out. A small black helicopter had just buzzed into the picture. Its guns were blazing, shiny shell casings spilling out and raining down on a group of soldiers arranged in a semi-circle, guns pointed out, muzzles winking white and yellow at the crush of walking corpses. Simultaneously, the helicopter slowed and made an exaggerated turn and the armored vehicle the soldiers were huddled atop rocked sideways, almost spilling them off. A thick bar of sun flared off the bulbous canopy as the helicopter settled into a hover directly over the frantic soldiers. Brook watched through the whirring rotor blades as half of the soldiers clambered onto the straight tubular landing gear she remembered hearing Cade call skids. Then, jiggling slightly under the newly added weight, the black helicopter shot straight up and whisked the lucky ones away. An identical helicopter moved in, gliding as if on ice, hovered above the remaining survivors and was still for a half second before buzzing off sans passengers. Then there was a flurry of movement, a strange commotion going on around the armored vehicle. *Things are going sideways*, Brook thought glumly.

A low murmur filled the room.

A quick look at the other monitor told her nothing had changed where Cade was concerned. Nothing she could do for him, so she rooted for the others—they needed it. While she'd looked away a Black Hawk, blades cutting a blurry arc, had moved in and was hovering over the surging dead. Then streaks of yellow and red, seemingly interconnected, blazed groundward, shredding into the dead. Dozens of Zs fell, but in seconds others took their place and were clambering over each other and grabbing and tugging at the remaining soldiers. And as Brook witnessed the Zs swarm overtop the MRAP, she prayed the doomed men would not have to suffer. It was all over in seconds. Death playing out in front of her eyes. Silent and exaggerated like some kind of old Charlie Chaplin film. Averting her eyes from the feeding frenzy, she glanced at monitor three, where the scene seemed to have been paused while she'd been watching brave men perish on the other. She'd had enough. Though part of her screamed to stay here and watch and root for Cade, she couldn't. The state of limbo was killing her. Time to shift focus and move forward because right here and now, from some four hundred miles away, there was nothing she could do for Cade and she knew it. Furthermore, she was out of her element. An interloper. Shut out of the loop, and judging by the actions of Nash, Shrill, the President, and every single person in uniform in the stifling hot TOC, she might as well be invisible. So, in order to avoid another *Faces of Death* moment like the one she had just witnessed—especially one featuring her husband and the rest of the Delta operators who had already risked so much for the country—she rose from her chair and bolted for the door.

The unsmiling Secret Service Agent, having already been spared a knee to the nuts twice today, instead received a laughable hockey check as Brook blazed by.

Then, succumbing greatly to Newton's applied law of physics, Brook bounced off the big man and redirected the unspent inertia— via her opposite shoulder—into the door's horizontal push bar. Squinting against harsh light thrown from the fluorescent tubes, she stopped in the wide corridor and heard the door shut with a soft squelch punctuated by a solid click that seemed to say, *You didn't belong here anyway. Now stay out.*

But she didn't want to show Airman Davis, who was most likely still waiting outside, that she'd been defeated. And going back to Raven knowing more than when they'd parted, but having nothing good to report, was out of the question. So she put her back to the wall and slid slowly to the floor. Extended her legs and bounced her head against the wall. Tap. Tap. Tap. Trying to knock some sense into her own head.

Under the watchful gaze of Schriever's finest from days gone by, Brook drew her knees up, planted her face in her hands, and listened for any kind of sound from the other side of the door that could possibly be interpreted as positive.

Chapter 27
South Dakota

Before the flesh-eaters could close the noose any tighter, Cade urged the gearbox into drive, tromped the pedal, and wrenched the wheel right. The truck jumped forward under power and then shuddered like it was suddenly starved of gas. Instinctively Cade checked the gauge. *Quarter tank.* Easing off the accelerator stopped the lurching but brought on an unusual wheezing sound. Then, after letting off the throttle entirely, the ticking intensified and the idle started to fluctuate wildly. Quickly he diagnosed the death rattle for what it was—the kind of sound an engine makes under duress just before it throws a rod and blows a piston into a hundred-cylinder head-killing fragments. It was no kind of sound any of them needed to be hearing in the middle of nowhere surrounded by the living dead.

"Sounds like a bad lifter," said Jasper.

Ari asked, "Checked the oil lately?"

"No reason."

"Why not?" queried Ari.

"Plenty more trucks just sittin' around," was Jasper's monotone reply.

"Well I hope this one doesn't die yet," Cade said under his breath. "It's got more problems than a bad lifter and *I* don't see *plenty* of suitable replacements in the vicinity."

Jasper made no reply. Remained stoic, seemingly unfazed by Cade's obvious jab at his provincial nature. Then, as quickly as the engine started acting up, it settled back into a rough idle.

Goosing the throttle, Cade said, "What do you think ... is she going to make it?"

Once again Jasper said nothing. Simply stared a thousand yards into the distance, with the same type of flat affect worn by the condemned.

A sharp elbow got Ari's attention. Cade mouthed, "Watch him."

The simple fact that the man had recently lost his wife and two kids to Omega made him a liability. A strong candidate to snap from the pressure. Cade had seen it before—before and after the dead began to walk. The saying *'You're only as strong as your weakest link,'* came to mind. Over the years, remembering this simple truth had saved his life on more than one occasion. In fact the words had been drilled into his head, early, and often. First by every grim-faced instructor at boot camp. Then by his future peers during the lengthy training process required to be accepted into the Ranger family. And most recently, by his friend and mentor, the late General Mike Desantos, during nearly every waking moment Cade served with him on the *Teams*.

Jogged by the thought of Mike and what his family must be going through, the realization that Brook and Raven must already know that he'd gone missing behind enemy lines hit him blindside like a three hundred and fifty pound nose tackle. *What does Brook know?* he thought. *Was she even aware that Oil-Can made contact with us?*

Considering how quickly this could go tits-up, not to mention the fact that Brook and Major Nash had already butted heads—on more than one occasion—Cade figured there was no way in hell a woman as calculating as Nash would be stupid enough to bring Brook into the loop at this stage of the game. At the very least, out of respect for him, the major would probably play the CYA—cover your ass—card and inform Brook of the very minimum and then sugar coat it until more information came to light. But whatever the case, Brook was pretty good at reading between the lines. She'd intuitively know something was wrong the second the Osprey thundered over the base without the slower Ghost Hawk in tow. Then he pictured her big brown eyes and million dollar smile, and at that very moment the urge to be with her had never been stronger. Just the thought of his family so far away and how all of this would affect them should they get overrun by the dead set his guts to churning.

"Agent Cross, I need you to be my eyes and guide us through this shit show," Cade said as the truck rolled forward under a new head of steam. "'Cause we're going home."

Risking his face being raked by the claw-like hands of the dead, Cross hung his head around the cab into the weak slipstream and began to call out navigable seams through the warren of vehicles. "Take a hard right here and then loop around the silver compact at your one o'clock. Then you'll have to ride the shoulder a dozen yards. Got to be careful though. The slope on the right isn't very steep, but as loaded down as we are ... wouldn't take much to roll us over," he said.

"Roger that," Cade answered back. "Easy does it on the shoulder." After traveling a dozen yards, he scraped the rear bumper of a dirty gray Hyundai, made the required left and cautiously slipped past a handful of vehicles on the right shoulder with the wheels on Jasper's side worming dangerously through the browned grass and soft topsoil.

"Getting close," said Cross, who at this point had his boots wedged under the weight of Tice's stiffening corpse and his upper body angling over the pick-up's roof. "OK ... now you'll serpentine between a few more cars and then it gets tight."

How can it get any tighter than this? thought Cade.

Then, as if reading Cade's mind, Cross added, "After you bull through it'll get even tighter ... we're going to have to squeeze between a red Suburban and the school bus on its left."

Making a face, Cade asked, "And after that?"

"Wait one," Cross answered back as he stood tall, and peered through the 3x magnifier atop the SCAR. Beyond the yellow school bus he could see the cause of the roadblock and their objective which lay just beyond it; it appeared exactly as Dover had described. A sight for sore eyes for sure, and the only sane reason to be risking getting stuck in this gridlock of death. "Good news ... it's mostly clear of Zs," he said. "Now get us there."

Wheeling slowly past a pair of horribly mangled vehicles, Cade swung a hard left at Cross's insistence and then motored on, the engine still wheezing, ticking, and steaming.

"Once you split this gap, angle diagonally to the left," said Cross. "After that, follow along the breakdown shoulder to our objective. A hundred yards is all ... then we start phase two."

You'll serpentine between a few more cars and then it gets tight, Cross had said. Following the vague instructions in his head, Cade maneuvered between a half-dozen small and medium-sized cars, creasing a good deal of sheet metal and smearing a pack of slow-moving Zs in the process.

"Sounds like we're riding around in a *pinche* icebreaking ship or something," said Lopez to no one in particular as the sound of breaking glass and the unnerving rasp from grinding metal vibrated the air all around.

"It's bound to get worse," replied Cade as a burst of rifle fire rang out from the bed.

"Ain't going to make it," said Ari at about the same time the pick-up's bumper got tangled with the rear fender of the car to the right.

"A little more warning next time?" Cade said as he shifted down into the near-worthless towing gear. He gave it gas. Then there was a groan, followed by a loud clap as the two vehicles parted and the truck surged forward a few feet.

"Didn't think we were going to get through that one, Captain," said Ari.

Jasper grunted, then muttered under his breath, "There's too many of them. Too many cars. Too many corpses. Too many to bury."

Cade ignored the babble. Continued scanning the road forward. *What was it that Cross had said in his ear back there? Red Suburban on the left and then turn right? Or was it yellow?* All of the running-and-gunning squeezed around the horrific crash was beginning to take its toll on his short term memory. He was about to eat crow by asking Cross for a refresher when the Secret Service man unknowingly bailed him out. "These two," Cross said. "Part the bus and Suburban and we're almost home free."

Save for a good deal of camping gear visible through the window, the battered Suburban appeared to be empty. On the roof were mounted a pair of hard plastic gear carriers, empty and hinged open like the wings on a beetle.

Looking at the overloaded rig, Cade said, "Wonder what campground they were headed to?"

"Doesn't matter," replied Ari. "Looks like they didn't make it ... did they?"

"Plates are from Kansas," added Jasper. He buried his chin in his chest and a low ominous chuckle filled the air. Then, sounding eerily like a little girl, he said in a high falsetto, "Toto, I've a feeling we're not in Kansas anymore." Which was followed immediately by an over-the-top belly laugh a la Robert De Niro in Cape Fear.

After the bizarre display of emotion from the undertaker, Cade made a fast and hard decision and whispered in Ari's ear, "Disarm him."

Ari nodded subtly, and then, still semi-numb from the shoulders to his fingertips, pitched forward, spilling the broken emergency radio from his lap. "Shit," he said, feigning disgust.

Taking the bait, hook, line, and sinker, Jasper leaned forward and grabbed for the radio as it bounced off the transmission hump, slid down the slick plastic slope, and came to rest against his muddy boots.

Simultaneously Ari squared his shoulders, and in one fluid motion ripped the Velcro, drew his Beretta from its holster, and had the pistol cocked and trained on the undertaker.

Radio in hand, Jasper hinged up and realized at once what was happening. In half a beat the flat affect disappeared and his eyes went wide and crossed slightly as he stared at the gaping muzzle pointed between them.

"Pistol first," said Ari, the Beretta's barrel wavering slightly.

Averting his eyes from the gun in his face, Jasper placed the .22 on Ari's lap and then gently laid the radio next to it.

"And the machete ... pass it through the slider to them," said Ari nodding towards the men in back. "Now the shotgun ... butt first. Finger away from the trigger."

Jasper complied and then, as if a switch had been flicked, he folded forward and let loose a sorrow-filled wail.

Cade replaced the Glock on his lap. Steering one-handed, he rooted around in a cargo pocket, withdrew a pair of oversized zip ties, and passed them through the slider. "Stick your arms through," he said, taking his eyes from the road just long enough to show Jasper he meant business.

Ari leaned left as Jasper thrust his corded forearms through the opening.

"Zip him, Lopez," Cade said. "And make it quick."

As the engine hit another low point, nearly stalling, the sound of the Hercules tooling the air somewhere out of sight reached Cade's ears. He watched through his side vision as Lopez performed a task perfected in training and used in the real world hundreds of times. In seconds Jasper's hands were bound palms together and he was sitting down in his seat, sobbing like a baby.

"Thank you, Lopez," Cade intoned.

Slowly Ari lowered his sidearm. "Sorry, friend. It was for your own good."

Chapter 28

There it is, Cade thought. *Yellow school bus on the left.* Then he committed and entered the narrow canyon of metal and glass and colorful camping gear. He powered down the window, craned his head out, and gaped at the whale-sized vehicle. On its rear end above the clouded-over back window was a vinyl sign. It was stretched tight and tied down. Hand lettered in red were the words, *Camp Carefree, Sioux Falls, South Dakota.* Below that, in much smaller font, was a web address and a phone number, and lastly, an unfulfilled promise: *You can entrust your little ones with us.* And judging by the number of pale, stick-thin arms probing the air through the open windows—about a hundred unlucky parents had.

"Looks like they made it to camp," said Cade, taking a sliver of solace from the fact that it appeared the bus had been heading away from Sioux Falls, which he took as a sign the little ones had enjoyed one final summer camp fling before joining the ranks of the dead.

"Nothing worse than seeing little demonios," whispered Lopez into the comms, while tiny ashen fingers massaged the air inches from his face. He whistled, long and drawn out. Instantly the rasps of the entombed dead rose in volume and new faces pressed the glass, filling every available void.

"Fucking wrong," exclaimed Hicks, who usually left the talking to others. "Looks like they all died away from their families."

"That's why I am so glad I didn't have any kids before the shit hit the fan," added Cross. Then he swung the SCAR around and dropped a pair of Zs that were creeping up on their six.

Considering himself very fortunate, Cade made no mention of family as the sneering faces of three dozen undead grade-schoolers slid by.

Always the cruise director, Ari said, "Hands and arms inside the vehicle, gentlemen. It's gonna be a tight fit."

"Hang on," Cade said, aiming the Chevy at the Prius-sized gap between the school bus's right fender and the tubular grill guard wrapping around the Suburban's front end. He buried the pedal and after a slight hesitation the full force of the engine, nearly two hundred horsepower, was applied to the road. Consequently the nearly half-ton of flesh, bone, and sinew—living and dead—sardined into the six-by-eight box behind him caused the Chevy's front end to rise slowly like a boat planing water. A wisp of steam curled through the grill and a cacophony of metallic gnashing rang out as a direct result of the added stresses. Then the rig nosed back down and, with the racket of two colliding locomotives, punched into the Suburban. Headlight glass shattered. A length of fender trim was sheared from the mounts securing it, curled back and probed the air.

In an apparent miscalculation on Cade's part only the Suburban's grill guard budged, bending back at a forty-five degree angle before the Chevy pick-up was wedged tight between it and the bus's enormous front tire.

For a few seconds the Chevy fought valiantly to break free, spinning the rear tires until the engine stalled out and died. Then, lured by the close proximity of fresh meat, the undead tykes returning from *Camp Carefree* pulled away from the bus windows and, like a single-minded organism, surged into the stairwell and crashed headlong into the bi-fold doors.

Chapter 29
Eden Compound

Duncan parked the Land Cruiser under the Black Hawk's drooping rotor blades, grabbed his radio and shotgun from the passenger seat, and willed his weary frame from the plush confines of the high-dollar SUV. He slung the Mossberg, pushed the door closed, and spent a couple of extra minutes covering the Toyota with some of the excess camouflage netting used to conceal the helo.

Better safe than sorry, he thought as he set out across the clearing, eyes searching for a clue as to the whereabouts of the camouflage blind concealing the entrance to his brother's underground compound.

The afternoon sun was just beginning to bake the back of his already sunburned neck when a fella he'd met a couple of days prior, Edward, emerged from the tree line laboring to carry a pair of bulging nylon duffle bags. A tick south of morbidly obese, the man had the neck of a firmly entrenched politician, wide and rolled with fat. And as he drew nearer, huffing and puffing, Duncan could see that the man's clean-shaven face was becoming redder by the second. Worried Ed might be close to having a massive coronary, Duncan stopped walking and asked if he could help carry the bags.

Eyes downcast, Edward said nothing and kept up his steady, lumbering pace.

"Wouldn't be a problem," said Duncan as their paths crossed. Edward still made no reply.

148

Incredulous, Duncan stopped and watched the man toddle away, bags swaying, shotgun banging against his considerable backside.

"What the hell did I do to you?" Duncan muttered as he stood in the middle of the clearing watching Ed approach the two Cessnas chocked adjacent to the Black Hawk. When Ed reached the nearest of the civilian aircraft—a shiny white item emblazoned with letters and numbers denoting its FAA identification and a black stripe running from nose to tail to add some flash to the rather pedestrian aircraft—he tossed the bags behind the narrow seats, and then with a great deal of effort climbed up and wedged his frame behind the controls.

We need a bigger plane, thought Duncan, adapting a line from Jaws to best describe what he had just witnessed.

***

As always, Duncan had to work at finding the concealed entrance. Once he located the camouflaged netting, he pulled it aside and passed on through. On the other side he smoothed and straightened the edges and corners, making sure the foliage looked as natural as rent-off sticks and leaves and clumps of bushes could.

With his footfalls deadened by the thick carpet of pine needles, he padded down the dirt ramp, passing through bars of light and dappled shadow along the way. The smell of damp earth filled his nose as he worked at the latches to open the outer steel door. When he entered the compound anteroom he performed a ritual he'd learned years ago in the jungles of Vietnam but had dusted off only recently. He stood still, eyes wide, letting them adjust to the dark. He lowered his breathing and listened hard for any kind of movement. And while he stood there in the low-ceilinged container, feeling a little like Indiana Jones invading some other culture's temple, he caught a tear-inducing whiff of his own body odor. The sour stink of fear-tinged sweat mingling with traces of bodily fluids and cordite clung to him like a bad reputation.

Standing there wallowing in his own stench, with the events of the day careening through his head like a Michael Man flick, a prolonged stint under one of those Frisbee-sized shower heads with pinprick jets of steaming hundred and forty degree water pummeling his skin and soothing his muscles had never sounded better. Hell, he thought. He'd even defy his own personal man code and put a loofa pad and some girly-smelling hair conditioner to use given the chance.

Once his eyes finally adjusted to the low light environs, he discarded the spa treatment fantasy like an old razor, propped his shotgun beside the vertical hatch, and tried the handle. And as expected, the door was unlocked and opened quietly on oiled hinges. *Should be a Klaxon sounding right about now*, he thought, shaking his head. For some lame brained reason, before he'd arrived at the compound, the group decided on a show of hands that during the day the doors would be latched, but not locked from inside. And given the fact that an average team of operators could neutralize the outside security, leave all of them cut from ear-to-ear exsanguinating on the ground and be gone like ghosts in a matter of seconds, he let it be known whenever possible how adamantly opposed he was to the ludicrous decision.

But since Logan was a big boy and the compound was his, Duncan had decided to save the battle for another day. Unfortunately for Logan, today was that day. Push had come to shove, and Duncan had been forced to do the shoving—albeit with a number of .50 caliber rounds—up on the road, and now he was going to do some pushing and revisit the issue with his baby bro.

He ducked into the next cramped Conex container which doubled as the compound's security and communications center, took two exaggerated strides, staying in the shadows, and stopped directly behind Logan, who was tethered to a Ham radio by a pair of bulky Hi-Fi headphones that were cinched tightly on his head and covered both ears.

While Duncan wrestled with the notion of teaching Logan a lesson on breaking and entering and the dire consequences that came along with it, he let his eyes wander over the facing wall; it was taken up by rows of shelving on which all manner of unused radio gear sat dark and silent. A bin at eye level was filled with electrical cords, speaker wire, and a myriad of colorful cables secured by plastic zip ties. Next door to it sat a half-dozen Motorola two-way radios taken off the bodies of the Huntsville dead. A polymer Glock pistol belonging to Logan sat within arm's reach next to the radios.

Arranged side by side on the desk below the shelving were a pair of closed circuit television monitors, each one partitioned so that six separate feeds could be displayed simultaneously. Frozen on the monitor on the left were mainly color images of conifer trees at ground level. The second screen displayed six grainy images. One showed Duncan and Edward passing. The next was a long, pulled-out view of the airstrip, mostly greens and browns with trees at the far end of the runway and a thin sliver of blue sky overhead. At the bottom on the left was another image, snapped from behind, of him entering the woods near the hidden entrance. The latter half of the partitioned monitor caught the white Toyota and a flash of his face in three separate frames at three different locations as he approached the airstrip via the dirt and gravel road coming in from the State Route.

Worrying his handlebar mustache with one hand and working the lighted dials and switches bristling from the ham set with the other, Logan continued his chat, totally oblivious to Duncan's presence.

Twenty-five years ago, when Duncan was in his early thirties helping his aging parents raise Logan, he would have jumped at using a golden opportunity like this to "*toughen*" the boy up.

Instead he leaned against the cool wall cloaked in shadow from the waist up and listened to the conversation Logan was having with someone whom he guessed was a ham radio operator somewhere out in America.

But after less than a minute of eavesdropping on this side of the exchange, Duncan got bored and acted on his earlier impulse. Slowly but surely he covered the distance, cutting the angle just right so that he remained outside of Logan's field of vision. Forming up behind the man, Duncan curled his hand into a rigid claw and then clamped it firmly down on his mark's shoulder.

Caught totally by surprise, Logan let out a yelp and involuntarily launched an inch off of his seat, a move that sent the headphones tumbling from his head crashing into the Pringles can he'd been using as a penholder, scattering chewed-on Bic pens and Sharpies all over the plywood floor. Then, teeth bared, the usually demure Logan turned to confront the unseen prankster.

Laughing at the sight of his baby brother's dome-shaped hat-head, more so than the adverse reaction the sneak attack had elicited, Duncan laughed and slapped his thigh. When he'd finally calmed down he wiped the tears from his eyes and waited for his comeuppance.

Casting a glare that quickly morphed into a full blown smile, Logan shook his head and said, "I guess that conversation was over." He hung the headphones up on a peg and pushed his chair backward, a discordant screech of rubber on plywood that could have woken the dead. He reached to the shelf and retrieved the Glock, which he slipped back into its black leather holster snugged against his right hip. Snatched the bowler hat off the shelf and positioned it precisely on his head. Finally squared away, heartbeat nearly back to normal, he sat back down and made a face at Duncan that said in no uncertain terms, *Grow the fuck up.*

"I'm still not used to how everything echoes down here," said Duncan, ignoring the look he knew all too well. "But you gotta hand it to me, Oops. The way I snuck up on you ... I still got it ... don't I, baby bro?"

"Lucky I didn't pop a cap in your ass," Logan said, patting his Glock. "Left you to bleed out on the sheet wood."

"Good thing I wasn't a real rotter. Or one of those hillbillies from Huntsville. You would have lost first-blood either way," drawled Duncan. "Shoulda had one ear listening to whoever your friend was there and the other tuned in to your surroundings. Better yet, that main door *should* be secured at all times."

"Your parenting days are over, *Old Man*," Logan said. He switched off the ham radio and stored the folding chair under the desk. After straightening the papers on the desk, he turned back to face Duncan and added, "But thanks for caring."

Looking over the top of his bifocals, Duncan said, "I thought we were done playing the nickname card."

"Earlier today, if I'm not mistaken, it was *you* who referred to me as *Oops* over an *open* channel in front of God and Jaime and anyone else who might have been listening in."

"Well you pissed me off by insisting I take Chatterbox Phil for a ride," said Duncan. He craned his neck, checking the two adjoining containers for anyone within earshot. He lowered his voice and went on. "Hell, halfway to Huntsville I couldn't decide how I was going to murder the man. Swear to God, if the Toyota had been a Huey that boy would have been getting flying lessons ... know what I mean?"

"He that bad?"

"Yeah ... I couldn't decide between duct taping his mouth closed or dropping his motor mouth ass off in the middle of 39 and leaving him there until I finished the recon."

Logan put his hands in his pockets. Shrugged his shoulders and cocked his head off to the side as if saying, *Finished yet, old man?*

Wondering if he should recount the story in its entirety, which would have to include indicting himself by divulging his new-found Achilles heel, Duncan worked his silver goatee, smoothed it out and then ruffled his knuckles cross grain against the whiskers. "You know, bro," he finally said, "I was proud of myself today. Wanted to shove old Phil into a wood chipper on the way back. Head first so he'd remain silent. So anything he said couldn't be held against him ... ever."

"And?"

"And I turned the other cheek. Took the high road. Asked him to channel his inner mime ... and ... how do you younger folks say it in a text message? S-T-F-U."

"Before smartphones became useless paper weights and texting a thing of the not-too-distant past, it was an acronym meaning *shut the fuck up*," Logan said, wholeheartedly wishing Duncan would get tired of talking and do so as well. "That was mighty big of you, brother. 'Cause once you're past Phil's annoying quirks he's a pretty good guy."

"Agreed. Young man saved my bacon on the road down there by Huntsville. And again ... if it wasn't for his help on the bend up there ... no way I could have handled all the rotters that had gathered since we left," Duncan admitted. "Gotta come clean with you, Logan. When the dead started walking, missing my exam at the VA was wayyy down on my worry list. Like not even registering, down on the list. But today, my diminished peripheral vision nearly got me killed."

"And you think you're OK to take the Black Hawk up?" Logan said, his brow hitching up an inch. "You know damn well the Army would clip your wings in a New York second."

"This is different, Logan. You, baby bro, are not the Army. Besides, I didn't have any problem flying that thing here from Colorado Springs."

"I've been meaning to ask you about that. After all that time away from the controls, how'd you manage that? Did it all come back to you like riding a bike, or did you have to consult a manual or something?"

"I saw a hundred hungry rotters heading our way and I started flicking the obvious switches. Then I prayed a little and hit the APU and the bird fired right up. Figure my success came about from a combination of things. One, I was rated in the Huey and I've had some stick time in a Cobra. Two, dumb luck. And three, a combination of the prayer and a couple more helpings of one and two thrown in for good measure. But in all seriousness, except for the electronic doo dads, the Black Hawk's controls were pretty much the same as the old slicks and gunships. Plus ... having the Grayson fella in the left seat was a Godsend."

"How so?"

"He worked the navigation and communication gear. Knew what he was doing. Even gave me some pointers ... apparently he's logged a lot of hours riding around in helos. And the unit he's in does a lot of cross-training ... they're kinda like the jack of all trades in the Army—only they're very deadly and they pretty much master everything."

"So just say it. The Grayson guy is Delta Force."

Before Duncan could confirm or deny the assertion there was an out-of-place noise in the adjoining room. A metallic sound complete with a drawn-out, hollow resonance as if a gong had been struck somewhere in the gloom. Then a few choice curse words and the echo of approaching footsteps.

Chapter 30
South Dakota

Cade's view of the little Zs, with their faces and bodies smashed against the green-tinted safety glass, reminded him how the late Hosford Preston had gotten him and Daymon trapped in the attic of the old farmhouse in Hanna, Utah. And just as the centuries-old glass between them and the dead had failed then—he presumed the glass inches from his face would do the same at any moment.

He tried the key. *Nothing.* Then he turned the ignition all the way off and cycled forward, engaging the starter. It produced a strong-sounding effort as he pumped the gas, but didn't live up to its name.

"Use caution," mumbled Jasper. "Floods easily."

"That's the least of our problems," Cade replied. Nonplussed, he repeated the process with the same result. Released the key, silencing the starter, then sat in brooding silence, breathing in gasoline fumes from the now-flooded carburetor.

Jasper made no reply.

"Let it rest for a minute," Ari said. He glanced up at the rearview and noticed Lopez engaging the dead, face-to-face, smashmouth combat, bashing in their skulls with the fully-collapsed butt stock of his M4. Hicks and Cross were standing shoulder-to-shoulder firing round after round from their pistols. After seeing the destruction the operators were wreaking on the dead, Ari flicked his gaze back to Cade. "I think we're going to survive this."

Looking over his shoulder, Cade said, "Do you know something I don't? Can't exactly call in *danger close* if we have no kind of air support." He looked at his watch. *Two minutes.*

"Roger that, but we've still got the Hercules."

"No use to us here, Ari," said Cade. Sitting there with a dead numb ankle in a dead truck surrounded with walking dead led to his thoughts wandering off to a dark place. A place where he kept all of his mortal worries. A place his pre-mission mental rituals were supposed to have sealed off. But the mental trap had failed. The proverbial dike had sprung a leak, leaving him with no defense against reflecting on his family's future without him. He took comfort in knowing that this deep into the outbreak, Brook had proven herself adept at taking care of Raven. His girls had run a hundred and thirty mile gauntlet through the dead-plagued countryside from South Carolina to Bragg, and then from that seemingly impregnable stronghold, Brook had delivered them to Schriever without a scratch. *Hell*, he thought, as the dead crowded, rocking the truck on its springs, *Brook had even ventured outside the wire on her own—twice—returning unscathed on both occasions.* In his mind, two words described her: *Mission capable.* Raven, on the other hand, was a raw piece of clay that still needed a good deal of shaping. Sure, she had already been taught how to listen to her intuition when it came to right and wrong and good or bad. But this wasn't the fourth grade, and when it came to the living dead she was still dangerously naive. She knew the basics but not the specifics. Thanks to Mike Desantos she was crystal clear on the one-bite rule. She was also very familiar with, *when it's night, douse the light*, a newly made-up mantra of Brook's—corny but effective. Bottom line, was she to be taken outside the wire to see firsthand the drive the dead exhibited once they locked on to fresh meat? To know more than anything that every encounter with infected humans had the likelihood of becoming a true kill-or-be-killed fight to the death?

Slowly he was resigning himself to accept the fact that someone else was going to have to see them through in his stead. A hot tear rolled down his cheek as he realized how terribly he was going to miss them. He hefted the Glock. Pulled the slide back. *One in the pipe.* That, plus the glint of brass in the well, assured him he wasn't going out alone. Sadly, he couldn't remember how many shells were sandwiched between the one he could see and the spring-loaded follower. *You're slipping, Wyatt.* So while Ari recited a prayer, Jasper rocked silently in his seat, and the dead scratched against the hood, he dropped the mag from the well, catching it in the palm of his hand. He turned it around, counting the available rounds showing in the see-through holes designed into the back of the magazine. *Three, plus the one already chambered. That'll have to do. Two for Jasper and two for me.* He figured Ari would save one in the Beretta to fulfill his own exit plan when the time came.

The distinctive *crunch-crunch* of a twelve gauge round being chambered nudged Cade from his dark thoughts. He turned his eyes up to consult the rearview. At the same instant Ari and Jasper turned their heads in response to the unmistakable, universal sound that said *look alive or else.*

"We're dangerously low on ammo," Lopez said breathlessly into the comms as his rifle cut a blurry arc through the air, each delivered blow resulting in small eruptions of brain and fluids. "How much longer, Captain?"

"It's flooded. Thirty seconds or so and I'll give it another try."

"When it starts, put the pedal to the metal and leave the rest up to us," Cross said.

"Roger that," was all Cade could muster. Wondering what the President's man had in mind, Cade rolled his head to the left and locked eyes with one of the undead campers and then, for the second time in less than an hour, wished he knew more than he did about the properties of fuel—unleaded gasoline to be more specific.

Chapter 31
Eden Compound

The sound in the corridor was not foreign. In fact, every person who had ever set foot in the compound had heard the same thing at least once—either up close and personal or as an innocent bystander as demonstrated by Duncan and Logan. And most likely every person in either position had uttered or had to listen to a similar string of salty language.

So as the footfalls drew nearer and the epithets grew louder and more colorful, Duncan stuck a finger in the air as if saying *hold that thought* and pressed tight against the wall to allow whomever approached clear passage.

Three feet away, however, Logan was shaking his head and mouthing, "You'll regret it."

For once Duncan listened to reason, or Logan—whatever the case might be—and stood down.

A beat later, Daymon entered through the narrow doorway, stooped over, one hand slowly massaging his forehead.

Noticing he was not alone, he straightened up and regarded each man; first Duncan with a nod and a raised brow, and then Logan with a half-hearted glare. "While I'm not a fan of tight confines, I usually find a way to adapt and overcome. But this place of yours, Logan, it effin takes things to a new level of cramped."

Raising a brow, Logan said, "What's the problem?"

"Well, since you *asked*. I feel like *freakin'* Gandalf having to hunch over like an old man through every doorway. You design this place?"

Logan nodded. "You crack your head for the first time?"

"No ... that was the third. And the worst." Wishing ice was as easily obtained as before the apocalypse, he rubbed the growing knot and said, "Who'd you consult with on this underground tomb, anyway ... a bunch of *hobbits?*"

Duncan shot Logan a look that said, *I got this*. Then a conspiratorial smile crossed his face as he answered the question. "No, son. Their Shire was under siege so Oops here went low-budget and consulted the Keebler Elves."

"Smart ass," Logan snapped back. "Why don't you tell your claustrophobic friend here how *you* blew *your* half of the inheritance."

Duncan made a face, pushed off the cold steel wall, and paced ten feet to the far end of the container where a metal door sat propped open.

Sensing the rising tension, Daymon changed the subject and said, "Were you two having some kind of a secret meeting or something when I walked in here? Cause y'all went real quiet, real quick."

"Move along, sir. Nothing to see here, sir," Duncan said with a chuckle that echoed off the walls and ceiling. "There is no conspiracy taking place here because Logan prefers to run this compound by committee. With full *transparency,* of course."

Ignoring the disparaging comment, Logan said to Daymon, "We're getting the group together for a meeting at dusk. I'd like you and Heidi to be there."

"Where is there?"

"Far side of the clearing."

"Sounds great to this garden-variety-claustrophobe. But why outside after all that's happened around here today? Aren't you worried about drawing more attention to yourselves?"

"Gotta hold it outside," said Logan. "There's no way to fit all of us in any one room down here. And I'm pretty sure with the message Duncan sent our friends in Huntsville we're not going to have any visitors with bad intentions in the near future. Probably won't get any Christmas cards from 'em either."

"So should I invite Jenkins?"

"Already beat you to it," answered Duncan. "Logan says since Charlie is former law enforcement he's in automatically."

"And Tran?"

Clicking his tongue, Duncan said, "Hell, he looked like he was on death's door. Won't blame him if he doesn't feel up to attending."

"He's not as bad off as he looked when we got here," said Daymon. "He lost a lot of blood. Had a pretty bad head wound, but your Indian friend who patched him up said he thinks the little guy has a couple of broken ribs and a hell of a sprained ankle, but other than that there wasn't anything life threatening about his injuries."

"Though he holds a different opinion than me," Logan intoned. "It's true what my brother said, this compound is run like a democracy. Everyone is welcome and eventually gets a say in matters as long as they pitch in and can prove they play well with others."

"Rules me out then," said Daymon, cracking a smile. "I'd better pack up and leave."

"You and your friends are OK," said Logan. "The Old Man made an executive decision. Apparently he's already vetted you."

Nodding, Duncan said, "See you outside near the airstrip just after dark?"

"I'll be there ... can't speak for the others. I'll run it by them though," said Daymon.

Logan grabbed the legal pad from the desk, tore a yellow sheet from somewhere near the middle, uncapped a black Sharpie and began to draw. In less than a minute he'd knocked out a crude map complete with a hastily drawn SR-39, a thick, no nonsense scrawl looping around the compound. The airstrip, however, was a dotted black line bisecting the middle of the page and he'd drawn a pretty good-looking compass rose pointing north, denoting the compound's location in relation to Logan, Huntsville, and Eden.

Never one to pass up an opportunity to levy a quip, Daymon said, "Writing me a love letter? But we only just met." He took the map from Logan and held it under the overhead bulb. It was a crude overview of the compound, that much he knew after having seen the property from the air while aloft in the DHS Black Hawk. However, the hieroglyphic-looking markings scattered about the lined sheet meant nothing to him without a key. So he put the map flat on the desk and looked a question at Logan.

"Sorry Daymon, I'm not very artistic by nature," said Logan. "I'm more of a computer and numbers guy."

"No worries," said Daymon, leaning over the map. "What exactly am I looking at here?"

"Obviously a map of the compound ... but not to scale. First and foremost, make sure you go *nowhere* near the Xs marked *here*, and *here*, and the ones by State Route 39, *right here*," said Logan, black Sharpie acting as a pointer. "Each one of those indicate where we've dug rotter traps. Basically holes outfitted with sharpened sticks."

"Punji stakes is what we called 'em in Nam, Daymon. Real bad juju if you're not paying attention and step on one," added Duncan. "The VC used to dip 'em in shit. You get stuck by one, worst case scenario is you're going to bleed out and die. You find a way to free yourself, staunch the bleeding and move on, eventually Mister Gangrene will set in and you'll lose the leg. But we skipped the dipping 'em in shit part since the rotters are already basically gangrene walking anyway."

"Good to know," said Daymon, flashing a half-smile. "I'll be sure to steer clear of them. I had a thought when I was coming in here before I wracked my dome on the top of the doorway."

Logan began twirling his mustache and said, "What's on your mind?"

"You think we oughta be locking the outside doors after coming and going?"

Shuffling his feet, Logan met Daymon's gaze and said, "Funny you should mention it. Me and Duncan were just discussing that before you came in. Solid idea, friend."

"That's some Twilight Zone shit right there," said Daymon. "You know what they say about great minds." He folded the map, gave each man a solid fist bump, and then filtered through the space, ducking his head before transiting into the next Conex.

There was a brooding silence as Daymon's footfalls faded away.

Chapter 32

Logan craned his head and looked down the corridor. "Daymon seems like an OK guy," he said. Then he pulled a chair over and took a seat and looked up at Duncan still holding the wall up.

"I've seen him in action," said Duncan. "And he certainly can take care of himself. I think he'll be a heck of an asset once he gets used to the tight confines."

"I trust your judgment, bro," Logan proffered. Then his face opened up and there was a twinkle in his eyes as he went on, "Now tell me a Cobra Gunship story. Did it have the red and white shark's teeth on the chin?"

"Yes it did. And I'm sorry, Logan. There were lots of things about Nam I kept to myself ... better that way. Shit was bloody and brutal even from five thousand feet up." He went quiet for a beat. "Not to mention the fact that you were young and impressionable. I didn't want you to start idolizing big bro and get star-spangled-eyes and want to go off to war."

"Thanks for that," said Logan. "You know, Lev came back from Iraq a little different than he was when he left. Can't quite place how. But I can sense that he lost a part of himself over there."

"War has a way of changing a man. It's changing you too, Logan. You can't see it as it's happening, but one day you'll wake up and see the world through a different shade of glasses."

"Enough about me," said Logan quietly. I want to hear about the Delta guy ... Cade."

"Daymon says he spoke to Cade a couple of days ago and he's supposed to be making his way here. Damn good for us. Good to have a real ass kicker around when the shit hits the fan."

"Does he play well with others?" asked Logan.

"He's a little like you. Reserved until spurred into action. But his actions ... when he's spurred speak way louder than words and usually involve a gun, and a knife, and end with a trail of bodies."

"OK. Consider him vetted and approved. Can you promise me one thing though?"

"Depends."

"Just promise."

"In life, Logan, there are no promises."

"If or when he shows up. I was thinking before you go risking your life and anyone else's who hops in with you we oughta go find us a place to get you a new set of specs."

"You're not getting this old man inside a shopping mall for anything ... not even if my eyes get so bad I'm calling a cat a dog. No way. I ain't setting foot near one. I've seen how those monsters follow the roads. Sometimes staying inside the cars they died in even if they could get out and walk away."

"So what's your point?" asked Logan, a curious look on his face.

"My point, little brother ... the outbreak went full tilt on a Saturday." He paused for effect. "Hell, those mall walkers were at one time a couple of dead brain cells away from being a zombie before the outbreak anyway. So where do you think they went after they became real card-carrying, non-breathing zombies?"

"The mall," intoned Logan. "But I was talking about the eyeglass place at the strip mall in Eden. That's a bit different ... don't you think?"

Before Duncan could offer up another *hell no* in response to Logan's appeal, the equipment on the shelves began to sway minutely. One of the folding chairs skittered along the floor and a thumbtack worked loose from the corkboard, releasing a sheet of paper which fluttered to the floor near Duncan's boots. Then the vibration became a rushing sound with a resonance like an old box fan on the lowest setting.

Duncan mouthed, "*What the fuck is that?*"

"That's us losing some more people," answered Logan.

"What do you mean?"

Shaking his head in obvious disbelief, Logan said, "Edward's following up on his threat and flying his family out of here."

"Why?"

"Didn't like how you handled the folks on the road."

Duncan shook his head and sighed.

"It's not just you, Duncan. Ed thought this would be over in a day or two. And once he gunned down his first rotter and reality set in, he was already one foot out the door."

"Where does he think he's going that will be any safer than here?"

"Said he'd find someplace where there were no undead. An island or mountaintop."

"Swiss Family Robinson-type of pipe dream, that is. I've heard how far this thing has spread and how many of *us* have become *them*. And it ain't pretty," said Duncan. "The Shangri-La he's looking for doesn't exist. And the fact that he believes it gets much better than this is what might have just gotten him and his family killed."

The noise grew distant. Logan saw the plane in his mind's eye. Throttles pegged. Bumping along the make-shift runway. Flaps catching the wind. The plane rising slowly and then the moment of truth was near. He looked up at the container's metal roof and waited for it. Ten seconds went by. *Nothing.* Then ten more and nothing. No explosion. No sound of rending metal on impact. Thankfully, the not-so-svelte Edward and the loaded-down Cessna had cleared the trees and the fireball remained a figment of Logan's pessimistic imagination.

"They made it," said Duncan.

Logan replied, "Hope their luck continues."

Duncan looked at his watch. He noted the time, then pushed his aviator glasses to the top of his balding head and pinched the bridge of his nose. "In fifteen minutes, meet me in the interrogation room," he said, adding emphasis as well as air quotes around the word *interrogation.*

Remembering the bad cop/good cop ruse they'd played on the dreadlocked white kid from Huntsville, Logan cracked a quick smile. "Lev spells me in a few minutes, then I have to make my rounds outside to check our traps."

"I'll cover for you until Lev gets here. Who is out on security right now?"

"The girls are still up by the road. Chief is keeping an eye on the aircraft and the strip."

"Gus and Phil?"

"Walking the property," Logan answered. He handed over the two-way radio he'd been monitoring the others with. "Just changed the battery. 10-1 is the channel we're using."

"Good channel," Duncan said, remembering the trip through the gorge and high desert of Oregon. "I won't forget it."

"See you in fifteen," said Logan.

Duncan called out, "Sharp," at Logan as he walked off towards the exit. And as soon as the younger Winters was out of sight, curiosity got the better of the older Winters. He listened hard for the distinctive sound of the outside door latching, and a few seconds after the telling *snik* reached his ears he waited an additional minute, checked both corridors leading away, and then scooped up the paper that had fallen near his feet. On it were strings of letters and numbers seemingly thrown together. After a second he realized the column on the left was the call signs of two dozen or so ham operators. And in the next column there were abbreviations, three and four letters long, which Duncan gathered were the operators' locations. Finally, a third column held other notations scribed in Logan's clean, easy-to-read hand. Theoretically, thought Duncan, what he was holding in his hand was the contact information for survivors the world over that Logan had painstakingly gathered over the last three weeks. He hinged over, picked the thumbtack off the floor, and then pinned the paper to the corkboard in roughly the same location he remembered seeing it fall from. Then he listened hard again. Heard nothing. He looked down at the pad on the desk to steal a quick peek at the notations his brother had been making before Daymon blew through.

"Hell, I'm old enough to be his dad," Duncan said to himself, a weak attempt at rationalizing the transgression. He gave the first three sheets a cursory examination, smoothed them back down, and squared the pad away to where he thought it had been originally. Then, with the information he'd just acquired troubling him greatly, he made a mental note to confront Logan about it later.

Chapter 33
I-90 Near Draper, South Dakota

In order to allow the gas a little extra time to evaporate—or whatever term was applicable when dealing with petroleum products—Cade fought off the urge to turn the key after thirty seconds and instead waited a full three minutes. Sitting in the cab with morbid thoughts trespassing where they didn't belong, the seconds passed like hours—the entire three minutes seeming to take an eternity. And adding further tension to the wait, the undead bus driver had somehow forced its way past the undead campers and mashed its pale face against the vertical glass in the folding door. Then, as if driven by some leftover snippet of memory, the portly creature worked its fingers between the door's vertically-running weather seals and was slowly but surely working it open.

Ignoring the abomination, Cade said, "Fire in the hole." He turned the key and the starter whirred alive; then, to keep from making the same mistake twice, he kept his foot off the gas pedal, held his breath, and waited. Another couple of long seconds passed before the plugs sparked, setting the fuel in the cylinders afire. With a gunshot-like backfire the engine chugged to life and rattled on, sounding like it was hitting on only six of its eight cylinders. *Oh, what a beautiful sound,* Cade thought to himself as the power plant emitted a shrill squeal yet somehow maintained a ragged idle that transmitted a harsh vibration through the firewall, through the sole of the size-twelve boot he'd taken from Gaines, and deep into the damaged tissue, tendons, and bones of his newly swollen-to-size-fourteen left foot. Wincing from the incredible pain, he wiped beads of sweat from his brow and said a prayer, asking the Gods of internal combustion to keep the thing running.

Excited by the noisy engine, the undead driver thrashed against the door, opening it a few more inches. Then with its sneering face wedging the door open, it worked one of its blood slickened arms through the crack into the sunlight, strained forward, and raked its fingernails against the automotive glass.

With the Z's mouth longingly opening and closing registering in his side vision, Cade reached down and shifted the Chevy into *4x4 Low*. Trying his best to pretend the creature wasn't there, he shifted his gaze and watched the drama behind them playing out in the rear view mirror.

At the rear of the bed, his black body armor streaked with glistening fluids, Agent Cross stood tall, racking round after round through the shotgun. Five booming reports sounded and he dropped the empty weapon, drew a bulky-looking handgun and looked back and met Cade's gaze. Gesturing forward with the pistol, Cross said, "Keep the engine running and we'll get you through the gap." He turned, placed his free hand on the tailgate, and leapt atop the mound of fallen corpses.

The truck shimmied as Hicks and Lopez bounded out, following the agent's lead.

"They're *all* going to dismount?" Ari said incredulously. "If one of them gets bit, who is left to pull them back in?"

"If one of them gets bit," said Jasper. "You don't want them getting back in."

"You don't need to remind me how this works," Ari said. He looked at the slider. He looked left at the leering Z and the wall of yellow pressing against the door. Lastly, he looked past Jasper at the Suburban blocking egress on that side. "Newsflash ... we're stuck in here. And if those guys go down it'll only be a matter of seconds before the things are banging on the back window. Do you want that?"

"Relax, Ari. Cross's plan is solid ... they'll handle it," said Cade. "We are going home. I promise."

After putting down a dozen Zs and heaping their leaking bodies waist-high into some kind of rotten Maginot Line stretching between the Suburban's rear wheels and roughly the middle of the school bus, Cross, Lopez, and Hicks sat down hard on the rear bumper with their backs braced against the tailgate.

"OK Captain," Cross said into the comms. He paused for a split second to catch his breath, then went on, "I'm going to count to three and then you milk this bitch for all she's got."

"Solid copy. On three," replied Cade.

Cross started the count and when he got to *three,* with all their might, the bone-tired trio braced their boots and pressed a combined five hundred-some-odd pounds of flesh, bone, and muscle against the rust pocked tailgate.

Hearing Cross say *three* in his ear bud, Cade mashed the accelerator to the floor and crossed his fingers. Responding to the wide open carburetor, the trapped Chevy squatted under power, and a tick later the transfer case divided and unloaded the newfound torque to the differential, onward to all four hubs, and finally through the tires and onto the road. The truck surged ahead six precious inches, paused momentarily, engine roaring, until the forward motion and energy building behind it was greater than the series of bolts keeping the right front fender attached. A drawn out groan and a series of sharp metallic pings filled the air as the fasteners sheared, zipper-like, one by one and the Chevy's fender peeled away, freeing the pick-up from the clutches of the Suburban's twisted grill guard.

Sensing a little forward momentum building behind the sudden halt, Cross dug his heels in, straightened his legs until every muscle was burning, and yelled, "Push!"

Following the agent's lead, backs straining, neck muscles corded, Lopez and Hicks redoubled their efforts and as a direct result two things happened at once. The two-and-a-half ton Suburban rocked on its springs and shifted a few degrees to the right, and the pick-up shot forward, dropping them, to a man, flat on their backs staring at the azure Dakota sky.

Seeing the men slip from view, Cade jammed the truck to a stop, hollering, *"Get in, get in, get in,"* at the top of his lungs. As he sat in the truck trying to figure out what was happening with the team, the dead that had been scratching on the rust-streaked hood streamed into the newly-created passage and slammed full force into his window. Momentarily startled, he looked left at the crush of rotten bodies. Then, pushing the first tingling of a rising panic back where it belonged, he popped the testy differential out of *4x4 Low*, racked the transmission into plain old *drive* and gunned the engine to keep it running. "Jump in now!" he bellowed, flicking his eyes up to the rearview expecting to see Lopez, Hicks, and Cross piling aboard. Instead, he noticed a new flurry of movement behind and to the left as the bus door inexplicably hinged open and the undead driver spilled out, arms flailing, face first onto the interstate. Then in the next instant, just when Cade thought things couldn't possibly get any worse, undead kids began pouring from the stairwell, navigating the driver's prostrate body like a gangplank. "Check your six," Cade warned. Then, to add insult to injury, he witnessed Cross's makeshift barrier waver and then topple, corpses rolling like logs as more Zs stumbled and staggered over the top of them. Custer's last stand came to mind as Cade barked out new and more dire warnings to his diminished team.

Turtled, and nearly out of breath, with Cade's voice booming in his ear, Cross reached to his thigh and drew his Sig Sauer. *What next?* he thought as he tucked his chin into his chest, spread his feet wide apart and aimed between his boot tips at the creature nearest him. He steadied his breathing and caressed the trigger twice, only a second's separation between shots. The first .357 jacketed hollow point leapt from the muzzle at a blistering fourteen hundred and fifty feet per second on a diagonal upward trajectory, covering the eight feet to the soft spot under the female Z's exposed chin in the blink of an eye. Then the five hundred-plus pounds of kinetic energy behind the bullet wracked the stunted creature's head back at a sharp forty-five degree angle, the intense shockwave tearing an additional vicious half-moon-shaped gash below the initial entry wound. The second round punched in an inch to the right of the first, adding its own kinetic energy into the equation and rocketing the Z off its road-gnarled feet. As Cross shifted aim, he registered the limp body contorting into an upside down 'U', its newly misshapen head on a collision course with the pavement.

As expected, Lopez and Hicks' training kicked in and they entered the fray before the first Z struck terra firma.

Pistol bucking, spent shells tracing crazy arcs through the air, Lopez pivoted on one knee, walking fire left to right into the building crowd. Simultaneously, Hicks had noticed the same movement that had caught Cade's eye and crabbed sideways in order to engage the Zs tumbling from the bus. First, he stilled the undead bus driver with a double tap to the center of its pasty forehead, blowing brain and bone in a flat arc into the stairwell where it hit with a viscous slap. Time seemingly slowing to a crawl, he shifted his gaze to the tiny creatures tumbling from the stairway. He bracketed one about the same size and presumably the same age as his niece, Kylie, who he was certain was no longer among the living. But he found the resemblance uncanny enough to cause him a moment's hesitation, which had disastrous consequences. The round snapped low and right, and instead of striking the Kylie lookalike in the forehead where he had been aiming, the bullet blasted a hole the size of his fist in the side of her reed-thin neck. Pissed off at himself, and affected by a sudden flood of emotion, Hicks overcompensated and pulled the second shot high and right, sending the blazing lead dead center into the fire extinguisher which according to SDDOT (South Dakota Department of Transportation) mandate was strapped within easy reach alongside the bus driver's seat. The ensuing explosion of toxic chemicals took the path of least resistance, roiling out the door and coating both him and the Zs with a fine white talc. *This isn't what I signed up for*, he thought as the little monster crawled toward him. He fell to both knees with a ringing in his ears, eyeing his pistol. Ignoring the other pint-sized Zs, he stared, fixated on the spot where he'd blown the hunk of flesh from the Z's neck. *She certainly doesn't look like Kylie any longer*, he told himself. With its head attached by a thin cord of shiny muscle, and trailing shreds of yellowed larynx and emitting noises that sounded to him like a pissed off badger, it clawed its way toward him.

The last thing he remembered hearing before the extinguisher cooked off was the jangly sound of brass hitting the road intertwined with the dissonant *pop, pop, pop* of something sounding like a starter pistol. The air around him sizzled and then went quiet, an absence of sound he imagined persisted in outer space. And as the Z inched forward, its head bobbing to and fro like a damaged Jack-in-the-Box, suppressed thoughts and morbid visions began to loop through Hicks's head—a silent horror film comprised of visions from his past.

He relived the old folks' home outside of Atlanta. Beautiful day. Geriatrics choosing the lesser of the two evils. Leaping from the rooftop to their deaths, en masse, instead of facing the dead on its terms. The spree of mercy killings that followed visited him every night.

Then Pony Tail getting flying lessons courtesy of General Mike Desantos. The man's slight form, arms rolling up the windows on the way down, before being ripped apart by the dead without benefit of a mercy kill.

Did he deserve it?

Did it really matter?

No. Ponytail visited nightly anyway.

The visions from hell continued as the overloaded party barge capsized in his mind's eye and the water went red when bullets from the mini-gun he was manning shredded survivors and Zs alike into little pieces. *Nothing but chum.*

Then the bobble-headed Kylie imposter was on him. Grabbing and scratching, splintered shark-like teeth clicking. It got ahold of his off hand, drawing it towards its open maw. Then, barely registering, he felt a twinge of pain on his wrist. Like a bee sting. Or a scratch. Here, then gone. Nothing to write home about.

Reacting to the loud explosion and resulting white haze, Cross rolled onto his stomach and rose to standing. He looked to his right and let his gaze fall on Hicks, who was kneeling, arms outstretched, seemingly frozen; then he saw the broken creature, face down, writhing on its stomach. Instantly his sixth sense kicked in telling him that something wasn't right with the picture, so he crabbed sideways past the pick-up, Sig aimed at the stripe of white skin where the thatch of hair was pulled away tight in two separate directions, and finished the job Hicks had started with one well-aimed shot between the kid's once blond pigtails. Bile rising in his throat, he rushed to Hicks, pulled him to his feet and pushed him towards Lopez. Wide eyed, he hollered, "Get him in the truck." Then he took a knee and methodically pumped a dozen bullets into a dozen little faces, creating all new horror-filled visions to keep him awake at night. He dropped the spent magazine and jammed a fresh one home, while in his ear bud he heard Cade yelling for him to get in the truck. The sights and smells of death all around started his jaw to lock up. He swallowed hard against out-of-control salivary glands. Nothing doing. He was past the point of no return. He shook his head and went to all fours and emptied his stomach on the dashed yellow line.

***

While the twenty seconds of mayhem was happening at Cade's six, he asked Ari to hand over the pistol they had confiscated from Jasper. Handling the small black semi-automatic, he racked the slide back and checked the chamber. *One in the pipe.* Then he dropped the magazine from the well and counted the ten shiny .22 shells through the mag's side window. *Ten, plus one.* He slapped the magazine home and flicked the selector from safe to fire. Batted away a tiny hand with the squared-off muzzle and shot the offending creature through the eye.

"Next. Step right up," he said as the Zs milled around outside his window.

"Can't kill them all, Captain," said Ari. "You've got what? Ten rounds max in that pea shooter?"

Another creature gripped the window with both hands, canted its head horizontally and worked its slender face into the narrow gap between the drain sill and the window. Holding his breath due to the overwhelming stench, Cade placed the barrel in the Z's mouth and let the thing chew on it. He looked deeply into its dead eyes and found nobody home. The wheel was spinning but the hamster was missing. No spark of life.

Although he used to harbor a small shred of empathy for the dead, right now, with his ankle throbbing to a calypso beat and three dead teammates in the box bed, he felt nothing. No remorse. No sadness. No guilt. Nothing whatsoever when he pulled the trigger. "Every Z we put down right here and now is one less we'll have to deal with when it really matters," he said.

Knowing precisely what the operator was alluding to, Ari ejected the mag from his Beretta, thumbed one 9mm shell off the top, and reinserted it with a solid slap. "It's hot," he said, placing the black pistol on the seat next to Cade's thigh.

Like thinning a slow-moving line at the DMV, Cade emptied Jasper's pistol into the dead as they filed forward. Then he traded guns and methodically squeezed round after round from the Beretta into the Zs until their bodies were piled knee high in a rough semi-circle stretching from just outside his door and around the front of the school bus. Barrel still smoking, he handed the pistol back to Ari, who promptly reloaded his last shell into the magazine, slammed it home and racked the slide. "Insurance," he said with a quickly disappearing smile.

"We need to move it," Cade said again over the comms. He looked past Ari and regarded Jasper, who was rocking slowly back and forth. "Pull it together, big guy. We're going to need your muscle before all is said and done."

Nothing.

Cade tried reaching him again. "I'm sorry we had to cuff you, Jasper. But I couldn't risk having you bolt from the truck and let those things get inside here. You understand that, don't you?"

No response.

Cade noted three separate and distinct thuds and ceased trying to get through to Jasper. He checked the mirror just as Cross was crawling over the tailgate.

"They're in," said Ari, confirming what Cade already knew.

With the needle on the truck's temperature gauge pushing dangerously into the red, Cade stabbed the gas and wheeled around the few remaining Zs. Then, leaving the killing field in the rearview, he turned a hard, slow-rolling left and scraped by the bus perpendicular to the breakdown lane. Over the ticking engine he heard the Hercules make yet another pass. And then in his ear he heard Cross remind him to find the yellow bug and they'd be home free.

Chapter 34
Eden Compound

After inspecting the pull dates on two rows of canned food and then facing them so that all of the labels were readable and pointing in the same direction, Duncan snuck another look at his watch. *Three minutes overdue.* Even as a boy Logan had never been punctual, and if this was any indication then the zombie apocalypse had had little effect on the man. Duncan recalled the years he'd spent after Vietnam living back at home bouncing between jobs, women, and the horse track. Always searching for the answers to his problems in the next big trifecta or at the bottom of a bottle. Then one day, after a dozen years and thousands of nightmares and the fall of Saigon were behind him, he finally hit rock bottom and decided to clean up his act. With both Mom and Dad pushing sixty and Oops entering his teen years, Duncan found himself drawn to duty again— only this time it was to family instead of country. Once again he learned to straighten up and fly right and grab responsibility by the horns, only this time it wasn't due to a screaming drill instructor or the need to stay frosty in a theater of war. In hindsight, it had been Logan's unconditional love that pulled him from the abyss, allowing him to get a tenuous hold on his life. And that was why, over the last nineteen minutes, a hot mess of guilt had been gnawing at his gut like an Alien trying to escape. So, sitting here amongst the beans and soup and five gallon buckets filled with his least favorite food—white rice—he'd come to the conclusion that his best bet was to come clean and *then* begin the inquisition. After all, he was the big brother here and if he couldn't be trusted with the knowledge Logan was obviously withholding, then what good was he to the kid?

Just as he was finished facing the jumbo cans of cling peaches, the door swung wide and Logan swept into the room.

"Right on time," Duncan said.

Saying nothing, Logan slammed the door, setting the lone light bulb swinging.

"What's the matter, kid?"

Logan exhaled forcefully. "I'm a failure. That's what's the matter."

"Bullshit, baby bro. You designed and built this place single-handedly. If this is about Daymon and me busting your balls earlier then I'm truly sorry," said Duncan. He drew a deep breath. Held it for a second before exhaling and added, "After all that's gone down today, the last thing I meant to do was hurt your feelings."

"We're losing another family of four because they can't handle the violence. Good church-going people. Neighbors back in Salt Lake."

Like a cowboy in a western flick, Duncan leaned back against the wall, put his thumbs in his belt and said, "World's a violent place ... always has been."

Grimacing, Logan replied, "You know it's bad enough that we have to deal with the walking dead, but now we've got people ... bandits ... or whatever you want to call them, trying to take our stuff by force."

"Force *needs* to be dealt with by use of greater force ... violence of action. I don't like it either but the way I see it—we've solved our bandit problems for the time being. As for the unintended consequences—is losing seven or eight hungry mouths, with only two of them able-bodied men who bring something to the table such a bad thing?" He went silent. Worried his silver goatee.

Logan said, "You're *cold*, Duncan." He swallowed hard and looked away.

Duncan made no reply.

Logan said softly, "They have kids."

"I'm being practical, Logan. Besides, they made a choice. It's simple math as far as I see it, and with Daymon and Jenkins aboard it's a wash. Hell, I think the dreadlocked kid and the cop are worth four of your friends. Hate to be callous, but if we're going to survive ... come out the other end of this thing not hungering for human flesh ourselves, you're going to have to grow thicker skin. Forget about this democracy thing. Stop worrying about hurting someone's feelings, and take charge."

Logan's eyes went glassy. The overhead light reflected off the pooling tears. "I've already killed seven men since this thing started. Not rotters ... stopped counting them the day after Washington D.C. fell. It's the seven living, breathing men who are visiting me in my nightmares," Logan said, choking back the tears.

"Get used to it. It's gonna be multiples of those seven if you're lucky," drawled Duncan "And you know what that means?"

"No," Logan said, wiping his face with his shirt.

"It means you are still alive and they aren't," Duncan said. "This is not a Y2K type of event. What we have here is not what you and Lev prepared for. The police and military are not going to reconstitute any time soon. Maybe they never will. So right now I'm drawing a line in the sand. We've got to start treating this like the life and death situation that it is."

An outburst of laughter from a far corner of the subterranean redoubt worked its way forward, echoing from the walls and around the twists and turns and fading as it passed the storage room door.

"I've gotta come clean with you, baby bro. After you left ... right before Lev showed up, I snooped around a little. Found some radio info on a sheet on the floor, and couldn't stop myself from reading the notations on your legal pad. When were you planning on telling me or anyone else about the black helicopters those kids up north are seeing?"

"Initially I was going to wait until tonight when everyone was assembled. Then our conversation earlier and Daymon adding his two cents started gnawing on me. I *was* going to run it by you here. But, like always, you beat me to the punch."

Taking a can from the shelf and juggling it hand to hand, Duncan said, "Tell me about the names you scratched out."

"Those were groups of survivors that I'd been sharing information with since the outbreak. For some reason over the last

178

couple of days most of them have stopped transmitting. And they aren't picking up when I hail them."

"One try and you write them off?"

"No," answered Logan. "I'd give them a couple of tries in one day. Then try again the next ..."

"No answer they get scratched?"

"Yep."

"And this usually coincides with them seeing black helos?"

"The earlier ones all fell to the dead. I'm pretty sure of that. I was chatting with one fella in Salt Lake when his home was overrun. He left the mike open. I listened as they fought for their lives. Gunshots. Screaming. And then the moans and cries of the dead and dying ... and then silence. That was the last thing I heard of them." He shivered visibly. "Pleading for their lives and then silence."

"The ones you've been in contact with recently ... did they see the helicopters?"

"Yes. And some ground vehicles. All military."

"Was the Humvee I used to engage our Huntsville friends military?"

"National Guard—"

"Logan ... work the problem for a second," Duncan said, staring at him straight. "Take *nothing* at face value. Learned that over there. The peasants wore black pajamas. The Viet Cong wore black pajamas ... make any sense?"

"Perfect sense. I take back the parent comment. From here on out I want you to teach me everything you know."

"Copy that, baby bro."

"I think I know where to find a large cache of supplies. Weapons and gear and food. Enough to keep us going for a long time."

"Go on," said Duncan, a smile curling the corner of his mouth.

Ten minutes later, after Logan had laid everything on the table and they had war-gamed his idea together, a decision was made.

Chapter 35
South Dakota

With a slow motion procession of dead on their six, and glimpses of daylight peeking through the fender-to-bumper maze, the fabled yellow VW came into view. It was on the shoulder, right where Cross had promised. It served as the far left bookend to a row of stationary vehicles that were nosed up against a tremendous pileup blocking the interstate shoulder-to-shoulder. The burned-out hulk of some kind of tractor-trailer rig appeared to have been—initially at least—the main cause of the backup. It had jack-knifed with its trailer jutting to the right, partially hanging over the shrub-covered embankment. The tractor itself, Cade presumed, had at first ridden up and over a handful of cars, crushing them beyond recognition before the entire jumble caught fire. Intense heat had scorched the asphalt, causing it to bubble before cooling and hardening, leaving it looking like the surface of the moon. The conflagration had also scoured away any clues as to what make or model the nearest half-dozen automobiles had been. Everything flammable was gone. Vinyl, cloth, and plastic vanished in a cloud of toxic fumes. *Didn't matter though*, Cade thought. The people driving the little econo-boxes had probably died instantly. To him it was like they had almost been asking for it. Rolling coffins, he'd heard cars that size called. And the shoe fit because all that was left of them was skeletal remains—both human and vehicle.

"Cross, Lopez ... I need you two to cover Hicks at the next objective," said Cade as a burst of silenced automatic rifle fire sounded in his earpiece. He glanced at the rearview in time to see a flurry of movement as Hicks gunned a trio of Zs to the roadway, and in nearly the same instant unclipped the rifle, tossed it down, and the black pistol reappeared in his gloved hand.

"Copy that," replied Cross, eyes tearing up from the stench more so than the wind curling around his sunglasses. He sensed the truck begin to slow, snugged the SCAR carbine to his shoulder, and began dropping the nearest walking cadavers.

Then, before anyone could react, the sound of a hundred freight trains was again on top of them as Oil Can Five-Five skimmed overhead less than a hundred feet above the deck.

"This is Anvil Actual. How copy, Oil Can?" Cade called into the comms as the plane's pale fuselage flicked by and the truck was buffeted in its slipstream.

"Solid copy," replied a voice Cade recognized as belonging to the co-pilot who had introduced himself earlier as Second Lieutenant Norman Meredith.

"Are we still proceeding with Plan A?" Cade inquired. "Or does Nash have a Pave Hawk and some PJs (Air Force Pararescue Jumpers) enroute from Schriever?"

Meredith said, "If you have three hours to kill, we can arrange a Pave Hawk and a couple of PJs."

Cade grimaced and tightened his grip on the wheel as a child-sized flesh-eater appeared from out of nowhere and was instantly swallowed under the truck's front end. "Plan A works for us," he answered back, as the small form thumped and bumped along the entire length of the undercarriage. He relayed the question to Ari.

"Tell them my vote is for A," said Ari, who had been eavesdropping anyway and was never shy about adding his two cents. "They get us to Schriever and we're gonna owe them big time. Shit ... what are we up to now? Gotta be four or five cases," he added, answering his own question. He swiveled right. "Beer sounds good, doesn't it, Jasper?"

"Home stretch is coming up. We're committing," said First Lieutenant Dover in Cade's ear bud.

"Roger that," Cade replied, maneuvering the Chevy between the cable barrier to the left and the VW on their right while adding a few new streaks of yellow to the Chevy's growing palette.

Finally clear of the breach, Cade looked back at the sea of metal and shambling Zs he'd successfully navigated. Then he stuck his head out again and looked up at the Hercules which was making another slow turn to the south. He saw it level out and then noticed a barely visible grayish mist and knew instantly what he was witnessing. The thin, gauzelike veil was fuel spewing from the Herc's wings and mixing in the turbulent vortex and drifting to the ground. The broadening gray smudge kind of reminded Cade of rain falling from a distant cloud band as it fell to Earth.

Chapter 36
Colorado Springs, Colorado

At the precise location Sergeant Eckels had chosen to initiate contact with the dead, I-25 made a slight left-hand bend north by west. And beyond that bend, out of sight from his position, were three soccer-pitch-sized moats filled two knuckles deep with diesel fuel. And stretching in the opposite direction, beyond West Colorado Boulevard and the Auto Mall in which his command vehicle was parked, to an area in the distance near where he'd deployed the pair of M-ATVs and his lone sniper team, three similar-sized moats had been carved into the middle of Interstate 25.

The remnants of the excavation were piled head high on either side of the six lanes, and like parapets atop a castle wall, poured concrete Jersey barriers encircled with concertina wire snaked haphazardly atop the mounds of fresh dirt and fractured asphalt. To Eckels, the whole undulating affair kind of looked like an earthen sea serpent, or perhaps the Great Wall of China—but on a much smaller scale. To further augment his *kill box*, on the east side of 25 was some kind of slough, its brackish water moving at a snail's pace. On the opposite side, and of no interest to the shambling horde, stood a smattering of darkened fast food joints, their garish-colored signage offering up $4.99 value meals and Oreo Blizzards, Kid's Meals and the Chinese-made trinkets masquerading as toys so coveted before the world died. A block south was a thoroughly looted sporting goods store, its empty parking lot paper-strewn and glittering with broken glass. Next door, a half-dozen auto dealerships with a good deal of dust- and soot-covered inventory commandeered the equivalent of three long city blocks.

Eckels shifted his gaze to the dirt egress route the engineers had fashioned with their graders and diggers. Sandwiched between the ponds of fuel and the mini Great Wall, and barely wide enough for a single vehicle, the crude dirt path spooled out from West Colorado Boulevard and ran north several blocks past three more fuel-filled moats to where it disappeared underneath the West Bijou Street overpass which was the final piece of his elaborate puzzle. Holes had been drilled at all of the critical load-bearing points and then filled with high explosives. Once the charges were detonated, gravity, loading, and shear working together would bring hundreds of tons of concrete and rebar falling into the path of the dead.

"This is Jumper One-One, I have eyes on target. The lead grouping is nearing the first moat," said a sergeant who was manning the furthermost picket from inside one of the carefully-hidden M-ATVs. "The Zulus are four hundred meters from my position. How copy?"

"Solid copy, Jumper One-One. Hold and report any deviation," Eckels said, feeling a slight charge of adrenalin that was but a precursor to the flood he would experience once the operation was fully underway.

He ran through what *should* happen next. The squirter teams would continue to operate autonomously, continuing to communicate to each other while eradicating any Zs that broke ranks. And barring a big change in the direction of the horde, he would only listen in and keep up with their maneuvers on the continuously updating BFT. On the other hand, the movement of his pickets had to be timed just right because once he ordered them to spring into action, they would be close enough to reach out and touch the rotting tide of death. And to further complicate things, the moment the drivers in the forward-most pair of M-ATVs fired up the growling 7.2-liter diesel power plants, their positions would be broadcast to every walking corpse in the area and all bets would be off. One wrong move, Eckels conceded to himself, and the whole plan would fall apart. He looped around the front of his M-ATV and slid into the passenger side, gently ushering Hudson to the rear area of the vehicle usually taken up by a gunner or additional soldiers. He swiveled the BFT screen and double-checked Jumper's intel against the information already on the display.

"Two hundred meters," said the sergeant in Jumper One-One, tension evident in his voice.

Bearing in mind that the drivers in both Jumper One-One and Jumper One-Two were chomping at the bit and raring to go, Eckels checked the display one last time but at a greater magnification and then ordered them to engage the enemy at will.

Chapter 37
South Dakota

As Second Lieutenant Meredith finished crossing T's and dotting I's, Cade felt the cold tingle of anticipation course his spine. Six minutes. *Hell*, he thought to himself, marking the time on his Suunto. *Six minutes is barely the length of a Super Bowl commercial. Hardly enough time to take a piss, visit the fridge, and grab a fresh beer.* But to him and the rest of the men who had just been told by the co-pilot of the Hercules what needed to happen and when before an exfil was possible, those three hundred and sixty seconds were going to seem like a lifetime.

"This is Oil Can Five-Five," said the co-pilot Second Lieutenant Meredith. "After one final go-around we'll be light enough to come down and scoop you all up. I can't stress this enough, though. You only have six minutes to make it happen on your end."

Pounding softly on the steering wheel, Cade answered back, "This is Anvil Actual, solid copy on that. But would you please tell me why you can't give us more than *six minutes* to get the job done?"

There was a long silence. In his mind's eye, Cade could see the aircrew conferring. Going over the good-news, bad-news options before deciding how much the guys in the truck *needed to know*. But when Meredith finally answered back he gave it to them straight. No smoke was getting blown up anyone's keister. There was no gray area to be considered, and the co-pilot pulled no punches. "Not to put any added pressure on you Delta boys, but if you were up here and could see how many Zs are closing in on your position from the west, you and I wouldn't even be having this conversation. Six minutes *is* the fastest we can prepare the aircraft in order to carry out this type of landing. You take longer than six minutes to clear that stretch of I-90 and I'm afraid there will be too many Zs on the rollout for the pilot to even consider this extremely difficult proposition."

Cade heard a click and some static, then the droning white noise returned and Meredith added, "There is no cowcatcher on this bird. Only four very large guillotines ... so if you don't give us at the minimum two thousand feet to land we'll be forced to abort."

Cade did the math in his head. Two thousand feet equaled a distance slightly less than seven football fields. He thought harder. Converted that and came up with just over a third of a mile. "Solid copy," he said. "Do you have eyes on a suitable spot farther west or east of our location? Just in case? That is, if I can wring another couple of miles of forward travel out of this truck."

"Negative, Captain. That clusterfuck you just squeaked through goes on for miles behind the pileup. Farther on ahead of you is a no-go as well. Closer to the center of town, both lanes are choked up, not to mention the fact that some genius at SDDOT decided it'd be a good idea to erect what look like sodium halide lights down the center of the interstate every hundred yards or so."

Suddenly second guessing his decision to follow the interstate, Cade asked, "What if I go off-roading and get us to one of those feeders? Can you land and pick us up there?"

Hearing this and knowing from experience that the truck wouldn't survive an overland stint as loaded down as it was, Jasper came out of his funk and shook his head noticeably.

"Negative," said the pilot this time. "Side roads are too narrow. Plus there's more dead down there than you can imagine. They're all over. It's a good thing your bird didn't come down a half a *click* further. Because if it had ... all of your bones would be picked clean by now."

Cade made no reply. He let his silence do the talking.

"Captain, I assure you this is the only viable spot ... your only open window," added the co-pilot. "Use it or lose it."

"One miracle coming right up," Cade intoned, starting the timer in his head ticking off the precious seconds.

Ignoring the quip, Meredith craned his head and watched precious jet fuel sluicing from each wingtip and into the atmosphere. At 500 gallons per minute, per wing-mounted dump mast—of which there were two—a quick calculation told him the Hercules would be 13,500 pounds lighter in just under four minutes. And if all went as planned, the internal tank would be emptied and Dover would have them turning back to the west to start on final approach which would take a minute and change from touchdown to a complete stop.

Cade's ear bud crackled again. It was Meredith this time and he said: *"Just to be on the safe side, the flight engineer recommends an additional three hundred yards."*

Cade shook his head and didn't bother replying or reconverting the new distance. With the odds already stacked as highly against them as they were, what was an added football-field-length between friends. A little under half a mile of I-90 with Zs crushing in from both sides, four vehicles that needed to be moved, and a hair under six minutes in which to accomplish the feat. *No pressure at all*, Cade thought as he ground the pick-up to a sudden stop alongside a garish-looking lime green Camaro. Suddenly the truck's engine, which was ticking like a time bomb, seemed to have developed a mind of its own; the rpms fluctuated wildly between nearly stalling out and racing into the red. And to make matters worse, Cade saw another delicate curl of vapor waft from underneath the hood. "Go, go, go," he said into the comms while simultaneously holding the brake and applying a little throttle in order to keep the engine from dying. He watched Hicks, pistol in hand, leap from the back of the truck and hit the ground at a slow trot. "Stay frosty," Cade said to the SOAR crew chief, who had lobbied for this first leg after claiming to have run cross-country in high school and insisting he could still pull down a consistent sub-six-minute-mile. A tick later, Hicks was crouched low and peering inside the low-to-the-ground American-made muscle car. A second after that he flashed a thumbs up and called out that the car was *clear* and indicated that he was *going in.*

Cade experienced a sudden flood of relief as he witnessed Hicks fold his frame inside. A third second passed and he saw Hicks's upper body tilt sideways, searching the column and dash no doubt. Another two seconds passed and then Hicks said, "No keys." He put a hand on the sleek roofline and with a disgruntled look on his face pulled himself to standing.

Shit, thought Cade upon hearing the news he had been dreading. Who in the hell takes the keys with them during a viral outbreak when there isn't a snowball's chance in hell of getting roadside assistance?

"What now?" asked Hicks.

"Gotta push it," Cade replied. Then he did a quick computation in his head and figured the distance between the Camaro and the rally point to be a little over a half of a mile. So if Hicks hadn't been bullshitting about his running prowess, then making it from here to the rally point in less than two minutes was doable, and that was assuming he could first complete the most important part of his task in under four minutes. *A slim margin indeed.*

"Get it done," Cade said, shifting his focus to the second vehicle of the four which were spread across I-90 like a right leaning 'Z'. The green Camaro had been on the right-hand shoulder—the *tail* of the 'Z'. Their next objective, a copper-colored sub-compact sat in the breakdown lane diagonally opposite the Camaro, two hundred yards ahead.

As they motored along, Cade kept the wheel steady and the truck vectoring toward the distant compact. Then he shot another look over his shoulder just in time to see Hicks with his head down, back bowed like the St. Louis Arch, pushing the Camaro towards the embankment.

One down, three to go, Cade thought. Then he hailed the Hercules which had continued west, hanging a brilliant corona around the sun as the aerated fuel drifted gently groundward.

The reply from Oil Can Five-Five came back at once, with the co-pilot indicating the mission was still a go and the play clock was ticking. With the weight of the world pressing down on his shoulders, Cade checked his watch, duly noting the quickly diminishing time rendered in liquid crystal display. *Four minutes and thirty seconds.* He shook his head. *Not a lot of time,* he concluded glumly.

With one foot hopping between the gas and brake to keep Jasper's truck running, Cade took multitasking to another level by flicking on the wipers and giving the windshield a liberal spraying of cleaning formula. And as the blades scoured a portal in the thick glaze of detritus and bodily fluids, a quick glance towards Hicks sent a cold chill running the length of his spine. Dozens of monsters, having pursued them through the automotive maze, were now fanning out on the desolate roadway. Hicks, who seemed oblivious of the interlopers, was hunched over, hands on knees, his back visibly rising and falling with each labored breath as the Camaro slowly rolled away from him. A tick later gravity took over and the car rocked gently as it crossed over the rumble strips. Finally it cleared the shoulder, slid over the gradual embankment, and disappeared from sight like a ship swallowed by the sea.

"Good going, Hicks," Cade said into the comms. "No way I can come back and get you. So you're going to have to crack off a sub-two-minute third-of-a-mile. Can't let the Zs get in Oil Can's way ... so I'm going to need you to thin them out a bit before you bolt."

"Roger that," Hicks answered back. "Give me ten seconds and I'll be Oscar Mike."

With a fusillade of hollow-sounding gunshots coming over the open channel, Cade flicked his gaze forward and pulled in tight alongside the copper, two-door Japanese econo-box. Still belted inside the static Honda Civic were two very rotten creatures, and snugged down in the rear were a pair of unoccupied car seats. Whether the absence of the little ones who usually rode in them was a good sign or meant something more ominous Cade couldn't decide. "Lopez," he said. "I'm afraid you get the honors on this one."

"Why me, Wyatt?" the stocky operator asked. "You gave the flyboy the *empty* sports car. And I get this stinking *demonio* mobile?"

Not wanting to add fuel to the fire, Cade made no reply. Then, after a second of silence, the truck jounced slightly, a sign that Lopez had bounded out and was on the move. A quick peek in the mirror told Cade that the operator had forgone the M4 and was working his way around the Honda with a black semi-automatic pistol clutched in his right hand.

"What if there are no keys?" asked Jasper.

"He'll improvise. He's got plenty of time," Cade lied. A quick peek at the Suunto confirmed this, telling him another twenty seconds had slipped into the past.

As he pulled away from the Civic, he gazed towards the stark white Budweiser logo emblazoned on the flank of the eighteen-wheeler truck he'd already deemed the next greatest obstacle to their success or failure. But before he had driven twenty yards, a burst of static followed by Lopez's voice sounded in his ear. "Wyatt, I have a feeling you're discriminating against me," the Hispanic operator intoned. "First Desantos ... may he rest in peace ... makes me carry a demonio up from the CDC basement, and now I gotta deal with these."

"Sergeant, your orders are to *move* the car and then get your butt to the rally point," Cade replied sharply. "I don't care how you do it or if there are a dozen *demonios* crammed in that piece of tin. Just make it happen." Then, knowing how the mere sight of a festering, living corpse got under the religious man's skin, Cade made a conscious decision to forgive the glaring example of insubordination. The muttering and thinking aloud had become commonplace as of late, and for the most part everyone involved had learned to ignore it. Besides, Cade thought to himself. Lopez had already proven himself time and again and was far too valuable an operator to let a couple of apocalypse-induced idiosyncrasies alienate him from the team.

"I've got three walkers on our right. Four o'clock," said Hicks. "Engaging."

"Roger that," said Cade. He kept his foot on the brake and watched as Hicks prepared the optics atop Tice's M4. After swinging the 3x magnifier in place, he snugged the carbine to his shoulder, paused for a beat, and dropped all three Zs in a calm, controlled manner. Three muffled shots, spaced closely together, did the trick. Only three seconds gone, thought Cade as he cut the wheel hard right and goosed the ailing engine, an action that was met with an unusual vibration and yet another burst of white steam.

191

"You're up next, Cross ... sure you can drive an eighteen-wheeler?" Cade said, remembering his very own nearly failed attempt a week ago. Bouncing the dirt-brown UPS rig like a juiced Impala had been embarrassing to say the least. That he'd done it with Desantos sitting in the cab next to him made it all the worse. With the memory of his late friend fresh in his mind, he nosed the truck on a collision course with the humongous cab, more determined than ever to get everyone home alive.

"Get me close," Cross said.

Cade replied, "Roger that."

"*Do not stop*," added Cross, a touch of concern evident in his voice. "Just slow. Bring the rigs flank-to-flank and I'll jump out."

"And if you bust an ankle ... how are you gonna work the clutch so you can shift through all those gears?"

"We are running out of time, Captain. So please ... just slow down and I'll jump," Cross said, popping his head over top of the cab to get a better view. "Besides, the rest of the walkers are on to us now. And real soon they're going to be coming at us thick from our twelve o'clock."

"How many?" asked Cade.

"Too many to count," Cross said at once. "Definitely too many of them to take on toe-to-toe. Looks like the pilot was right ... the window is closing on us."

Cade grimaced and nodded. Then, still smarting from the sting of the answer, took a quick mental inventory of their weapons and ammunition. The latter of which they were already low on after having had to fight their way out of the NBL in Winnipeg. They'd lost the other two M4s along with his backpack and the satellite phone when the fuselage had ripped open upon impact. With the dead moving in from all corners, there had been no time to search the area around the crash site. He considered it a blessing they were able to recover Tice's body before fleeing. Hicks and Lopez had completely burned through their spare magazines, meaning both of their M4s were out of the fight. So that left them with the SCAR Cross had adopted as his own, and however many magazines were left from the ones they'd taken off of Gaines's body. "Almost there," Cade said as the gleaming semi loomed near.

Gripping the bed rail with one hand, Sig Sauer pistol in the other, Cross planted a boot on the fender well and coiled his leg muscles, preparing to make the leap.

Chapter 38

"Didn't think this little guy could push that big 'ol Chevy, didja, el Capitan? So instead you give me this clown car of death to deal with," Lopez muttered under his breath as he approached the car in a combat crouch, pistol leading the way. Once he reached the car's rear quarter panel, he peered inside, keeping the 'B' pillar between the front and rear passenger doors between him and the Zs.

There were purple-ringed bite marks up and down both arms of the male demonio nearest him. He couldn't miss the deep crack running vertically from near the top of the glove box to the defroster vents where it had beaten on the dash. And there was a haze with all the opacity of Vaseline coating the windshield and side windows, everywhere the rotting cadavers could reach.

Lopez went to a knee, craned his neck, and sized up the undead woman. At some time in the past, blood had cascaded over its chin and chest and then dried to black, obscuring whatever silly saying was on the tee shirt. After determining there was nothing lurking in the backseat save for stale Cheerios, tiny articles of clothing and the two car seats, Lopez performed the sign of the cross over his body armor and wrenched open the passenger door.

Instantly a swarm of small black insects fled the overwhelming pong inside the car that started the contents of his stomach—however little existed—on an involuntary upward journey. *No vomiting for this hombre*, he told himself. And though he'd been nearly immune to the untoward effects of the stench of carrion since the first days of the apocalypse, the ripe nature of these two festering corpses nearly made a liar out of him. Fighting the urge to vomit, he stepped back from the invisible wall of stench and drew a bead between nose and brow. The black pistol roared two times as he delivered a perfect double tap.

With nothing but open road around the compact, and flatland around everything else, the tremendous noise from the closely-spaced blasts set his ears to ringing.

Breathing through his mouth to keep the vomit at bay, he ducked his head inside the car and peered past the destruction he'd caused. But there was no way to avoid having to look at the gray matter and splintered cranium that had peppered the female Z.

As he looked in, the creature hissed and strained and bucked, causing more of the dead passenger's scalp and brains to take flight, further sullying the interior. *Must have turned quickly*, thought Lopez, noticing the three-inch-length of jugular snaking from a fleshy crater on the driver's neck. He stuck the pistol across the male's corpse and put two quick shots through the female Z's temple. He said a quick prayer for the twice-dead duo and added a few words for whoever normally rode in the empty kiddie seats. He closed the passenger door and looped around the back bumper, and happened to glance down the interstate to see Hicks running towards him, arms pumping, black combat boots beating the hot roadway. Behind Hicks, a number of Zs littered the ground, sprawled out motionless in ever-widening pools of blood. And to make matters worse, he could see at least two dozen more picking their way slowly through the phalanx of blackened vehicles.

The driver's door was locked, so he pushed in the spiderwebbed glass with the reinforced plastic cap on his tactical elbow pad, hooked an arm inside, and popped the door open. He reached across the leaking corpse and poked the seatbelt release. The restraint reeled back of its own accord before snagging on what was left of the Z's face. Thankful he was wearing two pairs of the purple surgical gloves Cade's wife had given him, he grabbed the corpse by the neck and yanked it out onto the roadway. Then, anticipation mounting, stepped over the leaking corpse, literally slipped onto the gore-covered seat, and reached blindly around the steering column. "We have keys," he blurted over the comms a beat later. "On the move," he added after the engine caught and he slipped the car into gear.

Hearing this bit of good news, Cade prayed out loud, asking God for more of the same.

"He ain't listening," said Jasper in a funereal voice. "Hasn't been receptive to pleas of any kind for quite some time."

Making no reply, Cade brought the Chevy to a near crawl beside the beer truck and watched via the side mirror a surprising display of agility as the tight-end-sized Cross vaulted fluidly from the pick-up, planted both boots dead center on the big rig's running board, and grabbed a chromed bar affixed vertically head-high to him just aft of the driver's door.

Impressive, thought Cade as he cranked the wheel left, and as insurance against Mister Murphy, who had been absent for an inordinate amount of time, looped around behind the semi just in case Cross couldn't get it moving. Waiting for word either way, he looked left at the Honda which Lopez had already parked on the grassy median.

"The cab is clear but there are no keys."

Cade's heart sank. This was exactly what he'd been afraid of. And the reason he'd parked behind the semi. If a strongman can make the Guinness Book by pulling a 747 with his teeth, Cade reasoned, then pushing it aside with Jasper's truck shouldn't be outside the realm of possibility.

"Think your truck can push that truck?" Cade asked Jasper.

The undertaker shook his head. "Negative," he said. "No way."

Cade was about to call bullshit and give it a try when Dover's voice crackled in his ear bud, warning him that at the very least the eighteen-wheeler and the Zulus at the east end had to go. And to further ramp up the tension, he mentioned they were on final approach and counting down from two minutes.

"The semi will be gone in ninety seconds," Cade assured the pilot.

"And the Zs?" asked the co-pilot.

"We'll take care of those as well," Cade responded. "Anvil out."

196

He jogged the transmission to the lowest available gear and nudged the throttle. A groan, metallic in nature, emanated from the Chevy's front end where the bumper and grill met up with the semi-trailer. Simultaneously two things happened: The eighteen-wheeler rumbled to life and began to slowly pull away, and Cross said in his ear, "At Rawley they taught us more than just how to protect the principal."

**

While Cade had been conversing with the aircrew on the Hercules, Cross had been busy.

In the span of two seconds the operator had taken a quick glance inside, seeing if it was empty. Two more ticked by while he broke a window and climbed into the vacant cab. A dozen more seconds were burned searching the visor, glove box, and various cubbies looking for a hidden spare. Upon finding nothing, he wasted no time bemoaning his bad luck. Instead, he popped off the plastic shroud surrounding the inner workings of the steering column—two more gone. Then he unceremoniously yanked a number of multi-colored wires into a bar of sunlight where he could see them. They had been secured together with some kind of thermal shrink-wrap and were connected by a group of white plastic male-into-female couplings. Three more seconds were on the books by the time he located the correct wires. Then another ten rolled by while he stripped them using his multitool and touched them together.

He had broken into the truck and started it without a key in a hair over thirty seconds. A hell of a feat if he were being measured against a common car thief. Surely not the best time amongst his peers at the JJRTC—(James J. Rowley Training Center) just outside of Washington D.C. where he'd learned and perfected the fine art of Presidential protection—but hopefully quick enough to move a bomb-laden vehicle from the path of a Presidential motorcade if necessary. Which was exactly why he'd been taught how to hotwire every kind of wheeled vehicle, and why he'd continued to perfect the particular skillset even after the rigorous eighteen-week Special Agent Training Course he'd endured at Rowley.

Thankfully Valerie Clay was at Schriever safe and sound, he thought, working the clutch, gas, and the arms' length shifter like he'd been driving long haul his whole life. But the reality of the matter was that he and the others were here, in harm's way, with a large number of dead tightening around them like a noose on a horse thief's neck. Not to mention the added pressure of the multi-ton mass of metal that looked about as aerodynamic as a brick and much too plump to get airborne—let alone stay aloft—was relentlessly bearing down on them from the east.

After getting the eighteen-wheeler hot-wired and moving, Cross upshifted quickly, putting a head of steam behind the old Peterbilt cab-over. He eyed the maroon minivan, upshifted and then glanced down at the speedometer and saw the needle pass the thirty-miles-per-hour mark. Keeping the static vehicle positioned off the right fender, he upshifted again. *Thirty-five.* Then in no time the eighteen wheeler's speed surged past forty and there was no turning back.

***

Inside the Chevy, Cade and Ari had watched, mouths ajar, as the looming tailgate vibrated and the truck pulled smoothly away. With the shrill whine of spooling gears fading, Cade turned the Chevy back into the center of the interstate, looped around to the east, and steered straight for Lopez; at the last instant, he jogged the wheel a degree and slowed to a crawl, allowing the visibly-winded operator a chance to hook an arm on the bed and get ahold of the tailgate. Feet moving as fast as his bulky boots would allow, the stocky operator got a toe on the rear bumper and threw himself over the tailgate.

"Good work, Lowrider," said Cade, looking into the mirror.

Flashing a thumbs up, Lopez said, "You are going to have to pick up Hicks ... fool's high school conditioning is long gone." Then he spun around on one knee, looked eastward at about a twenty degree angle to pick out the gray speck on the horizon and said, "Better make it fast ... or Oil Can Five-Five is going to land on our heads."

In his ear, Cade heard the pilot say in his subtle Texan drawl: *"So far so good, Anvil Actual. Wheels down in ninety seconds. Great job, miracle worker."*

Hoping the pilot was understating the time to touchdown, Cade said, "Roger that," and pointed the truck towards Hicks, who was moving like his boots were made of lead, not leather. In a matter of seconds Cade had covered the distance, but when he pulled alongside and stood on the brakes, the Chevy's radiator finally went Old Faithful

Chapter 39
South Dakota
Aboard Oil Can Five-Five

Taking into consideration the elevation, pressure altitude, current outside temperature, present wind direction, and Oil Can's weight—which was considerably less after the high flow fuel dump—the flight engineer aboard the Hercules had been busy crunching numbers in order to work up the data necessary for his pilot to nail a successful Max Effort Landing.

After consulting the data written out on a sheet of paper in the flight engineer's easy-to-read hand, Dover watched the altimeter slip through one thousand feet AGL (Above Ground Level) and begin ticking down towards five hundred feet AGL. About to perform one of the most difficult maneuvers to pull off in the KC-130 platform, he strained against his straps, testing them in advance of the looming rapid deceleration. That he wasn't being shot at in the process was a plus. That he could see too many Zs to count slowly threading their way through the stationary vehicles at both ends of his runway set the hairs on the back of his neck at attention. *Two birds with one stone*, he thought as he looked through the portside glass and watched the eighteen-wheeler pick up speed on a collision course with the last remaining obstacle on his runway. And though his senses were overwhelmed by the plane's vibration and engine sound and the voices filtering in and out of his headset, he knew the impact between the truck and the smaller vehicle had been catastrophic. Glittering in the sun like some kind of an airburst firework, the silent eruption of broken glass bloomed and fell to earth, then bounced and skittered across the far lane. Next, the windowless shell of the van, its chassis shortened by at least three feet, followed the rapidly-spreading carpet of broken auto glass; after three full rotations across the black top, it bounced down the shrub-covered embankment, finally stopping with its grimy undercarriage pointing skyward.

Down on I-90, at the same time Hicks was being helped into the back of the Chevy by Lopez, the explosive sound of breaking glass and crumpling metal garnered Cade's attention. He jerked his head around towards the noise and then bellowed into the comms, urging Cross to bail out of the runaway rig. *Too late*, he thought as the Peterbilt with Cross behind the wheel pushed the minivan over the shoulder and into space.

Meanwhile, aboard the Peterbilt, Cross had just popped the door latch when Cade's voice sounded in his ear bud ordering him to bail out. With no time to reply, he dove from the cab, catching a glimpse of the speedometer on the way out. *Fifty miles per hour. Shit, this is going to hurt,* he thought as everything seemed to slow to a crawl. Taking note of every pebble and shard of gravel as the ground rushed up at him, he made a conscious decision and whipped his head left, hoping his body would follow suit. From the corner of his eye he registered the flash of chrome and paint as the semi barreled over the edge. Then he hit the sloped hillside like a missile, his right flank absorbing most of the impact. Instincts kicked in and he pulled his arms and legs tight and rolled, letting his helmet, tactical elbow, and knee pads take the brunt of the trauma as his speed bled off and he came to a grinding halt, on his back, head downhill, bruised and dusty—but alive.

He looked downhill; everything was topsy-turvy and upside down. His eyes picked up and followed the furrow of churned earth and broken bottles and dented cans, some still spewing geysers of foamy beer. His gaze walked the glittering wet trail all the way to the tangled jumble of metal where the tractor trailer had come to rest atop the newly flattened minivan. And there, staring him straight in the face, rendered in white, red, and black on the trailer's rippled sheet metal was a giant-sized bottle of Budweiser complete with golf-ball-sized beads of condensation. Suddenly reminded of how thirsty he was, he fumbled for the spout on his hydration pack and took a long pull. He dropped the spout and swished the water around in his mouth, letting it linger there, allowing the dehydrated pores to hungrily absorb the liquid for a second before swallowing. He ran his hands up and down his legs and inspected his arms one at a time, fully expecting to find a fracture or three, but discovered nothing obvious. Nothing bad enough to keep him from clawing his way back up to the interstate. But before he started his ascent he needed to get his wind back. He closed his eyes, breathing in and out, shallow breaths at first, listening hard to his surroundings. His heart hammered against his sternum, sending a tidal surge of blood flowing through his head, a whooshing sound that was slowly subsiding. Then, two distinct and very familiar sounds caught his attention— one more so than the other. From uphill and to the right he heard the inbound Hercules—a welcoming noise that came across like the incessant buzzing of an angry swarm of bees. While downhill and to the left came the unmistakable, telltale sounds of the dead—the wanting dry rasp indicative of a first turn, to be exact—and without looking, he could tell there was more than one.

He rolled to his stomach, extended his left arm, and pushed off the sloping ground. Beads of sweat exploded from his forehead and a cold chill wracked his body as the initial surge of adrenaline started giving way to pain. Craning his neck around a chest-high shrub, prickly against his cheek and smelling like cat urine, he swept his eyes along the debris field and spotted the offending parties.

But not before they had noticed him.

Downslope, a dozen feet away, a trio of first turns navigated the shrubs which had been planted with little landscaping forethought in a basic grid pattern at roughly three-foot intervals. Beyond the trio, he spotted another dozen stumbling across the grassy median on the near side of the road paralleling the interstate.

"This is Cross," he said between labored breaths. "I'm OK, and making my way back up to the interstate. How copy?"

Nothing. There was no response. Then he realized he hadn't heard the usual click from the voice-activated throat mike. The subliminal hiss of white noise usually present in the background was also absent. He felt his right ear for the ear bud and found it missing, torn away presumably from the impact or the subsequent two-second spin cycle he'd ridden on the way down. *You're on your own*, he said to himself. He stood nearly erect, left foot planted on the downhill side, and though his right elbow and shoulder throbbed with a low intensity pain that was getting worse by the second, he aimed cross-body and double tapped the nearest of the three Zs in the forehead. And as the near headless abomination slid downhill through the remnants of its own brains, Cross sat down hard, dug both heels into the hillside, and drew a bead on the first turn making most of the racket. That it had recently made a meal of someone's entrails was a foregone conclusion, made all the more evident by the fact that its dirty blond hair was pasted to its head with a shiny coating of congealed blood and assorted other bodily fluids.

Cross took a deep calming breath and pumped two .357 rounds into its open mouth, rose to standing on shaky legs, and hustled uphill as fast as his battered extremities would carry him.

***

No sooner than Lopez and Hicks were safely in the box-bed, Cade had turned the wheel and accelerated. He looked through the sweeping turn and watched the tail end of the trailer disappear from sight. "Cross, how copy?" he said into the comms. *Nothing.* Nearing the point where the truck left the road, he tried hailing the agent again and was met with silence in his ear and the gnawing feeling that they would be burying yet another team member alongside Desantos and Maddox.

Slewing the truck sideways and halting parallel on the shoulder, Cade ordered Lopez to stand up and take a quick peek, stressing the fact that the Hercules was on its final approach.

Suddenly his ear bud crackled to life. "Anvil Actual, how copy?" said the disembodied voice.

Cade answered, "Solid copy, Oil Can Five-Five. Miracle accomplished."

"Roger that," said Dover. "Better rally to the extraction point. We will be wheels down and rolling out in less than one minute. And be advised you have Zs entering my runway to the east."

"Solid copy," Cade replied. "We will take them out ASAP. Anvil out."

The truck rocked on its suspension as Lopez stood on the wheel well in order to see down the hill.

"I see the truck," said Lopez. "And it don't look good, Captain."

"Do you see any signs of Cross?"

"Negative," Lopez said at about the same instant Cross— dust-covered from head to toe and limping like he'd been beaten— rose from behind a shrub twenty feet downslope. "Disregard, Captain. I have eyes on Cross."

"Roger that," Cade answered back. "Is he ambulatory?"

"Affirmative," Lopez answered back.

"Just what I needed to hear. I need you and Hicks to help him get up here on the double ... our freedom bird is forty-five seconds out." He looked past Ari and out Jasper's window and saw the Hercules, nose down at an impossible angle, its barn-door sized flaps which ran along two-thirds of the wings' trailing edges already deployed at a ninety-degree angle. His first impression of the plummeting aircraft was that something wasn't right. The Hercules looked like a giant gray lawn dart about to spear the ground. But while Cade gaped like a bystander at a fatal wreck, the Herc slowly nosed up out of the dive, and landing gear wrapped with huge black tires that looked like they could take a pounding sprouted from the nose and amidships.

"Captain, Hicks is not good to go," said Lopez into the comms. "He's mumbling something about someone named Kylie. I think he has snapped or something."

"You're on your own, Lopez."

Without a word Lopez bounded from the truck and ran down the embankment and disappeared from sight.

"What's the matter, Hicks?" asked Cade, twisting around in his seat in order to try and establish eye contact.

Silence. The Ghost Hawk crew chief was sitting on the wheel arch with his legs draped across the dead, eyes transfixed on something in the far away distance. *A sudden onset of PTSD?* Cade wondered. If he was correct, it was a long time coming, considering all they had been through since Z-Day. At any rate, he concluded, Hicks was now no more useful than Jasper had been at the onset of his episode, and considering their current predicament there was nothing he or anybody else could do until they were all safely aboard the Hercules. Then, splitting his time between watching the incoming bird and casting looks back at Hicks, Cade ticked off the seconds in his head. And when he reached ten he said, "We gotta go, Lopez. We need to be clear of the road." He cast his gaze right and saw movement to the east near where the Hercules would be coming in. Looking like flocked Christmas trees and contrasting dramatically against the sooty black wall of metal, the little summer camp zombies were approaching at twice as fast a pace as the others. Then he looked left and noticed a new group of Zs emerging from the nearby snarl of vehicles in twos and threes, rapidly spreading out across the Interstate.

Chapter 40
South Dakota
Aboard Oil Can Five-Five

Setting his gaze on the hundred-foot-wide swath of scorched interstate, Dover noted the numerous burned-out automobiles and the looming tractor-trailer rig that his tail would need to clear prior to setting the Hercules down on the two-lane. Slowly he started bringing the flaps into play, throttling back simultaneously, eyes flicking over the gauges and indicators. He flipped a lever bringing the landing gear out of their housings, and when the proper indicators lit up he said, "Gear down. Flaps full. Holding max effort threshold."

To Dover's right, Meredith rattled off a few updates. He stated the current wind speed which was almost nonexistent. Then his voice changed timbre. Like he'd just been surprised, he said, "You've got Zs east side on the inbound approach."

"Roger that. I see them. Are those kids?"

"They were at one time," intoned the co-pilot.

Dover went silent for half a heartbeat. Craned his head trying to assess the situation, then said matter-of-factly, "Committing fully." And during that nanosecond in time when he'd made the final decision from which there would be no return, he registered a snapshot of the scene in his mind. Forty feet below the Hercules, the twisted and melted metal skeletons of what used to be cars and trucks sat fused together, a black tangle of instantaneous death by immolation. And just beyond the accident scene where the makeshift runway began, a couple of dozen zombies, child-sized and seemingly painted brilliant white, were frozen mid-stride. Then, the last thing that registered before he flicked his eyes up were their pale, sneering faces flashing by under the Herc's nose.

***

On Interstate 90

"Anvil Actual. You have exactly *thirty-five* ... that's *three* ... *five* seconds to clear the runway," said the Herc's co-pilot.

"Copy that," said Cade as he witnessed Cross's dust-coated black helmet break the horizon. A tick later, Lopez, who was a half-head shorter than the President's security man, came into view. He had Cross's left arm draped over his shoulder and appeared to be helping to steady him more so than actually bearing any body weight.

Making eye contact with Cade, Cross tapped his helmet over his right ear and then drew a finger across his throat, combined gestures that explained fully why the operator had gone radio silent.

"Help's on the way, Lopez," said Cade. Then he nudged Ari lightly, looked past him, and addressed Jasper directly. "Ari, cut Jasper loose."

After a triple take Ari flicked open his multi-tool and cut the undertaker's bonds.

Cade leaned across Ari. He looked Jasper in the eye and said, "Ari, I need you and Jasper to get out and help them in this vehicle. Throw them in if you have to ... you OK with that, Jasper?"

Nodding an affirmative, Jasper popped his door open, and with a burst of speed that belied his size, leapt out and was helping Lopez manhandle Cross into the back before Ari had gotten his legs untangled from the transmission hump.

"Forget about it," said Cade, placing his arm across Ari's chest. "That was a test. I needed to know if we could count on him to help move the bodies up the Herc's ramp when the time comes."

"By the looks of it I think he's passed with flying colors," Ari said as he watched the undertaker help Lopez into the back by physically lifting the operator over the tailgate.

OK. Now get your ass inside here, thought Cade as he watched Lopez helping Hicks to find a place to sit that would be safer than the raised wheel well. Finally, after a couple of the longest seconds of

Cade's life, he saw Jasper's fingers curl around the grab handle. Simultaneously, he goosed the throttle and hauled the steering wheel left, a move that rolled the truck hard to the passenger side on its tired springs.

Feeling the truck lurch and sensing the loading g-forces, Ari made a grab for the loose fabric of the undertaker's sweat stained shirt.

With one leg in the footwell and only half a butt cheek on the bench seat, Jasper snared Ari's extended hand, and after a hair-raising couple of seconds with the ground rushing beyond the open door pulled himself fully into the cab, crowded Ari, and slammed the door shut.

"Good work getting my men in back, Mister Literal," said Cade, ignoring the fact he'd almost turned Jasper into street pizza.

Jasper made a face. Opened his mouth but said nothing.

Cade used the opening. Flicking his eyes from the road ahead and the Hercules' reflection in the rearview, he said, "I owe you one for that. But we're not out of the woods yet. Cross ... he looks like he's firing on half a cylinder. Hicks is damn near catatonic. And—"

"I get it," said Jasper, his voice cracking slightly. "Whatever you need from me here on out, just ask."

"That's the spirit," said Ari, earning an elbow shot from Cade to his already more-than-tender ribcage.

Deviating from his course by a degree, Cade urged the truck to the right, sideswiped a trio of zombies and wiped them clean off the interstate. "I hate to impose," said Cade. "But I'm going to need your help transferring our fallen teammates to the airplane after it lands. Just be a little more gentle with them than you were with Lopez and Cross. Can I count on you for that?"

"Yes," said Jasper softly. "I'm sorry I lost it back there. That was the largest group of those things that I'd seen in one place, at one time, and that close. One of those things is bad enough ... especially when it's a family member. But back there, right then, seeing all those dead kids showed me the enormity of this great die-off. I thought I saw *my* kids back there ... it was all in my head. I know that now."

"Understandable," Cade replied as he eased off the gas. "You've been burying Draper all by yourself for the last two weeks. I've buried a few myself. Same thing probably happened to Hicks. He just lost his good friend Durant ... " Cade nodded towards the corpses arranged in the box-bed.

Jasper made no reply.

Once again Cade's ear bud crackled to life. "Ten seconds," a disembodied voice said with all the emotion of someone calling out bingo numbers.

This prompted Cade to crane his head out the window. He saw the Hercules clear the immolated tractor-trailer with only inches to spare, and just before its landing gear contacted the ground he caught a flash of the child zombies' upturned white faces tracking it as it buzzed over their heads.

Eyeing the breakdown lane, Cade kept the pedal floored. He watched the needle creep past *thirty* then on to *forty* and then risked another look over his shoulder.

"Wheels down," Dover said in his ear, confirming what he was witnessing. Blasted by the turbulence following the settling aircraft, several of the tiny flesh-eaters toppled and rolled, white dust devils spinning in their wake. For some reason the channel remained open and he heard someone in the cockpit say, "Reversing thrust." Then he heard nothing but the cacophonous roar of Oil Can's four humongous Rolls Royce engines rising to a crescendo as it rolled up on their six. He stole a glance at Cross and read his lips; the man was urging him to drive faster with a few eff bombs inserted between the pertinent words. He regarded Lopez and it came as no surprise to see the operator performing the sign of the cross over his chest. Hicks, however, had slumped over and was laying prone, head resting on the general's exposed entrails, staring wide-eyed at the sky.

Then Oil Can's engine noise changed pitch and the roar escalated to a sonic tempest he guessed was somewhere in the decibel range of a category five hurricane. "Come on girl," he said under his breath. "Don't die on me now." No sooner had the words passed his lips than the instrument panel lit up with small instantly recognizable symbols that basically screamed out, *"Too late for oil, kiss your engine goodbye."*

He pulled far off the interstate and jammed the Chevy to a stop. It listed to the passenger side as the shoulder settled under its weight. "Time to make a stand, boys," he said, killing the engine.

But it didn't want to die. The motor, as if demonically possessed, kept up a knocking sound for a beat and then finally seized up, belching blue-gray smoke, smelling like pit row at the Indy 500. Issuing a series of orders over the comms, Cade holstered his compact Glock and reached behind him to accept the M4 Lopez was passing through the rear slider.

With the Zs less than thirty feet away, Lopez grabbed another carbine and checked the mag. *Empty.* He reached beneath Tice's corpse and stripped the last two magazines from the dead man's chest rig. Dropped the empty from his M4 and seated a fully-loaded thirty-round mag into the well. In one fluid movement he charged the weapon, flicked the selector to single shot, and spiraled into a combat crouch. Weathered paint cracking under his weight, he rested both elbow pads on the sheet metal roof and made a conscious effort to calm his breathing. Snugging the carbine in tight, he said to himself, "Make them count, *pinche.*" He hovered the red holographic pip on the closest walker and his senses went into what he liked to call *quicksand mode.* At once his vision sharpened and he became acutely aware of every sound around him. First he heard the truck's passenger door creak open, then the scuffle of boots on pavement. A second later he saw and heard the driver's side swing open. And to the front the sounds the dead were making got exponentially louder, giving the Hercules running up on their six a run for its money.

***

Cade shouldered the door open, twisted his upper body, and wrapped both hands around the grab bar near his head. Then, with the steady reports of Lopez's silenced weapon reassuring in his ears, and the spent brass pinging off the hood and roadway, he tightened his grip and lifted his weight from the seat. Being careful not to bang his foot into the doorframe, he angled the bulky size twelve around, swung his good leg after, and pulled himself to a standing position.

Testing his ankle's ability to support his full weight, he let go completely, wavered but didn't fall. Next, with one hand on the door, he tested his full weight. The pain came on sudden and fierce. Pulsed up his leg, transited his ribcage, rattling his senses. Like he'd broken an age-old cardinal sin and stuck a fork in a toaster, the jolt attacked his central nervous system and was gone.

Hanging his head and taking slow, shallow breaths, he steeled himself for the test to come. Then, gripping the box-bed, he took three consecutive steps. Sweat beading on his forehead, he stopped near the rear wheel. He took in a lungful of rank air, pivoted on his right heel and immediately embarked on the three-step return trip. He certainly wouldn't be dancing anytime soon. But he was fairly confident if need be he could make it from the Chevy to the rescue bird unaided.

While he'd been testing his ankle, the Hercules had slowed considerably and was within a hundred yards, nose wheel rolling along the dashed yellow lines off to their left, its huge six-bladed propellers whirling so fast an optical illusion was created making them seem to bend and warp like something from Dr. Seuss's imagination.

He received a tap on the shoulder and turned to see Ari and Jasper standing behind Cross, his black uniform now a light shade of ochre. The special agent bent low and yelled to be heard over the airplane's engines. "We're going to have to clear the road." He pointed beyond the airplane which had pulled to a complete stop fifty yards to the fore and was just beginning to turn in place. "One of those kids gets chewed up by a prop and we might not make it home."

Cade glanced at the M4 on the seat next to him and shook his head at Cross while putting his palm up silently, indicating it was his problem to solve.

"I can take care of it for you, Captain," pressed Cross, his mouth an inch from Cade's ear.

Shaking his head side-to-side, eyes boring into Cross's, Cade mouthed, "I can't hear a thing." He cast his eyes to the fallen Zs littering the road in front of the pick-up. He watched Lopez swap mags and continue firing, then mouthed, "I'll take care of the little ones." Then he nodded and motioned Cross and Jasper towards the box-bed as the airplane's rounded wingtip scythed the air overhead.

Jasper acted first. Reaching into the box-bed, he wormed his arms under General Gaines and cradled the corpse close to his chest.

Using the M4 as a crutch, Cade limped away from the truck, hoping to find a spot with a clear line of sight towards the end of the makeshift runway. Finally, after laboring twenty feet along the shoulder, he found an acceptable location and took a knee. He swiveled his head, checking for stray Zs, and found only half a dozen in his vicinity. But they were thirty yards away, below his position, on the feeder road and probably wouldn't pose a problem. Wishing he had a spotter whom could watch his back, he drew the Glock—which held only one round—and placed it on the warm blacktop to his right. It would have to be his backup plan if the Zs caught hold of him. Next, he ripped his final magazine filled with thirty rounds of 5.56 hardball ammo from his chest rig, slapped it in the M4, and went flat to his stomach. He shifted around a little trying to get as comfortable as a guy with a pair of composite propellers slicing the air a handful of feet above his head could hope to get. Finding little comfort in the spot he'd chosen, he flipped the 3x magnifier in front of the holographic sight and searched for targets.

Chapter 41

Turning the KC-130 around in such tight confines took equal measures of skill and patience, and a couple of extra pairs of eyeballs watching out for anything that could snag a propeller, or wing pylon, or any one of the number of pieces of equipment mounted on the outside of the aircraft's fuselage.

First Dover had slowed and stopped the Hercules using the plane's built-in ability to reverse its propellers without shutting down the turbines. Then, slowly but surely, he rotated the Herc clockwise in place one-hundred-eighty-degrees, until the nose was pointed east away from the low hanging sun.

***

Lying in the shadow of the starboard wing, Cade went through the four fundamentals of marksmanship taught to him by his good friend and mentor, Major Greg Beeson.

Steady position: He splayed out his right leg and pressed his knee into the soft shoulder. *Check.*

Proper aim: To compensate for the drop of the bullet as well as the Z's lurching gait, he hovered the red pip a fist-width above the undead girl's head. *Check.*

Breathing: Taking steady, shallow breaths, he established a cadence. Inhaled slowly one final time, and then exhaled proportionately with his finger tightening on the trigger. *Check.*

Trigger squeeze: He drew back the last few ounces of trigger pull. There was a minimal kick to his shoulder and a shallow report which was lost in the noise created by the nearby airplane. A tick later he witnessed a puff of white and a mist of pink spray from the Z's shoulder area. *Fail.*

He glanced left and saw Jasper climbing the Hercules' cargo ramp with the general's limp body in his arms. Lopez rose up from the truck's roof, threw down the M4, and helped Hicks climb down from the box-bed.

"Captain Grayson," said Lopez. "Something's not right with Hicks. I'm wondering if he got bit."

Putting his eye to the optics, Cade repeated the Army's four fundamentals of marksmanship while answering back to Lopez. "Ask Cross if he saw anything."

"No time," said Lopez. "Cross is inside the plane helping the loadmaster secure the bodies. Dover says he wants to be wheels up in one mike."

"Roger that," said Cade as the first of the summer camp Zs went down, its little head disintegrating in a haloed cloud of flesh, brain, and splintered skull. He shifted aim right and dropped two more little flesh-eaters, and then noticed a new contingent of adult-sized creatures making their way onto the far end of the interstate.

Cade bellowed in order to be heard over the Herc's turboprops. "I need a sit rep from you, Lopez."

A second later Lopez replied. "Jasper just finished transferring the bodies aboard. I'm going in to check on Hicks."

"Listen," Cade said. "Even if you don't find any bites on Hicks, I want you to cuff him just to be on the safe side."

"Roger that. Time's running out, Captain. You need to get yourself aboard."

Cade made no reply. He drew a bead on the closest of the fast little Zs and dropped it to the road. He shifted aim and snapped off a dozen shots, enjoying a less than fifty-percent success rate on the others.

Then two things caught his attention at once: in his side vision he saw a fresh corpse cresting the embankment on his right, and from out of nowhere, barely audible over Oil Can's oppressive din, he heard an all-too-familiar sound. Craning his head all the way around, he ignored the fresh turn, looked over his right shoulder and saw the Chevy's crumpled and gore-spattered bumper and grill complete with the stove bolt Chevy emblem dead center bearing down on him fast. He followed the truck with his eyes as it swerved around him, peppering his face with hot rubber and gravel, then continued on a diagonal tack, narrowly avoiding the Hercules's outside starboard engine and deadly spinning prop. Then, at the last moment, when Cade was certain the truck was going to plunge over the embankment, whoever was driving course corrected and brought the rear-end back around, sending a rooster tail of dirt and gravel flying. There was an intermittent chirping from the tires as the truck drifted sideways, and finally a brief moment when the driver's full profile was presented and Cade learned that Jasper was behind the wheel.

He watched the truck for a spell and then squeezed a few more shots at the advancing monsters, and when the count in his head reached twenty-eight he swung the M4 a ninety-degree arc, flipped the 3x magnifier away and settled the holographic pip on the fresh turn's forehead.

For a brief second as the thing closed the distance, Cade second-guessed himself, wondering if he'd fouled up his count.

But thankfully his consternation was dispelled when the carbine responded to his trigger pulls and a pair of crimson holes appeared where the Zs eyes had been and the bolt locked open.

He threw the M4 aside, and as the dusty truck neared the far end of 90 near the burnt-out road block, Cade watched it swerve, double back, and drive back and forth from shoulder to shoulder across both lanes running down the remaining zombies.

"Brilliant move, Jasper," he said to himself. "Going out heroically and on your own terms."

But he wasn't alone. Catching him by surprise, two pair of hands, each grabbing an arm, hauled him to his feet and Cross and Lopez hustled him towards the Hercules.

Once aboard, Cade collapsed into a seat on the starboard side, cinched himself in, and closed his eyes. He barely detected the hydraulic whine as the ramp was closing. The engines spooling up were a vague memory, but the smooth g-inducing take off and subsequent gut-pressing sixty-degree climb were lost, because instantly he'd succumbed to unconsciousness after what seemed like a full lifetime's worth of running and gunning and adrenaline-fueled peaks and valleys all squeezed into a two-hour span.

Chapter 42
Schriever AFB

Overhead, fluorescents continued to serenade Brook with a steady, almost subliminal, hiss. She had no idea how long she'd been sitting on the thin carpet with her back to the paneled wall. No way of telling, since she'd gone off and left her watch on the nightstand back in Portland on that Saturday in July when the shit hit the fan, as Cade had been wont to say lately. What was supposed to have been a short visit with her parents in sunny Myrtle Beach had turned into a nightmare that she feared was about to get worse.

Scooting over a few inches, and risking a cauliflower ear if Tiny decided to leave his post, she pressed her head to the door and listened hard. No change. There was the same busy sound. The squelch of sturdy, military-soled footwear on carpet. The low murmur of concerned voices overridden occasionally by someone giving instruction. Issuing orders. But nothing new. Nothing suggesting Mister Murphy had hung up his spurs for the day after she'd learned Cade was still alive God knows how long ago. Minutes? An hour? Suddenly she wanted her watch. Then she could truly gauge how fast the odds were tipping in Murphy's favor. Like watching sand work its way through an hourglass, but instead it'd be relayed to her by a series of cogs and gears seemingly working in unison against her family.

She scooted back to her post against the wall, adjacent from the carefully-posed head shot of Schriever's base commander circa 1999. That had been a very good year. Newly married to a wonderful man. The love of her life. Pregnant, with a girl no less. A bit of information only she had been privy to up until Raven's birth. Cade wanted it to be a surprise. Said he'd love the baby regardless—boy or girl, it didn't matter. She had been so happy then.

A dull roar sounded from somewhere in the building, sending conditioned air through the vents overhead. The initial blast from above snatched her away from the swirling cauldron of emotions. Brought her back to the present. To face her problem head on. To face the people in the room and watch the rescue mission play out no matter the consequence.

She rose to standing and stood outside the door, one deep breath away from delivering a no-nonsense—let-me-the-eff-in—kind of knock, when an unfamiliar sound reverberated through the security door like a crashing breaker. The next thing Brook knew the door was open and a beaming Secret Service agent was ushering her inside.

Taken aback at first by the fact that Tiny was smiling, she was truly baffled when she noticed every person in the room was wearing a wide grin.

Maybe the Pueblo horde had been defeated?

But that supposition was squashed when she looked at monitor two and saw what looked like a war being waged in downtown Springs.

As she took a few tentative steps into the room and worked her way into a position where she could easily see the other monitors, another raucous cheer cycled around the room.

Maybe the aircraft bringing the scientists to safety had landed?

She looked at monitor one on the left and saw that the black Osprey was in fact back at Schriever and on the ground, its massive rotors spinning slowly, little figures spilling from the rear ramp.

Good for them. Then, fearing the worst, she let her gaze wander to screen three, where at first due to the smaller scale what was happening on the interstate near Draper was nearly impossible to decipher.

"Brook."

She looked around to see who was calling her name. A tick later the giddy Air Force personnel standing nearby quickly parted, and the equally diminutive Major Freda Nash appeared.

"They did it," said the major, smiling broadly and raising her arms getting ready to initiate a hug.

But Brook wasn't having it. She made a face and shook her head and said, "Who did what?"

"You weren't watching?"

Shaking her head, Brook said, "No. I was outside in the hall."

"Ari Silver, Cade, and two of his Delta team made it aboard the Hercules. Hell of a job on the pilot's part. Come with me and I'll fill you in."

Ignoring the major who had already turned and was hustling over to where the President was surrounded by her detail, Colonel Shrill, and a gaggle of personnel in blue and gray tiger striped Air Force camos, Brook instead bolted for the back door. Call her callous, but at this point she didn't want to know the details. That Cade was alive was all that mattered. With hot tears streaking her face, she hit the door running and retraced her steps to the rear entrance, where inexplicably Airman Davis was still waiting with the Cushman in the hot afternoon sun. She retrieved her M4 from the bushes where she'd left it and thanked Davis for waiting as she crowded in next to him. Then as an afterthought, she asked how long she'd kept him waiting.

"Not long," he replied.

Whether he was being truthful or just diplomatic in his answer she hadn't a clue. Time had a way of getting away from her. So she decided to collect Raven and get them both to the tarmac. She didn't want to miss anything else today.

Especially not giving her man a proper welcoming home.

Chapter 43
I-25 Colorado, Springs

Sergeant First Class Larry Eckels and his men held the first two moats for a little over an hour.

After springing the trap and successfully negotiating the graded dirt road paralleling moats one through three, the two M-ATVs, call signs Jumper One-One and One-Two, positioned themselves on either side of the middle overpass where they joined a pair of Strykers and a trio of Bradley fighting vehicles.

There they waited until a couple thousand more dead entered the new "kill box" before opening fire. And while they waited, heavy metal music serenaded them from a Humvee rigged with loudspeakers situated on a side street a quarter mile to their six.

During the first engagement, the M-ATVs employed a *talking machine gun tactic* whereas each vehicle would take turns firing while the other reloaded thus giving their machine gun's super-heated barrels time to cool down. The alternating crossing streams of fire, waist-high, pulverized the first echelon of dead with thousands of 7.62 rounds, effectively turning wave after wave of them into crawlers. Then, as Sergeant Eckels had predicted, the next surge of creatures helped to finish the job the 240s had started, crushing skulls and vertebra alike under the weight of their relentless advance.

Next, after the M-ATVs' ran out of ammunition, the two Strykers—eight-wheeled tank-like armored vehicles outfitted with the Protector M151 Remote Weapon Station, which employed both the

M2 Browning .50 caliber and an M240 machine gun—entered the battle. And in unison with the Strykers, the three M2 Bradleys brought their own M240 and 2,200 rounds of 7.62 mm into the fight. The result was devastating at first, because by the end of that first hour there were so many dead piling up that there was a clear and present danger the newly arriving Zs would disrupt the pre-positioned claymore mines and spill over the coiled concertina wire.

Since the objective was to keep the dead marching into the chute until they were decimated, Eckels had been forced to blow the claymores prematurely and start the diesel burning.

***

Now sitting in the idling M-ATV on the third overpass, he watched the Strykers and Bradleys continue to hammer away at the dead.

Several Black Hawk helicopters as well as a pair of Apache attack helicopters were taking turns orbiting over the horde, sending groundward steady streams of lead and cannon fire and further thinning their ranks.

Sergeant Eckels marveled at the drive the things exhibited. Hell, he thought. If Americans would have had half the tenacity when they were alive that they exhibited after turning, there would have been no way the country could have fallen as quickly as it did.

But what really got him was how the Zs kept trudging ahead even though they were ablaze. Finally being stilled only after all of their hair and skin and muscle was fully engaged and the resulting heat cooked their brains right inside their skulls.

As he watched they seemingly succumbed to the burning diesel. Just sort of bow down and sink in. No kicking and screaming. No fighting the licking flames. Total submission.

Suddenly, next to him, Huddie growled. A little tremor just to let his master know he was still there. Then the shepherd's tail thumped the seat. An action that always garnered a good scratching between the ears.

"All elements, we're oscar mike in two minutes," Sergeant Eckels said into the comms as he reached back and delivered the desired attention. "Proceed to the final staging area." He put the mike down and cast his gaze to the BFT display, and was pleased to see that the snaking red line had been nearly cut in half. Then, as the M-ATV began rolling and his driver maneuvered the vehicle between a Stryker and a pair of Bradleys, he keyed the mike, hailed Schriever and delivered a detailed situation report.

Chapter 44
Aboard Oil Can Five-Five

When Cade came to, he was disoriented and felt like his heart had transited his body and was now pounding away furiously deep inside his left ankle. Someone had removed his helmet and the comms along with it. The sweat matting his hair to his skull was drying and made his head cold. After a second it all came back to him, and he walked his gaze around the sparsely-appointed cylindrical cabin.

It was dim inside, and most of the team's tactical gear had been flung and left where they'd fallen. He could see helmets, gloves, elbow and knee pads wherever his gaze fell. Ballistic vests and weapons were piled in a much neater manner near the plane's cargo ramp. A few feet away, under an assortment of tarps used to cover cargo, were shapes he presumed were the bodies of Tice and Durant. There was also one corpse underneath an American flag. And judging by the bare foot peeking out at one end, Cade had no doubt that it was his old friend and teammate, General Ronnie "Ghost" Gaines.

He unclipped his safety belt, and under his own power trudged across the fuselage and sat down hard on the floor next the flag-draped body. He retrieved the thin box containing the Medal of Honor presented to him by the President. Opened the box and unfurled the ribbon attached to the polished pendant. He peeled back a corner of Old Glory and slipped the medal over the general's head. *Well deserved, my friend,* crossed his mind as he rewrapped the flag.

Oblivious of the eyes on him, he shimmied a few feet aft, drawing the Gerber. Then, with a sawing motion, he methodically sliced through the laces of his left boot. Wincing from the pain, he peeled the size twelve off of his swollen-to-size-fourteen-foot and then slipped the newly-stretched-out boot back on Ronnie's bare foot where it belonged.

He bowed his head and recited a few private words. For a minute or two he reflected on the mission as the plane droned on all around him, and when he finally looked up he realized that Ari, Cross, and Lopez had all been watching him. He looked around and then looked back and mouthed the words, "Where is Hicks?"

Cross pointed amidships in the general direction of the cockpit.

At that moment Cade noticed, though they were safely airborne and underway to Schriever, Lopez performing the sign of the cross. He looked left to where he thought Cross had pointed but didn't see Hicks; only the crew chief and the pilots and flight engineer farther forward were immediately visible. That the fuselage was wide open with virtually nowhere to hide a grown man was momentarily lost on him. Call it battle fatigue or denial or a combination of both. No matter which, he still wasn't following.

Until he realized that in addition to the general there were three separate, distinct shapes beneath the large olive tarp.

First Gaines and Tice. Then Durant. And now Hicks to cap off one hell of a bad day.

He made his way back to his seat. Strapped in and looked a question at Lopez.

Leaning in, Lopez said in his ear, "He got bit. Little teeth marks on his wrist."

"Same as Desantos," Cade said back. "Who put him down?"

With a tilt of his head, Lopez indicated Ari.

Cade shook his head and, thinking anything would be better than replaying the day's events over and over all the way back to Schriever, closed his eyes and willed himself to sleep.

***

Six Hours Later
Schriever AFB

"Is she asleep?"

"Like a rock. I wish you would have seen her riding that bike with Max herding her and the twins like they were his own personal herd of two legged sheep."

"Sounds like our Bird got to be a kid today ... really sorry I missed it," said Cade. "Where is the fuzz ball anyway?"

"Raven's still calling those four bunks we pushed together *Raven Island*. Max has taken to sleeping on the bottom bunks ... guess that would make that Max's Island."

"Appropriate," said Cade agreeably.

"How's the ankle?"

"Throbbing."

"You're lucky it wasn't broken."

"I'm lucky I made it home. And grateful you spirited me away before Nash could set her hooks into me." He activated the light and checked the time on his Suunto. Made a face because it was nearly midnight. "I've been out for a while," he said as the green glow dissipated.

"The pain killer knocked you on your butt. Do you remember the ride from the flight line?"

Shaking his head, he said, "No. Just the wheels hitting the runway and then you storming up the ramp ... and then Raven." A tear, unseen by Brook in the dark, rolled across his cheek and onto the pillow. "I don't remember much of the flight either. Just that it was a somber couple of hours."

"Want to talk about it?"

"We did our best. Still ... four men died." He crossed his arms behind his head.

She laid her cheek on his bare chest, ran her fingers through the soft hair there.

Something boomed far away. Muted, like thunder, but definitely man-made.

Cade cocked his head in the dark and listened hard. Hearing nothing more, he changed the subject and said, "What else did you and Raven do today?"

"Took her shooting. And you'll be proud—"

He interrupted her. "I'm always proud of you two."

Brook smiled then said, "I showed Sasha and Taryn and Wilson how to safely handle the M4. Got them shooting a little too."

"Zs?"

"Except for Sasha. She wouldn't get within five feet of a gun. Not even Raven's little rifle."

"We'll work on that." This made him think. "Do they still want to go with?"

"We'll find out in the morning. I'm going to send Raven over there to crack the whip. Get them packing."

"Not much to pack."

Remembering all of the crap Raven had taken to the aborted sleepover caused Brook to smile. She kissed him on the chest. "I hope they come along. Raven needs to interact with people closer to her age."

There was another low rumble somewhere distant, south by west. A helicopter transitted the base somewhere closer. Then, nearer still, someone was firing a carbine. Single pops, spaced apart, echoing through the crisp night.

"Sounds like they've got their hands full downtown."

"Pueblo Horde," said Brook. "Saw them on the screen in the TOC. Figure they'll be thinning them out for days."

"One step forward. Ten steps back," he said.

She sighed. "We'll be long gone."

"Yes we will," he said, propping himself up on one elbow. He activated the green glow on the Suunto, held it between their faces and looked her in the eye. "If Murphy doesn't intervene."

The light timed out and they shared a quiet laugh. Then she pushed him down flat. Shifted under the bedding and straddled him, being careful not to jar his ankle.

"How's that?" she asked.

Before he could reply, she leaned in and kissed him hard. Probed his mouth with her tongue. He offered no resistance as her body pressed into his. Even through her cotton tank-top he could feel her breasts brushing his chest.

Then she took over and guided him into her. They made love like that, quietly, without words, and when they were finished they lay side-by-side listening to the night sounds.

"What if we get pregnant?"

"What if?" he said. "Gotta go on living."

"Names?"

Cade didn't think long. "Jasper," he said.

Brook wanted badly to ask where he'd come up with the name. Decided to broach it later. Pick your battles and all. "What if I have a girl?"

"Gonna be a boy. Call it a gut feeling."

She couldn't resist any longer. Asked, "Why Jasper?"

"It's a very long story. But I promise to tell you all about it one day when we're both old and gray."

"I love you, Civilian Cade Grayson.

"Love you back," he replied. "Good night."

"Good night."

Chapter 45
Bushnell, Nebraska

Elvis left the house in Ovid and performed an end-around, bypassing the streaming horde of zombies and returning to Interstate 80 which was dotted with traffic snarls here and there but was still mostly clear of walking corpses. He motored west, putting some miles between him and Ovid, his only company the recurring visions from the basement from hell and his own mind continuously asking him what he was hoping to accomplish by rejoining Bishop.

Low on gas, he pulled up hard to the curb out front of a tiny, one-story, shotgun-style house. The yard was what caught his eye. Or rather the multiple bird baths and Buddha statues and garden gnomes of all shapes, sizes, and colors in the yard that were slowly being grown over by weeds and rambling vines. Gotta be a hose somewhere in there, was his thinking.

The search took him around the house where he found a length of hose and a badly decomposed abomination that had become hopelessly tangled up in it.

He wasted no time or energy on the undead monster. Instead, he cut the hose and was back in the pick-up and again tooling the side streets in no time.

The gas he siphoned from a couple of cars nosed in next to a darkened bakery.

He filled the truck's tank and the spare red can and then left Dix in the rearview, driving west until the sun was nearing the horizon and the sky was beginning to flare yellow and orange. From experience, he knew he had less than an hour of daylight to find sanctuary from the dead.

So now, six hours after leaving Ovid behind, he got off the 80 after deciding Kimball was too populated to go anywhere near. He jumped to the 30. Passed by a reservoir with a number of small vessels riding its still surface, and stayed on the two-lane for a couple more miles following the signs promising *Bushnell, Population 144* was somewhere close by.

The sun had fully set by the time he reached the town limits, but there was enough ambient light to see by so he ran the truck dark and slow. Passed by a few creatures hanging around the entrance to town. Ignoring them, he turned right on Birch Street. Saw a sign that said Birch would eventually become County Road Seventeen on the north side of town. *A good thing*, thought Elvis. A town on crossroads usually had at least one convenience store and a gas station. He took a swig of water, trying to placate his growling stomach, and continued cutting the town.

After driving around for a few minutes, passing the usual suspects dotting every little town in America, and with full dark blanketing Bushnell, he decided to drive back out to the 80 and sleep in the truck's cab, doors locked, one eye open. Better than getting trapped in a one-story, he reasoned. No way to drive a house away.

Chapter 46
Eden Compound

Sensing the first judder wrack Heidi's body, Daymon removed the surplus blanket from his shoulder and wound it around her tightly until she looked like some kind of medieval figure ensconced in an oiled travelling cloak. Finished wrapping her blonde hair with the second pass of the fabric, he tucked the trailing corner under her chin and delivered a covert peck to her cheek. He pushed a stray lock behind her ear and gazed intensely into her blue eyes. The simple gesture, though lasting only a handful of seconds, garnered a broad smile from the severely traumatized woman.

Painted gold and yellow by the licking fire, Heidi's face looked worlds different to Daymon than it did when they arrived at Logan's compound earlier in the day. The corners of her eyes had softened considerably and the perpetual set to her jaw had given way to an occasional smile. And amazing as it seemed—considering how bad off she was when Charlie found her on the Teton Pass road, suffering from exposure and a near-death strangling—he'd been able to coax a couple of laughs from her. *If only he could turn back time,* Daymon thought. He would have never left her alone in Jackson Hole. Alone and at the mercy of Robert Christian, Ian Bishop, and the other buzzards that had descended on his favorite place on earth.

"Duncan ... you got a thing against the trees?" asked Daymon as he shrugged on his green Gore-Tex shell. Embroidered over his heart in red were the letters BLM, which stood for Bureau of Land Management, the government entity he'd worked for before the shit

hit the fan. The fact that his chief and fellow firefighters from the old firehouse in downtown Jackson Hole hadn't survived the Omega outbreak meant that his well-worn coat was the last link he had to his crew and former profession. *I'm probably never going to fight another forest fire*, he mused—unless old Duncan continued piling wood on the growing bed of white-hot coals.

But the flame and heat and the slim chance of an out-of-control blaze were the least of the tall, dreadlocked man's worries. All of the above couldn't be detected from the road which was a good distance away and separated by thick old growth. It was the smoke that had him concerned. It could carry on the breeze for miles, and if the wrong people got wind of it then another confrontation like the one he'd heard folks talking about since his arrival would probably happen sooner rather than later.

He glanced across the flames at the Vietnam-era aviator who apparently had not heard him over all of the crackling and popping. Zippering the green jacket to just under his chin where the collar battled with his lengthening goatee, he repeated his question. "Duncan ... why are you hatin' on the trees?"

Caught in the act with one hand curled around a well-seasoned piece of fir, Duncan grimaced and set it back down on the pile. "Ain't no hugger," he drawled. "But I don't hate 'em neither."

Daymon smiled and pulled the hood over his dreads. "The way you keep stoking that fire tells me you aren't worried about the friends of those dudes you killed showing up."

"They pretty much know where we are already," countered Duncan. "And if they come around we've got a few more surprises waiting for them."

"*When* they come around ... not *if?*" exclaimed Phillip. Punctuating the apprehension he'd just voiced, the rail-thin man ran his hands through his graying hair and shifted uncomfortably in the camp chair.

Looking up from the impromptu security huddle where Gus, the former Salt Lake County Sherriff, and Charlie Jenkins, the newly-arrived former Jackson Hole Chief of Police, had nosed their folding nylon chairs together, Lev said, "We've *got* to be ready for them. And

I don't recommend we go on the offensive with only Duncan's Humvee with the Ma Deuce and the handful of small arms we have."

"I concur," added Gus. "Whoever calls Huntsville home was probably just probing us again. What'd you say Duncan ... we've only got north of two hundred rounds linked up for the fifty?"

Resisting the urge to pile another log on the fire, Duncan instead took a long pull from his warm Budweiser before answering. "I linked about a hundred more. Still left Logan with enough for his Barrett, which we're going to need as a standoff weapon when we do move on Huntsville. Hell, it'd be effective deployed from the Black Hawk if we take her up."

Jamie leaned in, pushed a stray strand of dark hair into her watch cap, and walked her gaze from one person to the next before settling on Duncan, whom, in the short span of time since he'd been at the compound, had become the go-to guy for advice amongst the group. "I say we go in quiet and slice their fucking throats," she hissed, the licking flames sharpening her already-angular features. With her eyes still fixed on Duncan, she went on. "I'm looking at this thing from a woman's point of view," she said, throwing a quick glance in Jordan's direction. "There is no doubt in my mind that those hillbillies we got the jump on at the hunting cabin the other day were part of the gang we ambushed today. Same brand new Toyota SUVs. Same MO, the way they had Jordan zip-tied and hooded. It doesn't take a genius to deduce what kind of party they had planned for her. And then from Chief and Lev's description of what happened at the Gudsons' property the other day ... where once again they were driving the same new SUVs and a couple of National Guard Humvees—it all seems to tie them to the dead National Guard soldiers Duncan and Phil found at the roadblock. But what I can't shake. What really pisses me off and makes me want to act"— she paused, neck veins bulging, all eyes on her—"is what those animals did to Mr. Gudson and his little boy." Her words trailed off quietly, and with a rare display of emotion she choked up and then, offering no resistance, she allowed Logan to pull her in close. After a tick she shrugged off his arm, palmed away the tears, and then finished her thought. "My mind keeps going to Mrs. Gudson and her teen daughter. Where are they? Are they still alive? And if they are, what's happening to them *right now*? I *really* don't want to know the answer to that. Although I think I already do. But you know what? If we stay here with our thumbs up our asses and do nothing, we might as well expect the same treatment when they return and we find ourselves with our backs against the wall. We're on the side of *good* ... that means we help the other *good folks*—or die trying." Jamie had locked eyes with Lev as she delivered the 'or die trying' part of her sermon slash appeal slash call to action. She softened her gaze and then melted into Logan, awaiting a rebuttal from the young combat veteran.

Taking the high road and choosing not to confront the young woman's opinion here or now, Lev rose slowly, shouldered his AR-15 and walked in the direction of the compound's camouflaged entrance.

Sensing the tension in the air, Heidi tightened her grip on Daymon's bicep. He gave her a sidelong glance, a quick smile to put her at ease, and resumed following the group's conversation, waiting for the right time to mention Cade Grayson's impending arrival.

Meanwhile, Jenkins, who had been listening intently to Jamie's heartfelt declaration, peeled away from the LE—Law Enforcement—huddle and claimed a spot a foot closer to the fire. Save for the occasional hiss and pop from veins of pitch cooking off inside the wood, the clearing was quiet. It was if the group had taken a collective breath and had yet to exhale. He looked at the sad sight of Tran warming his battered and broken body by the fire. Then he passed his gaze over the men and women he'd known for only a short time: Seth, Phillip, Logan, and the two women—Jamie and Jordan—all of who seemed capable and had automatic rifles lying by their feet. Finally he locked eyes with Duncan—the fella, he noted, who people seemed to look up to.

"As much as I'd like to see those vermin eradicated. We've got to be careful and not act on emotion—not develop a case of tunnel vision. Because it's not only the living we have to contend with," Jenkins said in a low voice. "We're going to need all the firepower we can rustle up. Except for the one fortified town we passed through ... Etna, if I remember correctly, everywhere else between Jackson Hole and this compound was abandoned and teeming with walking corpses ... or *rotters,* as you all call them. I hate to sound glum but we are on our own. And I don't mean just *us*"— he thrust his hand out palm down and made a swirling motion with his arm which seemed to signify everyone in attendance—"I mean the entire *country* is on its own, and that means the U.S. Army is *not* going to reconstitute itself any time soon—if ever—and come rolling through here and restore order. And lastly ... there is a ruthless and vicious killer on the loose." He went on to describe the siege of Jackson Hole, Robert Christian's hostile takeover, and how merciless Ian Bishop, the former Navy SEAL, had been when meting out punishment in order to keep the population in line. Without thinking about Heidi's ordeal in the 'Valley of the Crosses', as Daymon had deemed it, Jenkins included a very graphic description of the hundred or so people he had seen crucified next to the Teton Pass road. "Ian Bishop escaped Jackson Hole alive, and I'd bet he and his paramilitary group went west, not east."

"I concur," added Daymon. "I've seen his handiwork. That fucker is pure evil, and if any of you cross paths with him, you'll see what I mean; he and his men will make the goons you've been dealing with look like a church group."

There was silence.

"I agree," Duncan finally said. "We've got to be very careful whenever we venture away from the compound." He paused and looked over at the newly-arrived former Police Chief of Jackson Hole, who had been forced by Christian and Bishop to keep the locals in line. "I can think of no good reason Bishop would set up shop *closer* to Colorado Springs," he went on. "If I were him and I'd just jabbed a stick in the eye of the United Stated government, I'd surely go the other way as fast as possible. Somewhere densely wooded and sparsely populated with an airport or airstrip nearby."

"I would be willing to bet the farm that he's set up shop somewhere along the Idaho/Washington border," Jenkins said. "I've had dealings with him. He ain't stupid. And by that I mean he's nowhere near the coast. Hell, seventy-five percent of the world's population lives near a coast."

"And there's no way he'd go anywhere near any of the big cities," said Chief. "Too many rotters ... that'd be same as committing suicide."

Leaning in towards the fire, Jamie said, "Why in the hell are we even talking about some dick that we have no reason to believe is anywhere near here?"

Surprising everyone, Tran sat forward in his low-slung folding chair and said forcefully, "Because you need to be afraid of the man. He *is* nearby and he *is* pure *evil*."

All heads turned and all eyes fell on the slight Asian man, whom Daymon's small group had come across on the outskirts of Victor, Idaho. He had been in the back seat of Daymon's old International Scout, unconscious, bloodied, and battered, and looking every bit as bad as one of the walking dead—the latter of which had almost earned him a face full of hot lead. However, mere seconds from leaving this world, Tran had snapped out of his stupor and asked for help, a feat the dead were not capable of, but a simple act nonetheless that spared his life on the spot. But the fact that Tran had been Robert Christian's Boy Friday didn't sit well with Jenkins and Daymon. Finally, it was Heidi's revelation that Tran had eschewed the violence and bloodlust the billionaire's henchmen regularly engaged in that mellowed the contempt both men felt towards him, and the sole reason he was here with them now.

So after saying only a handful of words during the entire trip from Victor to the road outside the compound, and then having spoken only half as much since being welcomed here, Tran stunned everyone around the campfire by going on to say, "I think I know where Ian Bishop is."

There was another short span of silence followed by Heidi springing to her feet. "Spit it out, goddammit," she cried as she stalked around the ring of stones toward Tran, who was still sitting down.

Feeling his stomach go cold, Daymon stretched his lanky frame, found solid footing and rose to his feet. He approached Heidi, who was standing over Tran and obviously waiting for an answer to her question. Daymon grasped her hand and, after a little resistance, gently guided her back to her seat.

After watching with rapt attention, Duncan tipped his beer, draining the suds onto the dirt.

"The lady said spit it out," he drawled, staring directly at Tran.

After a moment's hesitation, Tran told them everything he'd overheard during his time at the 'house' in Jackson Hole. And though he couldn't speak to who was with Bishop nor pinpoint his location accurately by name or a GPS coordinate, he did say unequivocally that Northern Idaho was a place they should avoid at all costs.

"Whole lotta help that was, Tran," said Lev. "I'm no map maker but I'd guess the Idaho panhandle has got to be several thousand square miles of mostly rugged terrain. Locating this Bishop would be like trying to find a needle in a haystack."

"Proving my point, Lev. Like I said ... who the eff cares about Bishop until he's our problem. I say we clean house close to home first."

"Jamie is right," interjected Logan. "All in favor of dealing with Huntsville first raise a hand." He put his hand up, looked around, and counted silently in his head. "In favor of hunting down Bishop?"

Only Heidi's hand went up.

"The majority has spoken," stated Logan. "I'm sorry Heidi, but that's how we've agreed to make any decision affecting the entire group."

"So it's settled," added Duncan. "We hope the bastard stays away for now and continue to forage and get the compound ready for winter."

Heidi leapt up, said, "Fuck it," and stormed toward the moonlit clearing in the distance.

The reaction was exactly what Duncan had expected. Knowing there would be a time and a place to worry about the Bishop fella, and accepting that the time was not now or here, he bit his tongue and watched the blonde disappear into the shadows. Once she was gone, he met Daymon's gaze, nodded at the younger man, and made himself a mental note to follow up with him later.

"Wait a sec," Daymon called out, trying to free himself from the poorly-balanced camp chair. Once he'd untangled his legs he sprinted off into the gloom.

Logan made a face and then looked up through the canopy at the field of stars winking light years away. "I've got an idea. It's a long shot but worth a try," he said, shifting his weight to the edge of his chair. "If we're going back to Huntsville we're going to need better gear. More firepower, and something to help us to see in the dark."

"Is there a Cabela's nearby that I don't know about?" asked Gus.

"No, sadly, there is not a Cabela's nearby, let alone a K-Mart that wasn't ransacked early on. But a couple of months after I bought this land, I was in town trying to find an excavator to dig the holes for the Conex containers and to prep the clearing for the airstrip and the like, but I kept having to compete with this crotchety old guy named Lenny who was also making preps for the Y2K bug. Bastard was always renting the earth-moving equipment I needed right out from under me—"

Cutting Logan off, Duncan said, "Hate to interrupt your yarn, baby bro, but cut to the chase. Is Lenny alive or isn't he? Been over a decade since you broke ground here. And just how do you think your former competition is going to be of any help to us now?"

"It was the whole sneaking in and slitting their throats thing Jamie said that gave me the idea. Figure the fella might have some night vision equipment he will loan me. If he's still alive, that is. He's gotta be seventy or so by now. I'll see if I can find what ham frequency he transmits on—"

"You haven't contacted him since this thing started?" asked Gus. "Not even for a welfare check?"

"Not that kind of a relationship," added Logan, shaking his head. "We were kinda prepping adversaries. He was expecting more of a fight from the authorities than I was, if you know what I mean."

Lev poked his nose into the exchange. "What makes you think he will just hand over the goggles?"

"He's not a bad guy. He's just reclusive ... used to live in Huntsville, so if he's no longer there then he's got nothing in common with the brigands who are. Stands to reason he'd be more than willing to help out if I word my proposal the right way. We might even be able to barter with the man. Give him something he needs ... maybe a shiny new Toyota."

Duncan leaned in and said, "So where is his place, Logan?"

"I don't know exactly but I have a good idea. I remember seeing him towing an excavator eastbound down 39 behind a big Dodge pickup. For some reason it stayed with me that the excavator's tracks were clean at the time. Then the next day when I was in town at the *Rents All* place waiting for him to return the thing so I could get my hands on it, he brought it in and caught hell because the tracks were still caked with *red* dirt. And I think I know where to find that type of dirt."

"Finish yer never-ending story," drawled Duncan. "I'm getting sleepy."

Logan added a few more details and then excused himself. Whether or not he had saved the scribbled numbers that would make finding the retreat that much easier was the biggest unknown. What with a bunch of new people pulling duty in the security and communications container, he feared anything could have happened to the scrap of paper on which he'd written the man's ham radio handle and frequency on.

Chapter 47
Eden Compound

Searching for Heidi, Daymon left the flickering campfire behind and made his way towards the far edge of the clearing where the aircraft were parked.

As he neared the dark blue DHS Black Hawk where he figured he'd find her, the moon peeked from behind high, scudding clouds, washing a single engine Cessna and a lone Bell Jet Ranger helicopter in its brassy yellow glow.

After a short search, he found her sitting in the grass, legs drawn underneath her, back braced against the helicopter Cade had procured for Duncan a week prior.

He ducked under the camouflage netting draped over the rotor blades and sat on the grass, his shoulder touching hers. "What's going on?" he asked.

She said nothing. Only burrowed in close against his warmth.

Daymon savored the moment. He kissed the crown of her head. Breathed in the scent he knew so well, which was slightly masked by the distinct odor of wood smoke clinging to both of them. And when she didn't respond, he stared off into the dark, fearful she was about to divulge more details about her ordeal at the mansion.

They sat listening to a cricket's scratchy serenade and the distant murmur of people talking around the fire. After a handful of minutes Heidi finally broke the silence. "Sorry I stormed away."

"No worries," he replied.

"What Tran said back there surprised me ... I was in a good frame of mind for once, and didn't have my defenses up. Then he had to go and mention Bishop—" She threw a violent shudder that wasn't a by-product of the chill in the air. "—I lost it."

Daymon asked, "Anything I can do for you right now?"

"I'm OK," she said, looking away. "I need to learn how to stop stuffing my feelings. That's all."

"Heidi," he said, looking her in the eyes. They were moist and tears were running down her cheeks. "Anything at all ... I'm not good at this intuitive stuff so you have to let me know."

"I didn't mean to take it out on Tran." She went silent for a moment. "But Bishop—" she went on, putting a sharp edge to her words. "—I want *anyone* connected to him and that house on the bluff either six-feet-under or walking the earth without a pulse."

Feeling the steady beat of Heidi's head thumping the helicopter resonating through his body, Daymon said, "At least you know Lucas and Liam are dead. That's a good start."

"And I have Tran to thank for it. But now that I know Bishop is still out there ... changes everything. With or without you, I don't feel safe here."

"I won't let him hurt you," Daymon said. "And if he shows up here we'll run him off."

"I thought your friend Cade was going to be here."

"That's what he said. Something must have come up. If he's not here by tomorrow I'll call him."

"I thought the phone he gave you died."

"Logan found a compatible charger in his box of electronic odds and ends. Thing's so full of wires and stuff looks like he looted a Radio Shack."

The low voices began to fade and Daymon could see dark forms passing in front of the dying fire. Embers flared and angry orange sparks shot towards the heavens as someone stirred the coals. From the way the form was stooped over, he presumed it was Duncan.

"When I talk to Cade I'll fill him in about Bishop."

"How is he going to help?"

240

"Can't be sure he will. He was on a mission to apprehend Robert Christian last time I saw him. I dropped his team off at the mansion so I figure he kind of owes me one."

"I don't want anyone to know what happened to me at the mansion, let alone a stranger."

"I can understand that," Daymon said. "I've got something I need to get off of my chest. Something I've been keeping inside since the day I met Cade." He talked about being trapped in the attic of the farmhouse in Hanna, Utah. Sparing none of the details, he told her how the lawyer, Hosford Preston, had gotten the three of them trapped. Then he admitted how he'd had a breakdown in his core values he'd never be able to forget.

"You didn't put the man out of his misery?" Heidi said incredulously. "I've seen you kill twenty rotters at once without even batting an eye."

"That's different, There's nothing in their eyes. They're not human anymore." He paused and took a deep breath. Looked away towards the dying fire. "Hosford was still alive. He was already bitten but he was still alive. Cade said, 'Shoot him,' but I couldn't."

"Why?"

"I was pissed at him for getting me trapped with my thoughts and my claustrophobia in that fucking hot and stuffy attic. It was black as night up there." His breathing quickened. "So I let the monsters have him."

Shaking her head, Heidi asked, "That's not you, Daymon." She sat up straight. "Does Cade know?"

"He seemed pissed at the lawyer too."

"Pissed enough to let him suffer?"

"He was fucked anyway. One bite's a death sentence. It just seemed right at the time."

"Doesn't make it right, Daymon."

"I know," he whispered.

She held him for a few minutes, then, with her left hand, tugged his shirt from the front of his pants where the leather belt was cinched tighter than she'd ever seen it. "You lost a lot of weight," she stated.

He sat up straight as her right hand pushed under his fleece shell and then between the tee shirt and his skin. "Does this hurt?" she asked, tracing a finger across the raised scars while imagining, in her mind's eye, the thick pink cords of mending flesh.

"Not anymore, thanks to Jenkins," he said. "Who would have thought a salve meant for horses would work so well?"

"Former 4H member Charlie Jenkins, that's who," she said, throwing a true shiver against the nighttime chill.

A sly smile curled Daymon's lip. *Ammunition*, he thought. *Let the hazing begin.* Although he respected Jenkins and Gus and Cade and men like them, he still received a great deal of satisfaction from finding chinks in their armor. He supposed it was because firefighters had always deferred to the authority of lawmen, and this was his way of playfully letting them know that the playing field had been leveled. Just then he felt a vibration on his leg. He pulled his shirt and fleece back into place, fished the Motorola from his thigh pocket, and thumbed the talk button. "Daymon," he said.

"Coming inside?" came Duncan's soft drawl followed by a little electronic squelch.

"Gimme five," was Daymon's reply.

"That's *all* the time you're gonna need?" the grizzled aviator quipped.

Daymon made no reply. Only listened to Duncan's trademark cackle for a second, then silenced the radio.

"What a *dick*," said Heidi as she rose. "I thought you said he was one of the good guys."

"He's not so bad. Just likes to bust my balls," said Daymon. "Probably didn't think you were listening."

"Let's get back. I'll put some more salve on your wounds."

"Is that all?" Daymon asked, a mischievous tone to his voice.

Heidi made a face in the dark.

"That *is* all ... *for now*," she answered quietly. "It's still too soon."

He held the netting and let Heidi pass. He followed suit and they walked hand-in-hand towards the foreboding black wall of trees demarking the clearing's edge. Alert to any out-of-place sounds or odors, Daymon kept his head moving on a swivel as the moonlight-washed clearing disappeared behind them. Then, with the gnarled branches seemingly reaching and clutching for him, he slowed his pace, looking longingly over his shoulder at the flat earth and grass. Finally, he gazed up at the infinite openness of the nighttime sky and was suddenly compelled to turn around, find a spot in the tall grass and sleep out in the open. He wouldn't let on, but truth be told he feared the metal-walled embrace of the low-ceilinged Conex container. He feared having tons of topsoil symbolically pressing the air from his lungs. Fighting the initial stirrings of his ever-present claustrophobia, he took point in front of Heidi and fumbled his way in the dark towards the compound's hidden entrance. Once there, a predetermined series of knocks gained them entry.

Chapter 48
Outbreak - Day 17
West of the Rockies

Wondering what his second-in-command and old friend Carson was doing at the moment, Bishop rolled over and peered out the window and across the lake where the partial moon was reflected off its shimmering surface.

The king-sized bed he had commandeered was empty and would remain so until the right woman came along. He'd already made a pact with himself that she'd have to be the one to approach him. He was not Robert Christian. And, though he was no stranger to brutality and killing, taking a woman against her will was something he didn't partake in.

However it was something he'd learned to turn a blind eye to where his troops were concerned. Carson and Joshua knew where he stood on this, and were instructed to keep the men under them in control and the practice out of his sight. But as the old saying went, *boys will be boys*. And they had been *boys* with a handful of the locals, undoing all of the inroads they'd already made by purging the area of zombies for miles around. Truth be told, he hadn't ordered his men to waste bullets on the monsters to gain favor with the locals. He just couldn't stand to look at one for even a second. *Out of sight, of mind* was his new motto.

So in addition to sterilizing the area, his men, with help from the locals, had fortified the lake road, blocking entrance to the creatures but also to the rightful owners of the lakefront properties on either side of his new home.

And the reason he couldn't sleep was the vulnerability he felt with his most trusted men away and the underlying current of hostility growing stronger with each passing day.

He looked at the nightstand and for a beat thought about picking up the sat phone and recalling Carson and the boys from their foraging mission. Then as quickly as the impulse had come, it was gone. *Hell*, he thought to himself. *You've spent your entire career behind enemy lines. How is this any different?*

He rolled out of bed. Padded to the humongous walk-in closet, and selected from the former owner's wardrobe a pair of plain gray sweatpants and a similar long-sleeved sweatshirt—both a size too small. Squeezed into them, and as penance for allowing fear to even crack the door, left his pistol by the bed and went for a midnight jog around the lake.

Chapter 49
Colorado Springs

Though it was full dark, for Sergeant Eckels to see the action in front of him, night vision goggles weren't necessary. The half-mile-long funeral pyre lit up everything for blocks around and cast a soft, dome-like glow over the entire battlefield.

He stood outside his command vehicle and watched the squirter teams in their M-ATVs engaging small groups of Zs that had inadvertently escaped over the rubble and concertina barriers, their top-mounted CROW turrets dishing out quick bursts of second death.

He popped another AMP. Took a long pull and felt the instant caffeine rush hit his system. It was almost the same feeling he'd enjoyed earlier when he found out all of his teams had made it back here—to the final rally point—without a single casualty. His chest swelled with pride at the way they'd executed his plan as designed. Then he made himself a mental note to thank Major Greg Beeson for the heavy-metal-music-idea the next time they crossed paths.

Finally, he drained the last of his AMP energy drink in one gulp and then said loud enough so that all of the soldiers standing nearby could hear, "Good job, men. Now mount up. The night's still young and our job is far from over."

Chapter 50
Schriever AFB

Cade had been awake since first light. Already he'd written the after action report for the Winnipeg mission and then, after handing it off to Airman Davis, he'd gotten a ride to the lonely corner of the airbase where Desantos and Maddox were buried and put some more of his friends and teammates into the ground.

Now, hours later, sore and sleep-deprived, he sat on the bottom bunk adjusting the Velcro straps on the orthopedic boot Brook had scrounged up for him the night before. He strapped on the thigh holster and snugged the Glock 17 home. He looked for a handhold above his head suitable to haul himself off the bed but found nothing.

"Raven," he called out.

"Yeah Dad."

"Will you please bring me my crutches? Your mom propped them by the door when she left."

Repeating something she'd no doubt heard him say to her a thousand times she called back, "You leave them laying around?"

Cade made no reply to that. No use. Because he had no good defense.

Max rounded the corner ahead of Raven. He came right up and sniffed the black monstrosity wrapping Cade's ankle.

"I'm a robot dog catcher, better watch it." To which Max growled and backed away.

"Where'd Mom go?"

"Mess hall. But she said she'd send Davis to give me a ride."

After handing over the crutches, Raven asked, "Where are you going?"

"Got a couple of errands to run. How about we drop you by so you can light a fire under your friends."

"That wouldn't be nice," she said, taking him a little too literally.

"OK. Let me rephrase that," he said as he rose unsteadily from the low-slung bunk. "So you can make sure they're good and ready and packed when we all come by to get them later."

"I can do that. Can Max come?"

"I don't see why not."

"Can I leave now, ride my bike over there?"

Teetering on the edge of saying no, Cade said, "Yes ... if you take Max. But be careful and hurry back. I'll leave mom a note so she doesn't freak."

After clapping her hands and doing a happy dance she wheeled her bike forward. "Dad, can you get the door?"

He creaked over to the door and held it wide as she bounced the mountain bike down both stairs. Without looking back, she straddled the bike and pedaled off towards the mess hall.

After watching her and Max zipper down the walk he went back inside, popped a couple more Ibuprofens and laid back down, waiting for Airman Davis to arrive.

***

Max ducked and dodged and nipped at the knobby tires the entire way, twice almost getting his tail caught in the whirring spokes.

"Beat you, Max," crowed Raven triumphantly as if Max had been privy to the challenge. "A personal best unaided by a golf cart."

Near her feet, Max turned a happy circle. Partly because he was a dog and had heard his name. But also there were familiar scents on the other side of the door.

Leaning her bike against the wall beneath the silent A/C unit, she chased down Max and offered him a sausage—or health missile, as her mom referred to anything cylindrical and ultra-processed originating from the base mess hall.

"Stay," she said to Max. Then she climbed the steps and tapped a timid-sounding announcement on the screen door.

A handful of seconds passed. Finally the inner door sucked inward, and Wilson hinged the outer door toward her. He looked down and then left and right, completing a ragged circle and then said to her, "What are you doing here, Raven? And where's your mom?"

Raven processed the questions which, if asked separately and under the right set of circumstances, would come across as fairly benign. But the way Wilson posed them—rapid-fire and sharp-of-tongue, their meaning took on an entirely different context—making the leap from caring and thoughtful to an indictment of sorts.

"Can the inquisition wait until I'm inside?"

There was a peal of laughter. *Sasha*, she thought. Wondering what kind of teenage things were going on inside brought her up on to her tippy toes in order to see past Wilson.

"Come on in," he said, turning sideways in the doorway.

She walked past him and was nearly blindsided by Taryn, who had a stack of board games two-feet-high balanced precariously in her arms.

Rushing to her aid, Raven called out, "Hold still."

"Thanks, said Taryn. "I'm glad you showed up."

"You are?" replied Raven, more than a little surprised the seemingly bad girl even knew she existed.

"I'm so tired of losing at Monopoly to the red twins."

Tilting her head to see the titles, Raven said, "I've never played most of these."

"How about Candyland?"

"Who hasn't," admitted Raven.

From across the room Wilson called, "She won't play the game I want to play. That's why I keep reverting back to good old Monopoly and my pewter roadster."

"They stopped making lead toys before I was born, genius," said Sasha.

"Quiet, Sash ... bust it out, *Tee*," he said using his new pet name for Taryn.

Tee, thought Raven. So Taryn and Wilson *were* an *item.* At least that's what she'd heard her mom refer to people who were dating or going steady.

"Sit down at the table, Raven," said Wilson. He extracted an ominous-looking black box from near the bottom of the stack. Pulled up a folding chair and sat down opposite her. "Tee ... Sash ... look who's chicken now?" he called out.

Raven said nothing, just watched him empty the box. Inside was a folded game board which he opened and placed flat in front of her. On the cream colored board, in a strange, old-fashioned black font, were the words *Yes* and *No.* Below the words was the entire alphabet, two slightly curved rows consisting of thirteen letters each. And strangely, below the alphabet were the words *Good Bye.*

Raven asked, "What kind of game is this?"

"Ouija," answered Wilson as Sasha and Taryn pulled up chairs of their own.

"What?"

"Wee-Ja," said Sasha, sounding it out slowly. "It's a spooky game that supposedly lets you talk to the dead."

"Lots of them to talk to these days," said Wilson, trying to be funny.

The room went so quiet you could have heard a pin drop.

Wilson placed a plastic spade-shaped game piece the size of a deck of cards on the board. It was white, with three casters and a plastic window she could see the game board through.

"What's that?" asked Raven.

"I think it's called a planchette. Allegedly the spirits of the dead move it around the board," said Taryn, sounding highly skeptical.

"Tee, you and me first," said Wilson. He placed his fingertips gently on one side of the planchette.

Taryn followed suit.

"Ask a question," he said.

After a second's deliberation, Taryn smirked and said, "Dad ... are you there?"

Slowly the game piece moved away from Wilson's corner on a diagonal trajectory. It slowed over the words *Good Bye* then continued upwards and onward and finally parked itself over the word *Yes*.

"Shut up ..." said Sasha, her face going white.

Taryn sat up straighter but made no reply.

After a pause, she said, "Your turn to ask a question."

Wilson said, "Are we leaving today?"

The planchette began to move towards *No* but reversed course and resettled over *Yes*.

"Game's broken," quipped Sasha. "We're never gonna leave this boring piece of asphalt."

"Wrong," said Raven, shaking her head.

Looking up from the game, Wilson said, "What do you mean?"

"That's why I'm here," answered Raven. "This time we really are leaving. Dad sent me to tell you all to get ready."

"When are we leaving?"

"Pretty soon, *Tee*," said Raven, testing her *item* theory.

Taryn flashed a wan smile. Tilted her head by a degree but said nothing.

Confirmation, thought Raven.

"We all can't fit in one of those golf carts," Sasha said.

"Mom will figure out something ... she always does."

Looking up at Raven, Taryn said, "We'll be ready."

"Raven, do you want to ask the next question?"

Shaking her head and grabbing ahold of the door handle, Raven said, "No, Wilson ... I promised my dad I'd be right back."

Sasha said, "OK. We'll see you later."

As Raven was closing the door on her way out she heard Taryn's next question, but didn't stay to see the resulting answer. Taryn had asked in a soft voice: *Dad, are you still here?*

Inside the room the game piece skittered a few inches across the board towards *Good Bye*, but abruptly changed directions and once more stopped right over *Yes*. Taryn glared at Wilson.

"I didn't do that," he said with a wild-eyed look, "at least not consciously."

Taryn pursed her lips. Said, "Besides me and Brother and Mom, what did you love the most?"

The planchette started moving. It stopped over the letter *H*. Then it continued on, crossed its own path and stopped on *O*. Finally, in the span of three or four minutes, it had stopped and hovered over the letters, *T, R, O, and D*.

After the last letter was revealed Taryn gasped and released the game piece like it had somehow burned her.

"Hot rod?" asked Wilson.

Taryn said nothing. She stood up, wearing a look of incredulity, and bolted for the door with Wilson calling at her to come back.

Chapter 51
Schriever AFB

After five minutes had elapsed and Davis still hadn't arrived to pick him up, Cade left his billet behind and began to walk aided by the pair of crutches.

He'd made it a dozen yards before the Cushman, Davis at the wheel, finally rushed up on him.

A short ride later, Davis pulled the Cushman tight to the curb just outside the glass and steel facade of the TOC. He stilled the propane engine and squirmed around, reaching into the back seat for Cade's crutches.

Seeing this, Cade put a hand on the airman's shoulder, and grabbed his own *walking sticks* as Raven had taken to calling them. Planted his boots on the ground—one a Danner model, the other that ungainly plastic thing—and then slid off the seat and rose to standing. Wavering on the crutches, he turned his body a degree, looked over his shoulder and said, "No telling if our paths are going to cross again, so I wanted to say thank you for going above and beyond for me and my family the entire time we've been here. Means a lot ... especially when I was away." He went quiet for a moment, obviously searching for the right words. "So if there's anything I can do to repay you, just say the word."

"Go easy on the major, that's all. She's been beating herself up for failing to save her daughter, Nadia, on Z Day. For a hell of a tough lady who is used to running the show, I imagine that was a bitter pill for her to swallow."

"Understood," said Cade, who wasn't wearing a uniform for the first time in days. No rank or insignia anywhere on his person. Instead he had on tan fatigue pants and a black tee shirt. In his pants pocket were the captain's tabs he'd ripped from his soiled uniform the night before. Those he would once again be giving back to Nash.

Though it wasn't customary, but because he knew Cade was leaving on another mission, Davis snapped a smart salute.

Seeing this alone sent an impulse from Cade's brain to his arm, and because of years and years spent giving and receiving them he almost returned the gesture. But instead he reached out—and though it felt unnatural as hell—shook the airman's hand.

With Davis casting a quizzical look in his direction, Cade hobbled into the low, squat building through the double doors and made his way along the warren of halls, passing a number of identical doors set into walnut-paneled walls. His crutches sounding a creaky cadence, he covered one-half of the rectanglar-shaped perimeter of the TOC's nerve center. In his mind's eye he could see the airmen and women on the other side of the wall, tapping away at keyboards, looking up at the multiple big screen monitors, riding herd over Nash's diminished fleet of satellites. He arrived outside of the major's door and listened hard.

Nothing.

He paused for a moment, massaging his armpits where his hundred and eighty pounds had been grinding unnaturally against the thin strip of rubber trying to pass as padding. He could feel his heartbeat throbbing unnaturally in his left ankle. He looked down at his toes, bruised black and blue, swollen and tingling. He could hear Brook's voice in his head as he'd labored to write the after action report the night before: "*Take two of these every couple of hours for the pain.*" And finally, every time he'd tried to perform a task to hasten their exit, she would repeat the following ad nauseum like some kind of parrot: "*Stay off your feet. Keep it elevated so the swelling stays down, and most importantly Cade Grayson, quit getting up and down.*"

But he'd recently come to find that at thirty-five years of age, the magical healing properties of youth were no longer serving him— no matter how hard he tried to follow *nurse's orders*. Still smarting from a probable fracture to the nose from the ladder mishap in

Hanna, and now the ankle, he was afraid someone else was going to have to do the heavy lifting, so to speak, for a couple of days. And that person was none other than Nurse Ratchett herself.

For a full minute he stood in front of the all-too-familiar battleship-gray door, jaw set firm, hand clenching and unclenching, trying to work up the nerve to face the diminutive major for the first time since the Black Hawk down incident. Avoiding her at the sunrise funeral this morning had been easy. He had arrived late and left immediately after, blending into the crowd which had been considerably larger than when Desantos was laid to rest.

Then he burned another minute mulling over all of the good reasons for him to be summoned here on such short notice, and could think of none. The F-650 was gassed and loaded with food and water and various other supplies. And thanks to a generous donation from Colonel Shrill and an off-the-record after-hours free pass into the base armory, he wouldn't be wanting for weapons or ammunition for quite some time. So, in his mind, he and his family were good to go. That the kids would be accompanying them was something he was going to have to learn to accept. He'd been outvoted by the girls—Brook's vote counting for the customary two—and if Max could have voiced his opinion it would have been a solid four-to-one margin of defeat.

With way too many questions swirling through his mind, and looking forward to having one of them answered, he removed his ball cap and delivered three sharp raps to the door.

"Come in, Wyatt," came Nash's voice, muffled by the steel core door.

The door was unlocked. He turned the handle and pushed through elbow first, aluminum crutches banging against the frame on the way in.

"Graceful."

"I try."

"Take a load off."

And he did. Thankful for the offer, he took the chair closest to the door. A decision subconscious in nature more so than tactical. He noticed it immediately for what it meant—he didn't want to be here. And he felt a great amount of guilt for allowing Brook to think—through omission—that while she and Raven were saying goodbye to Annie and the girls he was at the TOC saying his own goodbyes.

Twisting around, he propped the crutches against the wall. He returned forward and regarded Nash with an inquiring look.

As if reading his mind she said, "Why am I here?" Slowly— enunciating each word.

"I won't lie to you," he answered. "The thought did cross my mind."

"I have something I want you to see before you *leave*," she said.

"Did you find the flight recorder?"

"No. Jedi One-One was a complete loss."

Good, thought Cade. Then, deciding to turn the tables and go on the offensive, he said, "I need to ask a favor from you before I *leave*."

She furrowed her brow and shot him a look that implied it was going to cost him. "Go on."

"Let me start by saying that you already know that we don't need to play this quid-pro-quo game any longer."

Nash crossed her arms and swiveled her chair so that her upper body was facing away.

Noticing the body language which screamed, *I don't like where this is headed*, he stroked his ample goatee and said, "If you need me for a worthy cause, a game changer that's on par with Slap Shot—if you locate the missing nukes for example—then I'd move heaven and earth to help find them. But we don't need to continue this charade of chit redemption any longer. We're both above that."

"And Brook?"

"She's squared up with you and Shrill so let's leave her out of this."

There was an uneasy silence finally broken by the faraway rumble of thunder.

Nash swiveled her chair around. Placed her hands palms down on the desk blotter. She looked Cade in the eye and said, "What do you need?"

Cade regarded her hands which shook with a slight palsy. Then he noticed that her fingernails were chewed on, bloody around the cuticles. With downcast eyes he said, "I know how far back you and Tice went. And how closely you two worked together when the CIA was running black-ops out of Bagram. And I'm sure you're still coming to grips with how he died. Hell, I know I am. Fucking freak accident like that. It's all still so fresh. And that's why I hate having to bring up his name in your presence."

"But?" said Nash.

"I need you to look into the after action reports from the Jackson Hole mission."

"What the hell has that got to do with Tice?"

"I gave away his sat-phone to a friend who was a great asset to us on that op. I need to know its number so I can contact him on it."

"The Daymon kid?"

"You read the report?"

"Yes. And if I remember correctly, you indicated in the report that Tice lost the phone."

"Means to an end. Tice had nothing to do with the omission ... lie, whatever you want to call it. He was a good operator. For a spook."

Nash smiled.

"For what it's worth," added Cade. "I'm sorry."

"Is this Daymon guy the reason you're leaving again?" asked Nash, shaking her head subtly.

"In a roundabout way. He'll be at the place where I'm going. Plus there is another guy there who I owe a great deal of gratitude to. He helped me reunite with Brook and Raven. They're both holed up in a compound in Utah with some others." Cade paused, thinking. "It's somewhere near Eden, which is outside of Ogden." He passed her an envelope with the GPS numbers scrawled on the outside. "I figure me and Brook and Raven can stop off there and resupply and recharge the batteries. Maybe pay it forward a little, helping them fortify their defenses while we're there ... if they'll accept my help. Pretty self-sufficient group of folks from what I've seen so far."

"So we're talking about people who were mere strangers to you three weeks ago"—she flipped open the laptop sitting to her right, powered it up, and cast a steely gaze across the desk—"and that's where your allegiance lies now?"

"No, Freda. Like always, it begins and ends with my family. And I don't think I need to impress the importance of family upon you."

Nash grimaced. "No you don't, Cade Grayson. No you don't," she said, voice wavering. "I wish I had balls the size of yours three weeks ago. If I did then I would have dropped everything at once and commandeered a bird and went cross country and rescued Nadia. Hell, California was a shitshow all up and down the coast, but the area around USC wasn't that far gone when the Joint Chiefs stopped issuing orders. I could have done something for her without repercussions. I should have lifted a finger. But I didn't. I was caught wearing two hats. One of a worried mom and the other of a patriotic Air Force lifer. We both know which hat I discarded."

"Hindsight's twenty-twenty, Freda. If you knew how bad things were going to get out there, I'm sure you'd have been on that plane."

"I did know, Cade. I had a bird's eye view as the largest cities in China fell. I called around looking for her but got no answer. Should have left then ... but didn't. Then I watched the voracious dead march across the border and set India on fire with the Omega virus. Then there was the limited nuclear exchange between them and Pakistan. Kashmir was no longer the issue ... it was the twenty million infected Indians storming across. Russia, the U.K., France, Germany, they fell like dominos. I still didn't lift a finger to find her."

A flash of heat lightning winked outside the window, illuminating the dusty horizontal slats behind Nash's head. A tick later thunder boomed and crackled, the clouds overhead colliding like runaway freight trains.

Nash took a deep breath and said, "As long as we're coming clean"—the look of curiosity reappeared on Cade's face—"let me tell you what really happened after the crash. It's been eating away at me." She cleared her throat. Dabbed a tissue against her eyes, wiping away the tears, then went on, "When the satellite finally came on station over South Dakota—"

Cade interrupted. "Draper," he said.

"After One-One missed two radio checks and went silent, I thought the worst. Shrill went the other way, chalking it up to comms failure."

"He always has been a glass-half-full kind of guy."

"At any rate, we agreed on one thing. We both decided to focus on recovering the Osprey and the scientists who were the sole reason we went into Canada in the first place. They don't get back here, then there's no chance of replicating Fuentes's antiserum."

"Agreed. So you called off the Hercules after hearing their description of the wreckage. Is that the decision you made?"

Nash said nothing.

"I hope so, because it was the correct decision. I'm going to put myself in your shoes," said Cade. "Jedi One-One had been radio silent for some time. You're waiting for your satellite window to open up, but before it does Dover brings Oil Can Five-Five on station. Is that correct so far? Am I leaving anything out?"

"Correct," said Nash, averting her eyes.

"And when the Herc picks up the burning wreckage and saw no obvious signs of life and then the sat feed also confirmed this, which was because we were already on the move, you took that available intel and made a hard and fast—albeit difficult—decision to have Oil Can RTB."

She grimaced. Said, "Correct."

"Major, you made the right call so stop beating yourself up over it."

"No," she said shaking her head. "If I would have turned the Osprey around right away they would have heard the dustoff call and General Gaines might still be alive today. Hell, I passed on a second chance to turn Ripley around when Oil Can called in the smoke. She could have put the Rangers aboard her bird on the ground and they would have seen the obvious signs that you fought your way out of there. Then Ripley could have aided Oil Can in the search and extracted your team and Hicks wouldn't have gotten bit."

There was a long silence.

"I let you all down."

"Shoulda, coulda, woulda ... didn't. Can't change the past."

"I keep repeating it though."

Cade shook his head. "First off, Oil Can didn't receive the dustoff ... our radio was roached. Secondly, we're all gonna die sometime, Freda. Some sooner than others." He could see that though the decision Nash had made could never be reversed, the inner conflict it started was still waging a hot war within her, its collateral damage broadcast on her features. Her brow was tight and her eyes bloodshot. Her jaw had a Mount Rushmore set to it— granite and unmoving. He said, "I fucked up too. It was my call to destroy the Ghost in place. But it had unintended consequences ... drew more dead in from the interstate, forcing us to leave the scene. So my decision was the reason your satellite found no proof of life."

There was another long silence.

"I accept all of the blame for leaving the crash. My decision." He fished the envelope containing his captain's tabs from his pocket and placed them on the desk top.

Nash made no reply. She looked at the envelope. Looked at the laptop screen, then her gaze lifted and settled back on Cade.

The look directed his way was one he hadn't seen in a great while. He could almost hear the gears clicking in her head. *Here it comes*, he thought. He was certain a question he'd been dreading was about to be hurled his way.

"How did the Ghost go down?"

There was no hesitation on Cade's part. He held his gaze locked to hers and said, "Engine failure. Due to bird strike. Just like it says in the AAR—after action report—I had Davis deliver to you." Though it was a half-truth, he felt bad using it on Nash. She'd always been aboveboard with him. *And then there was one*, reverberated in his head. Ari had suffered enough loss. That it all happened during a time of war absolved him in Cade's mind. Couldn't fault the Night Stalker for wanting to keep his edge.

"Engine failure, and that high above South, Dakota—"

"Draper," said Cade interrupting.

"Whatever ... he couldn't recover?" said Nash with a raised brow.

"I'd strap into a bird with him at the controls any day."

"Ringing endorsement," Nash said cryptically. "Be careful what you wish for."

Cade made no reply.

Nash added, "If it's any consolation, I didn't ground either Ari or Dover. I wanted to but we can't afford to have anybody on the sidelines. And that's why I hate to see you go. But I understand. I really do." She picked up the phone, and after a second or two had a conversation with someone on the other end of the line, telling them to bring the files pertaining to the Jackson Hole mission and a trio of encrypted sat-phones.

"Thank you," said Cade as soon as Nash placed the handset on the cradle.

Swiveling the laptop around so that the monitor faced him, she tapped the enter button which started a video playing and said, "No ... thank *you*."

***

Once outside the major's office, phones in hand, Cade thought hard about what he had just witnessed on the laptop screen. Part of him was happy how it went down. The other wished it wouldn't have been so cut and dried. Either way, he thought, game over.

***

Nash closed the laptop with enough force to produce a satisfying snap. She leaned back and gazed at the photo taken on the first day of college of her and Nadia in much better times. Sane times. Happy times. Then a tear traced her cheek and she looked away, settling her eyes on the blotter in front of her. She studied the GPS coordinates for a moment, then picked up the envelope Cade had left her. She could feel through the paper something flat and square that intrigued her. She found a letter opener, sliced one end of the envelope, and dumped its contents on the desk. And once again, gazing at the Captain's tabs laying there on the blotter, it hit her that Cade Grayson was leaving the fold again.

Chapter 52
Eden Compound

After one night sleeping underground, Daymon thought he was going to go insane. Being housed in the cramped Conex container with Heidi alone would have been barely tolerable considering his mind's near-inability to process the crushing feelings of claustrophobia. That he and Heidi were cooped up with Jenkins and Tran made the ordeal register just one step north of hell on his comfort meter. What with Jenkins farting and Tran whimpering and crying out with pain every time he coughed, sneezed, or rolled over, the odds were very low that he could make it through another twenty-four hours without murdering one or both of them.

So he arranged the surplus wool blanket so that it covered Heidi entirely, threw his legs over the bunk's edge, and searched the floor in the dark for his headlamp. He worked it over his dreads, cinching it tight. Flicked it on and ran the stark white beam over the floor, found his boots where he'd left them. Rounded up a shirt and the black cargo pants which were getting a little ripe and needed replacing, pulled them on and strapped on the 9mm Beretta that Duncan all but insisted he wear at all times. Careful not to jostle the love of his life, he pulled the Carhartt tee over his dreads, laced up his boots, and made his way towards the door, being mindful that its top-notch fell about forehead-high to him.

Hearing the usual sounds coming from his left flank, he swept the lamp's beam over Tran, who was in a deep REM sleep, eyes twitching back and forth beneath slack lids. He ducked his head and held his breath transiting the airspace near Jenkins, who was snoring away on the bunk above Tran.

Thankful he'd given the hinges a shot of WD-40 before turning in, he swung the plate door open and stepped into the connecting container. He flicked off the headlamp and navigated the compound by the light cast from the overhead bulbs. Noting the steady purr of the entombed generators and a rustle of movement from one of the other living spaces to his left, he passed by darkened store rooms and the armory, then took a right where he ran into Phillip sitting in Logan's usual spot, under a dim cone of light, the remnants of an MRE scattered on the desktop in front of him.

"Heading topside?" asked Phillip through a mouthful of pound cake.

"Too cramped to sleep."

"Sleep? The sun's up."

"Couldn't tell back there in the *tomb*."

Phillip swallowed, took a swig of water and said, "You'll get used to it."

Daymon made no reply. Flashed the man a quick smile that said you don't know *Jack*, and ducked through the doorway.

***

Once outside the compound, Daymon dogged the door tight. Zombie tight, not human tight. Then he heard the metallic snick of the internal lock that told him the Phillip guy was halfway competent. He took a deep lungful of damp air and relaxed a bit with the knowledge that Heidi was safely ensconced inside and he no longer had God knows how much dirt over his head. He looked through the conifer canopy at the lightening sky. Drew in another deep breath, stretched hard, sending a popping noise up his spine. Curiosity piqued by harried voices and the occasional grunt coming from the direction of the makeshift airfield, he stowed his headlamp and moved towards the sounds slowly, letting his body become fully awake.

He stopped just inside the tree line, cracked the top off a bottled water and finished it in two drinks, being careful not to let the plastic crackle as he sucked down the last mouthful.

Enduring constant drips from above, he loitered under the drooping boughs and watched the activity taking place.

With Duncan acting as supervisor, Lev, Gus, and Chief rocked the DHS Black Hawk back and forth incrementally until its wheels rolled up onto the half-inch plywood sheets they'd laid down over the wet grass. Then, like some kind of chain gang boss, Duncan began to deliver a Vietnam-era marching cadence in order to get the men working in unison.

After a couple of minutes of watching the men slipping and sliding and wondering who the hell Ho Chi Minh was, Daymon sensed someone's approach. He glanced over his shoulder as Logan, wearing the black bowler hat Daymon had never seen him without, materialized from the shadows, one hand held up in greeting. The fatigues he was wearing, light khaki with brown splotches and black dashes, clashed with the hat and did little to help him blend in to his surroundings.

Following closely behind Logan were the two younger women whom Daymon had been introduced to the day before on the road outside the compound.

Standing a few inches over 5-feet, Jamie wore black cargo pants and a long-sleeved shirt in U.S. Army woodland camouflage—an interlaced patchwork of brown, green, and black leaf-shaped patterns. Her features were strikingly sharp, angular cheek bones with a small aquiline nose set above thin, pursed lips. Her eyes, like the lock of hair snaking from under her boonie hat, were dark brown with very little of the whites showing. And cradled comfortably in the crook of one arm was an AR-15 style rifle, black, with a scope of some sort attached on the upper rail.

Jordan, on the other hand, was far from imposing. A mere tick over 5-feet, she had soft, rose-colored cheeks and an open and inviting face. Eyes the color of glacial runoff were set closely above a slightly upturned nose. Matching her lashes and eyebrows, a shock of honey-blond hair was pulled into a short pony tail and stuck out the back of her black ball cap. A scoped bolt action rifle was slung over her shoulder, its synthetic stock done up with a woodland camouflage. Daymon was struck at once with the impression that he was in the presence of someone's kid sister on the first day of deer season.

"What's the old man up to?" asked Daymon.

Shouldering the M4, Logan replied, "He's been talking about taking that thing back up and I think he's finally making good on the threat."

"Threat?"

"Because he's been complaining about his vision lately. I don't think it's safe for him to be flying."

"Have you looked around lately? The dead are walking. Some murderous motherfuckers ... pardon my French, ladies," Daymon said flashing a half smile. "With these douche bags wanting to kill you and take your compound and all of the stuff in it, I think your brother's eyesight should be the least of your worries."

"We *all* look out for each other here," Logan replied. He reached back and handed a fob full of keys to Jamie and nodded towards the Jackson Hole Police cruiser.

"Duncan gave me a lift to Driggs in that helicopter. Flew it like a champ," said Daymon.

"Well, we are siblings. He watches my back and I watch his."

"Sounds like you're watching his like a helicopter parent."

Logan watched the girls walk across the dew-bent grass, their passage disturbing the low-hanging mist making it swirl and eddy. "No ... I watch him like he's all I've got left in this world. Because that's the truth of the matter," he said.

Daymon put his hands on his hips. "Where are you going?" he asked.

"Now who sounds like the helicopter parent," Logan said with a grin.

Obviously feeling rather sheepish, Daymon kicked at a blade of grass, transferring beads of dew to his boot. "Didn't mean to pry."

"No worries. The old guy I was talking about around the campfire ... the prepper," answered Logan. "We're going to see if we can locate his bug-out retreat."

"You know where it's at ... or at least the general ballpark?"

"Within ten miles or so. There are a couple of old mining operations east of here. I figure he staked a claim on one of them.

Probably locked it up with a long-term land lease before breaking ground on his compound."

"And you're basing this supposition on a certain type of *soil* you saw on a rental tractor?"

"I remember seeing the bright red dirt and hearing the clerk complaining about it like it happened just yesterday. And yes, I suppose I'm right about it because it's as solid a lead as any. Like I said, this fella is one of the extreme end-of-the-world type of *preppers.*"

Scratching his head, Daymon asked, "Isn't there a National Guard armory in these parts? Wouldn't you think there's a better chance of finding the equipment you're looking for there?"

"Camp Williams south of Salt Lake is where they kept their gear and vehicles. Other than that, there are a few local garrisons scattered about," Logan said. "But none nearby. Besides, odds are every unit went out loaded for bear when martial law was declared. Lev and Chief came upon a roadblock east of here near Woodruff. That's where they got the pair of high-tech headsets off of a couple of dead Guardsmen. But the rest ... their weapons and ammo and medical kits had already been picked clean."

"You're driving there?"

Logan nodded towards the black and white Tahoe.

"Taking Jenkins up on the offer, huh?"

Logan shifted his weight from one foot to the other. "You spying for the Old Man or something?"

"No ... just shootin' the shit, that's all."

"I was surprised Jenkins offered it up," said Logan.

"I'm not," Daymon shot back. "I drove us here from Victor in that thing. Seems like a switch was flicked and Charlie has put his policing days behind him."

"Grateful just the same," said Logan. "I figure the light bar alone gives us a little clout if we encounter any survivors. Besides, I can't stand those creampuff luxury Toyotas."

"You'll like this one. She sure drives nice. Lots of power and the beast will stop on a dime and give you a nickel change," said Daymon. "Years ago, who would've thought that the *po-po* would be rolling around in lowered SUVs."

"Sorry, Daymon. I'm going to help them push the chopper," Logan said. "You coming?"

Saying nothing, Daymon pulled up his shirt and exposed the wormy-pink scar tissue forming over the wounds where the fence at Schriever had chewed into him. Shiny and thick as a lamp cord, he'd carry them for the rest of his life as a grim reminder of the hold his fear of captivity and confined spaces had on him.

Logan made a face, turned away, and jogged across the dirt strip, carbine banging his hip with each footfall.

Shivering against the morning chill, Daymon watched Logan toss his rifle into the police cruiser's open window, methodically roll up his sleeves, and join in the effort.

Wishing he'd had the foresight to don something thicker than a tee shirt, Daymon rubbed the goose flesh on his arms and set out towards the action—partly to get his blood flowing, but also to see if there was anything he could offer in the way of help.

Aside from the manual labor there was nothing else he could do. And he'd already learned the hard way how even the slightest bit of exertion could reopen the vertical gashes on his abdomen. So he stood back and gawked at the men as they struggled and cursed and pushed until finally the Black Hawk's rotor disc and tail boom was clear of the tree line. Amused, he watched as Lev and Gus ran around the chopper policing up the half dozen plywood sheets that weren't still trapped under its big tires, then carted them over and stacked them neatly near where the ship had originally been parked. On the return trip, they dragged the camouflage netting back to the chopper and tossed it over top and stretched it taut so that it covered the drooping blades and vertical tail rotor.

Getting Duncan's attention wasn't easy. The way the grizzled aviator had been walking around issuing orders and slapping backs like some kind of conflicted *shop steward* prevented Daymon from just walking up and tapping him on the shoulder and asking for a minute of his time. So Daymon waited and watched Logan pass a couple of emergency gas cans into the back of Jenkins's black and white. Then he looked on as Duncan and Logan held a brief huddle, arms around shoulders, faces stuck well into each other's personal bubble of space.

Oh, to be a fly on that bowler hat, thought Daymon, wondering what kind of master plan those two were hatching.

Then the girls entered the vehicle—Jamie, whom he barely recognized out of her ghillie suit, riding shotgun, and Jordan, taking the spot behind Logan. Thanks to a shaft of daylight lighting the squat vehicle's interior, Daymon could see Gus in the back seat opposite Jordan.

The doors thumped shut and the Tahoe's tuned engine burbled to life. Daymon saw Duncan clasp Logan's hand and give him a parting hug through the open window. Finally the loaded-down Tahoe pulled away and bumped across the spongy soil towards the gravel feeder road, its needle antennas whipping the air. Then a white Toyota SUV with Chief at the wheel and Lev in the passenger seat transited the clearing and entered the feeder road close on Logan's bumper.

***

Approaching with a broad grin on his face, Duncan locked eyes with Daymon and said, "What are you doing out here dressed like that? You're gonna catch cold."

Wanting nothing more than to regurgitate Logan's *who's the helicopter parent now* quip, Daymon restrained himself and said, "I didn't remember the Farmer's Almanac calling for an early autumn."

Duncan cackled morbidly and replied, "I didn't remember that worthless rag predicting an undead outbreak either."

The comment brought another half-smile to Daymon's face. Rubbing his shoulders he said, "Touché'. Still think we ought to cut a few more cords of wood. Probably gets pretty cold up here in winter."

"That's near the top of our to-do list," said Duncan. "Hate to change the subject on ya, but I'm gonna. What are you *really* doing out here? Everything OK with you and the girl?"

"It's getting to be more OK day by day," Daymon said. He palmed his chin, thinking, *What are you my dad?* Then he grabbed the back of his skull and, twisting against the resistance, cracked his neck. Rolling his head in a full circle, he grimaced and then asked matter-of-factly, "You taking the chopper up?"

"After I thumb through *this*," said Duncan, holding up an inches' thick ream of papers held together by three enormous silver rings, on its cover the words: *Aircrew Training, Utility Helicopter, H-60 Series,* and under the header in bold red letters the warning: *Property of Department of Homeland Security, United States Customs and Border Protection.*

"That kind of reading is bound to put a fella to sleep," quipped Daymon.

"This old guy doesn't need any help," said Duncan behind a guttural chuckle.

"You gonna want an extra set of *eyes* when you go up?" asked Daymon.

"More than you know," Duncan said, clapping the taller man on the shoulder. "You're more than welcome to tag along."

"I'm going for a walk."

"Watch out for the traps," said Duncan, hitching a brow.

Daymon pulled out the crude map Logan had drawn for him. "I think I'll be able to steer clear of them thanks to this," he said.

Duncan made no reply. Instead handed over his two-way radio.

"What's this for?"

"Call if you get in trouble," answered Duncan. "It's OK to ask for help." He winked and turned an about-face and, carrying himself like he didn't have a worry in the world, ambled towards the compound's entrance.

After drawing in a couple of deep lungfuls of crisp morning air, Daymon consulted the map, racked a round into the stubby combat shotgun that used to be Duncan's, and then bled into the forest, quiet and confident as could be.

Chapter 53
Bushnell, Nebraska
Interstate 80

Elvis woke up with an immediate need to empty his bladder, but quickly found a more serious and deadly problem staring him in the face.

Overnight, more than a dozen walking cadavers had surrounded the GMC, and now the truck's windows were completely blocked by their ashen faces.

He tried to figure out where his plan had gone wrong. The road had been clear when he stopped here hours ago in the dark. Therefore the only logical answer was that they'd followed his taillights all the way from downtown Bushnell. *Tenacious fuckers*, he thought as he did a modified pee-pee dance on the bench seat while gripping his junk tightly with both hands.

He thought about driving away and finding a spot nearby to hang it out, but he really had to go. So, with the dead banging the hood and both doors, he whipped it out in the truck and shot a steaming yellow stream into the passenger footwell.

"Sorry, Farns," he said with a chuckle. "We'll have the motor pool guys clean that up."

While he pissed, he looked out the windshield at what, the night before, had been nothing but gray asphalt illuminated by the truck's headlights. Now he had a panoramic view of flatland dominated by farms with faded patches of lawn and waving fields of corn. And in the distance, illuminated by the rising sun, he saw even more lurching corpses moving about the roadway in loose knots.

He started the engine, turned his Huskers cap backwards, and in no time the dead were behind him and he was pushing eighty down the center of the interstate belting out an awful rendition of Judas Priest's *Breaking the Law*.

***

After Bushnell came Pine Bluffs, and that was where he saw it. Blaze-orange and sitting on the side of the road with the driver's last service call, an earth-tone Chevy Malibu, still attached to the wheel lifts.

Elvis pulled ahead of the wrecker, a newer model Dodge 550, and parked his urine smelling pick-up, and jumped out.

He found the tow operator a dozen yards away. In the grass beyond the shoulder. The old fellow had been attacked and died, and then apparently reanimated paralyzed from the chest down.

Elvis spun a circle and didn't see any additional threats, so he ignored the crawler and inspected the truck. He found the doors unlocked, a half-eaten PB and J sandwich on the seat and the keys still in the ignition.

He climbed inside and found what he'd been looking for. A square navigation unit hardwired somewhere behind the dash. He cycled the ignition. Nothing. Not even the last gasp whir of the starter draining the final volt from the battery. *WWFD?*

Elvis jumped from the cab. Checked the crawling corpse, and found it had moved only a few inches along the hardscrabble ground.

He jumped in the GMC, performed a K-turn and nosed it to the Ram. Sourced a pair of jumpers from the wrecker and attached them to the two trucks. *Red on positive. Black to ground. Kinda like 'lefty loosy, righty tighty'*, mused Elvis. *Some things you're taught stay with you forever.*

The Ram started up right away. And so did Elvis' relationship with his new road dog when the GPS came online and a voice, soft and feminine but with a tiny bit of robot thrown in, said: *Searching*.

When the display finally refreshed and the unit appeared operational, Elvis cycled through the menus until he found one where it appeared ready to accept a string of coordinates. He dug in his pocket and withdrew the scrap of paper covered with a mess of numbers written in his hand.

He input the numbers exactly as he'd written them down, hit enter, and watched as the computer brain set to thinking.

Thirty seconds later a new map refreshed, on it a wealth of information. His current location was noted, and connecting it with the final destination were a trio of squiggly yellow lines denoting the routes available to him.

One look at the driving mileage, though, made his heart skip. He zoomed in by tapping the + button on the screen. Scrutinized the offerings and then chose the one that would take him farthest away from the large cities.

He hopped down from the cab, went around back and gaped at the controls, trying to determine how to release the disabled Malibu.

It took a moment but he worked the correct levers and the vehicles parted ways.

Heading to the cab, he noticed a number of plastic gas cans strapped next to the rear of the cab with rubber cords. A quick tap on each told him they were full.

After transferring his meager belongings from the GMC and climbing back into the idling truck, he adjusted the seat and mirrors, checked his watch, and said aloud, "Well, little lady. If I'm gonna get us there before tomorrow then I'm gonna have to drive like a trucker on meth."

Chapter 54
Eden Compound

Coming and going from the compound had always been stressful for Logan—more so now after learning that the stretch of two-lane fronting the feeder road had been under surveillance by the Chance kid, who was now lying dead a dozen yards away, his bullet-riddled carcass buried under two feet of dirt.

Logan brought the Tahoe to a crunching halt short of the foliage-covered lattice that served to keep the compound's entrance safe from prying eyes. Leaving the engine running, he slid out of the driver's seat and jogged to the fore, parted the makeshift blind, and looked the length of the state route, east and then west. For as far as he could see nothing moved. The air was still and heavy with a ground-hugging fog that was just beginning to burn off. He brought his binoculars to bear, walking his gaze up the grassy slope before settling on the distant tree line. Swept them left to right, and then, using hand signals, silently motioned Lev forward. The two men conferred for a moment; then, after setting their radios on the same frequency as Phillip's, who was on duty in the security container, they shook hands, and Lev darted across the road in a low crouch.

With a couple of quick twists, Logan removed the wire holding the blind in place. He unlocked the padlock and pushed the hidden lever that allowed the gate, lattice and all, to swing freely on well-oiled hinges. It was a pretty elaborate set up which he had designed to keep the place hidden from humans during a world-rocking financial crunch brought upon by the supposed computer-killing Y2K bug. And for the first few weeks of the zombie apocalypse it had been worth its weight in gold, as fleeing survivors and the rotters following them from Ogden had passed right on by. Now, however, it was merely a pain in his ass as he stood out in the open vulnerable to attack.

With the specter of a set of crosshairs settling on his forehead, he pushed the gate open and hustled back to the Tahoe. Climbed behind the wheel and rolled forward at walking speed as Chief closed and latched the gate and secured the lattice in place.

After taking a left into the rising sun, he lowered his visor and flicked his eyes to the rearview, where he saw his old friend scale the fence and disappear from sight.

***

Logan watched the odometer tick ahead, and when three miles had spooled out behind the truck, thumbed his two-way and informed Lev that they were nearly out of radio range. To save batteries he powered down the device. A steady clicking sounded to his right as Jamie thumbed all thirty rounds from the earth-toned polymer Magpul magazine. She corralled the loose shells on the seat between her legs, where they produced a brassy tinkling with each dip in the road. She turned the spare mag upside down, blew into it a few times to dislodge any debris that might gum up the workings, and then painstakingly clicked all thirty shiny cartridges back into place. Tapped the mag against her palm to seat the rounds, swapped the mag with the one in her carbine, and repeated the process until all of her spare mags were good to go.

Like a kiddie rollercoaster, the two-lane wove through forested hills, rising and falling minimally, and then shot a straight line for a couple of miles before taking on a steeper pitch where the road snaked through, what were obvious to Logan, man-made slots in the hills.

Getting closer, he thought. Patches of reddish rock where the elements had eroded the native grasses and topsoil were becoming more evident the farther away they went from their valley.

As the Tahoe's transmission geared down, a sign flashed by on the right. It was the usual beehive cutout with writing in black indicating they were currently travelling on Utah State Route 39. The first heading on the sign read: *Woodruff, 11 miles*. The next line had a smaller beehive that was labeled *SR-16* with *Randolph, 22 miles* and an arrow indicating the town lay to the left. And below that, using the same reflective letters and numbers, the third entry read *SR-16, I-89 South, Bear River, Wyoming, 24 miles* with an arrow indicating the town was to the right.

From the back seat, Gus said to no one in particular, "Where do you think all the rotters went?"

"No idea," answered Logan. "But I'm grateful we're not in the thick of them. I had a feeling we'd be seeing herds of them this close to the junction."

"Well, Logan, I'm glad your hunch is wrong," said Jordan. "Feels strange being out here all alone, just the four of us."

"Not to worry. As long as we keep moving we'll be alright," he said back.

Stowing the extra magazines in a cargo pocket, Jamie asked, "What about humans?"

"In our neck of the woods? Aside from Huntsville, Etna, and a few other holdouts still broadcasting on ham radio, there's nothing but rotters left."

Suddenly Logan slowed the cruiser, hunched over the steering wheel and said, "The roads aren't clearly marked so keep your eyes peeled. One of them climbs off to the left and the other is on the right ... both are probably a little grown over."

"My money is on the left mainly because staking out the high ground makes more sense to me. With just a couple of competent snipers it'd be way easier to defend."

"I like the way you think, Jamie," said Gus, earning himself a quick jealous glance from Logan via the rearview. "But on the other hand"—he added, meeting Logan's eyes—"the Ogden River runs along 39 to the south. Water is necessary for mining. And from a survivalist's perspective, definitely a must have for any kind of self-sufficiency."

There was a break in the scrub brush on the left and Logan slowed to a walking speed. "Left now or do we look for the river road? Let's put it to a vote. Jamie first."

"Left," she said.

"Jordan?"

"I don't know, Logan." Then, after seeing an animated Gus pointing towards the passenger side, she added, "I vote for a right turn."

Stopping the SUV on the centerline, Logan twisted around and caught Gus' eye. "How do you vote, Gus?"

"The river side makes the most sense to me."

"I'm with Jamie," said Logan. She cracked a smile and placed her hand on his thigh. He went on, "It's a tie, so why don't we flip a coin?"

"Here," said Gus, handing over a gold-hued Sacajawea dollar coin he carried around with him for occasions such as this.

"I hated those things," stated Jordan. "Always mistaking them for a quarter."

"Heads or tails, Jordan?"

She looked to Gus for help. He shrugged. She said, "Tails."

Flipping the coin, Logan said, "C'mon *heads*." He caught the coin rather theatrically, peeked under his palm and blurted out, "Heads. Left it is." He reversed a few feet, set the brake and stepped from the truck.

Jamie watched from her seat as Gus exited from the rear passenger door, looped around the hood, and joined Logan on the road's shoulder. The two scrutinized tire tracks in the crushed red rock of the entry, scuffing the chevron-patterned ridges with their boots. They looked closely at the puddles remaining from the night's thunderstorms. Then Gus crouched down on his haunches, fussed with the low scrub on either side of the rutted track, turning the branches over in his hand. He looked up at Logan, shook his head, and then rose.

A ton of information was conveyed between the two men with very few words, and Jamie was dying to know if turning *left* was the correct decision. And then, answering her unasked question, the men climbed back in, slammed their doors in unison, and Logan cranked the wheel to the left and sped up the unimproved road.

"Well?" said Jamie.

"Well, what?" said Logan.

"What did all that detective work tell you?"

"Left is as good as right," answered Logan as the SUV dipped into a deep pothole jostling everyone like ragdolls.

"We found some tire tracks. No telling how old they are because of the rain," said Gus. "So we decided it would be best to check it out since we're here, and if this isn't the right place we check it off the list and move on."

"And we spare ourselves a twenty-mile backtrack if Sacajawea is right," added Logan.

With no guardrail between the Tahoe and a deadly drop off, the narrow road twisted back and forth on itself and gained several hundred feet in elevation before leveling off at the gated entrance to what appeared to be a long dormant mining operation complete with an old, water-filled quarry, the rising sun glinting from its surface.

Logan pulled up close to the gate, which was adorned with a host of colorful OSHA safety signs. One, red and black, read *Hardhat Area*. Another depicted an exploding stick—complete with lit fuse—that could only be construed as *Danger - Dynamite!* Under the picture, for the low IQ crowd, were easy to read bold letters stating that blasting took place on the premises. Topped with razor wire and at least twelve-feet-tall by his estimation, the fence looked pretty formidable—but Logan had an ace up his sleeve. Craning his head to see the top of the fence, he said, "See that?" to no one in particular.

"See what?" said Gus as he chambered a round into the Les Baer AR-15 sitting between his legs, barrel pointing downward towards the SUV's floorboard.

"Up there."

Jamie clucked her tongue and said, "Those are the same black domes on the ceiling in Wal-Mart and Target. Security cameras. See them Jordan? There's one on each corner."

"Oh ..."

"And this ain't the movies," Gus interjected. "Those things aren't going to pan our way and let us know we're being watched. They've got a wide field of view so they don't have to."

Jamie made a face. Looked out her side window. "Are we—" her brow furrowed as she looked up "—being watched?"

"One way to find out." Logan jumped up and down waving and smiling at the camera.

They waited a few minutes, and when there was no response Logan asked Gus to cover him. He hustled around back, popped the hatch, and came out with his *ace*. And by the time he looped back around—massive red bolt cutters in hand—Gus was out and had his carbine trained downrange, aiming at dead space beyond the chain-link fence.

"I'll watch our six," Jamie said, stepping onto the ochre roadbed. "Jordan ... you stay in the truck and keep your eyes peeled."

Jordan made no reply. She was watching Logan, who was leaning forward, elbow splayed out, working the tool with all his might. She didn't see the lock fall away but knew it must have, because Logan motioned Gus over and the two of them rolled the fence in opposite directions, creating an SUV-sized gap. A tick later there was a pneumatic squelch from the gas struts as the hatch was closed, followed by a heavy *clunk* as the latch dogged shut. Simultaneously, Logan and Jamie slid into the front seats, and then Gus was crowding in on her from the right. The doors slammed shut—three consecutive solid thumps—and just like that they were rolling through the breach.

"Moment of truth," said Logan as the Tahoe squeezed through the gap with only inches to spare on each side. Wincing at the idea of a flurry of bullets coming their way, versus a lone chunk of lead with just his name on it, he goosed the engine and caught flashes of silver from the wind-rippled body of standing water rolling by on the left.

"There's your water source," said Gus. "You could probably roll a 747 Jumbo Jet in there and it'd sink from sight."

"A mining op this size has gotta have the pumps to draw the water out," said Logan.

Jamie cut in. "What about filtration?"

"Before the shit hit the fan, there were tons of sites on the web where you could download plans on how to build large scale water collection and filtration systems," answered Gus. "Couple of plastic barrels and charcoal are about all a person would need. So easy even a caveman could do it." He smiled but the quip was lost on everyone but him. "You know that Government Insurance commercial ... with the Neanderthal?"

Crickets.

A frown furrowing his brow, Logan set the brake and slid from the truck. He hustled around and shut the gate, looped the chain through twice and returned to the Tahoe. Once they were moving again, Logan had to wheel around a series of water-filled potholes, all of which were large enough to swallow up one of the Tahoe's tires. He walked his gaze over a trio of swaybacked buildings. Behind the windowless, corrugated steel and wood structures, the red earth rose gradually, and then after a dozen or so yards shot up vertically at a ninety-degree angle for thirty or forty feet before rounding off at the hill's apex, where a tiny copse of gnarled junipers grew skyward.

To the right of the tired-looking sheds, backing up to a chain-link fence similar in construction and height to the front gate, stood a monstrous garage that looked to have enough square footage to accommodate a pair of full-sized fire trucks—or an Abrams battle tank or two. *Wouldn't that be awesome*, Logan mused. *Clank into Huntsville, bring the Howitzer-sized barrel to bear, and settle things once and for all.* He noted how weathered the facade was. The gray paint was chipped and flaking off, and what remained was tarnished by vertical fingers of rust, starting where the fasteners held the steel sheets together, and ending at the frost-heaved cement apron encircling the building. Two windows, grimy and yellowed with age, wrapped around the left corner. To the right of the windows, rising above the low cement stairs, was a banded metal door painted a pale shade of institutional green. Windowless, and secured with two serious-looking deadbolts and a padlocked latch thrown in for good measure, the entry looked more suitable for a correctional facility than protecting a mining operation's interests.

Offering another positive clue that the property had not been forgotten entirely were the two rollup doors, both about thirty feet square, stark white, obviously newer than the rest of the building.

"What's behind door number one, Vanna?" said Gus, poking his head between the headrests.

Making a face, Jordan looked at him and asked, "Who's Vanna?"

Suppressing a chuckle, Gus said, "Google her."

Twisting in her seat, Jamie shot the man a sour look.

"What? I'm just pulling her leg."

"Things are never going to be the same for her. Hell, for all of us for that matter, Gus. And we don't need you reminding us of it every two minutes."

Putting his arms up in mock surrender, Gus retreated into the back seat.

Trying to ignore the inane banter, Logan wrestled the steering wheel left and right, navigating the minefield of water-filled depressions. Head on a swivel and eyes moving, he pulled broadside to the double doors leaving thirty feet of separation and the Tahoe's push bar pointing towards the dilapidated outbuildings.

He took a peek in the rearview and spotted the *motor pool*. Languishing in a patch of briars, off to the side of the front gate, were a number of heavy earthmoving vehicles, colorfully-hued and rust-mottled. A couple of half-ton pickups, once *Ram Tough,* Logan guessed, were all but consumed by brambles, only the sheet metal of their sunbaked roofs peeking through.

Perfect cover, he thought. And as the seconds ticked by and the pieces of the puzzle fit together it was seeming more and more likely to him that this was the place they were looking for.

Chapter 55
Eden Compound

After a thirty-minute hike, a good deal of that time spent locating and avoiding Duncan's many pitfalls, Daymon was standing inside the tree line overlooking the gently sweeping curve of State Route 39 that had earlier been the site of so much death and destruction. He swept his gaze along its entire length looking for rotters. *Nothing.* He looked at the blacktop, noting the spilt blood which had dried to black; rambling Rorschach patterns marking where Duncan's antagonists had fallen and died. Equidistant from either side of the road at the apex of the curve were four oily black splotches where a vehicle had burned, its tires melting to pools; the skeletal remains now sat partially blocking the road a few hundred yards to the west—a warning to anyone else who dared bring their bad intentions on a road trip from Huntsville.

On both shoulders bracketing the charred asphalt, still evident and partially filled with brown water from the previous night's rains, were the four manhole-sized craters produced when the buried propane canisters marking the beginning of the end for the marauders had been detonated. And across the two-lane, beyond a barbed wire fence on the upslope of a small grass-covered hillock, he could see the freshly tilled dirt concealing the corpses of the dozen or so dumbasses who had pushed their luck one bad deed too far. Nearby, above ground, was where the group had set fire to a couple of dozen rotters. He could see blackened skulls, their shadowy eye sockets staring blankly, sitting atop a wide debris field of knobby vertebrae and razor-edged rib bones.

The whole morbid scene took him back to a turn of events that had taken place shortly after he was forced to give up the search for his "Moms" on the outskirts of South Salt Lake on the same day he'd first met up with Cade Grayson.

Nearly surrounded by the dead, and in danger of high-centering the old mint-green BLM Suburban atop a mound of the writhing creatures, he'd quickly jammed the transmission into reverse and blindly accelerated away before pulling the oversized rig into a violent 'J' turn.

But the evasive action had had an unintended consequence. By the time his front end had turned a full one-eighty, leaving the zombies in the rearview, an oncoming vehicle had been forced to swerve in order to avoid the collision with his much bigger rig.

The last thing he recalled, etched indelibly in his memory vivid with detail, was the minivan full of kids flipping onto its roof and skittering by, trailing sparks and kernels of shattered automotive glass. Then the immediate fireball, its heat warming the side of his face, followed a nanosecond later by an oxygen-robbing whoosh that seemed to tug at the Suburban. Finally, in super slow motion, always playing out in his side vision, were the backlit silhouettes of tiny arms, desperately fighting gravity and flailing and pounding against the spiderwebbed windows. And always present in his nightmares, right before he awoke sweating and breathing hard, were the innocent faces craning his way, flaming gas running like magma, melting hair and flesh away.

Thankfully the Motorola sounded in his pocket, a piercing electronic warble lasting long enough to drag him away from the awful scene playing in his head. "I can see you," said a male voice he didn't immediately recognize. "You're pretty good; I almost missed you."

With a mounting suspicion that Duncan's hearing was as bad as his vision and somewhat concerned the loud noise would draw rotters his way, he grabbed the radio's stunted antenna and pulled the trilling thing from his pocket. He quickly backed off the volume and thumbed the call button. "Where are you? And more importantly, who are you and why the games?"

"It's me, Lev. Up in the tree line. Your ten o'clock."

Daymon walked his gaze up the hillside, then panned his head left by a few degrees. In a grove of mature pines that had overgrown a good portion of the hilltop was a small sapling quivering to and fro, an exaggerated little dance. Then, dressed head-to-toe in some kind of camouflage netting, Lev stepped into the sunlight. Braced against his hip, throwing a long shadow across the grass, was some kind of scoped rifle. "I see you now," said Daymon.

"Where you headed?" asked Lev.

"Clearing my head, that's all."

The radio hissed again and Lev said, "Be careful of—"

"The Punji pits," said Daymon, beating him to the punch. "I know all about 'em. Logan drew me up a map."

"Call if you need anything. These things have about a three-mile range," said Lev. "I recommend you err on the side of caution and don't stray too far."

"Sheep and cattle stray," said Daymon sharply. "But thanks for looking out for me." *Again.*

"Don't mention it."

Daymon said nothing. He wanted the chit-chat to end so he could get going and spend a couple of hours exploring the expanse of property that he'd been told fell off into a thickly-wooded valley heavy with game trails and split in two by a small creek. *Who knows,* he thought to himself as he strode off towards the west, *maybe I'll cross paths with a deer or wild boar along the way—either one would be better than the goulash Logan calls food.*

He set out on the gentle downslope following the fence line. He'd gone about thirty yards when something out of the ordinary grabbed his attention. Thinking he'd heard some kind of engine noise far off in the distance he froze mid-stride, slowed his breathing, and listened hard. *Nothing.* Then, a tick later, the dissonant buzzing, mechanical in nature, once again reached his ears. It droned on for a split second and then was gone. He stood stock still for couple of minutes without picking up the sound again. He thumbed the radio. "Lev ... you there?"

"Good copy. Lev here."

Cops and former soldiers, Daymon thought to himself. *Always communicating in the same clipped syntax—robot-like and impersonal.* He asked, "Did you hear some kind of engine?"

"Negative," said Lev, robot-like and impersonal. "Maybe it was the rotters moaning. Got a few approaching from your right. Saw you freeze ... thought you saw them. Didn't think you needed warning."

Daymon walked his gaze the length of the road. At the point in the distance where the blacktop disappeared into the canyon of trees, a number of pale forms were emerging from the shadows. He watched as they trudged silently uphill, past the immolated, now see-through, SUV. "Nope," he replied. "It wasn't them. I can't even hear their feet slapping the road from where I'm at."

"They're not moaning because they don't see you ... *yet*. What is it you think you heard?"

"I think it was a helicopter. Way off— distant. North and west of us."

"Military or civilian?" asked Lev.

Contemplating the question, Daymon shifted his gaze to the sky. Then he scrutinized the approaching zombies and determined from more than a hundred yards, based on their gait and decomposition, that they were all first turns, and were thus incapable of producing the sound that he had heard.

There was a brief burst of static and Lev said, "Well ... what was it?"

"Couldn't tell you," answered Daymon truthfully. "Maybe it was all a figment of my imagination."

The radio crackled again. "Maybe it's your Delta Force buddy trying to find the compound."

"He would have called first. He's a soldier just like you. Ducks in a row and all that jazz."

"Roger that. I'll keep my eyes and ears open. And Daymon—"

"*Yes.*"

"The rotters will move on as long you don't let them get eyes on you."

"Where are they coming from?"

"Nowhere really. They seem to just walk the road back and forth between Huntsville and Woodruff. Any of them that happen to be in the area when we come and go are drawn in by our engine noise. Engine noise travels a long way out here. Especially when it's the only man-made sound for miles. The dead have great hearing ... they triangulate in on sounds real well. Especially anything they associate with food ... which is just about everything."

I'm no dummy. But thanks anyway for the zombie primer, is what Daymon thought. "I'll be quiet," is what he said. He silenced the radio and melted back into the forest.

Chapter 56
Quarry

Leaving the engine idle, Logan slid from behind the wheel and met the others in front of the SUV's warm hood. "I've got a gut feeling this is the place we're looking for," he said. "Gus—you and Jamie check out the three buildings over there. I'm going to walk around the garage and see if I can find a window and take a peek inside. Keep your radios turned down low and call only if you need to."

"I don't have a radio. I thought you were grabbing them," said Jamie with a tilt of her head.

Feeling a little sheepish, Logan cast his gaze to Gus.

Shrugging his shoulders, Gus added, "I got asked to help move the helicopter. Figured since you were in the security container last ..."

"Forget the radios," said Logan. "We'll fan out and take a quick look."

Gus nodded.

"Lock and load," said Logan, shoving the now worthless lone radio into his pocket.

"What about me?" asked Jordan, subconsciously kneading the seatback.

"You've got the most important job," Logan said quietly. "I want you to get behind the wheel and lock your door. Then watch our backs while we check things out. While we're inside, if you see *anyone* or *anything*—living or dead—I want you to sound the siren. Can you handle that?"

She regarded him for a second. Her eyes narrowed, like she was deciding if this was a request or if she had just been issued an order. Finally, after a couple more seconds' contemplation, she shrugged her shoulders and said, "No problem."

To Logan it was fairly obvious the young lady was still trying to find her role within the group. And he took the hesitation for what it was, a manifestation of her deep-seated distrust of the male species. Given all she'd gone through as a captive of the hillbilly rapists, he couldn't blame her in the least. He killed the engine, slid from the truck, carbine in hand, and watched her loop around the hood with a newfound pep in her step. Obviously happy to finally contribute, Jordan flashed the group a smile and placed her rifle in the passenger seat before climbing behind the wheel.

Logan tapped the hood and mouthed, "Lock the doors."

She smiled. Cast her eyes downward and dogged her head side-to-side. A tick later the siren blared—hitting a shrill note that simultaneously forced Logan, Gus, and Jamie to clamp their hands over their ears. The noise continued, rising and falling unabated, until Logan banged on the hood and drew an index finger across his throat, a frantic slashing motion.

Heeding the pantomimed request, Jordan relocated the switch and silenced the siren.

"Shit," Gus said, shaking his head. He stuck a finger in each ear and jiggled them rapidly. "If there *is* someone here and they didn't know they had company, we sure as hell just lost the element of surprise."

Ears ringing from the sonic bombardment, Logan said, "She's a work in progress." Then he heard the satisfying *clunk* as Jordan actuated the door locks. He watched her get comfortable, adjusting the seat and mirrors, presumably so she could watch the gate without having to hang her head out the window. *Way to take the initiative*, he thought. After apparently getting everything dialed in to her liking she flashed the trio another smile punctuated with an enthusiastic thumbs up.

Seeing this, Logan said to Gus and Jamie, "Quickly, let's go ... same plan."

Chambering a round into his AR-15, Gus flicked off the safety, nodded at Logan, and with Jamie close on his heels, padded off towards the shed farthest left.

Cursing himself for assuming one of the others had brought along a second two-way radio, Logan struck off in the opposite direction; as he zig-zagged between steaming puddles, Duncan's voice sounded in his head, chiding him for the oversight, asking what the hell he'd been thinking. *Dot your I's and cross your T's*—one of Duncan's favorite sayings—resounded loudly, clamoring for attention, albeit a little too late. Then for the third time this morning Logan imagined a fusillade of hot lead lancing the air, every bullet with his name on it. M4 locked and loaded, its business end aimed in the general direction of the looming building, he straightened up and covered the distance in a full sprint.

Upon reaching the green door, he cut left and ducked under the window, slid down with his back against the wall near the corner of the building, and watched Jamie and Gus approach the outbuilding farthest left. Upon arriving, Gus searched the rear of the tiny structure, then reappeared and stood with Jamie by the narrow wooden door. They conferred and then Gus tried the handle. He looked over, met Logan's gaze and shook his head. He took a step and a half back, and behind a flash of black leather kicked the sweet spot next to the handle, destroying the lock and half the door.

Instantly, Jamie was through, Gus close behind. *Just like in the movies*, thought Logan. That no rotters or gunfire or screams came out of the shed was a very good sign.

Shifting his focus to the oversized garage, Logan craned his head and peered through the sun-yellowed horizontal blinds. Against the far wall was a low, wide desk, its dark wood lightened by a coating of dust. The rest was basic office equipment. There was a pencil sharpener fastened to one wall, and a bulky PC, probably brand new in the last half of the nineties, arranged on another desk alongside a printer. A water cooler, long dried out, stood close by. And occupying the left wall was a sagging, flame-orange sofa with three threadbare cushions and spindly walnut legs. Pinned above it, still displaying the month of September, last accurate in 2001, was a calendar hawking some kind of mining equipment.

All put together, everything Logan saw in the cramped office worked to negate his theory that the pristine garage doors were newly installed. Like a pendulum, his opinion began to sway away from prepper redoubt and back to this just being a long-idled mining operation.

He turned to check on the progress Jamie and Gus were making and saw that all three shed doors were hanging open on bent hinges, splintered wood where their single locks had been, and the two of them were heading his way.

When they'd closed to within earshot, Logan said, "What did you find?"

"Spiders," said Jamie, checking her hair and clothing for eight-legged passengers. "Lots and lots of spiders."

Shaking his head, Gus answered, "Decades-old equipment. Nothing that points to anyone planning on riding out the apocalypse here."

"I didn't see anything inside the office that makes me think any different. But these doors are brand new," added Logan. He looked at them. Long and hard. "But the rest of this. It's the type of picture I'd try to paint if my place was out in the open like this."

"Good point," said Gus. "But I'm thinking we should leave now and check the other site. This just doesn't pass the smell test."

Logan cast his gaze towards the Tahoe and saw Jordan, alert, head panning side-to-side every couple of seconds.

"Stay here," Logan said. "I'm going around back." He turned the corner at a slow trot, passed the rusting north-facing wall and crabbed sideways through the narrow space between the building's northeast corner and the chain-link fence to his left. He stopped and gazed down the narrow chute and saw more of the same: razor-wire-topped chain-link on the left, the building's rusting rear flank to his right. Boots sucking in the mud, he sprinted thirty yards or so, rounded the next corner and spotted something that tugged the pendulum back in the direction of thinking a prepper was at work here.

The six windows on the south side appeared brand new. They were double-paned, with sturdy metal cages on the outside and stark white vertical blinds on the inside. He moved along the wall until he found a window with a finger's width of clearance between the blind and the sill.

He knelt down and was pressing his face against the warm metal, peering inside, when something slammed violently against the window, vibrating the blinds and visibly bowing the glass outward.

Reacting instantly, Logan leapt backwards as if he'd just come upon a pissed-off rattlesnake. His bowler hat flew from his head and landed in the mud as expletives began to flow from his mouth.

While the trapped rotter continued slam-dancing with the windows, Logan retrieved his hat, brushed it off as best he could, and then rejoined Jamie and Gus around the corner.

First to notice him round the corner, Jamie said, "Whoa, Logan. Looks you've seen a ghost."

"That bad, huh?"

Gus said, "You should see yourself in a mirror. You've got the albino look down."

"What'd you find back there?" asked Jamie.

"Brand new windows. Someone was calling this place home."

"Was?"

"Yeah, Jamie. Was," said Logan.

"What's in there?" she asked with a tilt to her head.

"Something we're going to have to deal with. I'm going to grab the bolt cutters."

Chapter 57
Quarry

As Logan worked the cutter's maw into position to snip the lock, he could hear their *friend* on the inside banging into the roller door.

"What makes you so sure that thing or those *things* won't come storming through the door?"

Stopping what he was doing, Logan rested the cutters on the cement stair and looked at Jamie. "First off, rotters never *storm* anything. I'd be willing to bet that's the old guy banging the door. He probably got bit somewhere outside and then came back to his castle and turned inside there all alone."

"What makes you think that's only one rotter in there?" said Jamie. "Sounds like five."

"I was having lunch in Huntsville a while back and I heard a couple of blue hairs talking about him. Supposedly he's got no family around here except for a daughter and granddaughter in Logan."

"And a little lunch counter gossip makes you certain that's him and he died in there all alone?" said Gus, who suddenly went quiet and cocked his head to the west.

Logan made no reply. He also looked to the west.

Crinkling her brow, Jamie asked, "What's up guys?"

Gus asked, "Anyone else hear that?"

"From this direction," said Jordan, pointing across the standing water that had lost all of its On Golden Pond allure and was now as black as midnight. "Maybe a car or truck— but I only caught it for a second."

Logan listened hard. Shook his head. *Nothing.* "Stay in the truck ... same routine. Hit the siren *only* if you see something," he said to Jordan. He waited a second for her to respond, then, after seeing her nod, turned and addressed Jamie and Gus.

They discussed the best way to go about getting inside without any of them getting bit.

Worst case scenario, Gus argued, was that there were two, maybe three rotters in the garage. Why they were in there, and what they may have been protecting, was a matter of opinion. Even after Logan had pointed out the recent improvements to the building, Gus was not convinced it was worth taking the risk to find out. The girls, on the other hand, were both in Logan's camp, so sticking with the whole democratic process thing they moved to formulate a plan. After exploring every avenue, they came to the conclusion that the armored windows were a no-go. And since the roller doors weren't going to budge without utilizing the Jaws of Life, they would have to breach the outer door. With the plan hashed out, the only thing left to decide was which one of them was going to open the inner door and let the dead—however many there might be—come to them. Then, taking everyone by surprise, Gus asked for a volunteer.

Solely to beat Jamie to the punch, Logan agreed to the task. Last thing he wanted was to lose her based on one of his stupid suppositions.

***

Standing on the first step, with everyone watching, Logan swept aside the broken padlock with his toe. Then, mimicking Gus's technique, he reared back, took a stabbing half-step forward and lashed out, planting the sole of his right boot on the green door dead-center between the two catches.

But the follow through and splintering wood didn't happen. Instead, the steel door and Schlage bolts held fast. The energy behind the kick—which had to dissipate somewhere—surged back through the waffle-patterned sole, vibrated up his fibula and tibia, and then shot through his femur, an electric current juddering every bone north from there.

A half beat later he pitched backwards off the steps, landing square on his tailbone; the bowler flew off again, adding insult to the pain making his eyes water.

Sitting in a puddle—with the lady he fancied looking on, and the intact door looming over him—was the most humiliating moment of his life.

Jamie went to her knees. "Are you okay, Logan?" she asked, cradling his head with both hands.

Looking her straight in the face, he said, "My brother comes onto the scene and all of a sudden I can't do anything right. I forget the radios. Ed and his family leaves, and now this ... I've always been in his shadow."

"It's alright to look up to him, but in my opinion you should stop living in his shadow."

He said nothing.

Trying to stay out of it, Gus walked away humming a ditty only he knew the words to.

Jamie offered Logan a hand up and said, "We're only people until we're one of those *things*. Then all this bullshit minutiae doesn't mean a thing."

"I know, I was the only one counting, but that was strike three right there." He made a face. Looked at the others one at a time, shook his head and said, "I don't think I deserve another chance."

Gus couldn't hold his tongue. He said, "I was counting. And that was strike four if you take into account Little Miss Premature on the siren over there."

Logan made no reply. Tried to wipe the mud from his hat but only smudged it further. Red-faced, he gave up and slapped the bowler back on, dirt and all.

Seeing this, Gus said, "Forget about the door. I'll take care of it." He made a shooing motion and went on, "I want you two to get behind the cruiser. And tell Jordan to keep her head down."

With a little help from Jamie, Logan limped back to the SUV, rubbing his backside.

Gus stood at an oblique angle ten feet right of the door, snugged the AR tight to his shoulder, and aimed for the one-inch strip between the locks and frame. He took a calming breath and squeezed off four consecutive shots, a second or two between each.

While the sharp reports were still echoing around the quarry, Gus approached the door and finished the job with one swift kick. He took a quick peek inside and noticed the interior door was shut. He looked over his shoulder at Logan and said, "Step right up. It's redemption time."

Logan paused for a beat, put down his carbine and drew his Glock. Pulled the slide checking for brass.

"Just fling it open and get your butt out here."

"Pronto," added Jamie, "I wouldn't want to lose you."

After limping up the steps, Logan hesitated once again and cast a look at Jamie that said: *I got this*. Brandishing the Glock one-handed, tucked close to his body, he crabbed past the desk and grasped the brushed-nickel knob. Once again he hesitated. Then for reasons known only to him, tapped the 9mm against the hollow door—an action that received an instant response. The first impact rattled the door, jiggling the knob in his grip. The monster had no chance at a second attempt because Logan flung the door open and backpedaled out of harm's way, a mass of black flies buzzing after him.

The creature stumbled through the inner door and caromed around the office, moving the flimsy desk a couple of feet and sending the antiquated IBM PC to the floor in the process. Then another rotter—female, elderly, and grossly overweight— emerged from the inner sanctum trailing several feet of its own greasy intestines.

The two abominations pin-balled off each other, causing complete devastation to the small room before finally finding their way through the open door and into the sunlight.

The male rotter, also elderly—early sixties, Logan guessed— and rail-thin with ashen skin and a scraggly white beard, locked on to him like a heat-seeking missile. *If these two were a couple in life*, he thought bringing his Glock on line, *then the age-old adage, opposites attract, must have been at play.*

Stumbling down the steps and over the pitted ground, coveralls black with dried blood, the male zombie covered a handful of feet before meeting a pair of 9mm Parabellums head on. The first projectile, travelling at a blistering 1,200 feet per second, struck the monster on the sharp ridge of its lower jawbone. The bullet's kinetic energy snapped the creature's head back like a Pez dispenser, discharging a geyser of flecked bone and tooth through the pulpy chasm where its sunken cheek used to be. *Strike five*, Logan thought pessimistically even before the effect of his second shot had become evident.

A thousandth of a second later, the latter half of Logan's double-tap found its mark, entering directly under the rotter's mangled chin and exiting diametrically opposite behind an airburst of skull, hair, and gelatinous gray matter. Relief washed over him as the thing fell in a heap in the red mud near his feet.

No sooner had the remains of the rotter's brains dribbled from its skull than a flurry of gunshots sounded from Logan's right flank.

Wobbly and unsteady, like a drunken sailor on liberty, the second rotter had trundled down the stairs on the heels of the first, inexplicably ignored Logan, and trudged directly towards Jamie and Gus and into the hail of hot lead fired from their carbines.

Trying to avoid an imminent tsunami, Logan sprang back as the plus-sized flesh-eater, its face a bloody red mess, fell headfirst into a mud puddle.

But Logan's reaction time had been lacking and he was deluged with enough displaced dirty water to wet him from crotch to sternum.

Crouched low and moving sideways, Gus stepped quietly over the leaking bodies. Then, craning his head to see through the doorway, he swept the business end of his rifle inside, cutting the room off by degrees. *Nothing.* Still, he waited and listened and watched the darkened doorway for a full minute, and when nothing else emerged, his law enforcement training kicked in and he called out, "Clear."

Chapter 58
Schriever AFB

"So what do you think the compound will be like?" Cade asked Raven as he tossed an empty backpack on the bunk and worked at undoing the top enclosures.

She bit her lower lip. Looked at the floor for a second, searching for an answer. Finally she said, "I don't know," and looked up and locked eyes with him.

"No idea at all?"

"The word *compound* kinda makes me think of a castle. Maybe there will be a wall and a moat." She added a couple of tee shirts and a pair of khaki cotton pants her mom had scrounged up somewhere to the pile of clothes going with them and added, "Sasha thinks we'll be able to explore city ruins on the way. Says it's going to be fun ... like their trip from Denver. She says there will be a ton of zombies but she's not scared at all. I don't really believe her though."

Cade rolled up a black tee shirt, stuffed it in a zippered side pocket, and said, "Are *you* scared?"

"Kind of."

"What do you think the countryside near the compound is going to look like?" he said as he stuffed the rest of the clothes in the main body of the pack.

"I kinda think it'll look a lot like where Robin Hood lives ... the Starwood Forest."

"Sherwood Forest," said Cade, correcting her. "But you're close. There's a lot of trees and a creek and a grassy clearing with a landing strip. I've seen it mostly from above ... when I was riding in a helicopter with some people you're going to get to meet."

"You think we can build a fort or a tree house in the forest?"

"The compound is more fort than castle," he said. "But, yeah. I'll help you build a tree house. With a garage for your bike, how's that sound?" Then he went over most of the details he knew from Duncan about the compound, leaving out the part about it being buried underground. *No telling how she'd take that kind of news*, he thought. So he decided to leave her free of worry for now and wait until they actually arrived there and then see how she took to the place and its subterranean nature.

"So we'll all be safe from the zombies there?"

"Yes sweetie. And we will be with people whom we can trust." Then, one at a time, he made sure each Glock pistol had a full mag and a round in the chamber. The 17—minus the suppressor— was holstered in the drop-down on his left thigh. The compact 19, however, went under his arm in the quick-draw rig. "Good to go," he said aloud, out of habit more so than to reassure Raven.

"Yes we are," she replied. She rose and crossed the room, Max by her side; as she opened the door she let out a little squeal. "Yeahhh ... Mom's back."

Marveling at the girl's uncanny ability to hear what he could not, Cade grabbed his crutches, rose creakily, and followed her outside.

The Cushman ground to a halt just as he reached the bottom step. He hobbled over and, after Brook silenced the engine, said, "We're ready when you are." Behind him he could hear a ticking as Raven pushed her mountain bike from around the side of their billet. Then the swish of knobby tires through damp grass.

"Pinch me," Brook said, beaming from ear to ear. "I can't believe we're actually leaving this fortress of boredom and deceit."

Nodding his head in semi-agreement, Cade placed the lone backpack behind the passenger seat next to hers and loped around to the driver's side. With most of his weight supported on his right foot, he slid his crutches into the back seat and sat with the walking boot sticking out slightly. "Hey hon," he said, once he was situated.

Brook swiveled around to face him. "Yes," she answered.

"You're going to have to do the heavy lifting for a couple of days. Starting with the Bird's bike."

"And the rifles?" she asked as she placed the lightweight bike on the back where, on a normal golf cart, a couple of baskets would be corralling a pair of overstuffed bags full of golf clubs.

"Already in the truck."

"The Whipper guy didn't lay claim to it while you were gone ... did he?"

"No. He's not so bad. He's just wound pretty tight. Like we all are these days." He went silent for a beat, then added, "We had a talk and we're on the same page now."

Wondering if she could coax the rest of that story from him one day, she secured the bike with a couple of lengths of paracord. She whistled and hollered, "Come on Max."

Just as Raven was taking her seat next to Brook, the Australian Shepherd bounded from the grass, his coat covered with dew. After a couple of quick convulsions which sprayed everyone with a fine mist, he snaked under Raven's legs and claimed a spot between mom and daughter.

"Home, James," said Cade in his best British accent.

Pigtails flailing like medieval weapons, Raven whipped her head around and blurted, "Really?"

"No sweetie," answered Brook as she started the Cushman. "Dad was using a figure of speech. I'll explain it to you once we're on the move. Reminds me," she added, speaking over her shoulder. "Am I driving that monstrosity part of the way?"

"To start. We'll take turns. Maybe the Wilson kid can take the wheel a little."

"Over my dead body," replied Brook, recalling the terror-filled moments during which their U-Haul convoy had gotten gridlocked in the gated community southwest of Colorado Springs.

The statement elicited an impromptu meeting of the eyes between father and daughter. Cade made a face and shrugged. To which Raven bugged out her eyes, then turned forward and sat rigid in her seat just as the cart started moving.

***

After transiting the base via the smooth asphalt drives past the community resource center, the medical clinic and the mess hall, Brook snugged the Cushman to the curb behind an identical model Cushman and silenced the engine. "You or me?"

"Me," answered Raven, who was already half out of the vehicle.

Brook watched her bound up the steps and knock on the door—a furtive flurry of tiny knuckles playing out like bongos on the hollow-core door. After a few moments it opened a crack and Raven disappeared inside.

"*Password please*," followed by a curt, "*Enter*," was all Brook could think of as she watched the interaction play out. Then, like a limo driver delivering a diplomat to a high level meeting, she sat back and prepared for the long wait; her experience was that anyone under twenty seemed to think *quick* applied only to powdered flavorings for milk or the speed at which paint dries. She turned to face Cade and asked, "Since I'm doing the driving, is there anything I should know about this new truck?"

"It's a beast ... that's for sure. You know our Sequoia?"

"Hated driving that thing," Brook answered without hesitation.

Fully expecting the sentiment he'd heard her utter a hundred times, he cracked a smile and said, "We can't expect to run an undead gauntlet in a VW."

"No ... really?" she said smartly.

"I know it's bigger than my old truck, but I think you'll warm to it."

"I don't have to like it to drive it," was her answer to that. Then, parroting something Cade always preached, she said, "I'll adapt."

"You've done great so far," he said, giving her shoulder a soft squeeze.

She looked at her watch. *Seven minutes.*

The door opened and Sasha emerged carrying a bulging, utilitarian-looking, tan canvas bag over her shoulder.

Max's ears perked and he sat up as Raven emerged with a wooden baseball bat clutched in one hand and a tan leather handbag with some kind of logo dotting nearly every square inch in the other. Everything was placed in back of the other cart and Raven returned and took her place next to Max, who greeted her with a gentle butting of his head, a move that was reciprocated with a good scratching behind the ears.

"What's keeping the other two?"

"Taryn is inside on her bed hiding under the covers," answered Raven. "Wilson said she had *cold feet*. That mean she's sick or something?"

"Something," answered Cade. He'd been afraid something like this might crop up. Better to find the possible weak link here behind the wire than out there on the road. His first inclination when Brook proposed letting the kids come along was to scream *Hell no*, but he'd caved like he was prone to when Brook turned the screws or turned on the charm. Now he wished he'd listened to his gut instinct, which was usually always right.

But three against one was long odds so he said nothing more. Looked at his Suunto and did a quick calculation. *If we get going soon*, he thought, *then we might make Mack*—the small town straddling the border between Utah and Colorado—*sometime around dusk*. Just in time for a hot meal, and if the scuttlebutt he'd heard from some 4th ID soldiers who'd spent time there was correct—a hot shower just might be over the horizon.

The door creaked open and Wilson stepped into the flat light of morning. Mist swirling, he gently closed the door, head hanging low, eyes hidden by the brim of his boonie hat. Then he tossed his meager belongings into the back alongside Sasha's and, without looking at Cade or anyone else, took the wheel and made a shooing motion, urging Brook to pull ahead.

The carts started in near unison.

Brook edged around and nosed in the direction of the humongous aircraft hangers piercing the fog in the distance.

"Taryn's not coming?" Raven asked.

Once again Cade shrugged. He had no power over people—unless the circumstances required him to abduct or kill them. He tried to make eye contact with Wilson as they passed by the idling

Cushman, but only registered the funereal-look parked on the redhead's face.

Chapter 59
Quarry

After dragging the near-headless bodies out of sight, the three of them proceeded single file through the office and into the garage itself, leaving Jordan behind as lookout.

Once inside, another dichotomy presented itself. Although the exposed beams and rafters were obviously roughhewn old-growth and original to the building, Logan noticed that everything else was brand new and modern. There were work benches along two walls complete with peg boards and a plethora of tools, each outlined and hanging in their own assigned location. Sitting in the corner near the far overhead door were two enormous Honda generators—both shiny and red and still in their shipping packaging—crated in knotty yellow wood with Styrofoam showing at the corners. The floor they sat on had been painted a pale gray and was flecked with some kind of traction aid—which did wonders considering the slug tracks created by the female rotter as it had dragged its intestines everywhere. Aside from the slimy floor and streaks of body fluids and scraps of flesh and guts on the insides of the garage doors—every other surface in the place looked clean enough to eat from.

Gus, who trailed in last, flicked the wall-mounted switch—a move both rote and highly optimistic considering the electrical grid had been down since day two of the outbreak. However, he was rewarded for the effort as the overhead fluorescents flared to life, bathing them with a stark blue-white light. "Smart old guy ... installed himself a solar collection system on the roof," he said, looking up at the ceiling which had to be at least thirty-five feet overhead. "And I'd bet the farm that he probably installed twelve to fourteen panels at a hundred plus watts each. Hell, a kilowatt will go a long ways if you only have the essential stuff drawing from it."

Jamie looked at Gus. Made a face and said, "What were you doing, reading up on water filtration *and* solar arrays in between handing out speeding tickets and lounging around the donut shop?"

"Ha ha ... so easy to crack on a cop with the donut jokes. Pretty original, Jamie." His smile faded and he added without one scintilla of remorse, "That's exactly what I was doing, and that's why I left my badge and cruiser on the freeway near Arsenal and decided to take Logan up on his offer. And I'm glad I did. Wouldn't change a thing."

"I'm glad you did too," said Logan.

"Enough with the mushy stuff," Gus said sharply. "I think we ought to dismantle this system and load it onto those trucks along with the generators and take it all back with us."

The trucks Gus mentioned were nosed in to the back wall. Both were American-made rigs with dealer invoices glued to their passenger windows. The white Dodge was a factory-prepped extended cab 4x4 with a pair of whip antennas presumably for a citizens band radio. It was shod with dual rear wheels and oversized tires all tucked under widely-flared fender wells. The other, a black Chevy Silverado 4x4, was equipped similarly with a big Vortec engine sans the dual rear wheels.

Looking around the space, Jamie said, "So where's the video feed from the front gate end up?"

"Good question," answered Gus. "Surely they weren't monitoring it on that old IBM in the office."

Nosing around the far side of the hulking Chevy, Logan called out, "Over here."

Jamie worked her way around, Gus in tow, and arrived just as Logan was kicking aside a charcoal-gray area rug that looked like it belonged in the high-traffic entry of an auto parts or hardware store.

Gus said, "Whatcha got?"

"I found a door," he answered, pulling his shirt over his nose. "But there's something dead down there. Your turn to do the opening, Gus." He backed away.

Shouldering his AR, Gus approached the trap door which looked to be eight to ten feet long, and wide enough for two decent-sized men to stand atop shoulder-to-shoulder. He knelt and grasped the handle, pulled hard and swung it cleanly to the right and allowed it to rest against the workbench.

Simultaneously a cloud of flies, thicker than the first, enveloped his head while the air from below, thick with the stench of death, blasted him in the face. Throat constricting, he fell backwards and rolled onto his stomach. Instantly a torrent of vomit and bile sluiced from his mouth, running in rivulets over the edge of the shadowy opening and down the stairs which he'd caught a fleeting glimpse of before the unexpected two-pronged assault.

Grateful that a rotter hadn't followed the swarm from below, and certain he'd be as good as dead if one had, he slid on his butt away from the stairs and pulled a flashlight from its carrier on his belt. *Once a cop, always a cop*, he thought, as he twisted the bezel and swung the beam over the stairs. Wood treads—not quite as high tech as the rest of the garage—disappeared into the ground. Suddenly on the verge of hurling again, Gus said, "Someone open up a door. Let some of this stink out."

There was a clunk and then a discordant metallic rattle as Logan raised one of the garage doors upward in its tracks.

"Going in," said Gus, wiping his mouth with the back of his arm. Feeling like a tunnel rat in Nam, he fully collapsed the stock on his AR, clamped the tactical light between his teeth, and moved down the steps one at a time, careful to tread on the sides only, heel first, slowly transferring the weight to his toes.

Nine steps later he was standing on the metal floor of a buried Conex container. He walked the flashlight's beam left to right, illuminating the walls which were covered with small colorful murals, each with its own theme, painted by someone barely graduated from stick figures. Suddenly three light bulbs a yard above his head came on.

"How's that," Logan said, his voice thin and reedy in the stair's confines.

"Bright," answered Gus. He squeezed his eyes into slits until his pupils adjusted, and when he opened them fully he saw the source of the pong. Huddled in the far corner were two putrefying corpses, a boy and a girl.

The boy was tow-headed, thin in the face, and looked to have been about ten before death caught up to him. His hair was meticulously combed and he wore a pin-striped three-piece suit which was bulging at the seams from post mortem bloating. His shirt's top button had popped, dropping his clip-on tie into the biohazard soup wetting the front of his jacket and slacks.

The second corpse looked a spitting image of the boy. *Identical twins?* Gus noted that her blond hair had been cropped short—harder for a rotter to get a hold of, he guessed. Both wore masks of contentment, like they'd gone to sleep on Christmas Eve with visions of sugarplums banging around in their heads and simply failed to wake up.

On the floor near the kids was a woman of about forty, her body curled in a fetal position atop a once-yellow sleeping bag that had done a wondrous job of soaking up copious amounts of her bodily fluids. The sight reminded him that on average the human body held ten pints of blood, all of which had run in a continuous rivulet from the woman's slit right wrist, following the natural slope of the floor a number of feet before pooling and drying to black in the opposite corner of the container.

His gaze followed the nearly straight black line back to the sleeping bag. Then, full of sadness, his attention was drawn back to the woman. Nothing about her face was placid or calm or content. Her lips, thin bands of blue, were bared over a picket of crooked teeth. Her eyelids were frozen open but the windows to her soul were gone—having been usurped by a writhing plug of shiny maggots turned the color of ivory by the bulbs overhead.

He took a step closer, knelt down and took a pill bottle from under the sleeping bag near her head. He read the label. *Percocet. Prescribed by Doctor Jeff Malone. Quantity: 40 tablets, 5 milligrams per.* Enough to put the kids to sleep forever, he reasoned. But not enough for mom. So she resorted to slicing her wrists the correct way—vertically—thus taking the tendons out of the equation.

After covering the dead woman with the sleeping bag's top flap, Gus searched around and found a fleece blanket in a stuff sack which he used to fully conceal the kids.

Using the AR's flash suppressor he pushed open the next door, flicked the light switch and peered inside. *Clear.*

Following the same procedure he'd learned at the Academy and perfected from years serving the citizens of Salt Lake County, he searched the entire compound which was a warren of shipping containers, placed end to end like the Eden compound, but half the size. The technology, however, had not been skimped on. The security cameras at the front gate were indeed real, and broadcasting a steady image of the gate in one corner of a large flat-panel monitor.

Once he had checked the catacombs for more rotters, and after he'd taken a cursory inventory of the dead man's preps, he called out for the others to join him.

Chapter 60
Quarry

But only Logan came down the stairs. "Big enough for the two of us?" he asked.

"Judge for yourself."

"Wow, old man was keepin' himself busy."

"Where's Jamie?"

"She's doing the same thing you did."

"Puking?"

"And crying."

Gus made a face. "Let's see what we have here," he said. He pulled aside a number of hard plastic Pelican cases lining the wall opposite the glowing monitor, and with Logan helping, delved into them.

Inside the first box they found ammunition of various calibers as well as two sets of communication gear that rivaled the voice-activated units Lev and Chief had taken from the National Guard rotters. The next container held a half-dozen pairs of the earliest generation NVGs—not the best, but better than they already had, which was zip. The third case was filled to the top with medical supplies, arranged in neat little rows from meds on the left to bandages and sutures on the right.

Gus said, "Follow me," and led Logan into another room where—Eureka!—ballistic vests in multiple sizes hung on wooden hangers. Extra sets of camouflage clothing in kids and adults sizes were piled high. And above them, a host of pistols were affixed to the wall in the same manner as the hand tools up top. Each weapon had its own outlined place with hooks holding them in place. Standing up on the adjacent wall were a couple of scoped bolt-action sniper rifles, a half-dozen modern automatic rifles prepped for close quarters battle, and a trio of riot shotguns.

Then, stacked neatly along the wall below the guns were, by Gus's best estimation, several thousand rounds and at least thirty loaded magazines—mostly for the CQB rifles.

"This could *not* have been the old man's hideout," said Gus behind a low whistle.

Logan whistled also and spun a circle in the dead prepper's armory. He wanted to say, *I told you so*, but refrained. Instead he intoned gleefully, "Let's load this into the three trucks and get back to the compound ASAP." He picked up one of the head sets. Looked closely at the disc-shaped throat mike and smiled. "These will do. Don't you think?"

Eyes narrowing, Gus returned the smile, and nodded.

Jamie entered the room, still wiping away tears. Seeing this, Gus said, "I covered them up for your protection."

"I looked anyway. Shouldn't have though." She began to bawl—a mournful, hair-raising dirge.

"Come here," Logan said. Held his arms wide, took her in, gently wrapped her up and held on tight as sobs racked her body. After a couple of minutes she took a deep breath, fixed her red-rimmed brown eyes on his and mumbled, "Why? Why did she have to do that?"

"I'm guessing she couldn't find it within herself to go upstairs and kill her folks ... I'm guessing the rotters were those kid's grandma and grandpa," said Logan, nuzzling her dark hair. "And if she did, then she'd have to expose the kids to the world up there."

"Let's get cracking," urged Gus. "We've got lots of stuff to hump upstairs ... and we are burning daylight down—"

His appeal was abruptly interrupted by the long, drawn-out wail of the Tahoe's siren.

Gus backtracked to the container with the electronic gear, bent at the waist and looked hard at the monitor. "The gate looks clear," he hollered. "Maybe she's just lonely. You two get going. I'm right behind you."

***

With Jamie in tow, Logan snaked through the unfamiliar labyrinth, dodging hanging bulbs, piled-up stores, and bare metal bed frames along the way. As they entered the death room and passed the bodies of the woman and her kids, he sensed her slow and fall behind.

But he continued on.

He hit the stairs. Took them two at a time, and when he reached the top was blessed with a lungful of crisp clean air, nearly blinded by the light streaming in the open roller door, and greeted with two different noises. The first was familiar and in his face—the high-pitched piercing wail of the Tahoe's siren a dozen yards in front of him. The other was less distinct, much farther away. At first it struck him as perhaps coming from a big-rig compression-braking on the state route below. But countering that theory was the fact, that save the quarry drive, there were no steeply-graded hills to necessitate such an action.

So he stood under the half-open overhead door, squinting against the light and waving, trying to get Jordan's attention. But she was looking everywhere but in his direction. The siren blared on and then suddenly she turned her head and looked directly at him. Instantly her mouth formed a perfect 'O'. A beat later the blue and red lights went dark and the siren went silent. At first the crushing silence hung heavy over the quarry, but without the competing racket of the siren the noise he'd first chalked up to brake compression increased in tempo, the decibels rising. Then a blur, all glass and matte-black paint entered his side vision and began to slew and slow incredibly, almost in defiance of gravity.

Somehow over the whine of the gas turbine to the fore, he heard from behind the resonant clatter of something metallic striking the floor. Then the distinct rattle of a swivel attached to a rifle's sling. Next: the *schlack-schlack* of an AR charging handle being pulled back and sent home. Finally, urgent footsteps as Jamie and Gus formed up, one on either side of him.

Jordan had done her part.

Now his mind was racing—but not nearly as fast as the source of the second noise which had just ripped by mere feet above the steaming red earth, made a tight turn, and was now heading straight at them.

Then the noise rose to a pitch where he couldn't think or even hear his own voice, which if he could, would be telling him to move, to take action.

But his feet seemed rooted, and to add to the sensory bombardment, gritty, silt-laden water blasted his eyes and face, blinding him further, feeling like a thousand needle pricks on his exposed skin. Then the air around him crackled—sonic tremors whose origin he had a hard time placing. He heard the person to his right groan like the wind had been knocked from their lungs. But before he could look in that direction he felt his bowler hat lift from his head. And then the last thing he felt—before the world went black—was a hand, soft and feminine, grasping ahold of his.

Chapter 61
Schriever AFB

Continuing the age-old battle between night and day, the sun had risen a few more degrees in the sky and, with each passing second, prevailed in burning off more of the unusual fog that had descended on the airbase overnight and seemed hell-bent on sticking around until noon.

Cade held on tight as Brook turned a hard right that caused the cart's wheels to squeal against the glossy cement floor of the near-empty hangar whose jumbo-jet-accommodating-doors seemed to always be open. As she zippered between a number of static aircraft, Cade noticed a pair of the 160th SOAR Squadron's MH-60 Black Hawk helicopters, panels popped open, their innards—wiring and hydraulic tubing and anodized aluminum fittings—exposed for all to see. Then his gaze found the lone surviving Ghost Hawk, its silhouette low and sleek, carbon fiber rotors drooping, sad looking— he could almost sense it yearning to once again get airborne.

But it wasn't a living thing. A helicopter wasn't capable of emotion. Maybe he was sensing Ari, somewhere, lamenting the fact that he'd been passed over for the job of ferrying a Special Forces team on a mission back East to find some very specialized equipment for the scientists who had just begun working on the Omega antiserum.

"*Cade*. You have that look. What are you thinking about?" asked Brook as she slowed the Cushman and craned around, searching for the massive black Ford F-650 pick-up that had been nosed in against the wall when last she'd seen it.

"Change."

"Been lots of that lately."

"Where's the truck you told me about, Mom? Can't be that big," Raven said, moving her gaze around the hangar, a mirror image of her mom, "I don't see it anywhere."

Over the puttering engine noise and squeak of rubber echoing from the high rafters, Cade called from the rear seat for Brook to stop.

Brook complied. Flicked the switch, silencing the engine.

Cade untangled his crutches, rose to standing and clacked over to the spot where the truck had been parked. He checked his pockets and came out with the keys with the blue oval on the fob. Veins on his neck thick like cables, he turned a ragged spiral and then reared his head back and bellowed, "Whipper!"

Chapter 62
Eden Compound

Daymon continued hiking south along the fence line, consulting the map provided by Logan every now and again. He'd only been at it for a few minutes, and was making good time when he encountered the rotter. Trapped from the knees down in one of Duncan's Punji pits, the thing hissed and clacked its teeth, straining mightily against the sharpened stakes in an attempt to get at the nearby fresh meat.

"Talking loud. Ain't saying nothing," said Daymon, drawing his machete from its sheath. He shrugged off the shotgun and approached the creature with caution. He didn't know exactly how the traps worked, nor what they could do to a human, so he edged closer to get a better look.

But the undead thirty-something began to follow him—first the eyes—shark-like, never wavering. Then by twisting its torso around, exposing to Daymon presumably how it had died. Like most first turns he'd seen, it had defensive wounds, nicks and scratches and bites all up and down its arms. But that hadn't killed this one. The coup de gras came in the form of a massive bleed out. Like many of the others he'd seen since fleeing Utah in the early days of the outbreak, this one's neck had become someone's meal. He could see vertebra and shiny corded muscle and veins, masses of little snaking capillaries still clogged with congealed blood swaying and whipping with its every movement.

And as it flailed and grabbed at him, the sound of tendon and sinew snapping as rotted flesh and muscle was pitted against the sharpened saplings made Daymon wince.

Gotta do it. "Sorry, man," he said as the machete scythed the air. He winced again as the sharp steel cleaved into the rotter's temple and stuck there. Then he held on tight to the handle and let the weight of the monster and gravity do the rest.

As the thing hinged over, both bones in its lower leg snapped at odd angles, letting the body fall completely flat and causing Daymon's blade to pop free.

Daymon wiped the blade on some nearby grass. Looked east up the road and saw that the other rotters were still cresting the apex of 39 near where Lev was. He swung his head around west and saw nothing to be worried about. Then he fished in his pocket and brought out his map. He rummaged in the other and produced a Sharpie on its last legs. He marked the map with a tiny faded *DR*, his own little reminder that the dead rotter was there and would have to be dealt with later.

***

Though Logan had only been gone for a short time, Duncan rotated the volume knob up a couple of clicks, thumbed the call button on the two-way radio, and tried to hail him.

Initially there was no response. He double-checked that the Motorola was tuned to channel 10-1, then tried a few more times, still getting nothing but static. He was about to give up when Lev came on and said Logan was out of radio range and wasn't expected back for a couple of hours. "Copy that," replied Duncan sharply. Reluctantly, he turned the volume low and tossed the radio on the chopper's left seat. Took a sip from a bottled water. Lastly he scanned his surroundings and reburied his head in the technical manual for the DHS Black Hawk while trying his best to push the worry he was feeling for his baby brother to the back of his mind.

Chapter 63
Schriever AFB

Exactly ninety seconds after Cade began braying the first sergeant's name, he heard distant footsteps, a kind of high-speed shuffling interspersed with harsh squeaks echoing from the steel ceiling and walls. He looked up from the scrolling black digital numbers on the face of his Suunto and fixed a smoldering gaze on the older man who had sworn days earlier that their differences were a thing of the past, and, in the man's own words, *"The hatchet has been buried."*

That Brook and Raven were covering their ears and no doubt mortified didn't even make a blip on Cade's give-a-shit radar. He was beyond livid and—like Luke being beckoned to the Dark Side by Vader—was in danger of losing out to his anger and following up on an earlier threat, the result of which would be one man dead, and him locked up in the security pod.

Cade cast his gaze on the second Cushman, where Sasha looked on mouth agape and Wilson was slumped in his seat, knees cresting the short windshield, only the top of his boonie hat showing.

Refocusing his attention on the approaching man, dressed in greasy coveralls and kneading a similarly-soiled rag, Cade stood tall as possible—considering the crutches jammed into his armpits—and said through gritted teeth, "Whipper, where in the eff did you put my Ford?"

"I'm hooking it up for you," the crusty first sergeant answered with a sly smile.

"What ... you up-armoring it for me?"

"No need. Nothing's getting into that thing. And last I checked, the Zs aren't planting roadside IEDs."

Grimacing, Cade said, "You'd be surprised at what you'd encounter outside the wire."

Whipper made no reply.

Cade looked at Brook and shook his head. He jangled the keys at Whipper and said, "I have these. How'd you move the rig?"

"Same way we move aircraft around here. Follow me."

Wanting to exhibit zero weakness, Cade clunked along double-time and caught up to Whipper. They passed the Ghost Hawk, with the procession of Cushman carts creeping behind them. Then they passed by Whipper's battered yellow door and stepped onto the tarmac with the carts still shadowing them. "Here she is," said Whipper proudly, like he was showing off a piece of artwork or a new grandkid. "They're just about finished with her."

Chapter 64
Eden Compound

The second Daymon's eyes snapped open, a vague sense of unease descended over him, a feeling that something was definitely wrong—but he couldn't quite put a finger on it.

Considering the nightmare he'd just been starring in, and the fact that he was once again inside the metal cocoon that, for the time being, he begrudgingly called home, the realization that he wasn't perspiring profusely or fighting his demons for every breath came at a great surprise to him. *Amazing,* he thought to himself, *how a copious amount of fresh air coupled with a good deal of strenuous exercise can knock a guy out.* But the same thing held true when he'd been fighting fire in his old life. Cutting back brush and preparing fire-breaks had always had the same exact effect—instantaneous deep sleep—no matter the cramped one-man-tent nor his proximity to the all-too-real danger of being burned to death.

He passed the time waiting for the cobwebs to dissipate by listening to Heidi's breathing and staring towards the ceiling that he knew was there but couldn't see. Her respiration was measured—slow, and steady—and from the sound of it, she was experiencing a good round of much needed REM sleep. For a brief second he contemplated waking her, and just as quickly decided to let her be. That it was nearing noon had no bearing on his decision. The woman had been through a lot since the fall of Jackson Hole. Nothing wrong with a little sleeping in. *Besides,* he thought, *down here, without a watch, there's no way of knowing whether it's day or night.*

After finding his boots in the dark, he felt around and snatched up his shotgun and machete. Maintaining a modicum of stealth, he made it through the door and into the outer passage, leaving Heidi still sound asleep inside.

Meaning to go topside, he turned the corner, passed by Phillip who was still pulling time on the radios, and ran headlong into Duncan.

The two men, moving in opposite directions, bounced off of each other.

Rubbing his sternum, Daymon said, "Whoa, Trigger." He hiked up his shirt and was relieved to find that his pink "pet worms"—as Heidi had taken to calling the scars on his abdomen—hadn't split open again. Then, as he set his gaze on Duncan, a cold ball formed in his gut. Since the virus and its undead consequences had swept the nation, he'd seen this look on people's faces more times than he cared to remember. The usually rosy-cheeked cowboy was pale—stark white—like he'd just rubbed elbows with Death himself.

Duncan removed his glasses and wiped the lenses. Then, as if fighting some dire emotion, he took a deep breath and said, "This is one of those be-careful-what-you-wish-for moments, because I'm here to tell you that I'm taking you up on your offer."

Saying nothing, Daymon pinned his dreads behind his ears and held his breath. Finally, mind going a mile a minute, he exhaled but remained silent, stoic in the face of the coming fight with Heidi which he knew making the correct decision here and now was apt to bring on. But still, he owed the old man for going out of his way and delivering him to his little house in Driggs. For if he'd never made it home and got ahold of Lu Lu, he'd never have made it to Jackson Hole and reconnected with Heidi in the first place. So, though he'd expected the reconnaissance flight to be tomorrow, he had no choice but to say yes right here and now.

"Take some time. Mull it over," Duncan said with a thick drawl. "And then I'll see you topside in five." His face relaxed a bit but his body language—stooped shoulders, head hanging ever so slightly—was unchanged.

The sound of a chair scooting back broke the silence, and Daymon noticed Phil staring at him from behind Duncan's elbow.

"Yes, I'll go up with you," Daymon finally said, causing Duncan to double-take and make an instant about-face where he stood. "But why today? Why right now? And why in the eff do you look like you just saw a ghost?"

Chapter 65
Schriever AFB

The twin-engine, tandem-rotor Chinook MH-47, measuring ninety-nine feet from nose to tail, and nearly thirty feet from tarmac to the top mast of the rear rotor, made the oversized Ford F-650 parked alongside look like a child's toy.

At first glance, Cade couldn't see what Whipper and his ground crew had done to the rig. But by the time he had hobbled within spitting distance, it was obvious to him what the wispy-haired sergeant had in mind. Before he could mount any kind of a protest, Whipper had closed the distance and started yammering—more in the interest of self-preservation than an act of cordiality. When the small talk was out of the way, Cade said, "What the hell has gotten in to you, Whipper?"

Whipper smoothed back the white hair that to Cade seemed to be getting lighter and thinner by the day. He raised his hands shoulder high and said, "I'm sorry. I thought I'd take the initiative ... do you a favor. I kind of feel like I still owe you for what you endured the other day. Losing Sergeant Maddox on your watch and all."

Checking his rising anger, Cade made no reply.

"Hear me out," said Whipper, hands on hips. "I did some thinking"—*for a change*, Cade thought—"even in that big rig of yours, the second you get outside the wire you've got three things working against you—"

"More like three hundred million. And they're all dead," countered Cade. He flicked his gaze to Raven and then to Brook, who was giving him the look that all women seemed to have been born knowing how to deliver. It was obvious she wanted to be in the loop—*yesterday*. He shrugged, adjusted his stance on the crutches, and returned his attention to Whipper.

"First off, south and west of here there are still large groups of Zs that splintered off from the Pueblo herd. And if you go the obvious overland route through Manitou Springs, then you'd no doubt have an uphill battle just trying to avoid tangling with them. Secondly, northwest of here there are bunches of Zs leftover from the Denver horde, many of them radioactive. They've been roaming the no man's land between Springs and the Castle Rock craters since you Delta guys popped the nukes."

"I was told the 4th ID had a handle on the Zs," said Cade, flashing Brook his open hand, a silent plea for five more minutes.

"The ones from Pueblo for the most part. But it'll be months before they clean up the hot ones. They spread out north and east. Just kept walking leaving trails of footprints in the fallout. Hope is that the cold weather will slow them down. You know that Fuentes fella ... before he was killed he put one of them in the walk-in freezer in the mess hall."

"And?"

"It froze. Stopped moving ... until Fuentes thawed it out. Then ... business as usual."

Shaking his head, Cade said, "And the third thing going against me?"

"Nash," said Whipper with a certain twinkle in his eyes. "She's not really against you though ... unless you decline her overture."

"Which is?"

"She feels indebted to you, I would suppose. She ordered me to make sure you and your family get to Mack in one piece. Major Greg Beeson will be expecting you."

Smiling and shaking his head in disbelief, Cade heard Nash in his mind, the words spoken slowly and deliberately: *Be careful what you wish for.*

"Shall I have my men secure the sling?"

Eyes downcast and keeping his distance, Wilson filed by carrying a bat and a backpack. Apparently Brook had put two-and-two together and had gotten the *show on the road*. Another of Cade's pet sayings. "Go ahead. Looks like the call has already been made by my better half." He watched Sasha, loaded down with baggage, doddle along behind her brother and follow him up the Chinook's ramp.

"Done," said Whipper, beaming after having just killed two birds with one stone. He began backing away, but before he was out of earshot Cade called out, "Who's flying us there?"

"Not to worry ... he's a SOAR aviator. And I think he should be finishing up with the pre-flight on the other side of the helo. You should go on over and introduce yourself," Whipper answered rather cryptically.

Just then a fuel bowser, ungainly and heavy up top, rounded the far hangar and crossed the tarmac at a walking speed, its engine and overworked, whining transmission drowning out all other sound. It pulled a neat U-turn and parked between the Ford and the MH-47. Then a harsh squeal sounded from the fuel tanker as the driver applied the brakes and silenced the motor.

Deciding not to get in the way of the refueling process, Cade put meeting the air crew on hold. Instead, he covered the short distance to the Cushman and sat down next to Brook.

He told her everything Whipper had just told him, most of which she had already guessed. "A few minutes is all, and we'll be airborne."

"That helicopter can pick up the truck?" asked Raven, a touch of amazement in her voice.

"And then some," answered Cade. "I've seen one like it carrying *two* Humvees."

Having ridden in a Humvee once or twice, the visual of two of them taking the place of the Ford made Raven's eyes go wide.

"How long will the flight take?" asked Wilson, who had just returned after stowing his gear in the aircraft.

Cade guessed and said, "Two hours, tops."

"Anything you need me to do? I need something to take my mind off of Taryn."

"Care for a word of advice?" asked Cade.

"Sure," answered Wilson. "Can't possibly make matters worse."

"Not so sure of that. How old are you?"

"Twenty-one. Just turned before the rest of America *turned*."

"She won't be the last."

"Last?"

"Last one to break your heart," said Cade. He looked at the sun-painted peaks in the distance and then added in a near whisper, "I'd get used to it if I were you."

***

Ten minutes after it hooked up to the Chinook the fuel bowser pulled away, leaving Cade a clear view of the pilot; he already had his flight helmet on and was conversing with two men who looked to be the co-pilot and crew-chief. The three men were having an animated discussion, and by the time Cade approached to within earshot he recognized the very distinct voice of someone who he'd spent plenty of time with over the last week or so.

"Ari Silver, I'm not getting in that bird with you," said Cade jokingly.

"Not you again," Ari shot back over his shoulder. He had a few more words with his crew and then broke free from the pre-flight jaw session. "Nash didn't tell you I'd be shuttling you to Mack?"

"In hindsight, yes. But I failed to read between the lines."

"Surprised?"

"Yes, because you were pretty beat up yesterday. And no, because I went to bat for you ... *twice*. Once when I penned the watered-down after action report. Then when I had my *exit interview* with Freda Nash."

"Thanks. Means a lot," said Ari.

Arching a brow, Cade replied, "Even though you're stuck flying a *Shithook*."

"I'm just grateful to be on the stick. Plus, there's nothing for me to do here on the ground. Speaking of ground ... everything is onboard. Your monster truck is in the sling and ready to go." He looked towards his crew who had been standing just out of earshot, spun his finger in a ragged circle and shouted, "We're *oscar mike* in five."

"One question," said Cade, leaning in close.

Ari cocked his head but said nothing.

"How are you feeling ... your arms and shoulders?"

Ari smiled wide. He took a breath and said, "Couple of Ibuprofens and a deep tissue massage set me back on course. Besides, I'm flying, so everything is right with the world."

Everything? thought Cade "Honored to fly with you again," he said.

"Means a lot after all that's happened. Put 'er here."

They shook hands and Cade creaked away, leaving Ari to finish his pre-flight.

Chapter 66
Eden Compound

With Daymon matching him stride for stride, Duncan trudged a beeline across the grassy clearing, his gaze locked firmly on the vague outline of the borrowed Black Hawk helicopter. With a large swath of dark woodland camouflage netting stretched across the rotors and covering the cockpit glass like a veil of mourning, the chopper looked more like a widow attending a funeral than the utilitarian work-horse helicopter he hoped to have airborne shortly.

With help from Daymon who possessed a nearly ten-inch advantage in the reach department, they freed the helicopter from the fabric shroud. And as they dragged the netting a good distance away from the helicopter a stiff breeze kicked up, fluttering the fabric and prompting Duncan to add the mental note *Slight breeze from the west* to the flotsam and jetsam clouding his mind.

"You get the left seat," Duncan called out as he loped around the helo's nose and began his cursory preflight inspection.

"You're flying ... *right?*" asked Daymon pensively.

"Yes, Daymon. A helicopter is the opposite of a car, though. Pilot usually sits on the starboard side so he can see the tail rotor. The co-pilot sits on the left—"

Thinking back to his previous ride in the very same helicopter suddenly jogged Daymon's memory. "On the *port* side," he replied, finishing Duncan's thought. He popped his *port* side door open and clambered in, maneuvering his long legs around the stick before positioning his boots rather awkwardly into the footwell.

"What are you ... part spider?" asked Duncan, looking up at the former BLM firefighter.

Daymon made no reply. Merely flashed the old man a wan smile as he snugged the flight helmet over his dreadlocks.

Duncan smiled and continued his walk-around, taking in the condition of the helicopter's fuselage. Considering the previous night's rain, the amount of accumulated human detritus that remained was staggering. Bloody hand prints and slug-track-like streaks of unknown bodily fluids painted both of the helo's flanks and clouded nearly every pane of aviation glass encircling its rounded-off nose. He wet a rag he'd found in the chopper with residual dew off the grass. Made a few passes over the cockpit windows. Next, he inspected the moving parts on the tail assembly. From flight school on up to his days flying slicks and Cobra gunships with the 1st Air Calvary in Vietnam, this had always been his least favorite part of flying. But thankfully he was spared the task of scaling the chopper after learning from the DHS manual that, unlike the venerable Huey, this Black Hawk didn't have a Jesus bolt that needed checking prior to every flight. So instead of looking like a geriatric Spiderman, he eyeballed the drooping rotor blades from the ground. Finally, after determining that everything he knew enough to inspect prior to getting in the air appeared to be in working order, he opened the starboard side door and slipped behind the controls.

"Kick the tires and light the fires?" said Daymon.

Not in the mood for small talk, Duncan said nothing. He snugged on a pair of gloves left behind by the last aircrew, donned his helmet, and plugged his comms jack into the port.

"That's a line from Top Gun," added Daymon sheepishly.

After shrugging on the harness and snugging it tight, Duncan, who was growing more surly by the minute, finally answered, "Something like that." Then his hands went to work flicking switches that brought various systems on line and set a good portion of the cockpit lights and dials glowing in soft reds and greens. *Good to go*, he thought. The hour plus he'd spent reading the manual earlier had paid off. He brought the APU on line, which in turn fired up the turbines. They howled to a crescendo and the four rotor blades above their heads spun up, fast becoming a blur of white and black.

The second the rpms were sufficient for takeoff, Duncan pulled pitch and the chopper lifted gradually into the air and then pivoted on axis. "Hang on," he said through clenched teeth as the nose dipped, the engine noise increased, and the clearing fell away below them.

"How are the eyes?" asked Daymon.

"Fine."

"What's the plan?"

"Find Logan and give him a piece of my mind for not checking in."

"You're not his dad," Daymon proffered as the horizon changed drastically and the g-forces from the abrupt maneuver to port pushed him against the seatback.

Silence.

"Do you know where your bro was going?"

"Not necessarily. I'm operating on hearsay and innuendo and assumption here ... but it's all I got. From what Logan told me earlier, the old guy's place was rumored to be somewhere between Huntsville and Woodruff. That's thirty-six miles as the crow flies ... much farther on the ground." He paused for a spell as his hard-set eyes danced between the gauges and the gray stripe of road splitting the lush green canopy flicking by underneath them. He swiveled his head, then made the helicopter climb sharply before leveling it out and slowing considerably. "The compound is nearly smack dab between the two towns. Makes looking for them a little easier."

"Why's that?"

"Less of a chance of the old guy setting up shop near Huntsville because that's where he was renting his equipment from. Hell, if I was him I'd do the same thing ... throw anyone who was watching off the trail."

"So Woodruff is dead ahead?"

"About thirteen miles, I gather. Figure I'll just follow 39 and hope the cruiser shows itself."

Daymon nodded and continued scanning the road and forest to the right. "I see a little river down below. A few scattered groups of rotters as well."

"Probably traipsing back and forth between their old stomping grounds. I bet those things are thick down near Ogden on into Salt Lake."

"Like molasses," answered Daymon. "Seen them with my own eyes. South Salt Lake blew my mind. Dead everywhere. Rotters and half-eaten corpses."

"Too far gone to reanimate?"

Nodding, Daymon said, "And they were the lucky ones."

Turning the Black Hawk to port to follow a sweeping bend in the road brought a knuckle of red-hued earth jutting several hundred feet above the surrounding foothills into their path of flight. The high sun was flaring off of a substantial body of water that looked too symmetrical not to have been man-made.

"What the heck is that?"

"Let's take a gander," said Duncan as he increased altitude, bringing the rapidly-approaching top of the stunted peak directly into their line of sight. He was watching the Black Hawk's shadow riding over the tree tops, dipping and falling between breaks in the canopy, when suddenly his eye was drawn to a dirt road winding like a sprung coil up the southeast side of the red peak.

As the Black Hawk's rate of approach quickly halved the distance, Duncan nudged the nose gently to port in preparation for a high speed flyover. He leveled the bird out and passed his gaze over what he guessed to be a mining operation, its water-filled quarry reflecting the handful of clouds scudding through the cobalt sky, and sitting in front of an L-shaped grouping of buildings shielded by a grove of dogwoods was the black and white Tahoe, unmistakable with its blue and red light bar and needle antennas.

"That's Jenkins' ride," observed Daymon. "And they left all four doors open. Which I think is kind of strange, 'cause I can't see any movement down there."

Saying nothing, Duncan slowed the chopper and scrutinized the rest of the hilltop operation. Blocking access to the only road coming into the place was a good-sized hurricane fence on wheels. It was topped off with a double wrap of concertina razor wire. With his eyes, Duncan followed the lone set of tire tracks as they passed underneath the fence, ran up to and ended with the inert Tahoe. To the right of the quartet of buildings was a second fence bordering a massive briar patch with numerous vehicles trapped in its thorny clutches. As they got to within fifty yards of the trio of rundown outbuildings, Duncan held the bird in an unsteady hover and spun the helo on axis to give Daymon an unobstructed view.

"The biggest building looks like some kind of garage," said Daymon, confirming what Duncan was already thinking. "Slide us closer. I think I see something in the shadows between the garage and those three sheds."

"What do you see?" asked Duncan, trying to squint the scene below into focus.

Reverting back to the slang used by the soldiers at Schriever, Daymon replied, "Looks like a couple of dead Zs ... and someone took it to them pretty good."

"Setting her down in five."

The ground drew closer, the ripples in the puddles becoming white caps.

"Four."

The smaller rocks and pebbles became airborne under the force of the rotor wash, sandblasting the Tahoe's paint, making a mess of the interior on the driver's side.

"Three," said Duncan, half-expecting a hail of lead to be thrown their way, his hand ready to pull pitch and get them away to safety if the need arose.

The cyclonic wash emptied the nearby puddles of every drop of coppery-tinted water.

"Two."

Finger off the trigger, Daymon crunched a round into his stubby combat shotgun. He patted his thigh, double-checking that the machete was strapped there, and then placed his free hand on the harness release.

"One," said Duncan as the big Black Hawk's tires met terra firma and she bounced and crunched along the red dirt for a couple of feet before coming to a halt, the rotors still blurring the sky overhead. "I'm going to keep her running. I want you to stay here and be a lookout while I check out the big building."

Nodding an affirmative, Daymon twisted his torso around and plucked the binoculars from his bag on the floor.

Leaving his flight helmet on, Duncan unplugged it from the jack and then exited the noisy machine. With no means of communicating with Daymon, he flashed a thumbs up, hustled around the helo's nose, and made tracks for the abandoned Tahoe.

Chapter 67
Schriever AFB

The Chinook's interior was Spartan to say the least. Fold-up center-facing seats consisting of red nylon mesh pulled tightly over simple aluminum frames lined both sides of the fuselage. Though far from comfortable, Cade conceded, ninety minutes or so in the air and a slightly numb ass was a hell of a lot better than driving all day through a countryside teeming with roving groups of hungry dead.

He noticed Raven fidgeting in her seat. Gave her a gentle nudge to get her attention, and when she looked up, he planted a kiss on her oversized flight helmet.

The simple gesture prompted a toothy smile from the twelve-year-old. Already gone was the tight set of her jaw, thanks to a smooth-talking Ari who had taken her and Sasha around the outside of the hulking Chinook, pointing out all of the designed-in safety features. Then they received a grand tour of the flight deck, with Ari even allowing each of them to sit for a spell behind the controls. Then, pretending to be a male flight attendant, he had guided them to a pair of seats situated side-by-side, far enough away from the windows so they wouldn't be able to see the true nature of Omega's effect on the outside world—a brilliant move in Cade's humble opinion. Finally, after playing the attendant role to the hilt, Ari switched back into pilot mode and elicited a few laughs from them with the promise that he would fly like a *"grandma"* all the way to their destination.

Cade palmed Raven's helmet, gently turned her head, looked deeply into her eyes and said quietly, "This trip will be just like the time you and me and Mom flew Portland to Seattle. We'll go up and then we'll be landing in Mack before the drink cart gets halfway down the aisle."

Hearing this, Sasha flashed Cade a conspiratorial smile that implied that she knew what he was up to but wouldn't spill the beans.

Then, after looking the length of the helicopter, Raven shot back, "There is no drink cart, *Dad.*"

Cade smiled at her retort and the manner in which she said "*Dad*" which could be construed in one of many ways. But this time, judging by the inflection and tone, his mind automatically inserted the word *silly*. *Could have been worse*, he thought to himself. Thankfully she had never been prone to talking back like some of the girls who had attended sleepovers at the Grayson house. He rummaged in a cargo pocket. Pulled a Capri Sun he'd been saving for this occasion, and said, "Dad's drink cart is on board." Framed by the helmet, Raven's beautiful smile made another appearance.

He burned the image into his memory, then swept his gaze right. He caught Brook's eye and winked at her; a simple gesture that cracked the usual granite set to her jaw, producing a rare smile—also archived for use on a rainy day. *Because going forward*, he told himself, *things are certainly going to get tougher before they get better, and I want something I can call up—to get me through those tough times when things start getting dicey.*

He looked at his Suunto and felt a barely perceptible vibration pulse through the Chinook as the auxiliary power unit came to life somewhere within the airframe, powering the hydraulics and lighting the twin-turbines. *Right on time*, he thought as the rising high-pitched whine of the jet-turbines spooling and the slow but steadily rising *thwop-thwop* of the rotor blades reached his ears. A moment later the kerosene-tinged odor of jet exhaust wafted in from outside. Once again he got Raven's attention with a gentle nudge, plugged his nose, and mouthed, "Pee-eww," at her.

Suddenly the airframe groaned as power was applied to the engines. Consequently, Cade imagined the massive rotors feet above his head gaining rpms, their characteristic droop disappearing as centrifugal forces at work flattened them out and bowed them upward slightly.

As the noise inside the cabin rose, Cade regarded Brook. Her eyes were closed, the flight helmet making her look a little like a bobble head doll—albeit a very beautiful one. He passed his gaze over to Wilson, who was seated across from him next to one of the four widely-spaced porthole-style windows on the port side, wearing the same stoic the-world-has-gone-to-hell-in-a-handbasket look on his face. A look that aged him a decade at the least.

Through the porthole, above and left of Wilson's shoulder, Cade could see Cheyenne Mountain—President Valerie Clay's fortified redoubt—and the undulating spine atop the Rockies' western front stretching north toward Denver. Then he craned around and regarded the Ford which was sitting on the tarmac a dozen feet from the Chinook's starboard side.

Sun flared from the copious amounts of glass and chrome and black sheet metal. The thick straps of the cargo sling securing the truck to the helo's underbelly were fluttering madly, buffeted by the hurricane-strength rotor wash. On the tarmac, one of Whipper's men was standing near the Ford, sending some kind of instructions via hand signals to the aircrew in the cockpit.

Suddenly, in his flight helmet which was connected to the ship-wide comms via a thick cable plugged into the bulkhead, Cade heard the co-pilot—who was a doppelganger to Agent Adam Cross—call out, "Thirty seconds to launch." Then Ari broke in over the co-pilot and said, "Welcome aboard Night Stalker Airways *and* vehicle transport. Next stop, Mack, Colorado. We will be cruising at one hundred and thirty knots at one thousand feet above ground level—" *Let's keep it that way*, thought Cade, "—with an estimated flight time of one hour and forty-five minutes. Please stow your tray tables and put your seats in their upright positions, and then after a brief test hover we will be underway."

Reacting to the announcement which everyone else heard broadcast inside their helmets, Cade mimed folding up an imaginary tray table, an impromptu act which seemed to lighten the mood, drawing laughs from the girls but not from Wilson, who was now bent at the waist, face buried deep in his hands.

As the rotors bit into the air and the turbines strained to generate the torque necessary for lift off, the noise in the fuselage rose exponentially. Then, simultaneously, as if the move had been rehearsed in advance, both Raven and Sasha shot furtive wide-eyed looks around the cabin and clamped their hands over their ears on the outside of their loose-fitting flight helmets. Brook, however, merely closed her eyes and settled in for the harsh flight—this being her third stint aboard a Chinook since the outbreak and all.

As Cade looked on, the horizon outside the window seemed to shift slightly as the Chinook's front gear left the tarmac. Then the craft leveled off, and the buildings and perimeter fencing in the distance steadily slipped from sight. In his mind's eye, Cade could picture the strapping affixed to the pallet under the truck going taut and the cargo finally leaving the ground. But instead the comms crackled, and he heard the co-pilot say, "Four o'clock starboard." Then the engines powered down considerably and Ari said, "Everybody brace. I've got to put her back down."

Suddenly the helo juddered and yawed sideways, losing a few feet of altitude in the process.

Hover test my ass, Cade thought to himself. With the cold presence of impending doom tickling his stomach, he regarded his family, and then uttered a prayer, asking the Man upstairs for a soft wheels-down landing. Because from experience he was well aware that it would only take a few degrees list to port or starboard to bring the rotor blades into contact with the asphalt tarmac and send thousands of pieces of disintegrating steel and carbon fiber flying through the air like angry hornets. Hoping for the best while bracing against the worst, Cade grabbed a handful of webbing between his thighs with one hand, and wrapped his left arm around Raven's narrow frame. "*Hold on,*" he said sharply.

Chapter 68
Quarry

Colt .45 in hand, Duncan climbed from the Black Hawk, ducked his head against the perceived threat of decapitation, and hustled in a combat crouch towards the Chevy Tahoe. After covering the distance as fast as his old bones would allow, he pulled up short next to the truck's rear quarter panel and peeked inside. Shoehorned in behind the rear seats was a black plastic Pelican case the size of a typical piece of wheeled carry-on luggage. The cruiser's molded-plastic back seat was empty; moving toward the front of the rig, he found the window rolled down and, like the others, the door hinged open. The keys were still in the ignition and apart from a half-full bottle of water, a poorly-folded road map, and a bolt-action rifle that he thought might belong to Jordan, he found no other personal effects.

But most importantly, what he failed to find in and around the SUV was what gave him a modicum of hope. Thankfully missing were obvious signs that a struggle had taken place. He saw no traces of blood. And there were no shell casings inside or around the SUV. And so far, other than the two dead rotters between the farthest of the three outbuildings, there were no other corpses in sight.

After deciding to check the swaybacked structures first, he met Daymon's gaze; knowing that the former firefighter had no military training, decided that dumbing down the hand signals was the best way for them to communicate. So he pantomimed his

335

intentions by pointing at the shed on the left and then walking his fingers across his palm.

Message delivered, Duncan left the temporary shelter of the SUV's door and endured the blasting sand and water and continual popping of the rotors as he sprinted to the nearby building. Pressing his back against the roughhewn boards, he steadied his breathing and listened hard. But nothing distinguished itself over the noise of the chopper and the whoosh of blood surging between his ears, so, seeing as how any element of surprise had been squelched by their less-than-ninja-quiet arrival, he called out for his brother, quietly, at first.

There was no answer.

He tried again. Louder. More urgency in his voice.

Still he got no response.

Goddamn it, he thought to himself. *Why did I let him go out without me?*

With the business-end of his pistol out in front, he cleared the tiny buildings starting left and working right and, like the lonely Tahoe, found all three abandoned and empty.

He popped out of the third building closest to the garage and scanned the perimeter one final time, walking his gaze along the fence line to the gate, then back to the brambles and the long-idled heavy machinery. He looked over at Daymon and placed his hand up, palm out, fingers spread slightly—another silent signal telling him to stay put. Then for some reason something about the damp earth's appearance a dozen yards behind the Tahoe piqued his interest. But seeing as how he was closer to the garage, he made a mental list that placed examining the disturbed ground between checking the garage's perimeter and fully sweeping its interior. The latter he decided, based on the sheer size of the place, he wouldn't be doing alone.

When he neared the pale green door, which rather ominously was blood-spattered and hanging ajar, he couldn't help but notice the destroyed lock and bullet holes puckering the steel where presumably Logan or one of the others had used their weapon to gain entry. Seeing only cheap-looking furniture inside the gloom, he moved on. With the .45's muzzle tracking his gaze, he cut the corner wide and wound around back, along the way making all of the same observations and assumptions as Logan had concerning the newness of the roller doors out front and the recently-installed windows on the far southernmost side.

Duncan was nobody's fool, and possessing a strong intuition and usually infallible gut instinct ran in the Winters family. And as he stood near the corner of the building and watched the rotor blades cut the air above the chopper, the mental note hit his in-box, spurring him into action.

He ambled onto the crushed rock parking lot where he followed a zig-zag pattern to the spot of disturbed earth that he'd noticed earlier.

One look was all it took for all of the pieces of the puzzle to fall into place. He walked a wide rectangle, boots crunching a cadence, his mind wrestling with a new set of clues. Positioned in a sort of semi-circle, blending in with the like-colored earth, were a dozen brass shell casings, all of them 5.56 and probably from an AR or M4-type carbine. *Not good*, he thought as he continued the search. A dozen yards from where he found the brass, on the periphery of the disturbed area, he spotted a number of black playing cards that had found their way into the puddles, became waterlogged, and were now sitting at the bottom.

Instantly his stomach constricted. A frigid tremor wracked his body as he bent over and plucked one from the water. It was an Ace of Spades. *Death cards*. He'd seen them before in Vietnam usually accompanying the mutilated corpse of one of his brothers-in-arms. He turned it over and over in his hand—thinking—but still didn't recognize what the blood-red logo on the opposite side represented. The image was of some kind of medieval warrior in full battle dress, wearing a plumed helmet with a thin slit for eyes. He pocketed the card and the .45 went back on his hip in its high-riding holster. He ducked his head, covered his face and sprinted back to the helicopter. Yanked the door open and shut the Black Hawk down. Meeting Daymon's eyes and noting the perplexed look on the man's face, Duncan snatched up an M4 carbine from the back compartment, nodded in the direction of the garage, and mouthed, "Follow me."

Once the turbines had quieted down and the rotor blades were stilled, and he and Duncan were twenty feet from the bird, Daymon asked, "I saw you inspecting the ground. What did you learn?"

Duncan halted, turned towards Daymon, and hung his head. He removed his glasses and pinched the bridge of his nose. Finally he replaced his glasses, met the younger man's gaze, and replied, "Whoever *was* here, ain't here any longer."

Trying to ruffle away the dome shape the helmet had pressed into his dreadlocks, Daymon said, "Can you elaborate? 'Cause I'm no good at guessing games."

"A couple of helicopters set down over there behind Charlie's cruiser. One had skids like a Huey, only different. The other marked the ground up just like ours. The wheels were side by side and there was also a wheel out back. Probably a type of Black Hawk, which leads me to believe the other ship was one of those Little Birds ... like those special ops helos I saw flitting about Schriever. "

"Begs the question then ... who were they? And where did they spirit your brother, Gus, and the ladies off to?"

Like a portent of things to come, a stiff wind gust banged the office door against the wall.

"I'm not so sure they've been taken." He hinged at the waist, placed a hand on his knee and took a couple of deep breaths. "I don't like what I've seen so far. In fact, my gut is telling me something I don't want to hear."

Resting the shotgun on his shoulder, Daymon opened his mouth like he was going to say something, but thought better of it and remained silent.

"Found some spent brass back there. Now I'm terrified to set foot in that building," Duncan said, gesturing at the creaking door.

"I'll go first," Daymon said, leveling his weapon at the doorway. He took the steps in one stride and covered his mouth against the pungent reek of death that hit him the moment he crossed the threshold into the low-ceilinged room.

Seeing this, Duncan put his boot on the first step.

Voice muffled by his free hand, Daymon looked back and said, "You better not. I'll do this alone."

***

Three minutes later, by Duncan's watch, Daymon emerged from the door carrying Logan's crushed and bloodied bowler. Looking every bit a walking corpse, ashen-faced and speechless, the dreadlocked man sat down hard on the top stair.

Then, without saying a word—because none could describe the pain he was feeling—Duncan turned and slumped against the rust-streaked wall, riding it to the ground where he sat with his arms wrapped around his head for a good ten minutes.

Chapter 69
Schriever AFB

In order to leave the landing pad clear for the Chinook and put the Ford back down in roughly the same location it had been before launch, Ari had to make the unannounced but very necessary sideslip maneuver—that even to Cade, who was used to riding in all types of aircraft, had seemed very uncharacteristic at the time, considering the helicopter wasn't taking enemy fire.

"Bad choice of words," Ari said over the shipwide comms as he leveled the bird out. "Whipper tells me he has an important passenger on the tarmac who we need to get on board."

Cade's mind ran in circles as he craned around and looked outside to see who might be waiting. The first candidate that crossed his mind was Colonel Shrill. Maybe the man had decided at the last minute that he wanted to pop in on Major Beeson unannounced and conduct a surprise inspection in person. If so, Greg was *not* going to be happy. Maybe President Valerie Clay and Major Freda Nash were going come aboard and put on another full court press to try and convince him to stay at Schriever and continue running ops for them. If so, *Brook* was not going to be happy. *No use speculating*, he told himself. Resting his head against the bulkhead, he watched the scenery outside the window crawl slowly upward as if their takeoff had been recorded and was now being played back in reverse.

The mountains were momentarily visible through the small porthole window. Then the Zs crowding the distant fencing gave way to blue sky, which was quickly blotted out by the flat, squared-off rooftops of the nearby aircraft hangars. Lastly, a supernova-like glare illuminated the helo's dark interior as they put down next to the truck which had spun a few degrees while airborne and was now sitting perpendicular, almost as if it were about to T-bone the helicopter, its newly-cleaned windshield simultaneously reflecting and amplifying the ascending sun.

Finally the Chinook came to rest, its bulbous tires and substantial hydraulic shock absorbers making the landing even softer than Cade had prayed for.

Then the stone-faced African American flight engineer unhooked his safety harness, strode aft along the metal gangway, and hit a switch that started the rear ramp on a downward journey.

Accompanied by a steady hydraulic whine, inch by inch the metal maw parted, allowing in harsh white bars of light which temporarily blinded everyone inside the helo.

When a semblance of normal vision finally returned, Cade panned his gaze aft at their new passenger and was suddenly flooded by a feeling of been-there-done-that when he recognized the fully-framed silhouette.

Chapter 70
Utah

Though Duncan had skipped the section in the DHS flight manual concerning the Black Hawk's performance thresholds, judging by the intermittent blips and bleeps coming from the cockpit warning systems as they hammered along a couple of hundred feet above the treetops pushing one hundred and fifty knots, it suddenly occurred to him that whatever they were, he was probably nearing or exceeding many of them.

With the turbines whining, high-pitched overhead, and the main rotor beating a sad cadence against the moisture-laden air, he nosed the Black Hawk on a westward heading, keeping the livewire glint of the Ogden river off to their left and SR-39 meandering lazily below.

Then for at least the tenth time during the short flight, he looked over his left shoulder just to make sure he wasn't stuck in a never-ending nightmare. But sure enough, Gus's and Logan's corpses were real and still back there, lying crossways in the cabin, wrapped in sheets stripped from the bunks in the subterranean shelter. And even in his side vision, Duncan could see that the crimson blooms, roughly center mass on each of the bodies where the murderers had scored tightly-grouped shots, were steadily spreading across the white fabric like some kind of unstoppable virus.

Daymon adjusted the boom mike and asked, "What's on your mind, sir?"

Twisting his head owl-like and fixing a no-nonsense stare in Daymon's direction, Duncan drawled, "No, you didn't. I will *not* have you and Phil both calling me sir. Duncan works for me. Or Winters. Hell ... you can even call me Chief if it's OK with *the* Chief."

"Sorry," replied Daymon.

"In reply to your pansy-ass try at pulling an end-around of my defenses, I'll honor the effort and lay it all out on the table for you."

Save for the air rushing by the cockpit, and the din of the engines and the complex mechanicals all working in unison to keep the five-ton aircraft aloft, there was a long uneasy silence. "*Revenge* is on my mind," Duncan finally said. "No more live-and-let-live bullshit. I should have gutted that Chance kid when I had the *chance*." He chuckled at his play on words—the sound low and menacing. "Scorched earth is my new policy. In fact, right now all I want to do is channel my inner Genghis Khan and burn Huntsville to the fuckin' ground—man, woman, and child. And then I want to skull fuck every one of the corpses of those animals that killed my little brother. He was *only* thirty-five. I've got a Zippo lighter that's older than that boy. I was *not* supposed to outlive him, Daymon. And every second that the assholes who did this are alive on this earth and stealing air from the rest of us is an affront ... a slap in the face to how he lived his life. He-was-a-good-boy—"

Daymon watched with rapt interest as the old man's voice rose and spittle flew from his mouth and landed on the controls and gauges. Suddenly something appeared to jog Duncan's memory, and as if a switch had been flicked he stopped talking and looked around. Simultaneously he flared and slowed the helicopter, abruptly changing its course.

Daymon contemplated Duncan's lengthy diatribe, which, even when taking into account the recent turn of events, seemed way out-of-character considering the old man's usually unflappable demeanor and easygoing manner. He received a second's reprieve as his attention was drawn to a troop of rotters banging down the road toward Huntsville. Then he resumed trying to decide which approach he was going to use should Duncan's actions inch any closer towards unpredictability. And while the silent battle between doing nothing and stepping in and putting himself out there raged internally, the rotor sounds changed from a fast, high-pitched *whip-whip-whip* to a metronomic, almost hypnotic *whop-whop-whop*. What happened next was entirely unexpected, as he felt his stomach buoy up and lodge in his throat. In the same instant he looked down through the footwell and realized the ground was rushing up at him.

Chapter 71
Schriever AFB

Although Cade wasn't one hundred percent certain who was climbing the Chinook's loading ramp, judging by the slender form and the whipping ponytail his money was on the raven-haired girl he'd saved from a grisly death at Grand Junction Regional just days ago.

Wilson, however, was oblivious to her presence because he had reburied his head in his hands the moment Cade had reassured him that Ari's sudden maneuver had been planned and the chopper was in no danger of crashing.

So with his initial assumption having been confirmed by the instant reaction the new arrival invoked in both Raven and Sasha, Cade sat back, slightly amused, and waited for Wilson to catch on.

The flight engineer handed Taryn a pair of neon yellow muffs which she donned and benefitted from immediately as a shrill whine emanated from a nearby hydraulic piston. The rectangle of daylight quickly shrank to nothing, and a handful of seconds after the noise began the ramp bumped into the closed position and the whine subsided.

As Cade flicked his gaze between the engineer who was busy folding a seat down for Taryn, and Raven and Sasha who were giddy and beaming because their new friend had changed her mind and come aboard, Wilson hinged up and looked aft.

Moving faster than any operator or Chinook crewmember Cade had ever seen perform the task, Wilson pulled a move that would make Harry Houdini proud and was unbuckled, up and out of his seat, and embracing the young woman in record time.

Oblivious—this time of everyone *but* Taryn—Wilson emerged from his shell and, helmet be damned, planted a clumsy kiss on her lips. A kiss that was reciprocated and drew a couple of emphatic "grosses" from Raven and Sasha and a big ear-to-ear grin from Brook.

Looking down the fuselage at the spectacle, Ari broke in over the shipwide comms and said, "Night Stalker Airways would like to remind our valued passengers that this is *not* a Mile-High-Club-sanctioned-flight. Please be seated and we'll be resuming our hop to Mack momentarily."

Shaking his head, the burly flight engineer showed Taryn to the seat he'd prepared and buckled her in.

Chapter 72
Eden Compound

Coming in fast like he was landing a fully-loaded Huey into a hot LZ in the jungles of Vietnam, Duncan dropped them from the sky like a Yo-Yo and at the last moment flared the Black Hawk, settling it softly dead center on the expanse of green grass, wheels straddling the dirt airstrip.

Heart hammering in his chest wildly from the recent specter of riding another helicopter into the ground, Daymon detected the stars crowding his vision and finally remembered to breathe. Drawing in a lungful of fresh air, he cast his gaze around the clearing and noticed the lack of a welcoming party. And given the racket the helo produced, he knew the meadow shouldn't be deserted. He looked toward the compound's entrance but saw no movement.

Momentarily ignoring Daymon, who once again was as white as a ghost, Duncan pored over the instrument panel, checking all of the systems the manual listed as critical to staying in the air.

Satisfied, he powered down the turbines, setting the rotor into a slow spin, and said, "Get on the two-way and have someone come out and help with the bodies."

"All right," replied Daymon, fumbling in his pocket and hunting for the Motorola he'd taken off of Logan's bullet-riddled corpse. Thumbing it on, he asked, "Thing is set to 10-1. Is that the right channel?"

"Affirmative. Tell them to make it snappy because I'm hoping to catch those Huntsville bastards with their pants down." An awful vision of Jamie and Jordan enduring Lord knows what at the hands of their captors flooded Duncan's mind. Shaking it off, he glanced back at his *cargo*. Because that's what he believed the two human bodies had been reduced to. Minus the soul or spirit or whatever the moniker du-jour, they were just shells leaking blood onto the cabin floor. *Logan and Gus*, he thought, *were somewhere much better*. At least he hoped they were. And that's where his faith kicked in. He had to remain faithful considering the times he was living in.

"This is Daymon," he said, thumbing the call button on the two-way. "We're back and we need a couple of extra bodies out here in the clearing."

A second passed, then the radio crackled to life and Phil indicated that he and Chief were coming topside.

***

Less than a minute later, Daymon watched Phil and Chief emerge from the foliage, change course and set off on a sprint towards him.

Rifle in hand, sling flailing wildly against his leg, Phillip, who was rail-thin and lighter by at least thirty pounds, led the two through the rotor-wash-whipped grass. Brandishing a stunted shotgun, his glossy black ponytail bouncing with each footfall, Chief, who was built like a fireplug and at least a head shorter, somehow matched Phil stride-for-stride.

Sans helmet or weapon, Daymon ran full tilt and met them halfway, about fifty yards from the idling chopper, where they could talk and not have their words drowned out by the din of the rotating blades.

Taking it slow, sparing no detail, he filled them in on the events at the quarry, where Duncan's state of mind was, and where he feared Logan's murder was about to take the man. Using Apocalypse Now as a reference, he said, "Think Colonel Kurtz times a thousand." Succinct and to the point, Chief and Phillip grasped the statement's full meaning. Then Daymon heaped upon them the unenviable task of moving the bodies inside one of the abandoned vehicles where the animals couldn't get to them. Lastly, he asked them to carry the black Pelican case inside, stating that it would be well worth their while before imploring them to peruse its contents.

348

And just when he was finished talking he caught a flash of movement in his peripheral vision.

Heidi was standing near the entrance, dappled in sunlight. He had no idea how long she'd been there but she was a sight. Sparing her from seeing the grim task Chief and Phil were about to undertake, he strode across the meadow to her side and guided her behind the blind where they shared a much-needed embrace.

After a couple of minutes passed, Daymon pulled away first, looked down into her eyes and said, "Logan and Gus are dead." Without allowing the words to fully register, he pressed on. "And Jamie and Jordan are missing."

"Missing or abducted?" she said, her voice rising.

Just as he'd feared, she was right back to square one—he could detect it in her eyes. The sparkle had been extinguished with his words still hanging in the air.

"I'm going to help Duncan look for them," he lied. Truth was, he was going along *only* to save Old Man from himself. He'd been there before. Rage alone made him allow Hosford Preston to get eaten by the dead. As the old saying went, *the devil made me do it.* Or in this case—not do it. It was the black Glock bucking in his fist and the exploding faces of the three hissing corpses that always visited first. But it was the inevitable cameo appearance of the lawyer's fear-etched face that woke him from his nightmares every time. If only he would have listened to Cade, things would have turned out different. His soul would be a little bit cleaner. Done was done. He couldn't change the past. But he might, however, be able to help keep Duncan from making the same kind of mistake. One he might regret for the rest of his life.

"Jordan and Jamie?" reiterated Heidi.

"We're not sure," said Daymon, a million different thoughts running through his mind. "But there were only the two bodies so at least there's a chance they may have fought the bad guys off and escaped." The lies—which even by omission counted just the same—continued to pile on as he left out the condition in which they'd found the Tahoe and the fact that Jordan's rifle had been left behind.

Heidi said sharply, "Tran was right. They're still out there." She pulled away from him and back-pedaled, a look of incredulity on her features.

"I'd be willing to bet it was the same people they tangled with the other day. Stirred them up too much." He went quiet. Steeled himself for what might end up being yet another lie. "Don't worry, hon. Me and Duncan ... we will find them alive."

Heidi made a face. "And that's almost worse than dying," she spat. "'Cause I'm living it."

Daymon made no reply. He watched her disappear into the compound. He didn't follow, and when she was gone, he retrieved the compact Thuraya sat phone from his pocket and thumbed it on. He checked the display and came away pleased because he had reception. He scrolled through the incoming calls. Found the most recent one from Cade days ago. Took a deep breath and hit the green call button. Three electronic trills later, the call was answered by a computerized female voice telling him to leave a message after the tone. A tick later the voice was proven right, and a sound that some focus group somewhere had determined would lead to the most people resisting the urge to hang up beeped in his ear. Hanging up for Duncan's sake, hell, for all of their sakes for that matter, was a luxury he could not afford. So, grudgingly, he began to relay the happenings from the last couple of days. Halfway through recounting the story, but before he'd even touched over the most important fact of the tale, the same sound blared in his ear. In disbelief he thumbed the phone off and back on and then immediately hit redial, hoping this time, assuming Cade didn't pick up, that he'd be able to relay the pertinent information in the allotted time.

He listened to the same three electronic trills, then waited for the long dead focus group's chosen tone to sound. After the beep, he cut to the chase, spilling about Logan and Gus and the missing girls. Then he slowed down and voiced his concerns about Duncan. He finished by nearly begging Cade to call him back ASAFP—as soon as fucking possible.

He killed the call and pocketed the phone. A beat later he detected a sudden change in pitch to the Black Hawk's twin-turbines. Simultaneously the rotor swish picked up, rising to a crescendo. On

350

the move, he jammed the phone in a cargo pocket, rounded the blind and couldn't believe what he was looking at. The Pelican case was on the ground a dozen feet off the Black Hawk's nose. Beyond the helo, near the tree line, Phillip and Chief were struggling to fit one of the wrapped bodies into the rear of the white Land Cruiser. And the helicopter was bouncing, light on its wheels, with only Duncan at the controls. Then the rear boom lifted to horizontal, and just like that the Black Hawk was airborne, rotor thumping out man-made thunder claps, clawing its way into the azure sky.

Waving his arms frantically, Daymon ran across the clearing trying in vain to get Duncan's attention. He made it to the dirt strip just as the craft banked sharply starboard. He caught a glimpse of helmet, a sun-glint from Duncan's glasses, followed by a flash of recognition as the man turned his head and looked groundward.

Hinged at the waist, stomach heaving from the sudden spate of exertion, Daymon pivoted slowly, tracking the helicopter as it circled the clearing. Then he realized that Duncan was coming back around for him and he was standing in the man's landing spot. So he sidestepped a few yards, ducked and held his dreadlocks against the rotor wash, and clambered aboard once the helo settled on its landing gear.

The reception he received was about what he'd expected. Sure, he'd spent a little more time consoling Heidi than he probably should have. But deep down he had a feeling Duncan had been looking for an excuse to go it alone. Nobody to answer to that way, Daymon surmised.

Bringing the chopper around in a slow lazy half-circle, Duncan spotted the gray stripe of 39 through the trees and followed it west. "What took you so long?" he said, keeping his eyes forward.

"Had to tell Heidi what happened at the quarry."

"You tell her the girls are missing?"

"I kind of sugar-coated it. Painted a rosier picture than I'm seeing."

Duncan looked left. Fixed his gaze on Daymon. "So you lied."

"Omitted."

"Lied," pressed Duncan.

"Tomato, to-mah-to," Daymon shot back. "Didn't help. She went right back to thinking the boogeyman is waiting outside her door."

"And he ain't?" said Duncan. "Look down there." He slowed the Black Hawk and closed to within a hundred feet of the roadway, holding it in a ragged hover.

Below them, a group of thirty or forty creatures trudged eastbound away from Huntsville and the rather densely populated city of Ogden, a mere fifteen miles west of there. Slowly, collectively, their heads panned skyward and their dead eyes fixed on the noisy vessel they instinctually knew contained fresh meat.

"I'm talking about Bishop," said Daymon, throwing a shiver at the sight of the flesh-eaters. "He's the one who took her from work. Now he comes back in her dreams and haunts her nightly."

"What about the Robert Christian guy?"

"He's no threat to her now because he's out of the picture. Cade said he's locked up tight at Schriever."

Duncan went quiet and nosed the helo a few degrees to starboard. Panned his eyes over the scrolling countryside as the forest gave way to the same rolling hills he and Phillip had traversed earlier on their approach to Huntsville in the SUV. A tick later, still standing a stone's throw from 39 was the Shell sign, untouched and ridiculously bright yellow. But the gas station next to it, from the air, looked like something a kid had built out of an erector set and then torched in a fit of rage. Out back, shielded from the road, were a number of burnt-out cars and a drift of blackened corpses.

"Took care of them the only way they knew how," observed Daymon.

"Look what it got them. Burned the whole place down around them. It's a shame 'cause eventually, to gas up the rigs, we're gonna need to find a station like it, or a fuel truck or something."

Daymon made no reply. Kept his eyes on the road below until they came upon a rise and Duncan slowed the Black Hawk to a crawl.

"Down there," said Duncan, pointing out the carnage at the head of the massive bumper-to-bumper traffic jam, where, contrasting sharply against the blacktop, at least a dozen pale nude corpses lay. "Those ... were National Guard soldiers. I'd be willing to bet the same animals that killed them were the ones who killed Gus and my brother."

"Isn't that where the rotters almost got you?"

"Yeah. Phil saved my ass. I was winching the Humvee out of the ditch ... they didn't need it anymore."

"They're in a better place."

"I guess so," Duncan replied solemnly. "Just wish we could have taken the time to bury them proper." Suddenly the realization that he would be doing just that for his brother before long sent a cold chill up his spine. He shivered as his mind reeled and he reminisced over Logan. Saw in his mind's eye snippets of him as a baby, then a boy and finally as a young man with his curled mustache and black bowler hat. The scenes flashed by, morphed together like a photo montage at a wake, and then ended with an overhead view showing him rolling Logan's corpse into a shallow grave and then flinging the first shovelful of black soil over his slack, pallid features.

"Think we could hover here for a minute so I can take a look at the city with my binocs?"

"Better yet," said Duncan, working his thumb over a couple of switches on the contoured flight stick. He turned a knob bringing an image—like a fast-moving waterfall rendered in whites and blacks—into focus on the recessed, ten-inch screen mounted nearer to the left seat than the right. "That's the feed from the FLIR (Forward Looking Infrared Radar) pod. That round gimbal-mounted doo-dad under the chin? The DHS used it to patrol the border looking for little ninety-eight-point-six-degree hot-spots scurrying along the cold desert floor."

"How's it work?"

"I didn't pay too much attention to that part of the manual. I focused on the nuts and bolts of how to keep this thing in the air."

"Thought you said it's like riding a bike."

"This ship is like the Space Shuttle in complexity compared to my old Huey," said Duncan as the image on the screen moved in response to his manipulating the switches. Then by trial and error he managed to get it to zoom in and pan left.

"Wow," exclaimed Daymon. "Makes the city look like it's built outta black Legos."

"Those are the cool spots. Keep your eyes peeled for bright white spots. Especially real bright ones that are moving."

Daymon craned his head closer to the display.

"See anything?"

"Nope."

"I'll take us closer."

"You're not worried about us getting shot out of the sky?"

"Odds are against it. Besides, if you haven't seen anything yet then there probably ain't nobody home."

Pushing the stick forward and adjusting the FLIR pod with a nudge of the thumb, Duncan threw caution to the wind swung wide out over the reservoir's calm waters and approached the city from the north.

***

Up close, Huntsville was as dead as it appeared through the FLIR feed; except for a couple of dozen walking dead, nothing moved.

"Those rotters look fresh," said Daymon, binoculars pressed to his face as he watched a pair of zombies rending hunks of bloody flesh and entrails from a recent kill.

"I've seen nothing but first turns the last couple of weeks."

Still framed in the binoculars, the creature facing Daymon jammed a length of shiny intestine into its maw and, like a kid slurping spaghetti, ground away on the slippery white morsel, the contents of the victim's last meal dribbling from its working mouth. "Oh fuck," said Daymon, putting the field glasses in his lap. "Good thing I didn't eat this morning."

"Look at this," said Duncan. He had the FLIR pod trained on something in the distance. He zoomed in and spent a moment fiddling with the controls before finally figuring out how to switch from the infrared feed. The image on the monitor switched from blacks and whites to color. Licks of black smoke rose from the remains of a very large house that had been built high on the hill with a commanding view of both the downtown area and the surrounding reservoir . From the looks of the concrete footprint, the herringbone-

354

patterned brick circular drive, and the beautiful landscaping, Duncan guessed the place must have belonged to someone very important. A number of luxury SUVs were parked in front, and out back a swimming pool shimmered turquoise in the sun. "I'm going to take us downtown," Duncan stated as he skimmed the Black Hawk over a block of commercial buildings housing a diner, a drugstore, and what looked to be Huntsville's only U.S. Post Office—Old Glory still snapping smartly in the breeze.

After skirting the city along the water's edge, making a thorough recon to the south and finding mostly residential and not one living soul, Duncan spat a string of epithets into the comms. His drawl thick, veins bulging in his neck, he said, "We're going to check the McMansion and then I'm going to bury my brother."

Remaining silent, Daymon twisted around and retrieved the shotgun from the floor behind his seat. *Come on Cade*, he thought, *please look at your effin phone.*

***

Somewhere in Montana

Elvis had been following the yellow squiggle in the plastic box. Turn left. Turn right. Continue to blah, blah, blah and blah, blah—doing exactly what the lady said to do.

Hell, he thought, *with a name like Tom Tom she sure sounded pretty sultry.* He envisioned one of those brunette beauties from the forties or fifties in a low-cut top and hip-hugging shorts over fishnet stockings, all dolled up with lips pouting and red.

Mountains looming north by west killed his fantasy. He slowed, pulled over, and looked closely at Tom Tom's five-inch screen.

Then a song popped in his head. Something about coming around a mountain and she'll be there. God, how he hoped wherever Bishop was there were also a few ladies who sounded half as hot as the woman in the box.

With the trucker-on-meth mantra blipping through his head, he hopped out. Retrieved the final two full gas cans and emptied every last siphoned drop into the tow truck's extended range tank. Swept his eyes around and then tossed the empties behind the cab.

He climbed aboard and set the truck to rolling. Goosed the big engine and turned on the stereo. *Nothing.* Just white noise. So he hummed a few bars of an old Grateful Dead ditty.

Truckin' indeed.

Like a trucker on meth.

Chapter 73
Southwest of Colorado Springs, Colorado

While the Chinook hammered a nearly-straight line westward through the cobalt sky, Ari took the airline pilot shtick to the next level by pointing out the Garden of the Gods off to the starboard side. The reddish-orange rock formations, a byproduct of geological upheaval when the Rockies were formed, dominated five square miles on the western edge of Colorado Springs.

The new White House buried deep inside the NORAD Cheyenne Mountain Complex received a spirited introduction from Ari as the 9,656-foot-tall rocky crag scudded by on the port side.

While Ari provided the distraction no doubt designed to keep the younger passengers from keying in on the ongoing battle against the remnants of the Pueblo horde south of downtown Springs, Cade's full attention was on the dark smudge to the north, where the nuclear-scorched earth near Castle Rock and the hazy horizon met. That was in effect for him hallowed ground; the very place where his best friend, Mike Desantos, got bit and in effect lost his life. As the helo droned on, he kept a laser-like focus on the twin craters until they were no longer visible through the Chinook's tiny bubble window.

***

After having successfully tuned out Ari's voice for quite some time, Cade decided to be productive and power up the replacement sat-phone Nash had given him and see what kind of coverage it was drawing. He deployed the stubby antenna and thumbed the power button. After a long second, while the unit shook hands with whatever satellites remained aloft, the keypad flashed red and some kind of logo, colorful but vague, appeared on the tiny screen. He glanced at Brook, who appeared to be asleep, and when he returned his gaze to the Thuraya, the logo was gone and in its place were two identical ten-digit phone numbers—two missed calls that had come in back-to-back—both of approximately the same duration. But most importantly, the phone had recognized the number as the one Cade had assigned to the first slot in the contact list. And that could mean only one thing, Cade concluded—shortly after takeoff, Daymon had called him twice with the sat-phone Tice had given him in Jackson Hole.

Cade retrieved the earpiece that came with the new phone, removed the rubber dustcover from the headphone port, and plugged the jack in. He navigated the menu and selected the first missed call. After listening to the message twice, he scrolled to the second missed call and repeated the process.

Since the moment Cade withdrew the candy-bar-sized sat-phone from his pocket, Brook had been watching covertly from her side vision. And as she looked on, the expressions that crossed his features as he powered on the device and plugged in the ear bud said more than words alone. So she remained still and continued to watch his body language, which seemed to be changing by the second. His thumbs walked over the keypad and his shoulders seemed to inch closer to his ears. He clenched his teeth, and though he was wearing a flight helmet and had grown a partial beard, black and flecked with gray, underneath it all she imagined the muscles where his jaw hinged bulging to the size of golf balls.

Then the phone's keypad went dark; he glanced up and she was burned. Caught in the act, she mouthed, "Who was that?"

"Daymon," he mouthed back.

"Who?"

Providing a poor representation of dreadlocks, he waggled his fingers over his head.

She made a face, nodded, and closed her eyes.

"No more spying on me," he said behind a sly grin. Then, eyes bugged, he stared at her until her resolve cracked and she smiled, opened her eyes, and mouthed, "I love you."

Chapter 74
Huntsville, Utah

Hovering thirty feet above a copse of pines, and roughly a quarter-mile away from the mansion, Duncan put the FLIR pod through the motions. With the device set to pick up heat signatures he zoomed way in and slowly walked the optics right to left. *Nothing.*

Next he chose the setting that allowed them to see the image being picked up on the cockpit display in full color. "Where the hell are they?" Duncan drawled. "A good day spent killing and kidnapping, you'd think it's just about Miller time. Wish this thing had a rocket pod or two ... couple of Hydras into the middle of town might flush them out."

"I think there ain't nobody home," Daymon said. "Just walking rotters and twice-dead corpses. Can you zoom in on that garage?"

"You see something out there I don't?"

"Think about it, Duncan. You almost got bit because you didn't see a rotter ten feet from ya. The remains of the mansion is what ... couple of football fields away? The garage is another hundred feet."

"Quit bashing me and tell me what the hell you see and which side of the garage, the left or the right?"

"Left side," said Daymon. "A row of corpses. Lined up and stripped naked just like the soldiers at the roadblock."

With a little manipulation of the controls, the image on the screen grew in size and clarity. Duncan held the hover and craned his neck to see more of the display.

"They've all been shot. What'd you call it ... center mass?"

"That's how every soldier learns to engage the enemy in basic training," said Duncan, nodding an affirmative. "And that's exactly how those fucks popped Logan ... two to the chest." He grimaced as he heard his brother's last words echoing in his head: *Rotters don't shoot back.*

"Taking that into consideration, what does that tell us?"

"Boy should've been wearing a vest," whispered Duncan, a hot tear tracing the contours of his cheek.

***

After a slow fly by, during which no words were exchanged, Duncan set the Black Hawk down on the gently-sloped lawn in front of the still smoldering mansion. Newer grass clippings took to the air, creating a thin hazy veil that quickly dissipated after he set the power to idle.

With the hypnotic blur of the rotor disc overhead dissipating and the turbine noise a steady tolerable din, Daymon removed his helmet and shook out his dreads. Then he called out over the steady *thwop* of the rotor blades, "Why don't you stay here this time and let me do the lookin' around."

Ignoring what seemed to him more of an order than a question or statement, Duncan went about flipping switches that quickly silenced the turbines. He removed his helmet and hung his head for a moment, stroking his silver mustache. Then, after having come to some kind of conclusion, he reached around and grabbed his stubby shotgun from the back, swiveled around and shot Daymon a hard look. Held it for a couple of seconds like some kind of Mexican standoff and then, without a word, toed open the door and slid out of the helo onto the neatly manicured lawn.

Chapter 75
Huntsville, Utah

Without a shared word between them, Duncan and Daymon performed a thorough recon of the property. They walked slowly counter-clockwise from the static Black Hawk to the Olympic-sized swimming pool, stopping regularly so that Duncan could inspect the lush lawn.

Finally, breaking the heavy silence, Daymon asked, "What's with the lawn inspection?"

Without making eye contact, Duncan swept his arm on a flat plane indicating the expanse of lawn north of the razed structure and said, "Same thing happened at the quarry happened here. Helicopters put down right here." He pivoted and pointed at the Black Hawk. "And there also."

"How many?"

"Half a dozen," said Duncan, turning a full circle, eyes scanning the airspace all around. "There's a lot more room to land here. I figure the shit went down so fast at the quarry that they didn't need to land more than the two anyway. Puts the odds at like eight to four. Not winnable, especially if you get jumped like they did."

"And the other helicopters. What did they do?"

"Probably just orbited the place while my bro was dying."

"So you think these dudes in the helicopters are separate from the folks who've been attacking the compound?"

"Correct. We're up against more than just the Huntsville yokels. Using your terminology ... some real bad *dudes*."

Daymon bent down to inspect the lawn. Pulled a couple of blades, threw them up like a pro golfer might. "How can you be so sure?"

"Because those are the yokels over there. And they're dead as door nails. Ain't coming back. And ain't gonna bother us no more."

"I think I much rather prefer dealing with the yokels in their shiny SUVs over a group of bandits ripping around in helicopters."

"You and me both. C'mon," said Duncan as he set off around the pool, dodging the white wooden pool furniture someone had lined up as meticulously as those on the deck of a cruise ship.

Following a couple steps behind, Daymon kept his head moving—*on a swivel,* as he'd heard Cade say. And once they'd reached the garage which was standing open and filled with several new Toyota SUVs, all still tagged with paper dealer plates, it became obvious to him that Duncan's hunch had been correct. He cast his gaze over the prostrate bodies, all of which sported puckered little entry wounds on their torsos—*center mass,* Daymon thought to himself. Scattered about near the bodies were a number of playing cards that for some reason looked familiar.

"Like I said. It's obvious that these guys weren't soldiers," said Duncan as he rolled the rigid corpse of a twenty-something male over using the toe of his boot. He grimaced at the sight of cratered flesh and muscle and dermis all hanging in tatters. And contrasting sharply on the pale skin was spattered blood, congealed and dried to a very dark crimson.

Duncan went silent for a long moment while Daymon bent low to inspect the bodies.

Finally Duncan added, "These folks weren't fighters."

"And all the dead are dudes. There's not one woman among them," observed Daymon.

"And what do you make of these?" asked Duncan, holding up one of the red and black playing cards.

"Let me see." Daymon took the card. Looked at both sides and said, "I've seen these before. Had a run in with a young guy in the Silver Dollar in Jackson Hole. After I dropped him with a Reacher special—"

Looking bewildered, Duncan interrupted and asked, "Reacher special?"

"Broke his nose with my forehead. I'll loan you the books when we get back. He's more of a badass than that guy in the book you gave me."

"Mitch Rapp?"

"Yeah ... just one man's opinion though."

"What about the cards?" prompted Duncan.

"A bunch of military-looking guys, high and tight haircuts ... wearing camo. I'm pretty sure they were Bishop's men. They were near the door when I bugged out. They were playing a game of Hold 'em using an identical deck of those cards."

"And that's the *only* place you set eyes on them?"

"Except for right now. Right here."

"Well whose *eyes* are bad now?" said Duncan, extracting an identical, albeit slightly waterlogged specimen from his hip pocket. "Found this at the quarry. It was in a puddle a ways off from Jenkins' rig."

"And," said Daymon, "what the hell does it all mean?"

"To a veteran of the Vietnam war ... a warning to the enemy. A way to say 'don't fuck with us because we're the baddest motherfuckers in the valley.' Hell, I dealt a number of these myself after kicking some ass and taking some names—"

"And ears?" asked Daymon.

"Hell no. Not widespread at least ... that's mostly crap from the movies. But come to think of it, there were a couple of shadowy types I knew who might have dabbled in a little of that. But if I told ya then I'd have to kill ya." The ice between them finally broken, he smiled broadly. "Hell, right now I'd probably hack a few off if the opportunity presented itself and the ears that I was hacking off belonged to those dirtbags that killed Logan. And when we get back, after I bury him, I'm going to pick Tran's brain and see if he can't decide once and for all what it is he *really* heard Bishop say."

Daymon looked away, north by west, at the sun playing off the reservoir and asked, "What then?"

But the answer didn't come in word form. Instead, out of nowhere there was a tremendous explosion that sent him diving for

364

cover. And before he'd even hit the bricks there was a second percussive blast that stole his breath and set his ears to ringing.

Everything had happened so fast. A rotter had somehow gotten around his blind side. But Duncan redeemed himself for his own slipup at the roadblock and drew down on the freshly-turned monster.

"Motherfucker," said Daymon as he rolled over onto his back. "First thought I had when I saw you draw on me was that you were having a flashback from Nam. Then I thought ... Daymon, you're getting smoked by a big ass pistol."

Cordite smoke curling from the .45's gaping muzzle, Duncan reached his free hand out, pulled Daymon to his feet and, without missing a beat, said, "Once I find out where Bishop and his Hold 'em-playing buddies are, I'm going to go there and kill him ... *very slowly*, or die trying."

"Hopefully not the latter," replied Daymon, hands shaking from the near death experience. Never before had he felt the heat and shockwave nor the crack of a bullet passing by his head, let alone two of them closely spaced and traveling nine hundred feet per second. "I owe you one."

"No shit," replied Duncan. He clopped the taller man on the shoulder and without another word set out across the driveway heading back to the Black Hawk.

Chapter 76
Near Grand Junction, Colorado

Terra cotta earth and gnarled trees trying hard to survive the unforgiving high desert passed under the thundering Chinook. "We'll be over Grand Junction Regional in a matter of minutes," said Ari, his voice broadcast loudly over the onboard speakers. "I'm going to hover for a little while when we get there so that we can observe a moment of silence for a fallen hero. Because in this man's opinion, if it weren't for Sergeant Maddox's ultimate sacrifice, some of us on this ship wouldn't be here."

Nodding in agreement, Cade gave Brook's thigh a squeeze.

Though she truly was grateful for the man's sacrifice, Taryn's reaction to the news was different. Instantly she went rigid, the mere mention of her former prison tilling up an entire harvest's worth of new nightmares—more than enough to last her the rest of her young life. She sat up and drew her legs in and began a subtle rocking motion.

Drawing her near, Wilson matched the gentle swaying of her body and caressed her shoulder the way a mom might console a hurt child.

Phone still in hand, Cade turned it over repeatedly, wondering what good could come from inserting himself into the middle of the Duncan and Logan equation. He looked around the cabin, finally settling his gaze on Raven, who had somehow gotten ahold of some kind of electronic device. White wires snaked from under her helmet and her head bounced to a rhythm he couldn't hear. Next to her, Sasha was dozing, a large tan handbag filling in as a pillow between her head and the vibrating helicopter. Then he lingered on the two lovebirds across the aisle from him, who were still wrapped in the same mad embrace they'd been in since Taryn had come aboard.

Finally it hit him that if it weren't for the crusty aviator, Duncan, he might not be sitting here next to his lovely wife, with his beautiful daughter, loving life no matter how difficult it was—or was about to become. *Nope*, he thought. He'd have died on the highway near Boise if Duncan hadn't been there. Furthermore, he felt he still owed the man for going out of his way and plucking him and Daymon from either a slow death in the farmhouse attic or a fast death at the hands and teeth of the Zs that'd had them surrounded.

So he extracted the phone and extended the stubby antenna. He shifted his helmet aside and inserted the bud into his ear. Tapped out the unlock code and waited for the phone to indicate it was connected to a satellite. Meanwhile he scrolled through the *missed call* log, found the missed call entry labeled '1', and renamed it *Tice* out of respect for the man's ultimate sacrifice. Finally the compass icon flashed, letting him know a connection had been established.

He looked around the cabin once again. Then he peered out the window as the Chinook traversed the airspace over the outskirts of Grand Junction. Down below he saw dozens of Zs ambling the gray concrete side streets.

"Five mikes to Grand Junction Regional," said Ari, forgoing the usual hand signal.

No active military mission. No active operators aboard. Therefore, no need, thought Cade as he thumbed the send button.

Chapter 77
Huntsville, Utah

Two hundred and twenty-eight miles away, Daymon had just stowed his shotgun and was trying to find a comfortable angle for his legs.

"Why don't you adjust the seat?"

"You can do that?"

"Just like a car."

"All that way from Schriever to Driggs, and then today tooling around with my legs scrunched up like a dead bug, and you couldn't find it in your heart to tell me sooner?"

After a sharp cackle accompanied by a leg slap, Duncan said, "It's not my fault the last person riding in that seat was a shrimp."

Making no reply, Daymon instead fumbled around near the seat's edge and pulled a lever that sent the seat yawing right and tilting back on its rail a few precious inches. "Ahhh," he exclaimed at about the same time the electronic trilling of the sat-phone emanated from within his pants pocket.

Duncan watched Daymon squirm in the tight confines, a mad hunt for the phone. "Gonna answer the thing?" he said.

Daymon hit a key to talk and said, "Hello."

"Daymon?" said a disembodied voice that was hard to place with any degree of certainty.

"It is. Am I speaking with Captain Cade Grayson?"

"Affirmative. No rank is necessary ... Cade will do."

"Did you listen to my messages, Cade?"

"Affirmative. I listened to them twice," he replied.

"Well there's more," Daymon stated slowly.

The funny thing was that Cade wasn't at all surprised. Somehow he knew in the pit of his stomach that the two messages couldn't have contained all of the pertinent information. That would have been *way* too easy. And as far as he knew, Mister Murphy was loathe to take even a day off—at least where anything having to do with Cade Grayson was concerned. So he sat back, ears perked, waiting to hear whatever Daymon had to add.

"You still there?"

"Affirmative," Cade said back. "Lay it on me."

Daymon went over the newest revelations concerning the death cards, as well as the explanation Duncan had provided. Then, leaving no stone unturned, he described the massacre in Huntsville and the similarities it shared with the murders and probable abductions that had happened at the quarry. Once Daymon had finished his three-minute oration there was a full thirty seconds of silence on Cade's end.

"Hello. You still there?" said Daymon, trying his best to ignore Duncan, who had been sitting in the pilot's seat, hand out, palm up, mouthing emphatically, "Let me speak to him."

Playing keep away with the phone, Daymon leaned as far away from Duncan as possible and said, "So what's your take on the situation?"

"I think Duncan's a big boy and there's nothing I can do to help the *situation* from here."

"Where's here?"

Cade looked out the window briefly. "I'm staring at red rocks and walking corpses from a Chinook helicopter—" He looked at the altimeter on his Suunto. "—five hundred and two feet over the suburbs of Grand Junction, Colorado, where I've got some important business to attend to. And if all goes as planned, we should be wheels down in Mack within the hour."

Sweet, thought Daymon. He'd helped fight a complex fire there a number of years ago and knew the lay of the land pretty well. He imagined an overhead view of the area and did a quick mental calculation. "Hell, give-or-take, as the crow flies, you're only two hundred miles away from the compound. Can't you pull rank and bypass Mack and have them deliver you and your family to the GPS coordinates?"

Not wanting to go into too much detail, Cade said, "It's not that simple—"

Daymon interrupted him by saying, "Didn't seem to stop you from getting that Whipper prick to give up this Black Hawk I'm currently sitting in."

"That was General Desantos's doing. And that's a whole 'nother can of worms I don't want to open and revisit." Concentrating hard on how much he should divulge concerning his leaving Delta, he stared out the window and watched as the massive shadow of the Chinook and the blocky silhouette of the captive F-650 seemed to skim along the contours of the ground. Finally, after another full thirty seconds of dead air on both ends, Cade realized since Daymon stated he was in the Black Hawk, then Duncan *had* to be within arms' reach. "Put Duncan on," he said sharply. "But before you do, I think there's something you need to know ... and your girl Heidi needs to know. Robert Christian is dead. He's probably having dinner with Hitler as we speak."

"Were you there?" asked Daymon.

"No, I watched it on Nash's laptop. He went way too quick," Cade said, thinking about how Pug had left the world in an entirely different manner. "Christian didn't suffer."

"I'll tell her he did," said Daymon.

"You do that."

There was another long silence, then finally Daymon said, "I'm handing the phone to the Old Man."

Duncan snatched up the phone and drawled, "Hey Delta. How's it hangin'?"

Cade grimaced and said, "I'm finally free from the Green Machine."

"Out of the army ... no shit?"

"Affirmative," Cade said. "And I have a favor to ask of you."

"Shoot," said Duncan.

"Daymon filled me in on the happenings in your neck of the woods. I'm truly sorry to hear about your brother."

370

There was a long moment of silence on the other end, after which Duncan said, "I wasn't supposed to outlive him. It's not right."

"I figure I still owe you for the exfil in Hanna. I was hoping before you went and did anything you'd wait for me ... so that I can get in on the payback."

"It'll take the better part of the day to work up a load out and transfer fuel from the Bell to the Black Hawk. After that ... God knows how long to hunt the fuckers down," conceded Duncan.

Cade looked left and noticed Brook giving him the evil eye. Ignoring her, he said, "Daymon says you're pretty close to figuring out where they're operating from."

"Roger that," replied Duncan. "But close only counts if you're talking horseshoes and hand grenades ... not an entire state-in-the-union."

"Which state are we talking about?"

"Idaho."

"Been there, done that," said Cade, recalling their mad dash through the outskirts of Boise and then their subsequent flight from the dead aboard the National Guard UH-60. "It's a big state. Without me, who's going to work the satellite navigation gear for you?"

"You make a good point," drawled Duncan.

"I've still got the GPS coordinates to the compound." Cade paused for a beat, then went on, "Will you at least afford me forty-eight hours to get there before you go on the warpath?"

After another long spell of dead air, during which Cade could almost feel Brook's gaze boring into his soul, Duncan finally broke the silence and said in a funereal voice, "I'll grant you that ... but I will be wheels up if you're one second late. Even if it means I have to take on Bishop and his boys alone."

Imagining Duncan doing the same, Cade glanced at his Suunto and marked the time, then risked a surreptitious glance Brook's way and noted that her eyes were closed and her breathing shallow and steady. *Here we go again*, he thought, *out of the fat and into the fire*. And then, almost as if someone else was inhabiting his body and working his mouth, he replied, "Copy that ... forty eight hours. First light I'll be oscar mike."

Epilogue
West of the Rockies

Bishop sat bolt upright, swung his legs off the bed, fumbled on the nightstand in the dark and grabbed his pistol. Slowly, he expelled the breath he'd been holding, and then listened hard for any out-of-place noises.

Nothing.

He checked the glowing hands on his Luminox. *0422.* That the guards hadn't called set him at ease. *Probably just another nightmare,* he thought. So he replaced the Sig Sauer on the nightstand. Grabbed the bottled water sitting there and took a long pull.

Then, from somewhere across the lake, a car horn sounded— two long, drawn-out bursts of offensive zombie-attention-getting-noise. Unnecessary and irresponsible.

Forgoing boots, he grabbed his pistol and radio and ran down the stairs, taking them two at a time. He paused long enough in the kitchen to grab a pair of the newest generation NVDs from off the granite island and power them on. While he waited, he thumbed the two-way and ordered the guards at the gate to investigate. Then he donned the NVDs and padded towards the sliding glass door leading out to the back of the house and the boathouse and lakeshore beyond.

But before he could unlock and pull slider the horn sounded twice again, closely spaced. And just as he was about to locate a rifle with the ability to reach out and touch the asshole, he noticed headlights across the lake flashing a familiar pattern, then the sat-phone on the island came alive, emitting an electronic trill.

He backpedaled, snatched up the phone and looked at the lighted display, recognizing the number instantly. Then he cast his gaze at the flashing headlights and what he was seeing dawned on him. Three short. Three long. Three short.

S.O.S.

Message received.

A smile curled his lip.

Well I'll be damned, Elvis. You made it.

###

Thanks for reading *Mortal*. Look for Book 7: Warpath, the forthcoming novel in the *Surviving the Zombie Apocalypse* series in 2014. Please Friend Shawn Chesser on Facebook.

ABOUT THE AUTHOR

Shawn Chesser, a practicing father, has been a zombie fanatic for decades. He likes his creatures shambling, trudging and moaning. As for fast, agile, screaming specimens ... not so much. He lives in Portland, Oregon, with his wife, two kids and three fish. This is his sixth novel.

CUSTOMERS ALSO PURCHASED:

JOHN O'BRIEN
NEW WORLD
SERIES

JAMES N. COOK
SURVIVING THE DEAD
SERIES

MARK TUFO
ZOMBIE FALLOUT
SERIES

**ARMAND
ROSAMILLIA**
DYING DAYS
SERIES

HEATH STALLCUP
THE MONSTER
SQUAD